RIDE

THRILL RIDE

AMY RATCLIFFE

KENSINGTON
PUBLISHING CORP.

kensingtonbooks.com

KENSINGTON BOOKS are published by

Kensington Publishing Corp.
900 Third Avenue
New York, NY 10022

ISBN: 978-1-4967-5085-3 (ebook)

ISBN: 978-1-4967-5084-6

First Kensington Trade Paperback Printing: April 2025

10 9 8 7 6 5 4 3 2 1

Printed in the United States of America

To my fellow theme park adults, especially Aaron,
this one's for us

Chapter 1

Charlotte Gates took a deep breath and prepared to scream. The roller coaster smoothly approached the apex of the hill, nary a loud creak to be heard on the shiny silver track, and no, not everyone loved this sensation, but she couldn't get enough. To teeter at the top of a roller coaster, waiting for the inevitable pitch downward and twist of her gut brought her peace. Letting loose a scream from deep within, bubbling up from the diaphragm and just exploding. In those few beats before the roller coaster raced ahead to its next twist or loop or corkscrew, she felt like anything was possible. Worries about how she lost her job, her next paying article, her next bill, her next next next . . . it all fell away, chased to the outskirts of Charlotte's mind by that sense of lightness and freedom.

Charlotte pushed out a howl as she seemed to hang in midair above her seat for a moment too long before the cart tore down the hill at an unimaginably sharp angle. The rush of air cut the layer of humidity present in Orlando even in early January. It was an unorthodox time of year to debut a new ride, but the Cosmic Catastrophe Coaster had been a long time in the making, with Wonder World pushing the opening more than once. Now it was here and it was glorious. The cart sped around a tight corner, looping unnervingly close to the water below, sun sparkling off its unnaturally aqua-tinted surface. This was Charlotte's fifth ride on the complex, first-of-its-kind coaster, pushing even her iron stomach to lurch. But getting to know this coaster's nuances came with her job.

As a theme park reporter, her brand of research included everything from knowing how many water fountains the queue had to how likely this roller coaster would make a novice turn green. She regularly got asked questions like "But no, really, how scary is it even if I don't like roller coasters?" and "What if I don't like going upside down?" and "Will I feel claustrophobic in the over-the-shoulder restraints?" in every possible variation. When she couldn't rely on her admittedly skewed perspective of "intense" as it applied to a theme park ride, she brought a not-super-into-roller-coasters friend—read: plied said friend with their choice of theme park snacks—with her to gauge their reaction and interrogate them about their every thought on the ride as she took notes. One of those friends had stopped answering her texts.

Cosmic Catastrophe raced around its last corner and started the slow approach back to the launch point, a cavernous building themed to look like the galactic headquarters from the *Cosmic Thrill* movie franchise. She appreciated when a theme park included intellectual property in a thoughtful way like this. Charlotte pushed away the restraint bar and stepped out of her seat to the loading platform. Loosely pulling her chestnut strands into a messy ponytail and adjusting her romper, she took her time, a luxury on preview days like today without the usual crowds. And she needed that time. That fifth trip left her a little wobbly around the edges and she needed to find solid footing and water. She practically salivated thinking about the ice-cold bottle of water she'd shoved in the locker before her ride.

Charlotte nudged the exit gate on the loading platform,

the promise of hydration (so, so necessary in Florida) putting a bounce on her step. Focused on getting to her locker as quickly as possible, Charlotte didn't notice the figures looming at the end of the exit corridor.

One of them called out, "Charlotte! I was hoping I'd catch you."

Well, shit. Charlotte clocked her surroundings even though she knew she had only one way out of this area. She breathed, doing her best to pull her stomach out of the pretzel it knotted itself into.

His voice had that effect.

"Chad. I didn't expect to see you today." Charlotte hoped it didn't sound too much like she was pushing words through her gritted teeth. His blond hair was wavy, only slightly ruffled. There wasn't a sign of sweat anywhere on his face even in a long-sleeved shirt, tie, blazer, and pants. Chad Sandusky had the absolute nerve to be one of the ten people in the world who glowed in heavy, humid weather and looked as handsome as ever on this eighty-degree day. A tall man was with him, also in a suit but not faring so well in the heat. He had longer black hair with delicate curls forming in the sweat around his hairline. Dashes of red colored the tops of his cheekbones, and when Charlotte looked up, unreasonably deep green eyes with light gray flecks met hers. The brief glimpse sent a jolt down her spine that she couldn't attribute to the coaster. His tailored suit indicated he was an executive, but he wasn't someone Charlotte had seen around before.

"I'll email you later, Chad. Nice to see you," the striking stranger said and nodded at Charlotte, seemingly using this run-in as a chance to escape.

"Sounds good, Gregory. Thanks for coming by." Chad shook his hand and turned his full attention back to Charlotte as Gregory left. "Sorry, wrapping up a little business; you know what it's like. And even if it's the competition, it's a big day for Nia's team. They've been working on Cosmic Catastrophe for a while. I wouldn't miss supporting it," Chad enthused.

Charlotte wouldn't snort. She wouldn't. "How kind of you."

"So how have you been since . . . you know," Chad said.

Since you ruined my ability to trust another partner ever again when you cheated on me, just after I got laid off from my dream job? That's what Charlotte screamed in her head. Did she scream that only in her head? Chad stared at her, clearly waiting for an answer, so yes, that had been her inside voice. Small blessings.

"I've been keeping busy enough between freelance gigs, covering things like this opening for *Ride Report* and a little consulting, and helping with the family business," Charlotte babbled, putting a hopefully not too fake positive tone in her voice. She really did enjoy the work she was doing, even if it wasn't as satisfying or as prestigious as her old job at DreamUs, and she wanted Chad to know she was fine without him. "Definitely taking advantage of this time to explore some opportunities," she added.

"Oh, you're back in Lake Sterling? Lands of Legend is lucky to have you! I'm sure your family is thrilled. They always wanted you to stay there." Chad smiled broadly.

Sure, Chad. He'd never seemed to think much of Lands when they were dating. In fact, he'd insulted the park more than once by pointing out its modest acreage and how Charlotte was lucky to dodge a lifetime of trying to improve the park. Yes, while Charlotte had chosen to walk away from Lands to pursue work at DreamUs—much to her aunt, uncle, and cousin's disappointment—it wasn't because she didn't love the theme park.

Charlotte had not intended to tell Chad she'd moved back to her hometown and gone back to working for her aunt and uncle as a consultant at Lands; she knew he'd see it as a defeat, a move of desperation. And sure, Charlotte was a little desperate. Losing her creative producer position at DreamUs had been a blow. She felt unmoored, confused. She felt like a failure. She'd tied everything she was into her work. Running to the safe harbor of her home, her family, and Lands of Legend seemed like the obvious solution—at least in the short term. But Chad wouldn't see it that way.

She wrapped her arms around herself defensively, as if the gesture would somehow extend to her family and Lands of Legend. "It's been nice to be back, especially since Aunt Marianne and Uncle Frank want to retire soon. And they've been so receptive to my feedback and so welcoming. I've loved getting back to my roots."

Charlotte would not point out the park's lackluster performance this season or the previous year's abysmal attendance or the laundry list of improvements she'd recommended that the owners, her aunt and uncle, simply didn't have the budget to address. Never mind the ones her cousin Emily, the park's day-to-day manager, straight up ignored. All facts not relevant to this conversation.

"Of course they're listening to you. With your experience how could they not? I can't wait to see your fingerprints on the park," Chad said. As if he would ever visit Lands on his own. She had to drag him to the park during the single time he visited Lake Sterling, and then he proceeded to embarrass her all day with not-so-veiled cutting remarks about, well, *everything*.

"How are you?" Charlotte practically screamed, wondering the whole time why those words came out of her mouth. She wanted to change the subject, but why did she ask that? Stupid Midwestern politeness.

"Fantastic! I got that promotion so I'm leading the new themed area development at our new Paris location. I'll be leaving soon and spending most of my time in France for at least the next few years."

Well, the part about him being out of the country was a

plus, even if rage and envy clawed at Charlotte's lungs. She'd desperately wanted to work on the Paris project. The chance to break ground on a new DreamUs park and be involved from the beginning? It was everything a theme park designer could want. Charlotte had daydreamed about possible storytelling and experiences for Paris that would give her a theme park legacy, a place in the hallowed halls of visionary Dream Mechanics who everyone in the industry knew and admired. The difference she could make in creating other worlds for the park guests *and* be recognized for it! At least she'd have a strong connection there in Chad.

She swallowed her jealousy. "Congratulations. Any particular ride you're excited about?"

Chad smirked, his mouth covering up his perfect, straight teeth. That asshole actually smirked. "Now you know I can't tell you any secrets, especially since you're a theme park *reporter* these days," he said, condescension oozing through his words.

The time to end this punishing conversation had more than passed. She should have pretended she needed to go to the bathroom as soon as she saw him and ran past. Instincts were worth listening to sometimes. Who knew?

"Yeah, of course. Totally understand." Charlotte nodded. "Best of luck on the project. And speaking of my reporting, I'm sorry to cut this short but I have an interview to get to."

"I loved seeing you. Stay in touch? Who knows, maybe next time you'll be reporting on a ride I worked on and interviewing me about it!" Chad chuckled while he adjusted his tie. "Speaking of, I'll keep you in mind if anything opens up for my team in Paris. Wouldn't want to lose your talent to Lands of Legend forever."

Charlotte hated the feeling of hope that made her stomach leap—working on Dreamland Paris would be huge. She would not appear desperate. "I'd appreciate that. You know how to get in touch."

She nodded and gave Chad a tight smile and speed-walked to the lockers, rolling her eyes as soon as she turned her back. When Charlotte said best of luck, what she really meant was she'd be okay with him falling into a ditch and remaining there indefinitely. Who would miss him? He could have survival supplies—she wasn't a total monster. However, never having to worry about seeing him again would be a relief. But if it meant returning to DreamUs, especially in Paris, she'd swallow her pride and loathing.

She arrived at the lockers by the ride's exit, punched in her number, pressed her fingerprint to the keypad, and stepped over to the now opened locker. After pulling out her backpack with a touch of unnecessary aggression, Charlotte uncapped her water bottle and drank. As the cool water slid down her throat, she rested her back against the wall of lockers and squished her eyes shut as if to press that entire run-in out of her memory. Scrunching her nose, Charlotte thought of what her best friend, Melanie, would say. She breathed deeply and whispered to herself, "Don't cry. Don't cry. Don't give one more tear to that asshole."

Especially not now. Not when she had work to do. Professional, respectable, paying work. But seeing Chad reminded her of everything she'd lost six months ago.

After years of work at DreamUs, she was just let go. Layoffs, they'd said, citing a variety of economic and cost-cutting reasons. She knew layoffs weren't uncommon in the Dream Mechanics division; she'd seen it happen to colleagues. Sometimes temporary, sometimes not. Still, she thought she was too valuable an employee to be susceptible to those waves of layoffs and had asked her boss, Jeni, over and over again, why me? She thought Jeni might give her an actual answer beyond the corporate spiel. But she refused to give her one, legally probably couldn't, and when Charlotte had tried to pull the "hey, we're friends" card a couple of weeks after the layoffs, Jeni still ignored her.

That silence hurt as much as losing her dream job; Charlotte had thought she and Jeni were actual friends. And on top of it all, her boyfriend Chad, who hadn't been at the company as long as her, kept his position and didn't seem to understand Charlotte's hurt emotions.

"Charlotte, it's not like they made a decision to personally attack you and, in your words, 'ruin your life.' It's a business. They had to cut some fat," Chad had told her, somehow missing the part where he equated her with being "some fat." "You know these waves of layoffs happen from time to time and they rehire when they have new projects. Anyway, it's their loss. A competitor will scoop you up in no time and you can probably leverage all your experience at DreamUs for a more senior title and better pay."

His words had briefly comforted her, until she discovered no one across themed entertainment seemed to be hiring. Charlotte had hit up every one of her contacts in Los Angeles and in other theme park hubs like Orlando the week after she got let go. Two months later, nothing had changed. Everyone she spoke with respected her and loved her work, knew she was a gem, but sorry, they didn't have a place for her. Dejected after yet another lunch that ended in, "I wish I could help, but I just don't have anything right now," Charlotte abandoned her list of errands—Chad thought her unemployment left time for her to handle every household-related matter for their small bungalow in Burbank and she hadn't corrected him—and headed home.

Walking through the door early was one of Charlotte's best and worst decisions.

Chad wasn't clothed and he wasn't alone; Jeni was with him. Yes, former boss/friend Jeni. Which explained a lot of things, really.

Charlotte turned on her heel and left without saying a word, despite Chad chasing after her. Mostly she remembered how he caught his foot in a pillowcase—the pillowcase for her favorite, squishiest-in-all-the-right-ways pillow—as he ran toward her. He didn't fall, because of course he didn't, but he somehow pulled the pillowcase off with his foot and it dragged behind him as he staggered toward Charlotte. The end of three years represented by a seafoam-green pillowcase wrapped around Chad's foot, sliding inelegantly across the floor.

She moved out as quickly as she could and did the only thing that felt right: coming back home. A thirty-three-year-old running back to what she knew. To Ohio. Back to Lands of Legend. For now.

Chapter 2

Charlotte took one more deep breath and consulted the calendar on her phone; what she'd told Chad about having an interview coming up was true. She made her way down a plain concrete hallway toward the ride's exit—exit areas sometimes got the same attention to theming as the rest of the ride, but not here—and back into the frankly too brilliant for January sun. While digging her oversized sunglasses out of her equally oversized bag, she headed toward the Cosmic Wonders building for her interview with the coaster's art director. Afterward, she found a seat inside the blissfully air-conditioned space and pulled out her laptop while her thoughts about Cosmic Catastrophe were still fresh. The embargo for reporting on the coaster's opening was up in two days and *Ride Report*, the outlet paying her to write this story, needed her finished article as soon as she could so they could edit and schedule it.

"Charlotte!"

She turned her head and grinned at her best friend. "Hey, Melanie!"

"Leave it to you to be working in a theme park on a beautiful day," Melanie replied. "You know, life is happening here—rides, churros, me. You don't need to work all the time."

Melanie's tone was light, but it wasn't the first time Charlotte had heard that advice from her.

"I know, but I want to be prepared to turn this article in as quickly as I can," Charlotte answered while she saved the document and closed her laptop. She stood up to hug Melanie. Charlotte hadn't seen her fellow theme park reporter and friend in person in far too long. They'd first met when Charlotte was still working at DreamUs and had hit it off from the beginning. Jeni was concerned about Charlotte getting close with a theme park reporter, but it wasn't like Melanie was the type to dig for "scoops" or be sneaky for the sake of getting an article up on the internet first. Their friendship really developed once Charlotte was laid off in July and had an abundance of free time. She started to realize her work-martyr ways and, once she began to work on herself, she became a better and more available friend. Despite the hurdle of long distance, she and Melanie had become close. "I know intense roller coasters like this one aren't your favorite." She squeezed Melanie's shoulder. "How are you doing?"

"I rode it once and I consider that a win. I kept my eyes open, even during the loops!" Melanie pulled away and struck a defiant pose, her long platinum-blond hair, streaked with purple and green, in a braid that whipped over her slightly sunburned shoulder. Her friend looked as stylish as ever in a cute sundress with lacy shorts underneath. While Charlotte went for comfort first with rompers, hoodies, her favorite sneakers, and ponytails for days, Melanie blended fashion and comfort in a way that made her stand out in any crowd.

Melanie claimed she'd try any ride once, but that rule didn't usually apply to anything that went upside down or more than twenty miles per hour. Charlotte had once witnessed Melanie have a total meltdown about an unexpected but totally planned and safe drop in a ride. So, this marked huge progress. Melanie usually focused her theme park coverage on food and drinks. She'd built an impressive following on social media and her own blog with her photos and exceedingly honest opinions about everything from flavored popcorn to the more upscale restaurants in the theme park scene. Her training as a chef and history working in fine dining kitchens gave her a unique perspective among theme park food bloggers. Mel lived near the parks in Orlando, so she dropped by at least three times a week. And now she was expanding her portfolio beyond food to write more about rides.

Charlotte would not comment on how out of sorts Melanie looked despite her cute outfit. She thought Melanie was brave to face her fears, but she certainly wouldn't have thought any less of Melanie if she'd opted out. Thrill rides weren't for everyone.

"That's amazing! Look how far you've come. Ready to go on Interstellar Screamer with me next?" Charlotte joked.

Melanie's eyes expanded to at least twice their usual size. "Nope, nope, nope. Forever going to be a nope."

Charlotte laughed. "Well, the invitation stands if you ever change your mind. Have you started your interviews yet?"

Early press events like this usually included a handful of interviews with the people who'd worked on developing the ride from its inception, or maybe the sound designer for the entire attraction, or sometimes the food and beverage geniuses who concocted treats and drinks themed to the ride that would be sold in the ride's area of the park.

"I haven't, but I wanted to find you for a different reason."

Charlotte could tell from Melanie's cautious expression that her friend was holding back. "Because you haven't seen me for a month and missed me terribly?"

"Yes, of course. But also *Chad's* here." A sharp edge punctuated Melanie's last two words.

"Ugh," Charlotte spat out. "Yeah, I know. I just ran into him slash got cornered by him. He couldn't wait to tell me about his new promotion."

"Right? I think I talked to him for less than two minutes before he found a way to bring it up!" Melanie rolled her eyes.

Charlotte grimaced. "He told me he was here to support the Wonder World team, but it felt like he wanted to specifically find me so he could gloat about his promotion and sneer at my current career. Or, probably in his opinion, lack of a career."

"Would that surprise you?"

Charlotte sighed. "No, not even a little."

"Did Chad mention anything else?" Melanie had a questioning, almost cringing look on her face.

Uh-oh.

"Anything else like what?" Charlotte went on guard. "He said he'd be out of the country for a while to work in Paris, but that was about it."

"Ah. I'm sorry to be the person to have to tell you this—"

Charlotte interrupted. "Melanie, what is it?"

"It's about Chad and Jeni—"

"No. No. I refuse to hear any more." Charlotte covered her ears with her hands to show she was serious.

Melanie looked apologetic as she gently pulled Charlotte's hands away and held them. "Ignoring something doesn't make it not happen, you know. Being informed is good, especially when the information is coming from a kind person with your best interests at heart—that's me."

"You're right," Charlotte grumbled. "Tell me."

"They're moving to Paris *together*."

Charlotte looked down at the swirling stars on the carpet

and took a moment to process. "I thought you were going to say they'd gotten *engaged*, so all things considered, them moving in together, even if it is to Paris, the most romantic city in the world, isn't so bad."

"*Wellllll*," Melanie said in a high-pitched voice. Charlotte felt her gut drop as she leveled an inquisitive look at her friend.

"Yeah, you can guess," Melanie said.

"I'm shocked he didn't shoehorn that bit of news into our conversation, too. But hey, you know, good for them. I suppose? They'd better not invite me to the wedding is all I'm saying." Charlotte tried so hard to play it cool, to let this news bounce in and out of her mind without snagging on her anxieties. She would not dwell, damn it. It's not that she was lost without Chad. She'd cared for him, even loved him in a way, but their relationship had been about two people on a similar path with aligned goals who enjoyed each other's company and bodies. They moved in together out of convenience more than a burning desire to spend more time together.

But he'd found sparks with Jeni—sparks he didn't have with Charlotte and that made her feel less than in a way she didn't want to feel *right* after being laid off. The betrayal a mere month after that huge life change upended Charlotte's entire world. Jeni and Chad insisted their relationship had nothing to do with Charlotte losing her job, and she *knew* that was true. Still. She couldn't stop herself from wondering, then and now, six months later. At least she'd learned a valuable lesson about not dating coworkers and drawing a stronger line between work and life.

"Oh, they're eloping in Paris so no worries there."

Charlotte contorted her face to keep the tears at bay. She knew a wedding would happen, maybe not at this lightning-fast speed. She fucking knew it. Melanie put her hand on Charlotte's arm and gave a gentle pat. "I'm sorry I plopped that news into your lap out of nowhere, but I had to make sure you didn't hear it from someone else. How about we take a walk and get some drinks? I know exactly what you need."

Charlotte scrunched her nose and took a deep breath. "Only if we walk through the gift shop to maximize our time in air-conditioning."

She put all the Chad revelations from this trip to the back of her mind. For now, or maybe for forever. Who could say? Right now, she needed to focus on relief in the form of cold air on her skin, her friend, and a frozen apple slushie topped with a lemony foam.

Chapter 3

As Charlotte rolled her suitcase through the Orlando airport the next morning—both the best airport because of the theme park shops where she could grab her favorite snacks one last time and the worst airport because of all the wrung-out crowds who had been to those theme parks—she mentally planned her day back in Ohio. While she longed to hang around and soak in Wonder World's atmosphere and take one more ride on the Cosmic Catastrophe Coaster, she chose an early flight so she could get home and work. She had to turn in her article to *Ride Report* since getting a story up first on the internet, or at least in the first wave of stories, made a difference.

She made her way to her gate and sunk into a chair with an audible sigh. The satisfaction of being exactly where she was supposed to be and finally being off her feet lulled Charlotte into a cozy state. Of course, she didn't linger in that moment for long. Her brain was already spinning out with her to-do list for the next twenty-four hours. Charlotte had learned the only way to calm her mind in these moments was to pull out anything she could make a list on and get it all written down. She pulled up her phone's notes app and went step by step through everything, including what she could accomplish on the two-hour flight.

- Collect thoughts on Cosmic Catastrophe and make an outline to organize the chaos
- Transcribe interviews, starting with timestamps from notes
- Look through photos for any Easter eggs from the *Cosmic Thrill* movies

Charlotte was well aware that she put too much of herself into her work, no matter her title or role. Work consumed her identity. She didn't know how to be another way. Looking at the families waiting around her in clumps, it was easy to see why she did it. Kids clutching plush toys from Wonder World and Dreamland. Fellow grown-ups talking about when they could plan their next trip to the parks. The happiness the theme parks brought so many was palpable here, strewn out across plastic airport chairs.

For Charlotte, it started in her teens when she began working at Lands of Legend and saw behind the scenes how theme parks could bring together storytelling, thrills, and facades to create unforgettable experiences. Visiting the park had been special. But working at her uncle and aunt's park cemented Charlotte's path; she never wanted a career that didn't involve theme parks and her passion had become, for better or worse, all-consuming. Her whole life.

Lands of Legend brought together different corners of myths and fairy tales in a magical setting. On paper, the park sounded cheesy. Anyone in the theme park industry voiced skepticism about a small park in Southeast Ohio delivering on the themes and offering a quality experience. Then they'd visit, many at Charlotte's urging, and most of them ate their words. To walk into Lands of Legend was like entering a safe bubble from the rest of the world—a safe bubble for people leaving behind stress, loss, loneliness, anything heavy they wanted to cast aside while they gave in to escape and wonder.

Growing up with Lands practically around the corner, Charlotte spent a lot of her youth roaming between myths and fairy tales. She couldn't recall her first visit to Lands because she'd been in diapers, but one moment in particular years later cemented the special alchemy of imagination and a themed setting for her—not that she knew any of those words at the time. As she looked at a small boy putting on a puppet show with Wonder World toys from behind a suitcase, Charlotte remembered that moment.

It was a lazy, warm afternoon at Lands of Legend, right after the park celebrated the autumnal equinox. Charlotte ran ahead of her parents, skipping over the familiar cobblestone paths in her favorite part of the park: Fairytale Land. Sun sprinkled through the canopy of maple trees dropping spinning helicopter seeds onto the paths and people below. Charlotte made a game of catching the seeds before they hit the ground and launching them as high into the air as she could.

Ignoring her mother's call, Charlotte pursued her precious "helicopters" into Bluewhistle Meadow. As she scurried around the base of her most beloved tree, a tree she'd napped, picnicked, and read books under, she glimpsed a life-sized wing. With a bounce in her step, Charlotte raced ahead, nearly running into an otherworldly-looking faery wearing a flowing, gauzy dress in all the colors of fall, from dark reds to amber golds. Dried leaves and acorns stuck out from a crown adorning her short auburn hair. Charlotte stopped in her tracks. The faery bent down to Charlotte's level and held out her hand.

"I'm Flossleaf. Can I show you my realm?"

Flossleaf took Charlotte on a walk around the meadow, telling her about where she came from. It didn't matter that Charlotte had been to Bluewhistle Meadow many times before. She'd never seen it through faery eyes. Flossleaf painted a new land underneath Charlotte's feet. One teeming with faeries and fantastical creatures, with portals to other realms, with magic.

After she said goodbye to Flossleaf, Charlotte rushed back to her parents to tell them everything and to beg them to take her to the World of Faery. She didn't know then that the World of Faery was imaginary. That night Charlotte spread out crayons and paper on her bed and drew Flossleaf, her home, and the faery friends Flossleaf had described. Charlotte still had those drawings somewhere.

That's what a theme park could create. It could open those portals to other realms by engaging with imagination and fantasy. Charlotte would later learn the importance of making a story people could live within, a *theme* park, instead of only watching the story like an *amusement* park. She wanted to spread more of that specialness into the world.

An announcement from the gate agent, tinny and harsh, saying they'd start boarding soon pulled Charlotte back into the present and she took the time to note the effects of that specialness in the faces around her at the departure gate. She also took a breath to remind herself that there was more to her life than her work. Wasn't there? She'd never handled the work/life balance well, especially not when she was at DreamUs. Charlotte didn't even keep in touch with anyone from L.A. who wasn't a former work colleague, because she'd never met anyone outside of the Dream Mechanic office walls. She started her days early in the Glendale office, even earlier if she had to drive down the I-5 to the parks in Anaheim to be on-site. Sometimes she adjusted her hours to accommodate meetings with peers across the globe. Charlotte loved every minute, but it hadn't left space for much outside the office beyond sleeping and eating.

And she was in danger of doing it again. Between consulting for Lands of Legend and kickstarting her freelance theme park reporting career in the last five months, she had to remember to leave room for herself and her friends. (*Yes*, Charlotte, she mentally reminded herself, *you have friends now—well at least a friend*.)

Charlotte pulled her phone from her backpack and texted Melanie.

Charlotte: Already miss you.

Melanie: Me too!! When are you going to take an actual vacation and come here for more than just a little work?

Charlotte: I know!

Charlotte: I'll get on planning that. I promise.

Melanie: ☺

Charlotte: For real.

Melanie: Good!!! I also want to come hang at Lands again. It's been forever.

Charlotte: Anytime. Sir Cinna-Swirls on me.

Melanie: Be still my beating heart.

Melanie: Btw I forgot to ask! How is Lands doing?

Charlotte's thumb hovered over her keyboard, hesitating. She wanted to be honest with her friend because being vulnerable was important in building trust. Still, it hurt to type the words.

Charlotte: It's such a special place, you know that, but profits seem to have stalled. Attendance is down, revenue is down. I don't know if they're ever going to get Under the Waves open.

Melanie: Ugh, it has to be hard to keep all of that running. But your aunt and uncle always figure it out.

Melanie: Plus they have you to help, so they have an expert on their side.

Charlotte: You're sweet. I'll help them as much as I can while I'm there. It's temporary.

Melanie: I know, I know.

Melanie: I'm still keeping an ear out for theme park jobs down here for you and I'll let you know if I hear of anything.

Charlotte: Thank you.

Melanie: But Lands is good for you. Just saying.

Charlotte: Heard.

Melanie: ☺ Charlotte, do not even make me think of my restaurant days, istg.

Charlotte: ☺ ♥

She heard her boarding group being called, so Charlotte joined the line—which was only a line by the loosest definition of the word—and made her way forward.

Charlotte flipped through a news app on her phone while waiting in the jet bridge and saw a headline about another amusement park turning down Peak Fusion's offer to collaborate on its intellectual property. The story on *Ride Report* pointed out that the blockbuster television and movie studio had been trying to insert itself into what seemed like every amusement park across the United States. Well, according to sources, anyway, but Charlotte knew *Ride Report* had solid sources. Peak Fusion had a pile of popular intellectual properties that would attract families to amusement parks, but the nos stacked up and people weren't sure why. Speculation was that Peak Fusion was trying to foster goodwill on the public relations front. It was one of those companies that settled lawsuits quietly and passed investigations, but there had been recent rumblings about supply chain exploitation. The factory that produced toys for all the studio's properties was battling toxic work environment allegations. Reports of sexism and crushing hours in the visual effects departments for the company's *Heroic Patrol* movies and video games had come out, too. The potential skeletons hiding in the company's closet were apparently numerous enough to make business partnerships challenging. Charlotte vaguely remembered hearing about Peak Fusion making a proposal to DreamUs last year, but DreamUs was a powerhouse of a corporation with IPs of its own—it didn't need Peak Fusion.

The line had finally made it to the front of the plane; Charlotte put her phone away.

Once aboard, she settled in as much as she could into her assigned window seat. She preferred the right side of the plane for work trips, which were ninety-nine percent of her trips; she could position herself at just the right angle with her small laptop. Any other seat threw her off. Charlotte popped her headphones in to discourage any chitchat and pulled out her iPad mini to make notes until she could get her laptop out. She couldn't wait. She got so much satisfaction from blissful, undisturbed, distraction-free plane writing!

Over the two-hour flight, Charlotte managed to not think about Chad and Jeni more than a few times and knocked out most of her feature on Cosmic Catastrophe. That left her plenty of time to file her completed story well before end of day. Mentally patting herself on the back, Charlotte extracted herself from her seat and gathered her bags. Nothing about lugging a carry-on suitcase down a plane's small aisle was graceful, so she ignored the buzzing of her phone in her back pocket until she got to the relative open space of the terminal. She fired off a quick text to Melanie to make plans to catch up soon and opened her unread text.

Aunt Marianne: Will you be at Lands tomorrow?

Odd, her aunt didn't normally check in to confirm Charlotte's hours, but then again, as a consultant, Charlotte didn't have set office times.

Charlotte: Yeah of course, it's on the office calendar!

Charlotte's attempt to get the office staff to use a shared calendar was a work in progress.

Aunt Marianne: I just wanted to make sure! Just make sure you're still around at one.
Charlotte: Why, what's at one?
Aunt Marianne: We want to have a meeting before things get away from us with planning for the summer season.

Charlotte considered it a triumph that her aunt mentioned any kind of advance planning. As a family company, Lands tended to eschew corporate structure and scheduling in favor of on-the-fly brainstorms and check-ins. Maybe Charlotte's input was helping them finally get more buttoned up.

Charlotte: Ok! You know I'll be there. Looking forward to seeing you and Uncle Frank! <3
Aunt Marianne: Lv you, Charlotte.

Charlotte smiled at her aunt's signature abbreviation that had been born of a texting typo and then persisted to the point that it was how Aunt Marianne now signed birthday and Christmas cards.

Charlotte: Lv you too, Aunt Marianne.

Chapter 4

Charlotte got her things together and left the airport in record time. If she hadn't been in a rush to get home to snuggle her parents' cat Madmartigan and finish her article, in that order, she'd take her time in Columbus and stop to meander in her favorite bookstore, The Book Loft, with its thirty-two glorious rooms of books. And she'd probably get a Highlander Grog coffee from Stauf's next door, too. Charlotte daydreamed for a second about the blended aroma of books and coffee with caramel notes. A contented sigh escaped her lips. But no, she had to focus on doing her work for *Ride Report*. It's not like freelance reporting on theme parks was going to bring in buckets of money, but she wanted to keep establishing this as a side hustle along with her consulting work at Lands until the chance to return to DreamUs inevitably revealed itself. Temporary as her current situation might be, she always wanted to make a positive impression.

She spotted her small navy car from the parking lot shuttle and mentally went over her to-do list for the remainder of the day. Charlotte could rely on the to-do list in her head as much as anything she wrote on paper. Memorizing a list, regardless of the length, never felt like a challenge to her. The lists were on a carousel in her mind, and she could pull out a topic at will. Even so, she liked to write them down too—it felt orderly, and Charlotte loved order.

Her parents told Charlotte that making lists was a habit of hers from childhood. Whatever game her friends suggested playing—hide-and-seek, shop, knights and dragons—she insisted on making a list. Worst places to hide at Lands of Legend? Check. Best found items to use as safe weapons when pretending to be a knight saving a dragon from those who would do it harm? Check. And for the record, the best-found item to keep dragon-slayers at bay was always a large stick.

Lists became more mundane as she grew older. Less dragon protecting, more chores. More giving her structure that helped stave off anxiety. They were more like her list today:

- Feed Madmartigan so he doesn't murder me
- Finish writing article
- Unpack
- Read article one more time and submit
- Follow up with *Ride Report* about a "manufactured scents in theme parks" feature
- See if anyone made candles inspired by those scents and treat self
- Record business expenses from this trip
- Make dinner for Mom & Dad because they deserve it

Charlotte drove up her parents' driveway and parked off to the side, smiling at the sight of the gray farmhouse-style home she'd grown up in, its long covered front porch inviting as ever. Beautiful coneflower seed heads practically burst from flower beds—her dad kept the beds beautiful, even finding ways to make them special in winter. Charlotte followed a cobblestone path (built from extra material from a Lands of Legend project) around the back of the home in order to enter her basement apartment.

Her parents finished the basement ten years ago as a studio apartment and used it for short-term vacation rentals, mostly for tourists in Lake Sterling for Lands, before renting it to their daughter. It was a step up from returning to her childhood bedroom, which would have been impossible anyway since her mom converted the space to storage for her stained-glass studio. She felt indescribably grateful to have an affordable place she could return to and it was an extra bonus that she actually wanted to. The studio, though small, was welcoming with its well-loved furniture and buttery yellow walls.

As Charlotte piled her luggage by her desk, she heard what sounded like an elephant racing above her head. Madmartigan. She darted up the stairs, opening the basement door to find a prancing black-and-white tuxedo cat waiting for her. Madmartigan headbutted her leg and allowed Charlotte to pick him up and snuggle him. Her dad adopted Madmartigan while volunteering with the local cat rescue at an event not long after Charlotte moved back home. He couldn't resist Madmartigan's long, soft fur and sweet demeanor.

Madmartigan spent some time upstairs with her parents, but he'd quickly claimed Charlotte as his preferred human, curling up on her feet while she sat at her desk and hogging her pillow while she slept at night. It was probably her dad's plan all along, an attempt to give Charlotte some companionship outside of her job and after her failed relationship—not that they'd been the biggest Chad fans. And he wasn't wrong that Charlotte was lonely; not that she often let herself reflect on that or how she hadn't been on a date since she left Chad five months ago. She'd fully admit her dad's plot worked. Madmartigan had Charlotte wrapped around his fluffy black tail.

"Are you positively starved?" Charlotte asked Madmartigan.

He responded with an alien-sounding meow. "Hmm. I thought this might be the case."

Madmartigan walked Charlotte to the closet where her parents kept his kibble. He liked to make sure everyone knew where to find his food.

After feeding Madmartigan to his exacting standards, which included scratching his back while he ate, Charlotte went back down the steps to her apartment and snagged her laptop to continue the work she started on the plane. Talking to the creative minds at Wonder World had been both a delight and a pinprick of a reminder of what she used to do at DreamUs. The art director for Cosmic Catastrophe had practically been bouncing with joy as he discussed his work overseeing the coaster's look and atmosphere. Everyone's enthusiasm and pride in the work made it easy to write the feature and piece together information and quotes to explain how the ride came to be.

She stepped away from her work for long enough to unpack and consider whether she'd left anything out. A mockup of a seasonal park guide for Lands caught her eye. It was only winter, but they were already behind on planning for fall next year. Charlotte sent a quick note to her Lands email account to check the dates for quarterly planning meetings and move them up. She hit SEND, then shook her head and drafted another email to herself to first establish those quarterly planning meetings.

Coming back to Lands after working at DreamUs for so long had been jarring. Life as a Dream Mechanic came with structure—some would say too much structure and that it inhibited the creative process. But structure, meetings, and planning were all necessary to stay on schedule and make sure DreamUs's many parks evolved. Nothing about stagnancy was appealing. Not as a park-goer and not as a person behind the scenes.

While Lands wasn't stagnant, the business was on the disorganized side. So, in the few months since she'd been back at Lands, Charlotte had been trying to inject some structure. It was going over as well as she hoped—which was to say not particularly well. Aunt Marianne, Uncle Frank, and cousin Emily were resistant to anything that resembled what Frank called "corporate nonsense." Generally, that "corporate nonsense" was something innocuous like Charlotte trying to streamline meetings with agendas. She knew some baggage from the past over her obsession with working for DreamUs and *not* Lands of Legend played a role, too. When Charlotte so enthusiastically worked as many hours at Lands as she could during high school, her family thought she'd roll right into the business after college.

But then, sometime around high school graduation, Charlotte shared her DreamUs hopes and plans at the weekly family dinner with her mom, dad, aunt, uncle, and cousin. She thought everyone would be thrilled for her, pursuing a big dream and spreading her wings. And her parents did express support and pride; then again it was easier for them because (a) they were her parents and (b) they lent their time and talents to Lands between Mom's art and Dad's landscaping know-how, even though it wasn't *their* business. But Aunt Marianne, Uncle Frank, and Emily? They went through a range of emotions from surprise to confusion, and eventually, to something like betrayal. Emily took it hard and accused Charlotte of acting too good for Lands, which was an especially hilarious comment because Emily was home from her first year of college at business school and would not stop talking about her glamorous life in New York City and how much better it was than Lake Sterling. Marianne's and Frank's hurt feelings dissolved over Charlotte's years at DreamUs, but Emily found every opportunity to get in a dig about how Charlotte had "abandoned" them for greener pastures.

Charlotte and Emily had both spent hours running around Lands as kids and worked there side by side as teens for a summer, but while Charlotte would endlessly nerd out over her uncle's detailed notes and lore for the park, Emily didn't seem to care about that aspect, about the theming. Instead of sneaking onto rides after-hours with Charlotte at Lands, Emily switched to another part-time job at a local restaurant and spent her free time in high school with popular kids. When Charlotte chose to take her love of theme parks to another company, Emily had yell-cried at her. Emily had expected Charlotte would stay at Lands and eventually step into Frank's and Marianne's shoes, but if Charlotte wasn't interested, then it left Emily stuck to carry on the family business—the family business she would support because she loved her parents, but a business that didn't spark joy in her heart. From Emily's point of view, Charlotte was keeping her at Lands and trapping her in Lake Sterling where she couldn't make the most of her business degree.

Charlotte didn't think it was fair to shoulder that blame. If it was truly bothersome, Emily should talk to her parents about how she felt, but all these years later her cousin never had that conversation and Charlotte couldn't force her to. The tension between her and Emily tightened over time, to the point where Charlotte accepted it as part of her life. Usually, they avoided each other outside of family gatherings. Until Charlotte came back to Lake Sterling five months ago.

When Charlotte returned home and frantically planned how she would generate income, thinking about asking her aunt, uncle, and cousin for work at Lands increased her often-present anxiety to extremes. She would think about approaching them and unsettling tingles swept across her cheeks and her chest grew tight. Charlotte wrestled with it for a couple of weeks. But, for the most part, she'd had no reason to worry. Aunt Marianne and Uncle Frank were thrilled to have her join the Lands team again and bring her new experience and perspective to their operations. Emily tolerated Charlotte's presence, while regularly pointing out how they could have used Charlotte's expertise years ago to get their new land, Under the Waves, long in development, open, making the business more profitable. And Emily held profitability above all else.

Emily may not have wanted to be at Lands, or even in Lake Sterling, forever, but she still gate-kept the park and got territorial when Charlotte suggested ideas Marianne and Frank gushed over. Charlotte imagined Emily, to some degree, wanted to project to her parents that she was the one coming up with ideas, *not* Charlotte, because Emily always wanted to be the best. But Charlotte also suspected her cousin's attitude and actions weren't only about being competitive. She knew Emily cared about the park deep down, even while she rolled her eyes at her dad, explaining why he refused to charge guests more for simple things, like the decorated wagons they lent parents to haul their kids around the park. Part of Emily's sense of ownership was a bizarre need to keep proving herself.

Article turned in to *Ride Report* and other business-of-writing housekeeping tasks crossed off her list, Charlotte glanced at the time. She had just enough time to start dinner prep before her parents got home. They were perfectly capable of cooking their own meals, but Charlotte enjoyed cooking, especially for more than just herself, and it was nice to treat her parents after their days at work. She was only home temporarily anyway, so why not spoil them. Plus her parents paid for the majority of the groceries. Not a bad deal.

Her parents, Alice and Richard, were approaching retirement but not quite there yet, so they still put in the usual eight hours in their respective jobs at the nearby college, Grove Technical. Alice worked as the vice president of student affairs, while Richard had spent his career in the landscape architecture program. They carpooled to work when their schedules aligned and shared lunch together often. They had what Charlotte would call a wholesome, sweet marriage developed over years of companionship, arguments, and challenges.

She had one hand deep into a meatball mixture when she heard the key in the side door. Charlotte leaned back from the counter as far as she could and waved with the hand not covered in ground beef and breadcrumbs. "Hey, you two!" Mom stepped through the door first and smiled warmly as she placed her worn leather bag by the door and adjusted her oversized glasses. "You're back! How was your trip?"

"Oh, you know, rode a roller coaster so many times I felt unsteady, ate a lot of popcorn. The usual. I got to spend some quality time with Melanie, too," Charlotte replied. She didn't mention her run-in with Chad; her parents had met Chad only once and not been impressed with his attitude toward Charlotte's "quaint" hometown and "quaint" family theme park. "Did I miss anything while I was away?"

"Madmartigan cried pathetically at the basement door for so long we eventually let him go down there so he could see for himself that you weren't home," Dad joked. He ran his hand through his continually disappearing gray hair. "But other than that, nah. Nothing exciting going on."

Charlotte caught the forced nonchalance in his voice and noticed he wasn't making direct eye contact. Maybe, she thought, he'd decided to finally retire and wasn't ready to announce it to her because that would make it real. It's something he would do, but she knew pressing him directly wouldn't get her anywhere, so she tucked her questions away for later—maybe she could catch him off guard during dinner.

"That sounds like Madmartigan." Charlotte put on a face of faux concern and asked, "Do you think we spoil him too much?" Mom, not the cat's number one fan, adjusted her glasses and rolled her eyes. "I'm going to unwind on the porch with a glass of wine. How long do I have before dinner's ready?"

"About forty minutes," Charlotte said, and nodded toward the meatballs. "These are nearly ready to go into the oven."

Charlotte appreciated how her mother knew she didn't like to talk while working in the kitchen. They'd catch up later. If Charlotte would have told herself six months ago that she'd enjoy living at home again, she wouldn't have believed it. The reason why she'd moved back to Lake Sterling wasn't ideal, and society said living at home at the age of thirty-three wasn't cool, but she couldn't complain about spending more time with her parents. Mom headed toward the bedroom to change. Charlotte knew her dad would go to the storage shed to grab tools and do some kind of work out there until he had to come inside. He was like a child in that way, refusing to come indoors if he could be outside. Instead of playing with friends he was tidying his planting areas or placing new plants into the ground. Not all flowers either. His dedication to his ever-growing vegetable garden had been yielding quite the bounty. Usually, it produced so many vegetables they had plenty to share with neighbors and donate to the food pantry downtown.

After they sat and caught each other up on the last few

days, Mom pushed her spaghetti around her plate. "So, are you doing any work at Lands tomorrow? You haven't gone in for a week or so."

Again, Charlotte picked up on a weird edge to the conversation, something her parents were clearly leaving a wide space around.

Charlotte replied, "Yeah, freelance reporting life has been busy recently. But yes, I am. I'm planning to stroll the grounds in the morning and then work on a couple of ideas for winter social promotions in the office, see if we can get more folks in the park before we close for the season. I want to think more about spring activities, too. We need to see some serious growth in attendance if Uncle Frank and Aunt Marianne are ever going to get Under the Waves open."

Under the Waves would be Lands of Legend's fourth themed area and it had been a dream of Frank and Marianne's for years. Marianne thought of it as a space dedicated to learning about the ocean's mysteries with a mermaid palace, a dark ride through the ruins of Atlantis, a sprawling splash zone with sculptures of wild aquatic creatures, and most exciting of all, an ambitious roller coaster that would go underwater—or at least would look like it went underwater thanks to the art of illusion.

But despite elaborate plans, excavation, a man-made mini lake, and a huge chunk of completed construction following exacting engineering plans, Lands wasn't bringing in enough revenue to help Under the Waves inch toward completion. Aside from the roller coaster, each project in the area was so close to being ready for opening. So close she knew Marianne could feel it, and that the years the project had taken were discouraging her. Without an infusion of funds, they had to keep stalling and putting it off, with the projected opening date marching into the future. They'd never released the opening date to the public at least, so they didn't have to confront disappointment on that front. Alice looked at her, eyes crinkling around the edges with concern. "I'm sure you'll come up with something, and if not, who knows? Things may work out." She exchanged a heavy look with Richard.

Charlotte put her fork down, sat back, and looked at each of them directly. "Is there something you two aren't telling me? You've both been a little off since you got home." Mom suddenly found the rest of her meal fascinating. Dad stared at the table for a second and sighed deeply.

"We promised Frank and Marianne that we'd let them tell you tomorrow and I want to keep that promise," he said. "So, all I'll say is that you should be open-minded about change that will help Lands of Legend stay open in the long term and help them open Under the Waves in the short term." He reached out to put his hand on Charlotte's shoulder and repeated, "Open. Minded."

A thousand questions erupted in Charlotte's mind simultaneously with such force she could practically hear them bubble up. "Whatdoyoumeanopenmindedaboutwhat?" she pushed out in one long breath. "Is the park in danger of closing? Are Aunt Marianne and Uncle Frank okay? Is Emily doing something shady? Do we need to—"

"Breathe, honey. Take a deep breath," Alice cut her off and threw dagger eyes at her husband. "Your father . . . we . . . weren't supposed to say anything." More dagger eyes in Richard's direction. Based on Dad's pained expression, Charlotte was pretty sure Mom had kicked him under the table, too. "But since that cat's out of the bag, I don't want you to spiral all night. And we both know you will, with how much you dislike uncertainty. You know Emily has been looking out for investors for some time; she wants to get Under the Waves open so it can stop being a literal money pit. And that's on top of Frank and Marianne wanting to retire—

Marianne wants to get out and see the world before, in her words, her 'bones turn brittle.' "

Alice paused to make sure her daughter registered what she said.

Charlotte nodded.

"Well, Emily has found an investor for Lands. One with deep pockets. A firm called Ever Fund."

Charlotte exhaled. "Oh, that's amazing news. An influx of cash means opportunities for a lot of overdue upgrades in addition to opening Under the Waves . . ." She trailed off as she noticed her parents didn't seem joyful about this turn of events. At least not as happy as they should be. "What? What's the catch?"

Richard coughed. He was clearly deciding how much to divulge.

"It seems like the investors—I'm sorry, 'venture capitalists'—may want to make changes. They're as focused on the financial aspects of the business as Emily is, obviously, since they're providing money, and they'll want to make it back." Charlotte gave her father a quizzical look. "They want to claim a big stake in the ownership and day-to-day operations. Frank worries they want to make Lands more of an amusement park. They'll open Under the Waves but the concept of theming might be secondary to them. They want to do what will get people paying for admission. It's not clear if they share Frank and Marianne's vision. And Emily wants the park to make piles of money, so . . ."

"Is it a done deal? How long will Uncle Frank and Aunt Marianne stay involved in park operations?" Charlotte asked. Her throat suddenly had a lump she could barely swallow around, and those telltale anxiety tingles started to prickle her cheeks. She didn't know a person could crash from optimism to cynicism so quickly.

Alice replied, "I guess we've gone past not divulging details. Please, please act surprised tomorrow. From our understanding, the deal is mostly done. Emily and your aunt and uncle did a virtual presentation for the venture capitalist firm between Christmas and New Year's, and now that Ever Fund's had time to digest, they're coming to Lands to kind of sell themselves? They want to make sure the investment is a good fit for both parties. So, I don't know what that means for Frank and Marianne, but I'd be surprised if they keep working at the park beyond opening Under the Waves. It's either continue struggling to keep the park open, working long hours to do so and putting themselves under financial strain, or it's make this deal and help their life's work continue on in some way while they move on with their lives. Though I'll eat this fork if they completely step away. That park is their baby."

Charlotte sank deeper and deeper into her chair as her mom explained the stakes. If Ever Fund was coming to Lands tomorrow, that probably had something to do with the meeting Aunt Marianne texted her about. The news had somehow sucked out her bones because she melted closer to the floor like human-shaped goo. Could Lands of Legend even exist without her aunt and uncle's thoughtful oversight? What would happen if it was left to Emily's care along with this firm, Ever Whatever? Would Lands of Legend keep its ability to transport people to different places? Charlotte had been hesitant to go all-in with Lands since she'd been back; Emily hadn't put out a welcome mat and had excluded her from the big conversations—like this whole presentation to Ever Fund—and that, right or wrong, hurt Charlotte's feelings. Charlotte had been going along with the vibes, doing her best to help Lands, but trying not to overstep since she knew she wouldn't be staying forever.

But an investor. Marianne and Frank retiring. Emily as the heir apparent, taking over sooner than Charlotte thought. Maybe it was time to overstep. To insert herself into every ounce of Lands of Legend's business. While she was here, she'd make sure to put Lands on the right path and protect it from the investor and Emily putting carnival rides in every land.

She found her bones and straightened in her chair. She looked first at her dad, then her mom.

"Thank you for letting me know what's going on. I promise I'll act surprised when I see Uncle Frank and Aunt Marianne tomorrow. Would you mind cleaning up from dinner? I have work to do."

Chapter 5

*D*ing. *Ding*. *Ding*. Charlotte groaned. Her hand shot out from under the covers to snooze her phone alarm. Madmartigan meowed his displeasure at being disturbed as Charlotte rolled over on her back, slowly blinking awake. She'd stayed up past three a.m., googling Ever Fund (their website was generic as could be but did highlight their preference to invest in small businesses) and frantically texting Melanie and then making list after list as she worked on practicable, lucrative ideas to get more people through the Lands of Legend gates: food stalls, limited merchandise ideas, ticket packages. Anything that could bring in additional revenue or trim expenses—not that Emily was transparent about operating costs. It was yet another weird way she kept vital information about the park from Charlotte.

While making lists to still her racing mind, Charlotte saw that Lands would still need an investor. She didn't need access to a profit and loss statement that Emily wouldn't share anyway to know they were beyond the option of stacking small revenue amounts over time to open Under the Waves. She saw the need for an influx of cash. So she focused on what she could control and that was revenue-making ideas; she could share those with her aunt and uncle so that if—more likely when—Emily and the investors brought in suggestions that didn't hold true to the values of Lands of Legend, they would have appealing backups.

Her time as a Dream Mechanic had shown her the value of any idea, no matter the size. If it was innovative enough, guests would come to see it and pay money to do so. And while Charlotte knew it was an uphill battle with Emily, maybe it was time to bring her annual passholder idea to the table again. Emily had argued that the people who bought annual passes wouldn't spend as much in the park when they visited because they were coming so often, and was in favor of getting as much cash from visitors as possible. But with the right plans, the passholder program would be a constant, predictable stream of repeatable revenue and who didn't love that? Charlotte was sure Uncle Frank and Aunt Marianne had already had some of the ideas on her list, but she'd had the advantage and misfortune of seeing how DreamUs reached into the pockets of its visitors. She could employ some of the same tactics but in a more balanced way, which should be doable since Lands's prices weren't anywhere near as high as those in DreamUs parks.

Whatever happened, she would not let Emily and Ever Fund make Lands of Legend something it was not.

A calmer voice in Charlotte's head told her she might be jumping to conclusions about the investor's intentions and that maybe her parents were exaggerating, but she ignored it. She let a little anger roar through her at the thought of a bland, out-of-the-box drop ride marring the Lands of Legend landscape with some sort of Peak Fusion movie logo stuck on the side. Her brain could breathe life into a worst-case scenario with astonishing detail.

Charlotte texted Melanie.

Charlotte: Are you awake? I'm spiraling.
Melanie: You mean, am I awake after your texts kept me awake half the night? When you were also spiraling?

Melanie: (I say that with love.)

Charlotte: You could have put your phone on do not disturb.

Melanie: Please, you know I would never.

Melanie: What's up?

Charlotte: I'm too all over the place to be rational. How do you think I should approach this? Let Emily take the lead and tell me what's happening or???

Melanie: Uh, no. Emily is not the biggest Charlotte fan in the world and you know this.

Charlotte: You're right.

Melanie: Talk to your aunt and uncle first, alone if you can. See how they're feeling.

They're probably relieved about being able to move on with the park?

Charlotte: Hmm. Maybe.

Charlotte: It's hard to imagine.

Melanie: But you don't know until you talk to them. So do that first.

Charlotte: Has anyone told you how wise you are?

Melanie: Not often enough.

Charlotte: Thank you, Melanie.

Melanie: You're welcome. Keep me posted.

Charlotte put down her phone and got ready quickly. She wanted to get to Lands of Legend early enough to both soak in the park and talk to her aunt and uncle without her cousin present before the afternoon meeting. Charlotte went through her to-dos for the day as she showered:

- Check for any last-minute notes from *Ride Report* about my Cosmic Catastrophe Coaster article
- Feed Madmartigan
- Clean Madmartigan's litter box
- Walk around Lands, definitely ride Fairytale Canal

- Talk to Marianne & Frank
- Find a brilliant solution to the money problem to keep Lands pure and special

Charlotte made sure Madmartigan got his morning repast and then filled her to-go tumbler with the coffee her parents had left in the pot for her. They'd made her favorite kind of Stauf's coffee this morning, Highlander Grog, before they headed to work. It was their way of leaving her an encouraging hug. The coffee's butterscotch and caramel notes instantly lifted her mood and energy levels. Charlotte slung her crossbody bag over her shoulder and scritched Madmartigan's fluffy back before heading out the door. "Have a good day, sir, and try not to nap too much."

She pulled out of the driveway and drove the twenty minutes to Lands on autopilot. Charlotte had made this drive along the winding state route around farms, through Lake Sterling, and past the titular lake countless times. She knew just when she'd see the top of Hydra's Fury in the distance, beyond the flat fields and low hills.

Charlotte smiled every time it came into sight. She couldn't help it. The magic of Lands had never worn off since that encounter with Flossleaf, not even after she started working behind the curtain and seeing the hows and whys behind the front-facing magic.

She pulled into her usual parking spot at the far corner of the employee parking lot and took deep breaths. She would shove the meeting from her mind this morning and be present in the park. That was usually a reliable way for inspiration and ideas to find her. Charlotte already looked forward to getting one of the legendary giant cinnamon rolls from Sir Cinna-Swirls with its crunchy flaky edges and cinnamon-saturated gooey interior for breakfast. The more icing melting over the edges of the warm roll, the better.

Her mouth watered as she picked up the pace, remembering her recommendations from a year or so ago to push the cinnamon rolls—as much delicious food as possible, really—across the park's social media channels. She'd been at DreamUs then and saw how Instagrammable food was making the registers sing, so she'd also recommended that Marianne and Frank contract Melanie for help. The demand for quality and photogenic theme park food could not be overstated and Melanie's huge following, plus the popularity of a number of other theme park food-focused accounts and video channels, proved it.

The campaign was a success. Sir Cinna-Swirls's revenue followed an upward trajectory in the year since. Never mind that Charlotte probably shouldn't have meddled while working at DreamUs. Never mind that Emily did not once say thank you.

Charlotte reached the employee entrance at the end of the stone path from the parking lot. The path turned to dirt and went through a vine-wrapped arch into the woods. They had a more accessible paved option through the forested area too, so anyone coming to work for the day could transport themselves into a different world immediately. It made a nice transition from the outside world into Lands.

She greeted the security guard who scanned in employees. "Good morning, Owen! How are Mabel and Olive doing?"

Owen smiled. "Charlotte, you're back! Oh, they're fine. Trying to scam me out of more and more treats as usual."

They pulled out their phone to show Charlotte the latest Mabel and Olive photo shoot. Mabel and Olive, a sweet pair of corgi siblings, were Instagram famous for being (1) ridiculously adorable and (2) sporting stylish costumes Owen handmade for them. Owen took great pride in their work, designing the ensembles down to every last detail. They were in the process of getting Mabel and Olive certified for therapy so the precious pups could also deliver joy outside of social media.

"You made them mermaids while I was gone?! The way you designed the tail to look just like a tail but still give them plenty of mobility is impressive," Charlotte said.

"Thank you! It was tricky to figure out, but luckily they handle multiple fittings like pros." Owen beamed at the photos of their dogs. "Are you playing or working today?"

"Both," Charlotte replied. "But playing first, of course." She hadn't spotted Frank's battered truck in the lot; she had time.

"Well, enjoy these quiet minutes before the park opens. It's the best."

Charlotte couldn't agree more. She waved goodbye and followed the path—now a sidewalk—past the small building with administrative offices. It was more like a house than an office building. Charlotte decided not to drop off her things since she didn't want to encounter anyone else yet. She kept walking past the other operations areas dotted with various-sized buildings for employee breaks, a cafeteria, storage for costumes and seasonal decor, maintenance equipment, and more. It had been eye-opening for Charlotte back in the day to learn just how much went into making a theme park—even one of a modest size like Lands—operable.

She headed toward one of the secure pathways employees used to enter Lands from the behind-the-scenes areas and it dropped her into Fairytale Land, the park's oldest area. Frank had purchased a total of fifty acres, but kept the park's footprint small at first. Lands opened with Fairytale Land in 1985; back then it had a carousel (later renamed Emily's Carousel), a miniatures ride called Fairytale Canal, and Bluewhistle Meadow. Fairytale Land soon expanded and the park grew with two additional themed areas: Forgotten Beasts and Adventurer's Gate. Under the Waves, when it opened, would be the park's fourth "land."

Fairytale Land occupied a special place in Charlotte's heart. Besides being home to Bluewhistle Meadow and the entrance to the imaginary World of Faery where she'd met Flossleaf as a kid, the park's history sang loudly here among the smooth cobblestone passages and storybook-style exteriors. Everything here from the doors on the buildings to the rides to, yes, even the restrooms supported the land's theme of looking beyond the surface. Magic and mystery awaited anyone who paused to take a closer look.

Blog posts and YouTube videos documented the many hidden layers and Easter eggs, but park-goers hadn't found everything. Or if they had, they hadn't put it on social media. Charlotte appreciated the details still tucked away from the internet: The small, hidden faery door near the gift shop that opened into a small, curved passage. The shadow of a wizard in a pointy hat and robes that flickered on the door of the hat shop a handful of times a day.

Charlotte soaked in the space, unable to resist taking photos of the sun filtering through the trees just so to wash the area in the morning's warm yellow. Even after knowing Fairytale Land her entire life, she still got caught up in the magic, still felt transported elsewhere. And that was just from looking at open space without the hustle and bustle of employees, performers, and park guests.

She clutched her coffee mug close to her chest, closed her eyes, and leaned against the Sir Cinna-Swirls building, the delicate mix of cinnamon and pastry dough already wafting through the air. Charlotte inhaled. She still wanted to get back to DreamUs with its global footprint and ability to reach millions of guests every year, its massive workshops with Dream Mechanics imagining the most blue-sky possibilities and making them real from the simplest materials, like an actual Tony Stark in a cave with a box of scraps. No place she'd been thrummed with imagination quite like the Dream Mechanic office building. But she couldn't deny how Lands of Legend made her feel.

"Ah, excuse me," said a strange voice from behind. Charlotte turned around. She tried not to stare. First of all, this person's suit and tie didn't fit the surroundings; that happened at DreamUs because executives visited the park, but here at Lands, the executives were her uncle and aunt and they preferred flannel shirts and cardigans, respectively. Never mind that her cousin Emily did occasionally walk around the park in Louboutin boots. And also, he stood out. He was sort of beautiful. Tall, deep green eyes with light flecks of gray, blue-black wavy hair cascading to his shoulders—the hair's messiness at odds with his neat-as-a-pin tailored suit. Those eyes. They were familiar. So was the way his hair curled around his forehead. It reminded her of someone.

Shit, how long had she been staring and not answering?

Charlotte cleared her throat. "Yes?"

"I'm looking for . . . uh"—he glanced at his phone—"Sir Cinna-Swirls."

"You're in luck because you're here," Charlotte said. "Take a deep breath and enjoy." She mimed pulling the heavenly pastry scent into her nose and inwardly cringed. What was she doing and why was she doing it? This kind of awkwardness hadn't shown its ugly head since she met Chad in the hallway of the Dream Mechanic offices.

That tickled something in her memory. She knew this man! Those intense eyes had flitted through her mind more than once since her trip to Orlando. "Wait, do you know Chad Sandusky?"

"Huh? Uh, yeah, we went to school together. How did you know that?"

"You were with him at the opening of Cosmic Catastrophe two days ago. Gregory, right?"

Gregory appeared alarmed at her knowing his name and scanned his surroundings. "Yes?"

"I was there, too. We ran into each other before you left. Or I should say, I ran into Chad. I used to work with him and uh, date him and live with him." That was too much information, but it was apparently a morning of Charlotte making choices.

Recognition sparked in Gregory's green eyes. "Right? Right. So we did. I was, uh, not doing well in the heat so I was in a hurry to leave—I was there as a favor to Chad, I don't usually choose to spend time in Florida. I thought January would be cooler. Anyway, uh, sorry I didn't introduce myself."

"That's understandable, January usually *is* cooler," Charlotte said. While she wondered what the favor was, she decided it didn't matter at the moment. "Anyway, you're here early, the park doesn't open for five more minutes." That gave her pause. "Actually, how are you here?"

She couldn't believe she'd been so dazzled by this man's emerald eyes and confused by his connection to her ex that she hadn't realized park guests shouldn't be past the gates yet.

"Oh, I'm here for a meeting today and I heard about these cinnamon rolls and, uh, I needed food," he said. Why was *he* also being awkward? Charlotte had a hunch and, given that she'd been admiring his defined jawline while he talked, things had a high chance of continuing to be awkward.

"They are legendary cinnamon rolls; you won't regret it. Holly, our head pastry chef for the park, does exceptional work." Without changing the upbeat tone of her voice Charlotte said, "Are you meeting with Frank and Marianne Gates? You're the venture capitalist, I presume?" She tried to sound casual, all the while tugging at her worn jeans and favorite oversized sweater—not exactly on the same level as his formal business attire. That business attire should have immediately clued her in to him being their investor, but in fairness, his eyes were *quite* distracting.

He lifted his eyebrows in surprise. "I am. Uh, yes. I'm here for Ever Fund. How do you know Frank and Marianne?"

She knew it! She stuck her hand out. "I'm their niece, Charlotte Gates."

"The consultant. Of course, Emily mentioned you. Gregory Binns."

Did Charlotte imagine the hint of unpleasant emphasis on the word *consultant*? She wondered if Emily said less than flattering things about her, but she wouldn't worry about it. Charlotte could make her own impression. They shook, his soft hand firmly gripping hers. No, she didn't have a reason to think about this man's skincare routine. Charlotte practically jerked her hand away. Real smooth, she thought.

"Yes, I'm technically the consultant." She crossed her arms and stood taller. "I've been coming to this park since I was kid and worked just about everywhere in Lands in my teens before I went to college and grad school and worked in the Dream Mechanic division at DreamUs."

Why did she feel the urge to read her entire résumé to him? She had nothing to prove to him, this man wearing a crisp suit in a theme park, just like her stupid ex. She'd just wanted a sugary pastry.

"Anyway," Charlotte said with an edge to her voice, "I love Lands of Legend and know every inch of every land, and I feel very invested in its future—for my family's sake," she quickly added.

Gregory gave her an appraising look. "Is that so? Well, before meeting with them today I was planning to see as much of the park as possible—though that shouldn't take too long."

Charlotte's eyes widened in protest. Shouldn't take too long? No, Lands didn't sprawl across a ton of space. But it wasn't something you could see all of in less than half a day. Not if you were taking your time and appreciating it.

"Maybe you could be my guide? Give me the highlights reel. Show me what's so special about this place," Gregory asked.

"Umm." Charlotte pretended to check the calendar on her phone to buy herself time to think.

This was not how Charlotte expected her morning to go. She'd wanted to stop her thoughts from darting around like bugs skating on the surface of water by taking a peaceful stroll around the park after she stuffed her face with a cinnamon roll. Then she would find Frank and Marianne and have a heart-to-heart before the meeting at one. Charlotte pushed down the desire to tell this walking suit to have a terrific time exploring on his own, but she suspected he'd take a quick circuit around the park without any rides, shows, or meandering. He wouldn't get the real Lands of Legend experience. So why not use her powers for good? Maybe she could show him the magic of Lands, all the while reinforcing how special her aunt and uncle's vision for the park was. She didn't need to mention Emily's lack of interest in that vision.

Yes, that was it! She would give the best damn tour of Lands of Legend anyone could imagine. She'd win him over before the meeting even started and they'd get off on the right foot with the venture capital firm, assuming Marianne, Frank, and Emily liked what they heard from him today. A list ran through her head:

- Show Gregory all the best parts of Lands
- Explain the park's innovation and history
- Save the day

Easy.

Chapter 6

"Looks like I'm clear until the meeting. I'd love to show you around Lands—on two conditions," Charlotte said.

Gregory looked at her skeptically. "What conditions?"

"You will go on every ride I ask you to go on, and you will try to have fun."

"Ah. So you can tell I'm not the type who goes on rides, huh?"

Charlotte had her work cut out for her. "I didn't know for sure, but I suspected as much. The suit and tie don't exactly scream 'I'm here to toss my cares aside while I eat sugar and go on rides.'"

He had the grace to look embarrassed, the lightest pink creeping across his cheekbones. "Guilty as charged. To be honest, I'm only here because my mother, Evelyn, forced me to come. Mine's a family business, too. I haven't been to a place like this ever, I think?" He tilted his head back slightly, like he was going through memories. "Wait, I kind of remember my grandpa taking me to a park when I was a kid—you know, the target audience for places with rides and popcorn."

Charlotte didn't miss the dismissive tone in his voice.

If they had been walking, Charlotte would have stopped in her tracks. He clearly wasn't young at heart and since he couldn't understand why other adults would go to a theme park, he looked down on them instead. Every so often online discourse popped up about adults who adored going to theme parks even if they didn't have children to accompany them. It was a conversation Charlotte had had many times. And it exhausted her, yes, but it also prepared her for this moment. She took a deep breath.

"You're right. Kids do love theme parks, and families make up a large percentage of our visitors. But a ton of adults come without children. Groups of friends, childless couples. Between my time at Lands seeing visitors from day-to-day to working for DreamUs and reviewing demographics for all of the company's nine parks, I can confidently tell you adults love theme parks just as much as kids. Plus, they tend to have more disposable income, so they're especially valuable customers," Charlotte noted with a small, patronizing smile.

Gregory looked like he was going to interrupt. She didn't let him.

"Everyone needs an escape, right? Adults want to play in a world of imagination as much as kids. Some parts of society judge them"—she leveled a look at Gregory—"but they ignore the cracks and commentary from other adults who have forgotten how to play. We often treat adulthood as this sacred business, where every moment must be taken seriously—how are we 'earning' our way in life unless we follow societal standards? *Fuck* that. Life is fleeting. Play and happiness are important. Otherwise, what's the point?"

Charlotte pointedly did not think about how little time she left for play.

She concluded, "So no, kids aren't the sole target audience, and marketing with only kids and families in mind is a mistake for more reasons than lost revenue opportunities."

Gregory looked like he wanted to argue. Instead, a smirk

appeared on his all-too-handsome face. "Do you normally curse while in a theme park?"

Charlotte clenched her fists. *That's* what he took away from her impassioned speech?! She narrowed her eyes. "Don't even get me started on how curse words are arbitrary."

She gestured around them. "Also, no kids are around right now."

They stood in uncomfortable silence for a beat too long. Charlotte couldn't believe she'd agreed to show this limp noodle of a human around the park. It didn't matter how he turned standing with a slight lean into a work of art. Glancing at her watch, she noted she had three hours until the meeting Marianne texted about, and she still wanted to talk with her aunt and uncle before then. Plus, she did have some work to do before then, so she had maybe two hours. Two hours to make Gregory see the magic of Lands and be the ideal, hands-off money person who gave them a blank check and didn't interfere. As a bonus, maybe she could show him it was okay to experience joy.

It was going to be fine.

"Ookaay. Sir Cinna-Swirls is open now. Shall we start with cinnamon rolls?" Charlotte asked.

"Lead the way," Gregory replied.

Chapter 7

Charlotte regretted her decision to accompany Gregory around the park almost as soon as they sat down with their cinnamon rolls. Gregory started right in with throwing operational questions at her: How many employees worked at Sir Cinna-Swirls at any given time? When did they last increase the price for the cinnamon rolls? Was it necessary to stock so many optional toppings and did they charge for those, too?

She looked longingly at the cream cheese icing slowly melting down the side of the indulgent breakfast and held her hand up. "No. This is not having fun. This is not experiencing a theme park. I've done a lot of work to understand the difference, and trust me, this is treating magic like a balance sheet, and it is not the time for it. Not yet. Besides, shouldn't you ask Emily those questions? I'm just the 'consultant.'"

Charlotte glared to communicate that she would not tolerate another question. It shut him up.

Charlotte posed her plated cinnamon roll just so in the morning light filtering through Sir Cinna-Swirls's stained-glass windows to take a photo she'd later use for the park's Instagram feed.

"Is this experiencing a theme park?" Gregory asked as he gestured at her acting like a cinnamon-roll paparazzi.

A lock of wayward hair fell across his forehead, brushing the top of his left eyebrow. Even as Charlotte had an urge to touch it and put it back into place, she felt her mouth tighten as her glare returned. Charlotte ignored the question. She couldn't resist eating her cinnamon roll any longer. Leveraging the fork between the layers, she started peeling away the outermost circle of dough. It separated from the bun, revealing delicate pockets in between the pastry's layers, all of them dotted with brown spots of cinnamon and heavenly cinnamon sugar goo.

"Do you need a minute to be alone with your cinnamon roll?" Gregory asked.

How dare he take her away from her cinnamon roll reverie. "Yes, I would like a moment of peace while I eat the first few bites. Respect the cinnamon roll, Gregory."

He surprised her by saluting with his fork. "Note to self: do not interrupt Charlotte's cinnamon-roll time."

Charlotte savored the dessert (sure it was called breakfast, but) as she swept her gaze over the interior of Sir Cinna-Swirls. The stained-glass windows depicted idyllic forest scenes, one for each of the four seasons. Light sparkled against the red and orange leaves of the fall scene, and Charlotte knew the afternoon light would warm the glass purple blossoms of the spring scene later.

Gregory followed her gaze. He looked like he wanted to ask a question, but she could see him holding back to honor her request. Since she'd had a few quiet minutes to honor the cinnamon roll, she told him, "Go ahead."

"I noticed you looking at the stained-glass windows with such admiration and I know you've probably seen them a million times before. What makes them special?"

She didn't detect any sarcasm or hostility in his voice, but Charlotte still proceeded with caution. "My mother made these. She's been a stained-glass artist since high school, prac-

tically, and these windows are some of her earliest work."
Charlotte didn't try to keep the pride from her voice.

"It's something she's always done on the side, but over the years, she's made time for her art, learning new techniques. I think she's looking forward to finally focusing on her art full-time after she retires from her job at the local college."

Charlotte smiled. "Anytime she's here she finds a million flaws in these pieces. Just picks every square inch apart. But I think they're gorgeous. Are there some imperfections? Sure, but they make the windows all the more special."

She looked from the windows back to Gregory and was shocked to see he was smiling. A sweet, indulgent kind of smile, matched by warmth in his green eyes. The best crinkles appeared around the corners of his mouth and made him more attractive. No sooner had Charlotte noted the smile, it faded.

"That *is* special. And I don't notice any flaws with them," he said. "Does she have any other work in the park?"

"A few smaller pieces, right now. But she's been working on a massive triptych to go in the Under the Waves area. It has mermaids, underwater castles, all kinds of sea creatures. She's created at least a dozen elements for it over the last five years."

Charlotte couldn't help but get animated while speaking about the triptych. She'd seen pieces of it in Mom's studio; Alice had chosen the perfect hues of glass to emulate the ocean. Charlotte only hoped Under the Waves would indeed open one day so everyone could enjoy Mom's design, which she guessed Gregory was here to help with.

"I've heard a lot about Under the Waves from Frank and Marianne." Gregory looked like he wanted to get into more nitty-gritty about Lands, but he stopped himself. Instead, he asked, "You're really supportive of your mom's work, aren't you?"

"I am. She's an incredible artist!"

"And?" Gregory asked, apparently sensing Charlotte's over-enthusiastic tone.

"Well, I feel guilty." Charlotte admitted.

"Why?"

Charlotte considered for a minute. She wasn't sure why she felt comfortable telling this stranger her deepest thoughts. It surely wasn't because of that soft smile a few moments ago. She sighed. "I don't think she ever got to fully explore her art career because she felt like she needed to maintain a full-time job for me—she's worked at Grove Technical my whole life. Then I've done nothing *but* pursue my passion career. I know she's proud of me for chasing my dreams. She's come to the grand opening of every ride I helped work on at DreamUs, but I wish she would have been able to be only an artist all these years."

"Right, but you didn't make those choices. She did." Gregory's tone of voice said he thought this was a ridiculous way to feel.

And Charlotte was already well aware that she did not control her mother's decisions. She wished she hadn't said anything. It was time to change the subject. She didn't imagine Gregory to be the type to share personal details with a person he met minutes ago, but she found herself saying, "So, you said your mother sent you here and that Ever Fund is a family business?"

Gregory looked down and picked at the sugary remains of his cinnamon roll, a wrinkle forming between his eyebrows as he stared at his fork. "You know, I appreciate these bamboo utensils. Probably worth the extra expense to be able to compost these."

Definitely not a personal details type, despite Charlotte's question being pretty soft. His clumsy deferral was a bit endearing, though she was surprised to hear compostable forks were an expense he would support. Still looking at the fork, Gregory finally answered. "It *is* a family business. My grandmother, Sally, started Ever Fund ages ago with a goal of being different from other venture capital firms by investing in small companies on their merits and not just for what they were offering. She had to run a business, of course, but she was in it to help others realize their goals, not make stacks of money. Then my mother, Evelyn, worked with the firm right out of school, and continued to build it side by side with my grandmother. She took over when Grandma stepped down. My father was involved in the business until he split, but now my stepmother, Abigail, is into it, too."

That was *a lot* of family to be involved in the family business. "Not your grandfather? I noticed you didn't mention him."

Gregory turned his head away. "Nah, it was never his thing; he supported Grandma but he couldn't stand, as he put it, 'office jobs.' He passed away eight years ago."

Shit. It was obvious from Gregory's longing, mournful expression that he cared for his grandpa. "I'm sorry, Gregory."

He met her eyes and the grief behind those gray flecks in his pupils pierced her. "Thank you."

"And your brother's involved, too?"

"Yeah." She heard tension in Gregory's voice. Particularly when he kept going. "Ian took an interest in the company from high school and has been second-in-command for a few years now."

Charlotte processed the idea of a high schooler being interested in investing and it painted a picture of Ian.

"In fact, Ian's why I'm here. He's how Ever Fund heard about Lands of Legend in the first place."

Charlotte tilted her head. "How so?"

"He went to the same business school as Emily, and Emily reached out to him after seeing some report about him and Ever Fund in an alumni newsletter. A place like this isn't flashy enough for Ian's tastes, but he's a sucker for helping fellow alumni and he knew this kind of business is exactly what Grandma would have wanted to support. So, here I am."

Of course Emily leveraged a college connection; Charlotte had to admit it was a smart move. "So, why are you here and not Ian?"

Gregory bit his lip and looked like he was holding in a laugh. "Here? Ian here. That's a funny picture. Uh, this is too rural for Ian. He prefers the indoors. Ian wouldn't know what to do with this much fresh air. He sticks with investment opportunities in large cities."

"But this isn't too 'rural' for you?" Gregory's hair was the only part of him that didn't look out of place in Lands.

"No. It's not. I like being outdoors, though I don't get a chance with as much as I travel for work. The most I've been outside a stuffy office lately is when we helped this fleet of burger trucks open a restaurant. I spent days riding around in their trucks to learn more about the business. Thought I'd never get the smell of fryer grease out of my Armani suit—"

"Wait. Stop. You wore an Armani suit while riding around in a burger truck." That image was going to live in Charlotte's head forever.

"Only for the first couple days. It's important to my family that I project professionalism when representing Ever Fund."

Charlotte held in a smile. "I see. So, Ian brought Lands of Legend to Ever Fund, and then . . . ?"

"Right. Then my mom sent me here after your family's presentation during what was supposed to be our holiday break. She said it would be 'good for me' to get away from L.A., which doesn't make sense because I'm almost always away from L.A. for work, but here I am." Gregory shrugged.

"Here you are." And he didn't seem overjoyed about being here. Most people Charlotte knew would be elated to go to a theme park for work, but her data sample was skewed. "Whereabouts in L.A. do you live?"

"Los Feliz."

"Ah, cute neighborhood. Lots of places to get brunch, or so I've heard."

Gregory examined the ends of his hair. "I've heard that, too."

"How long have you lived there?"

"About seven years now. I'm on the road an average of forty-five weeks of the year. I haven't spent a lot of time exploring the neighborhood. I'm not even sure why I keep an apartment."

Charlotte recognized a fellow workaholic when she saw one. "Ah, I relate to that. Glendale for me."

"Right, DreamUs has a big campus over there."

"Mm-hmm, and that campus or the parks down in Anaheim pretty much encompass my knowledge of L.A."

The conversation fizzled like fire in a downpour as they both, presumably, dwelled on their respective life decisions. Charlotte pointed her chin at Gregory's plate. "Sooo, you all done?"

"Yes. You were right. It's one of the best cinnamon rolls I've ever had."

"I don't mess around when it comes to sugar, Gregory." Her voice was playful, but she hoped it implied she didn't mess around when it came to anything involving Lands. Screw it, she decided to be less subtle. This had been a perfectly fine conversation with Gregory sharing more than she thought he would, but she wanted to reset the tone between them. She locked onto his green eyes, ignoring the soft gray flecks, and kept her voice even. "And I also don't mess around when it comes to Lands of Legend or its values. Just so you know."

He waved a hand, as if to brush away her concerns. "Message received. But it's an amusement park. How serious can they be?"

Charlotte felt her jaw drop. The nerve. This was her aunt and uncle's dream realized. They'd literally built pieces of this *theme* park, not an *amusement* park, with their own hands. She could show him how important Lands's values were while she took him around the park. Charlotte speared the final bites of her cinnamon roll, shoved them in her mouth, and chugged the remainder of her coffee to wash it down. She pushed away from the table and took a deep breath. She looked at Gregory. The list she made earlier ran through her mind and she would still try to tick off every item. She'd even add one: teach Gregory that there was a difference between amusement parks and theme parks. Charlotte loved amusement parks too, but they weren't the same.

She'd focus on the tour ahead. But getting to know Gregory beyond the conversation they'd just had? Trying to make any kind of personal connection? Forget it. She reminded herself he was the money guy, and that's what Lands needed from him with as little of his interference as possible. Charlotte forced a small smile. "Shall we continue the tour?"

Chapter 8

They wrapped around the perimeter of Fairytale Land, and Charlotte gushed about her uncle's work. She'd shoved her annoyance with Gregory aside, putting her unimpeachable ability to compartmentalize to work. Plus, she couldn't help but get animated when she spoke about the park's history. The work Uncle Frank had done really was impressive.

"So he left his job as a draftsman for the city to open the park?" Gregory asked.

Charlotte appreciated the confirmation that he had been paying attention. "Mmm-hmm." She nodded. "He had a dream of creating a place where families could play together—something smaller than DreamUs's parks, something more intimate and homegrown but still with that level of quality and theming."

Uncle Frank sketched his ideas in notepad after notepad in the early mornings before he went to work, and the stacks of notepads expanded in his and Aunt Marianne's basement. Then one day while commuting home from his job in Columbus, he saw a Realtor's sign advertising land for sale. He drove by the parcel, noting its prime location and plenty of trees for shade. He knew right away that it would be the perfect place to bring his vision to life.

A call to the Realtor, a frantic weekend of turning his sketches and research into a business plan, and many, many meetings with the bank later, and her aunt and uncle owned the land. Three years after that, Lands of Legend opened.

Charlotte had taken on the unofficial role of Lands's historian as part of a college project. Lands had been open twenty-some years at that point, so she'd had plenty to dig into. She'd conducted hours of interviews with her aunt and uncle and the park employees who'd been there since the beginning, and learned that the park's early years came with a lot of painful, usually expensive lessons. It grew slowly but surely as word of mouth spread, each rise in attendance leading to new themed areas and rides. Charlotte had documented everything from that time until now in tidy binders with digital backups. She had found and preserved copies of every iteration of the park map, marketing brochures, the original tickets. The project had continued well past college into the present. Charlotte planned to design an exhibit about the park's history that Marianne and Frank could pitch to local museums for the next milestone anniversary.

All those hours digging into Lands's past meant Charlotte could call upon her memory to add historical data to her tour. She wasn't sure if Gregory would pick up on it, but Charlotte worked in the dates and phrases like "my uncle's long-time dedication" to the park often, just to remind him about its history and all the sweat that made that history possible. Being honest with herself, she didn't think she was being that sly.

"And this here was the first stone placed in the park—like many others, Uncle Frank placed it with his own hands," Charlotte explained.

"He must have had incredible patience to build the park so slowly. Especially since he presumably still had to make payments on the land while waiting to open." She could see Gregory turning over the numbers in his mind.

Charlotte felt a need to . . . she didn't know, make her uncle and aunt sound fiscally responsible? "Yes, but he had saved money for a while and had a bit of an inheritance to help out, and Aunt Marianne supported the family until the park opened."

Gregory had a questioning look on his face, but he merely nodded. The nod was just enough to push that one lock of hair out of place again. It fell into his face in defiance of his buttoned-up appearance. *Don't push it back*, Charlotte thought, *don't push it*. But he couldn't read her mind and lifted his hand and swept it back into place.

Too bad. The errant piece of hair softened his appearance and made him seem like less of a shark in a kiddie pool.

She walked Gregory to the front of the park in order to show him the guest experience from the entrance. The main gate opened into a clearing paved with smooth bricks. Trees surrounded the area, with wide paths splitting out of the clearing through the forest: one led to Wayfarer's Path with its gift shops, sit-down restaurant, and occasional street performers; the other paths meandered to each of the themed areas, Fairytale Land, Forgotten Beasts, and Adventurer's Gate (when Under the Waves opened, guests would access it through Adventurer's Gate). The hub-and-spoke layout was popular in theme park design because it worked.

Decorated arches framed each of the paths. A creeping sculpted beanstalk with broad leaves wound around the arch to Fairytale Land, the arch to Forgotten Beasts was carved with an intricate dragon-scale pattern, and the final arch looked like it was crafted from rough timber. The name of each land stretched over the arches in different fonts and designs. It had been important to her aunt and uncle to set the tone for each area with the entry points.

Charlotte explained to Gregory that the intent was for the visitor to come through the front gate and experience awe.

To feel the excitement of possibility and discovery. Marianne and Frank wanted guests to step out of the real world and into a place of wonder.

Refreshment stands stood along the paths: popcorn—each cart had traditional buttered popcorn and a unique flavor—ice cream sandwiches, and soft pretzels in shapes to go with each themed area. Charlotte particularly loved the dragon-egg pretzels with cheese-filled centers on the path to Forgotten Beasts. The offerings depending on the season: more chilled items like Positively Lemon, a lemon slushy, in the summer and cozier items like small bread bowls in the fall and winter before the park closed for a couple months before spring. Seasonal or limited-menu items always gave them an attendance boost from locals.

Contracting Melanie to help with the food last year had really paid off. She'd offered a lot of insight after the success of boosting Sir Cinna-Swirls. Lands of Legend's food items often got mentioned in the same articles as DreamUs's parks, no small feat for a small family-owned theme park in Southeast Ohio.

In the entrance clearing, small coffee kiosks sat to the left and the right for guests who needed caffeine right away; they'd partnered with a local roaster—Marianne and Frank supported other small businesses in town whenever possible. Under a sprawling man-made toadstool sat a large board displaying the day's events and showtimes. Park employees manned the toadstool all day to answer guest's questions and provide recommendations to help them have the best possible day. Depending on how long Charlotte was around, she wanted to suggest a Lands of Legend app to further assist guests with information and tips.

Charlotte had worked in positions throughout Lands and greeting guests from the toadstool had been her favorite role. She walked Gregory over. "This is one of the most fun places

to work in the park. I spent a few seasons inside the toadstool interacting with guests and telling them about all the
best secret places."

Gregory opened his mouth. Charlotte stopped him, "I know
that if I'm telling people about the secret places they are not
actually secret."

"That's not what I was going to say."

"No?"

He shrugged. "Okay, it's not all I was going to say. I was
going to ask how hot it got inside there in the summer." He
gestured at the toadstool.

"It's air-conditioned for the summer, heated for the winter.
Another reason why it's the best place to work." She continued, "We're not fully open in the winter since the outdoor attractions can't operate in the cold and the snow, but we keep
as much going as we can and also go all out with holiday
decorations. We end up closing for about two months, which
are coming up, because the attendance levels don't justify
having folks around."

"I know. I did do my homework," Gregory explained. "My
family expects nothing less. I would have come for your family's presentation in person and visited the park sooner if I
could have, but I was trying to take the holiday break off for
once.

"What kind of attendance do you see in the off-season?"
he asked. "It definitely drops off." Charlotte felt a little like
she was in court. Gregory had asked the question innocently
enough, but she didn't know if anything she said would be
used against her aunt and uncle. It's not like she could recite
the exact percentages and attendance numbers off the top of
her head, but regardless, she decided that wasn't Gregory's
business. Best to be noncommittal until the deal was inked.

She did want to brag a little so she added, "We've seen
great success with our fall and holiday celebrations. Especially in the fall—we partner with the Circleville Pumpkin

Show, a four-day festival that's nearby, and they get about four hundred thousand visitors. It always gives us a boost."

Charlotte led him toward the Adventurer's Gate path. "We'll start here and walk around the back of the park to Adventurer's Gate, go up Wayfarer's Path, check out Forgotten Beasts, and then head to the offices. Sound good?"

He nodded. Charlotte wanted him to fully absorb the atmosphere, pick up on the things he may not have read on the park's website or elsewhere on the internet. She guided him over to a bench tucked away from the path. "Sit down and close your eyes."

A stubborn look washed over Gregory's face. "I'd rather not, I'll get my suit dirty."

Charlotte pressed her lips together to stop herself from snapping and from pointing out his Armani suit burger-food-truck escapades. In exaggerated movements she took an ivory handkerchief from her purse and wiped it along the bench's surface. She held it up to Gregory so he could see the lack of dirt. "We have an amazing staff here and we all take pride in keeping the park as pristine as possible for our guests. I don't know what kind of parks you've read about, but maybe you shouldn't make assumptions."

He sat down without saying another word.

She took a seat on the other end of the bench. Of course he wasn't going to apologize. Charlotte should have known better. He did at least have the sense to look a little sheepish.

"Great. Now close your eyes." To her surprise, he did so without protesting.

"Take a deep breath through your nose."

He interrupted. "What is this, theme park mindfulness?"

"No," she replied, "but that *is* a program I'm working on pitching. Now, be quiet and follow my instructions. Take a deep breath through your nose and let it out through your mouth. Tell me what you hear."

His deep breath sounded more like an exasperated sigh,

but she'd let it be. He answered, "I hear the sounds of people walking by and talking. The music—it sounds like it's coming from behind us somewhere. The wind in the leaves. And maybe the sound of someone filling popcorn bags?"

"You don't hear any rides, right? No sounds of machinery or vehicles on tracks." Charlotte asked. His eyelashes were long, brushing the tops of his cheeks. Then there were those shoulders, not broad but still absolutely filling out his suit jacket. She blinked furiously. Gregory was talking and she'd missed it.

"Could you repeat that?" she asked.

"I don't hear any rides. I think I can hear some faint screaming but that's it. Can I open my eyes now?"

Charlotte started to nod, realized he couldn't see her nodding, and said, "Yes, you can open them."

"What was the point of that exercise?" Gregory asked.

Probably not for Charlotte to fawn over his eyelashes.

"The point was to show you how much thought my aunt and uncle have put into designing the park. It's not only about what guests see. They've considered the sound design for each area, from the music they hired a composer to create, to special sound effects, to how to build the park around the trees to soften the sounds from the rides. Everything you hear in any given place in the park is precisely what they want guests to hear. Every little part of this park is about immersion to fit the theme of whatever area you're in."

Gregory took all that in. "I wouldn't have guessed an amusement park would care so much about details like the sound. It seems like it's all about the roller coasters and the popcorn. Speaking of, how many roller coasters do you have here?"

It was Charlotte's turn to close *her* eyes for a moment. Not because she needed to appreciate the sounds but because she needed to process how he'd taken the lesson in both the exact right and exact wrong ways. She pinched the bridge of her nose as she remembered the relaxing morning she had planned for herself before talking to Marianne and Frank and mourned it before launching into a familiar lecture. Okay, maybe it was a rant.

"It's the details that can elevate the ordinary to the extraordinary. My aunt and uncle considered everything: the sounds, this bench we're sitting on, the look of the popcorn cart over there. Each part fits the theme of the land or the park to add to the immersion and wonder," Charlotte emphasized.

"And yes, some parks do focus on rides and having the tallest or fastest roller coaster. I love those parks. They pack in thrill rides and innovate as they try to outdo each other—and themselves—and they create fun places for families to play. We want people to play too, but we also want them to escape. To experience a world other than the one they live in every day and engage their imagination."

She paused for dramatic effect. "That's oversimplified but that's the where the difference between an amusement park and a theme park comes in. A theme park's rides and structures are rooted in a central theme, usually with different areas that have their own themes that connect to the overall one. It's about storytelling. Meanwhile, an amusement park's attractions are about entertainment. So, to summarize: theme parks are about storytelling and immersion; amusement parks are about entertainment and thrill that don't connect as part of a story. One isn't better than the other and neither theme parks nor amusement parks should be dismissed as only being about 'roller coasters and popcorn.' " She emphasized the last part with air quotes.

The last sentence came out as one long word. She'd forgotten to take a breath. As she tried to inhale deeply without being obvious about it, Charlotte glanced over at Gregory to see that he'd pulled a small memo pad from somewhere and was taking notes. Well, she hadn't expected that. She'd imagined her words flying through the air and right past Gregory's face. But no, it seemed he was trying to absorb what she said. He looked up from writing and Charlotte redirected her gaze to the ground.

With his pen poised for more action, Gregory said, "So, you're clearly very into this."

"I am. When I was a kid, I wanted to spend all of my time at Lands of Legend. And I did get to spend many weekends following my aunt and uncle around, summers with my cousin playing in the park and the employee areas. I have a number of memories from back then that still influence me. Growing up with Lands and seeing how it left, and continues to leave, its mark on those who visit, is what inspired me to pursue a career at DreamUs. I got to take what I learned here and scale it up to even bigger, more amazing experiences."

"I've heard you talk a lot about DreamUs but it sounds like you loved Lands. Why leave?" Gregory asked.

Charlotte scrunched her eyes shut for a moment. "My family wondered that, too—my cousin Emily especially. Sometimes *I* wonder about it, honestly. But I wanted a bigger canvas. I saw Lands of Legend make an impression on those who passed through its gates and imagined scaling that up with more parks around the world and working with the best of the best in themed entertainment while doing so. And to be honest, it was nice to be part of a place that got global recognition. I had my hands in projects that millions got to enjoy. It was an incredible opportunity and I miss it.

"Even if DreamUs is out of the picture for now, I don't regret anything about my path. And I want to be able to give others a taste of the magic I've experienced over the years," she continued.

"I'm sorry things didn't work out at DreamUs," Gregory said as he closed his notebook and tucked it away. "Sounds like that was really your dream job, pun not intended; I've known you for, what, barely a couple hours, I can see that you're good at what you do and that you love it, which I envy. It's clearly their loss."

Huh. Okay. A platitude? Yeah, maybe. But Charlotte didn't think it was meaningless. His eyes, the green mottled in the partial shade, looked sincere enough, and she could see a flair of the envy he mentioned—envy that must mean he wasn't head over heels about venture capitalism.

"You know what? It *was* their loss. But now I get to be here and help my family, plus explore writing about and playing in other theme parks. It worked out. I wish I hadn't been laid off. But it happened and it's okay."

Charlotte found herself believing those words after finally saying them aloud. She carefully left out her secret hope: that she'd go back to DreamUs in the near future. She still felt bitter about losing her DreamUs job, but the sting had lessened, the reality about the company's regular layoffs more understandable, somehow. Charlotte had thrown herself into freelancing as a reporter and as a consultant for Lands anyway, so that could be throwing a fuzzy blanket over a pile of dirty clothes—the dirty clothes being not processing the layoff, or thinking through if returning to DreamUs would be the right move, should the chance come her way.

"Thank you for explaining the difference between a theme park and amusement park," Gregory said. "I didn't come across that in my research."

"Sounds like maybe your research didn't tell you a number of things," Charlotte replied in a flat tone.

He nodded, the corners of his mouth turning up enough to bring back those mesmerizing laugh lines, evidence that someone (God, she hoped it wasn't someone and also questioned why she hoped that) or something brought out that smile frequently. "You're right. I hope to learn more from you," he said.

Huh. Gregory said she was right. Maybe he wasn't the heartless suit she'd pegged him as. They'd met such a short time ago, after all. He sounded genuine enough. Charlotte would see if that continued on their tour.

Speaking of, they needed to get going if she wanted to get to the offices with enough time to do some work before the meeting. They'd barely even started. She nodded toward the path and they got back on the way to Adventurer's Gate. The walkway slowly curved into a more open space, green tropical plants with broad leaves becoming denser as they went. Charlotte wondered if she should point out how even the landscaping started to lean into the Adventurer's Gate theme, exploring the unknown, with its increasingly unusual plants. Maybe that would be best saved for a later tour. She didn't trust that Gregory would take in that level of detail.

She could also mention how the walkway was a prime place for making out, if their teen guests were any indication. The shaded corners with small alcoves provided some privacy and when the lanterns above the walkway came on at dusk, the setting was a whole mood. Then again, Charlotte did *not* need to give Gregory any indication she had kissing on her mind. She stretched her peripheral vision to the max, trying to see more of his full lips.

Charlotte shook her head but failed to wipe away the thought of grabbing Gregory's hand and ducking under the leaves. She had to listen to Melanie and make time for more life, life that included dating. This physical connection—well, she didn't know if he felt anything—was clearly what came of Charlotte not making any time to romantically interact with others. There couldn't be any other explanation. Not one she would acknowledge.

The path got broader until it opened into a wide expanse of buildings and rides. Guests wouldn't know this, but her aunt and uncle had planned the land around existing tall, old trees. Their spreading branches partially obscured the corners of buildings and paths, hiding the scale of them in such a way that it created a mystery—you were never sure how small or big a particular area was until you got close.

A man-made small lake in the middle of Adventurer's Gate centered the area. They called it Gates Lagoon. Its dark blue water rippled over water plants and past the curving back of a sea beast emerging from the water, as Swings Ahoy moved in a pendulum arc back and forth. Early riders shrieked as they went nearly parallel to the water in the swinging ship. Charlotte thought riding Swings Ahoy first thing in the day was the best approach. Less chance of losing any meals that way.

Home to the spirit of exploration, Adventurer's Gate featured loose Medieval Scandinavian–inspired architecture and storefronts. Rustic roofs reached into the sky, settled onto their buildings like pointy hats. Between the lake, a log flume ride, and a dark boat ride, the slight smell of chemically treated "seawater" lingered in the area. Charlotte loved the scent, but she knew it wasn't for everyone, or at least not for a number of theme park YouTubers.

She led Gregory toward the waterside.

"Inhale deeply through your nose again," she instructed him. She wanted him to see the great and not-so-great about Lands, including this strange smell. Charlotte thought he might protest after the last such exercise, but he surprised her by being a good sport.

"What am I supposed to experience this time?" he asked with a note of sass. Okay, maybe not entirely a good sport.

Charlotte replied, "You tell me."

"I smell . . . well, it's not bad but it's not familiar. It's like being by the ocean but a little stale?"

Charlotte would give him that. Treating the water meant it wasn't the pure ocean smell they wanted. She'd been trying to convince her aunt and uncle to expand the piped-in aroma from the Journey of Discovery boat ride into the entire area to add to the atmosphere. She pulled out her phone to note Gregory's observance and showed him her screen. "I keep a running list of notes about each area of the park that I add to anytime I'm in Lands."

Gregory nodded his approval and pulled out his own note-book. The man took as many notes as her, and Charlotte could tell from the notebook's battered cover that he used it often. Glimpsing at the pages showed neatly tilted handwriting with subheadings. Subheadings! She relied on lists and notes to bring structure to her life and to soothe her anxiety; she wondered if he did the same or if it was more to jog his memory. Either way, it was a miracle that Charlotte's eyes didn't turn heart-shaped and throb out of her head like she was a damn cartoon. But the thought of him recording a negative note about Lands calmed down the mushy feelings.

"Don't count the stale water smell against Lands. It's something we can address," Charlotte said.

"That's not what I was writing down."

Charlotte gave Gregory a questioning look.

"I was noting your attention to detail."

"Ah. Well that's okay, then." Satisfaction crept through Charlotte's brain for some reason, and it made her skin flush with heat. She did not need to be splotchy in front of this man.

"Where are all the people?" Gregory asked.

That casual, but annoying, question was all it took for the redness to recede. Charlotte quickly considered how forthcoming she should be with Gregory. On one hand, he was going to get all the data he could handle if her family liked his presentation for Ever Fund today, so she could be straight. However, she wanted to use this tour to sell Lands of Legend and all its charms to Ever Fund and show its appeal as is, without a drastic makeover. It wouldn't hurt to put a positive spin on things, a spin with some realism.

"Well, clearly the stale ocean smell keeps them away,"

Charlotte joked. "It *is* early in the day and it's the offseason, but you're right. It's not as full as the other parts in the park and that's something we're working on. Adventurer's Gate is an area we want to revisit once we open Under the Waves. Since both areas have strong connections to water, we can leverage that to pull more visitors this way."

Gregory didn't look convinced.

She added, "I have a list of ideas on how to increase foot traffic in Adventurer's Gate. I'd be happy to send it to you *if* everything comes together." She gave him the fakest smile she could muster.

"*When* everything comes together, I would appreciate that," Gregory answered. "But is there a reason your aunt and uncle haven't implemented your ideas yet?"

He had to ask. Again, Charlotte didn't know how much to share. The continual struggle for the park to make large enough profits to do more than maintenance and the occasional new update was part of it, the biggest part of it, but Uncle Frank and Aunt Marianne also had a reluctance to change too much about the park. And to be fair, they often had Emily bringing them terrible suggestions. Emily wanted one thing: for the park to make money, even if her ideas didn't make sense for the park—ideas like building a conference area in the area behind the park for corporate team-building packages. So Frank and Marianne tended to get defensive anytime change came up, making it clear that they were desperate if they were entertaining Ever Fund.

"Oh you know, they've been focusing most of their efforts on securing funding for Under the Waves and building what they can of it for so long, and other updates aren't as high priority." There, not a complete lie. But was that too negative? She rushed to add, "Plus Lands requires regular maintenance as part of operations. Nothing out of the ordinary, just standard theme park stuff."

"Charlotte."

"Yes?"

"None of this is a test. I'm not going to hold anything you say against you."

"Is that a joke?" she asked. Charlotte couldn't read Gregory.

"It was an attempt at one. Okay, a poor attempt," he said. Those crinkles appeared around his eyes and mouth for a fleeting moment. Charlotte did not inwardly swoon. Nope.

He continued, "But I am looking at a bigger picture than only your comments when it comes to the park."

"I would hope so. After all, I'm still just the consultant," Charlotte retorted.

Gregory closed his eyes briefly, his lips forming into an almost smile. "You're not going to let me forget that, are you?"

"Doesn't seem likely." Charlotte smiled. "But it's okay, I'm giving myself a new title as of right now."

"And?"

"Vice President of Fun."

"Vice President, huh? Quite the promotion you just gave yourself."

Charlotte felt warmth jumping up to her cheeks again, liking this side of Gregory, and covered by kneeling down to pretend to adjust her shoes. With her face down she could let the smile turn into the full grin she was holding back. Teasing Gregory came so easily. She usually only loosened up like this around Melanie or her family—people she'd known for longer than an hour.

"Everything okay down there?" Gregory asked.

Why did she keep fumbling around him? He was the personification of a bag of money that may or may not have the best interests of Lands at heart.

"Yep, all good! A twig, branch, leaf-thing got attached to my laces." Improvisation was not Charlotte's best thing.

"Let me help you up." Gregory's hand appeared in front of her face. She thought of ignoring him and pulling herself up on her own, but she kind of wanted to touch his hand again.

Charlotte placed her hand in his and it felt so right she almost dropped back down to her heels. His strong grip saved her from the ground. She pictured his biceps flexing as he gracefully brought her upright.

"Thank you," Charlotte kinda gasped. "Think I got a little bit of a head rush." A lie. Holding his hand for three seconds had put her out of sorts, and that was going to be a problem.

Chapter 9

Showing Gregory the best of Lands went quickly, even with the list of ideas Charlotte wanted to share with her aunt and uncle running in the back of her mind. The tour was more abbreviated than Charlotte would have preferred, but she wore her love for the park on her sleeve and hoped Gregory got the slightest taste of what made the park something to cherish and uplift, not tear down.

He'd made a few comments along the way about potential cutbacks, and Charlotte danced around them. Anytime he said something remotely negative or too business-focused, she pulled him into some detail or another that showcased all the zeal and care her family put into the park and how much the guests enjoyed attending. Here was a small pond where baby ducklings showed up every spring; they even had a fan account on social media, LegendDucklings, did Gregory want to see? Also, here was a spot a couple got engaged recently; there was the space where they hosted special after-hours events, which Charlotte saw having huge potential for expanding, and on and on.

Charlotte basically made sure Gregory kept scribbling in his notepad. After that whole period of touching him for longer than she should have and not as long as she wanted to, she was staying focused on putting Lands in the best light possible in a timely fashion so they could get to the office with time left before the meeting.

She walked him through the Wintertide Trail in Forgotten Beasts and laughed as the animatronic dragon at the end of the trail made Gregory shriek. And she made him keep his promise to go on rides, saving the park's best ride for last. They strolled through Forgotten Beasts and walked by Mythic Glass, a shop full of blown-glass mythical creatures with a viewing area to watch the artist at work. Right now, Eva was the primary glass artist along with some assistants from Grove Tech, but her aunt and uncle switched it up with the season so the art would be ever-changing. Charlotte waved to Eva, settling in at her workstation, before leading Gregory to the entrance to Hydra's Fury, Lands of Legend's most popular ride in the thrill category. It was really their *only* ride in the thrill category, a problem Under the Waves would help since its centerpiece would be the Manta Diver, a coaster that appeared to go underwater. The story behind the coaster was about traveling to the Mariana Trench to look for signs of an elusive giant manta ray that had been attacking ships sailing anywhere near the area. To investigate what might be causing the creature to leave its home and chase away ships, the explorers—the people riding the coaster—have to dive underwater to look around. From the top of the highest hill, the Manta would race down a steep incline into a tunnel in the pool underneath with fountains shooting water up and away from the coaster as it entered to simulate a splash. The coaster would travel along the track in the tunnel inside the water briefly, slowing down to take in projected images of their quarry.

It was the kind of coaster that would bring in guests from around the country. The Manta Diver would be, by far, Lands of Legend's most expensive endeavor, and Gregory would learn about that coaster soon enough. But for now, going on Hydra's Fury would show him how impactful a thrill ride could be.

Charlotte stopped by the sign for the roller coaster, multiple Hydra heads and their gnashing teeth sculpted in perfect detail emerging from the wooden background. The sign was so large it was imposing, an intentional choice by her uncle. He wanted everyone to feel tiny and daunted going in, like how someone trying to defeat the Hydra in Greek mythology might have felt.

The sign looked like it was having the intended effect on Gregory.

He looked up and back down to Charlotte a couple of times, his eyes screaming doubt and fear.

His voice deepened with an obviously false bravado as he asked, "What kind of ride is this?"

"It's our best ride: a roller coaster called Hydra's Fury."

"That's right, I saw this on the park's website. Hydra like the beast Hercules defeated."

"The very one," Charlotte affirmed. "But the story of this roller coaster takes place before Hercules starts his labors. It's a time when the Hydra terrified the villagers around its home in Lake Lerna."

"The roller coaster has a story, *too*?" Gregory leaned in with interest. So close that Charlotte got her first solid whiff of his cologne. Given that nothing about Gregory gave "I like the outdoors" vibes, she didn't expect the eucalyptus layered with petrichor and a hint of evergreen. He smelled like the forest, a place Charlotte always wanted to run away to whenever her problems stacked up, a place theme park visits and work usually kept her from. She tried not to obviously inhale.

"Of course it does," she replied. "Remember, it's a *theme* park. Everything has a story, even the concession stands. My uncle found a story reason for every ride, every building he wanted to add to the park."

"Does that mean Sir Cinna-Swirls is an actual person in the park's story?" Confusion played over Gregory's face.

"Yes and no."

Charlotte liked seeing Gregory's face twist even further. She could tell he was wondering what he got himself into.

She put him out of his misery. "Sir Cinna-Swirls isn't a person you can, like, meet or anything, but we do have a story for the character that owns the business—and let me tell you, he's a real cad."

Gregory shook his head, worked his mouth, opening and then closing it. "This is a lot of belief to suspend."

"Not if you have an imagination. I can see you have questions," Charlotte said. "But it's not the time. Right now we have to go meet an angry Hydra."

"What do you mean they're 'angry'?" Gregory asked.

She pointed at the sign. "Hydra's *Fury*! It's mad because people are trying to kill them. Which, you know, is fair to be mad about. Let's go."

Gregory held his ground, a pale sheen to his face. He pulled at his tie. "So, here's the thing. I, uh, have never been on a roller coaster before."

He may as well have made a record-scratch sound; it would have had the same effect on her. She stopped and walked a few steps back toward Gregory. Charlotte had not expected the man *who was here to invest money into her family's theme park specifically to open a massive roller coaster* to say those words. "Uhhh . . . what? I'm confused. When I saw you with Chad at Wonder World, I thought you'd gone on the new coaster."

"No, absolutely not!" Gregory crossed his hands in front of him. "I was in Orlando for a conference and Ian wanted me to connect with Chad—they know each other from some stupid networking event."

She was relieved to learn Chad and Gregory weren't friends, but that piece of information wouldn't move her from her mission. Charlotte narrowed her eyes. "Are you stalling?"

"No." He looked defiant, but also nervous and like he was trying to turn into his feet into roots that would stretch through the concrete and prevent him from moving and therefore riding the coaster.

"But you said you did research!" Charlotte exclaimed.

"Yeah," Gregory admitted, "that was a lot of reading and watching videos online. I know that's not the same, but this all came together so quickly that I didn't have time to go to a park in person. And I have a thing about heights and how exposed roller coasters seem to be."

Oh. That explained why he'd crossed his arms and tried to make himself smaller. Charlotte wanted to handle this delicately. She disliked when people shamed someone for doing, watching, or reading something for the first time. She would be encouraging. Charlotte wondered if it would be too much to put a comforting hand on his shoulder (it would be). Instead, she said, "Hey, everyone has to have a first time riding a roller coaster. Luckily, you're with a pro! I take first-timers and people who don't super-enjoy roller coasters on them all the time. Look, you don't *have* to go on this right now, but I think you do need to try a roller coaster at some point and this one isn't so bad."

Best not to mention the friends who refused to be roller-coaster guinea pigs anymore.

Gregory didn't answer so Charlotte continued as she walked toward the queue. "Some find it helpful to know about every curve and hill so they can mentally prepare while others like to be surprised. Which do you prefer?"

He slowly followed Charlotte down the queue, past the red-figure style mural, typically seen on Greek vases, that depicted the mythical Hydra, its nine heads stretching over the brave souls trying to fight it. If it wasn't for his nerves, Charlotte would stop him to show off the art since it added to the ride's story, but she could read the room. Or the queue, in this case. She needed to get Gregory on Hydra's Fury as soon as possible. The chances of him turning around and dashing out of the line were high. Very high. She kept them moving.

"I think I'd rather be surprised." Gregory sounded anything but certain. "I mean, I don't want to know the ins and outs but maybe a general overview of the coaster and how long it will be?"

Charlotte chuckled inwardly at his contradictory answer. She couldn't fully get it since she loved riding roller coasters, but because of her jobs, past and present, she'd heard every variation of this statement. She knew just how to answer.

"You got it." She projected confidence and calmness. "So, you know how if you cut off one of the Hydra's heads it grows two more?"

He nodded.

"Hydra's Fury leverages that part of the myth. The riders, us, are battling the Hydra. When we attack, the track splits into two and we go off on one of the tracks. It's pretty innovative for a theme park of this size to have so much variability in a ride, actually, but that's because Uncle Frank . . ."

Gregory was looking around him, as if for a path of escape. This tangent was not helpful for his nerves.

"Anyway," Charlotte got herself back on course. "We'll attack with a sudden rush of speed, make the Hydra spawn two heads, go off in a surprise direction, and general roller-coaster things happen."

Best not to tell him about the stomach-dropping dips. Or the brief going-backward part. Thank goodness Hydra's Fury didn't go upside down. Gregory was not ready for loops, she could tell.

"It's about ninety seconds long, so it goes by quickly. I recommend trying to keep your eyes open for special effects and surprises, but if you can't deal, close your eyes and imagine you're doing cartwheels," Charlotte wrapped up.

"Do I look like the cartwheeling type?" Gregory dead-panned.

He didn't.

"Well, then imagine you're doing something you enjoy that involves motion. Then you can pretend you're doing *that* instead."

"Okay," Gregory said. "That I can do."

In a quieter voice he added, "But maybe we could walk a little slower. You know, so I can take in everything you just told me."

"Of course!" Charlotte assured him. "Of course. We can go at whatever pace you'd like."

A piercing sound rang out from the dim museum-style dio-rama ahead. Gregory yelled in reply and jumped.

"*What was that?*" he shouted.

Charlotte clamped her lips together so as not to laugh. It was too early in the day and too close to the season closure for the line to be full, so no people were talking and giggling to soften the queue's sound effects. The shrieks rang out much louder than usual.

"It's okay! It's only a sound effect. That's our take on what a Hydra might sound like." She could distract him with words. "My uncle consulted with some professors at Grove Tech—the college where my parents work—to develop a unique sound for the beast. You'll hear it on the ride, too. Pretty cool, right?"

Everything about Gregory's stance said it was not cool, but it didn't seem like he wanted to admit that. He swallowed. "Yeah, cool."

They got closer to the loading area and Gregory stopped walking. This was it, Charlotte thought, he was going to find a reason to get out of here. She wouldn't judge him for it. Or anyone. Her uncle had built in a discreet and easy to access "chicken exit" for anyone who changed their mind about going on the coaster. In typical Uncle Frank fashion, he'd made that exit hallway appealing by turning it into a baby Greek mythology museum; some people skipped the ride just to check it out.

It looked like Gregory might be heading in that direction. He gripped the divider that kept the queue moving in steady switchbacks and looked down. His knuckles were white. "I'm not— I don't know if I'm ready for this."

Gregory didn't sound pleased to admit what he perceived to be a weakness to Charlotte, but it reminded her that whatever his intentions were for Lands, he was a human, too.

She leaned on the metal divider across from him, the tips of her shoes touching his. "I get that. It's a big jump. Not everyone looks at a roller coaster and sees fun."

He glanced up through that lock of hair that kept falling across his face.

"If you don't want to go on Hydra's Fury today, no judgment from me," Charlotte said. "But if you're up for giving it one ride, I'll be right there with you the whole time. I won't pressure you to throw your arms up or anything."

Gregory straightened and took a deep breath. "Okay, okay. I can do this. It's not even two minutes. That's nothing."

Charlotte smiled at his self-pep talk. "Exactly. You got this. And remember, screaming helps, no matter what you're feeling."

She set a slow pace until they caught up with a handful of park attendees ahead of them. Thankfully they'd be on Hydra's Fury within a couple minutes. Charlotte knew from experiences with her friends that the waiting and anticipation could be one of the most torturous parts.

Gregory's face was still pale when they approached the loading area; Charlotte spotted light sweat on his forehead. She'd do him a solid and make sure they weren't in the front or back of the ride vehicle, styled to look like a chariot. The middle row is where they'd have the smoothest ride.

She waved at the attendant. "Hey, Beata. How's it going today?"

Beata waved back. "Charlotte! I haven't seen you in so long! We have to catch up soon, I have so many ideas to share with you." Her tone was exuberant, so very Beata.

Beata noticed Gregory behind Charlotte and gave Charlotte a quizzical look. Charlotte would swear he was standing behind her to try to hide from the roller coaster. Lands of Legend employed a number of people from Lake Sterling and the whole everyone-knows-everything vibe of a small town carried into the park; the employees knew Emily had been on the lookout for investors, so Beata probably put two and two together. "And it's been good so far today. More guests will be getting here soon," she said.

Charlotte always liked hearing Beata's feedback. She'd been working at Lands for summers between school for a few years and wanted to pursue a career in theme parks. "Excellent. We'll talk soon—I can't wait to hear what's on your mind."

Beata grinned. "Perfect. So, how many in your party?"

"Two," Charlotte replied, "And we'd like the middle row if possible." As she talked she tilted her head back slightly to indicate Gregory's hunched-over form behind her. Beata got it. She was even more accustomed to reluctant roller-coaster riders than Charlotte.

"You got it. Please step up to the yellow line."

"Thank you, Beata. See you soon!"

Charlotte moved forward then turned around to check on Gregory. "We'll board the next set of chariots. You doing okay?"

He straightened back to his full height. Determination filled his voice. "Yes. I'm fine. I'm ready."

Gregory didn't sell it.

The chariot rolled into place, its metal bottom scraping against the track. "This is us," Charlotte said. "I'll board first."

She stepped across the first seat and settled, shoving her empty coffee mug and her bag into the pocket in front of her. Gregory put a foot into the chariot gingerly. Charlotte wasn't convinced he'd go on the coaster until he brought his other foot in.

Once he got as comfortable as he could, Charlotte pulled the lap-bar restraint down until it locked.

"Does it come down any farther?" Gregory asked. The nervous energy coming off him could power a small town.

"Sure, but it might be a little uncomfortable," Charlotte said.

He replied quickly. "That's fine. I'm fine with that."

Charlotte pressed the lap bar down as far as she could, instantly regretting all the coffee she'd had. But Gregory visibly relaxed in his seat, despite the fact that he could barely move, so she'd accept the pressure on her bladder.

"Remember, you got this," she told Gregory, noticing beads of sweat around his hairline and a slight flush on his cheeks. She hoped he did, in fact, have it.

He kept his gaze locked ahead and grabbed onto the bar in front him so tight it made his knuckles white. "Yes, I've got this."

A wobble in his voice said otherwise.

The chariot set into motion. Hydra's Fury started slow and built up momentum, so hopefully it would ease Gregory into the experience. She heard him breathing through his nose and exhaling through his mouth. Charlotte nudged his leg with her knee. "Here we go!"

The chariot went through a small tunnel, past a mural depicting the Hydra they were about to fight. Charlotte knew shit was about to get real and she hoped Gregory would be ready. They exited into the daylight and rocketed up and down a series of small hills, Hydra shrieks punctuating each one, as they prepared to make their first strike against the beast.

Charlotte peeked to her right. Rather than closing his eyes, Gregory had opted to hold them wide open. His lips were closed so tightly that his upper lip was turning red from the effort. At least he wouldn't swallow any bugs, Charlotte thought.

The first animatronic Hydra head burst out of the bushes on Charlotte's left. She knew it was coming but she forgot almost every time and she yelled at the same time Gregory screamed with force. The chariot pushed forward in a burst of extreme speed to attack.

"Nope nope nope," Gregory repeated.

They attacked the beast on a small drop and the track split.

"*Eahahahhhhhhhhhh!*" Gregory yelled as they jolted to the right. Charlotte joined him, partially because she loved screaming on coasters and partially because she thought it might make Gregory more okay with making weird sounds in front of someone he just met.

The chariot approached a sharp incline and started slowly ratcheting upward, clacking the whole way.

"This is a big hill," Gregory shouted.

"It is. But it's the biggest hill on the coaster," Charlotte pleaded.

"You promise?"

"I promise."

"Okay, okay, okay," he muttered.

Charlotte tried to point out a detail off to his right but he shut her down. "You can tell me about the ride's story later. All I care about is whether we're almost to the top."

They were not.

"We're so close," Charlotte lied, both trying to make him feel better but also enjoying messing with him just a tiny bit.

The chariot clacked forward, and Charlotte threw her hands up in anticipation.

"*What are you doing?*" Gregory shouted while managing to grip the bar on the back of the seat in front of them even harder.

"The drop is my favorite part!"

Gregory looked at her like she was an alien. Charlotte put her hands back down so he wouldn't worry about her appearing untethered. She'd humor his fears, this time.

They'd arrived. The chariot teetered on the precipice for a second of spine-tingling suspension and then tilted downward at a sharp angle, gaining momentum.

"*AHHHHHHHH WHYYYY!!*"

Gregory's scream could have shattered glass. Charlotte echoed him, but her scream carried a note of "whee, isn't this fun!" while his said "I hate every moment of this."

Charlotte felt a sudden death grip on her right hand and glanced down to find Gregory's left hand covering hers. Nothing about the hand-holding was sexy. His palm was slippery with sweat, and he might be crushing the delicate bones in her fingers. But he was comfortable enough to reach out to her when he was scared.

Or he was too damn frightened to care. Probably that.

Regardless of the reason, Charlotte managed to flip her hand over and interlace their fingers. She squeezed back. She didn't care about him being an investor who could upend Lands and her family, only that he was not feeling great about the situation. Maybe putting the stuffy venture capitalist on a roller coaster that might make him ill wasn't the best idea in terms of really selling it on behalf of her family.

The chariot reached the bottom of the drop and bolted ahead, using the power from the descent to prepare for another attack on the Hydra.

Gregory relaxed his fingers slightly but didn't let go of her hand.

Charlotte's iron stomach flip-flopped, and the roller coaster had nothing to do with it. She didn't pull away either.

When they reached the part of the track that triggered a backward slide, he cried out in alarm. "Is it *supposed* to do this?!"

The temptation to lead him on was strong, but Charlotte didn't want to contribute to his never setting foot on a roller coaster again. She pushed words out forcefully as they cruised back, "This is intentional, meant to represent how a scared mortal would back away from the Hydra."

"You said 'intentional' somewhere in there, right?" Gregory said loudly.

"Yes!"

"*I don't like it!*" Gregory shrieked as they started to move forward again.

Charlotte laughed. "We're almost through, I promise," she said.

"You'd better be telling the truth, Charlotte!"

She was this time. The chariot slowed as it rounded one more curve that would take them back into the unloading zone. It came to a gentle stop and the lap bar made an unlocking sound. Gregory looked down at his hand as if he only now realized he'd been holding onto Charlotte for half of the ride. His gaze shot back up as he pulled it away and his cheeks flushed pink.

He wiped his palms on his pants. "Sorry about that. I, um, I may have freaked out a little."

Charlotte felt the absence of his hand more than she should have.

She brushed it off. "It's okay! It happens to the best of us. I've been the designated coaster hand-holder a number of times. It's an honor to serve."

Charlotte pushed the lap bar away and retrieved her belongings before carefully stepping onto the unloading platform. She offered a helping hand to Gregory as he shakily stepped out. It was proper manners and had nothing to do with her wanting to feel his touch again already.

He took her outstretched hand, pressing his palm into hers as he exited the chariot. He'd rubbed the sweat off seconds ago, but it had already reformed and it wasn't because of the weather. The day was unseasonably warm, true, but January in Ohio rarely made anyone sweat. But it didn't matter that his hand was clammy; holding his hand, helping him stand on shaky legs, being there for him—it all hit Charlotte's heart like a lightly tapping hammer. Charlotte couldn't contemplate the sensation for long because Gregory let go the second he was out of the ride vehicle. She led him toward the exit gate.

"So, what did you think of your first roller-coaster ride?" Charlotte asked.

Gregory walked at a slow pace, eyebrows furrowed in thought. "Umm. I didn't hate it?"

"That's something," Charlotte replied.

"I've never been on a ride so intense and my stomach tells me maybe it wasn't the best idea to have a giant cinnamon roll in my stomach."

Yeah, Charlotte hadn't thought that part through.

"But," Gregory continued, "I do see why people think it's fun."

Part of Charlotte had hoped he would be an instant fan of roller coasters after a single ride, but she knew that it rarely worked that way. His reaction fell in line with other adult first-time coaster riders.

"I'm impressed you went on it," Charlotte admitted. "The big question remains: Would you go on a roller coaster again?"

"I would consider it."

He dragged out every word of his answer, but Charlotte still took it as a positive sign. Some people swore them off immediately after their first one.

"That's good. Because if Ever Fund works with Lands of

Legend, you'll be helping to open a giant coaster and that means you have a lot more hands-on research ahead of you. Probably a whole trip to a DreamUs park, just to be thorough."

"I suppose you're right." Gregory said it like it was some kind of burden.

Getting a proper look at him, Charlotte noticed how the roller coaster had disheveled Gregory's hair; she spotted a small leaf clinging to it.

"You have a little souvenir from the ride in your hair," she told him.

He looked alarmed. "It's not a spider, is it?"

"Only a leaf. Right there." She pointed.

Gregory brushed the surface of his hair with his hand. "Did I get it?"

"Nope."

He tried again. "Now?"

"Still no. Lean over."

When he obliged, Charlotte reached over to pluck the leaf from his hair—his exceptionally velvety hair, it turned out. The inside of her arm brushed against the shoulder of his suit as she stretched up, and she was close enough to his face to spot an earring hole in the top of his ear. Like the long hair, an earring didn't line up with the buttoned-up man in front of her. She pulled her hand back and showed him the offensive bit of foliage before dropping it.

"Not an outdoors person, are we?" Charlotte asked.

Gregory didn't answer immediately. He leaned down to pick up the leaf and twirled it in his hands, and when he stood back up, wistfulness floated in his eyes.

"No, remember, I said I like the outdoors," he answered. "Love the outdoors. Or I used to anyway. But I do not love spiders."

The expression on his face seemed to be about more than a fear of a spider landing on his hair, but Charlotte didn't know him well enough to press, plus they had a schedule to keep. She checked her watch and the time had come to get Gregory to the office. "Well, then I'm glad we avoided any spider-related disasters. Are you ready to head toward the office?"

"Yes. I want to get settled before the meeting."

She pointed them toward an exit that would get them to the park's office. "Did you have fun this morning?" She mentally crossed her fingers that Gregory had connected with some of Lands of Legend's charm.

Gregory took long enough to answer that Charlotte stopped to look back at him. That wrinkle between his eyebrows was back. "Uh, I did." The awkwardness was back, too.

"I read a lot about the park online and looked at plenty of pictures. I had a certain image in mind when I came today," Gregory continued. "Seeing everything in person made me appreciate the potential more. I'm, uh, looking forward to getting to work, assuming your family wants to move ahead."

Charlotte translated his answer in her head, and she couldn't tell if it sounded like Gregory saw a serviceable blank slate that he couldn't wait to change. But Charlotte would lie down in front of Lands to stop the proverbial bulldozer and also maybe hear him out. Maybe it wasn't so urgent that she talk to her aunt and uncle before the meeting at one.

Chapter 10

They walked back to the same place Charlotte had entered the park earlier in the morning, before Gregory's arrival derailed her meandering morning. She turned around and gave Gregory a questioning look. "I'm guessing you know where the main office is since you made it into the park this morning?"

"I do. I left my things there before Emily pointed toward the way into the park."

"Ah. Did Emily show you the coffee bar this morning?"

"Excuse me, coffee bar? No, she did not." After their time together Charlotte still didn't know what to make of Gregory or Ever Fund, but she did know offering someone caffeine was a mark of human decency. They walked into the office, and every head in the room turned their way. Charlotte noticed her aunt's ever-present weathered gray cardigan wasn't on the coatrack by the door. Things were quieter than usual but the few employees hanging around weren't subtle. The collective inquisitiveness hung in the air as Charlotte wound past the cubicles and conference room to the office kitchen. People in suits were a rare sight in the mostly casual offices, but then again, maybe it wasn't only her who was appreciating Gregory's eyes. And hair.

She cleared her throat and gestured to the office kitchen. "It's not like those businesses that have a full-service coffee shop in their offices or anything, but we have a nice selection of coffees we rotate through for the drip coffee maker and an espresso machine with all the bells and whistles. My aunt makes a latte as good as any barista."

Uncle Frank's decades-old drip coffee maker looked sad next to the chrome and black of the espresso machine, but no one had the heart to upgrade it—Frank was attached and, like he often pointed out, it was dependable.

"When you said coffee bar, I was expecting a Nespresso or something, not an espresso machine. This is an exceptionally nice model. I appreciate how seriously you take coffee." Gregory might fondle the machine if Charlotte didn't keep an eye on him.

"Yeah well, Queen Emily insisted on treating the office after seeing a machine like it last time she visited her college roommate's place in the Hamptons."

"Queen Emily?" Gregory asked.

Charlotte winced at exposing her cousin's nickname to Gregory. "Yeah, it's a family joke—one she does *not* like, so you didn't hear me say that."

Emily had come home from getting her business degree with a different standard for living. She'd thrived in New York and Charlotte had been happy for her cousin finding her place; she knew Emily had felt a little out of step with Lands. To Emily, Lands was a business. Columns on a spreadsheet. A business that, albeit, made her parents happy and supported them and her, but Emily didn't understand the parts of Lands that made it special—the theming, the affordable prices so whole families could come without emptying their savings, the little character moments. She did excel in school, but she tried to wave her business degree like an explanation for every idea she'd brought up in the decade-plus since.

Ideas that, as far as Charlotte could tell, were often devoid of heart and full of dollar signs. It had caused Emily to butt heads with her parents over the business more and more.

While her notions for Lands rarely made it past the suggestion phase, Emily transformed herself and her home. Designer shoes and purses, Smeg appliances, endless comments about New York, where she visited often. If Charlotte didn't know how much of a bargain hunter Emily was to afford the luxuries she liked to show off, she'd think Lands of Legend was filling her cousin's coffers.

Charlotte waved to the whole counter. "Help yourself. I need to do some work before the meeting. I'm in that office up there if you have questions about the espresso machine or anything." She walked upstairs to her cozy but functional office and recited an item from the list in her head with every step she took, letting go of tracking down Frank and Marianne. She would see what Gregory had to say and go from there.

- Check emails
- Make sure the Cosmic Catastrophe article went up and share it with the Wonder World publicists
- Also read Mel's thoughts on Cosmic Catastrophe and then text Mel about her impeccable taste
- Look at the park's social media calendar
- Schedule some planning meetings for the summer season
- Stop thinking about Gregory's eyes

She stopped cold halfway up the stairs. Maybe she should pause on some of the to-dos for Lands until after the meeting? No. Any changes Ever Fund wanted to make wouldn't happen *tomorrow*. Charlotte had been so occupied with selling the unique qualities of Lands to Gregory, she'd temporarily forgotten the possible implications of an investor. All the things she freaked out about last night came roaring back.

Charlotte resumed her trip upstairs with less pep in her step. She rounded the corner for her office door and walked right into her cousin.

"Emily! Good morning—er, almost afternoon!" Charlotte greeted her.

"I saw you walked into the office with Gregory. Do you even know who he is?" Emily replied, businesslike as ever. "And good morning," she tacked on.

Emily had her hair, a few shades darker than Charlotte's, in her signature topknot, pulled so tight Charlotte often wondered if it gave her cousin headaches. She always dressed in either designer clothing or pieces she'd had expertly tailored so they looked like designer brands, but today she appeared extra sharp. Emily wore a black single-breasted Alexander McQueen suit that had not a crinkle in sight, no doubt for the meeting. At least Gregory wouldn't be the only one in a suit after all, Charlotte thought.

"Yes, I do know who he is. Funny thing. I ran into him outside Sir Cinna-Swirls. He was going to take a walk around the park on his own, but I gave him the full tour to show Lands in its best possible light," Charlotte answered. "I figured showing him what we offer would only strengthen the deal."

Emily crossed her arms and pursed her lips. "I see. Well, I was too busy with this potential contract and with prepping Mom and Dad to accompany him this morning, and he said he would be fine on his own. But I appreciate you stepping up since you apparently had loads of free time anyway."

Emily didn't hold Charlotte in the highest regard anyway, and once Charlotte no longer had a full-time job, she seemed to think Charlotte was lazy for not immediately replacing it with another full-time job, never mind that Charlotte's part-time "Vice President of Fun" role and part-time theme park reporter role combined was almost like working a full forty hours a week. Almost. But she knew Emily's attitude was more about Charlotte's mere presence at Lands after so many years away at DreamUs.

"Yep, that's me. All the free time in the world." Charlotte let her reply drip with sarcasm.

Emily uncrossed her arms and flared her nostrils. "How do you think the tour went?"

Charlotte grinned mischievously. "I took him on Hydra's Fury. It was his first roller coaster."

Emily's eyebrows jumped in alarm. "And did he like it or does he now hate theme parks forever? Will he even give Ever Fund's presentation today?"

"Don't be ridiculous, Emily. I'd say he tolerated it. Honestly, he was more open-minded about it than I expected. I also educated him about the difference between an amusement park and a theme park, so now he gets that, too."

Emily facepalmed, complete with a loud, smacking sound effect. "Of course you did."

"What? He didn't have any clue!" Charlotte defended.

Emily sighed. "Charlotte, you know how you get. It's like Dad. You can both be so intense. You're so zealous about it and I know that worked well for you at DreamUs, but it's not the same here. No one cares as much about the theming as you and my parents."

Charlotte had heard this all from Emily before. Repeatedly. And it wasn't true. Charlotte knew others cared, but Emily didn't understand so her cousin thought no one else did. She was bewildered by how Emily had learned so much from school and her time in New York, but not how to see beyond her own perspective.

Maybe Charlotte was guilty of that, too.

"I didn't veer too much into evangelical territory, Emily. I wanted him to get it. And I think he did." She remembered his surprise about Hydra's Fury having a story. "Okay, he mostly got it," Charlotte amended.

Charlotte kept going before Emily could chide her more. "Look, I was surprised to hear about Ever Fund. I know you've been looking for a way to get Under the Waves open for your mom and dad *and* for revenue, but I guess I didn't think it would come to having to get someone, a whole other company, outside the family involved. If this investment will help Lands move forward and stay open, I want to help that happen. If Ever Fund and Gregory can make a difference here, so be it. But not at any cost, I hope. I don't want Ever Fund to turn Lands into an amusement park."

Her cousin took a few beats to process Charlotte's comments. "I appreciate that," Emily mumbled. Emily wasn't known for talking about or even getting close to talking about feelings. Then her voice got clear again. "I am thinking about my parents, but more importantly, the longevity of Lands and making sure it brings in enough people and cash to keep running. Like I learned from Dr. Stevens at school, businesses have to make compromises, be flexible, ready to pivot. You're not even here full time, so while I hear you, your input will not necessarily stop those compromises. I have to look out for the park and those of us who will keep running it for years to come."

Everyone in the family had heard the name "Dr. Stevens" *many* times over the past several years. She was Emily's favorite professor at school, Emily's mentor, really. Charlotte was sure Dr. Stevens was a knowledgeable person, but she couldn't. She also couldn't deal with Emily being a shit to her right now.

"Emily, why bother?"

"Excuse me?"

"You want to make money? Wait for your parents to retire. Sell the park. Better to sell it than them watch you turn it into a personality-less park."

Emily stepped back like Charlotte had slapped her. Then she stepped close to Charlotte and hissed, "Just because I want to make this business that I'm stuck with successful and profitable enough not to be on the brink of closure all the time does not mean I don't care about my parents. They love this place, I know that, and they always will even when they retire. I can't and won't just let it go to someone else. I'm doing the best with what I have, and I don't need judgment from you. It's not like you'll even stick around this time."

Brink of closure. It sounded like the situation at Lands could be more precarious than Charlotte realized. Unless Emily was exaggerating. Charlotte didn't have the energy to continue the conversation, didn't have a whole lot of ground to stand on in regards to knowing the park's financial details. She could ask her aunt and uncle later. Besides, if she kept talking to Emily, the flames on her face would turn into words she'd regret. She took a step to the side to increase the space between them. "On that note, I should get some work done before the meeting."

Emily's jaw muscles went tight. "You aren't involved in the meeting."

"Uh, yes I am. Aunt Marianne invited me."

Emily arched an eyebrow. "I see. Well, it's mostly a courtesy anyway, just Gregory telling us more about Ever Fund and going over some initial thoughts for Lands's next steps."

Charlotte smiled because she knew it would annoy her cousin. "Can't wait."

"Do not ruin this for us, Charlotte." With a glare that would make flowers wilt, she pivoted on her heel and walked way.

Ooookay, Charlotte thought. Just like riding Hydra's Fury with Gregory, this meeting was going to require fortitude.

Chapter 11

With twenty minutes until the meeting, Charlotte walked to the coffee bar. She'd gone through some items on her list on autopilot, but she had enough time to start a fresh pot of coffee for the meeting (and for herself) and pulled out her phone to catch Melanie up on her morning.

Charlotte: Melanie. I have a problem. Remember that I mentioned Chad had some hot guy with him at Wonder World?
Melanie: Yes.
Charlotte: THAT'S the investor.
Melanie: !!! Small world.
Melanie: Also how hot?

Charlotte tried to look Gregory up online but she couldn't find him on social media.

Charlotte: I will take a picture for you later.
Melanie: You'd better.
Charlotte: I gave him a two-hour tour of the park this morning. But I can't tell if he gets Lands. He hasn't been to an amusement park before, except for maybe once as a kid, let alone a theme park. I'm worried.

Melanie: It's going to be okay. You'll figure it out.

Charlotte: If I'm allowed to stick around.

Melanie: Why wouldn't you be?

Charlotte: I don't know. I just had a Thing with Emily and I think she'd be fine not having me around.

Melanie: You've had a Thing with Emily for ages. Try not to worry.

Charlotte: Yeah, you're right.

Melanie: I've got to run. Keep me posted, okay?

Charlotte: I will. Thank you. <3

Melanie: <3

Charlotte slid the phone into her pocket and grabbed the full carafe of coffee. She placed it in the conference room and then went back to the kitchen to grab an assortment of mugs. Her aunt and uncle entered the conference room as Charlotte set the last mug on the table.

"Aunt Marianne! Uncle Frank!" She walked over to give them hugs despite having only been away from Lands for not even a full week. Knowing what the meeting was about too, Charlotte figured the occasion called for hugs.

"Your parents told you what was happening, didn't they?" Marianne asked while she embraced Charlotte, her stacks of beaded bracelets rattling as she patted Charlotte's back. It made Charlotte glance at the blue lace agate bracelet on her own wrist, a gift from Aunt Marianne who, when Charlotte had come back to Lands after the DreamUs layoff and Chad cheating debacle, had taken the bracelet off her own wrist and rolled it onto Charlotte's, emphasizing the crystal's ability to soothe anxiety. Aunt Marianne only gifted her bracelets when she believed someone needed them; it touched Charlotte so much she'd worn it ever since, only removing it to shower.

When she pulled back from her aunt, Charlotte noticed Marianne's long, Morticia Addams–style hair was limp—

hair her aunt had let her and Emily play with and brush endlessly when they were small. Aunt Marianne was the type to
give and give to others without thinking of herself, but it
wasn't like her to not brush her hair to a shine. Charlotte
would have to talk to her about a self-care day soon, something Charlotte herself had been trying to embrace in the
months since DreamUs let her go.

"My parents? Not keeping a secret? That doesn't sound
like them." Charlotte smiled as she pulled away and put an
arm around her uncle and looked into his piercing blue eyes
to get a read on his mood. Uncle Frank did not possess a
poker face; his every reaction showed on his face. It was
helpful, and often amusing, because everyone could see
what Frank thought of an idea in real time. "How are you
holding up?"

Frank became absorbed with adjusting the cuffs of one of
his ever-present flannel shirts and breathed deep enough to
move his shoulders, which he turned into a roll, squaring
them. Charlotte could see weariness in his movements. "I'll
be honest. I'm tired." He glanced at his wife. "We both are.
We want to get some kind of future settled for the park so we
can travel; it's time. You know we've been fixing up that
busted RV forever now. I don't do well with change, I know
that, but if I can make sure Lands is in a good place, I'd feel
okay about leaving."

Marianne raised an eyebrow and pursed her lips.

"Okay," Frank chuckled, "I'd feel better about leaving. I
wish we would have been able to figure out how to get Under
the Waves open with our own money, but sometimes you
have to admit when you need help. So, here we are. Was that
a long enough answer for you?"

Seeing her aunt's and uncle's demeanors made Charlotte
glad she didn't come at them first thing today and overwhelm
them more with her list.

"Hey, it was a complicated question. Sounds like you're

approaching this in a healthy manner. I'm proud of you for putting yourselves in a position to move on and retire," Charlotte teased. And she meant it; she really was proud. Uncle Frank had a legendary stubborn streak, so it counted for a lot that he was open to outside funding. That they would be in this conference room about to meet with a venture capitalist would have been unimaginable to Charlotte in the not-too-distant past. She patted her uncle's arm. "I know it must be a lot. Now I grabbed a lot of mugs, but I want to make sure: who all is joining this meeting today?"

Frank replied, "Just you and Emily and Ever Fund's representative, Gregory. Emily already has an idea about Ever Fund—she's the one who reached out to them, after all—but we wanted you in the room to hear what he has to say. But what we discuss today stays confidential. I don't know if we're going to agree to anything, and if not, no need to give everyone a scare, and if so, well, we want to tell the staff the right way."

"Are you telling me we're going to align on a communication strategy?"

Her uncle rolled his eyes and pulled out a chair at the table. Charlotte grinned. Her corporate lingo always had that effect on Frank, so this time she'd wielded her powers to lighten the mood.

Marianne and Frank were unusually quiet as they waited for the others to arrive. They sat next to each other, and Charlotte was pretty sure they were holding hands under the table. She studied the shadows around her aunt's eyes and the rigidity of her uncle's shoulders. This couldn't be an easy decision for them. Charlotte promised herself she would keep that in mind whatever Gregory said today. After all, she appreciated Marianne and Frank including her in this meeting. They certainly had no obligation to loop her in; Emily wasn't going to.

And speaking of, Emily and Gregory walked in, laughing

about something as they opened the door. They seemed more familiar with each other than Charlotte would have imagined. She considered Emily's feelings toward her family's business and the comment Gregory made that indicated to Charlotte he wasn't thrilled to continue his family's line of work. They were both too dressed up for Lands. Seemed like they had a lot in common, and Charlotte fought off an odd "I saw him first" feeling. Because no, Emily had. *Whatever*, Charlotte thought, letting the flash of possessiveness roll off her. She stood, lifted the coffee carafe, and broke the awkward silence. "Does anyone want coffee?"

At the nods from everyone except Emily, Charlotte poured as Gregory opened his laptop and plugged into the meeting room's screen. He patted his pockets, and when he didn't find what he was looking for, his mouth twisted in frustration. "I don't suppose any of you happen to have a clicker, do you?"

Her aunt and uncle looked confused, but Charlotte had this. Giving presentations was a common occurrence at Dream Mechanic, so most people had a clicker on their person at all times. Charlotte hadn't given up the habit of keeping one nearby; it was at her desk. "Yes!" Charlotte exclaimed too loudly. "Brb."

Had she really just said "brb" out loud? This meeting was going to go swell.

She rushed up to her laptop bag and back in a short amount of time, but the room had gotten quieter in her absence. Charlotte lifted the clicker up triumphantly. "Here you go!" She didn't know why she felt compelled to help this Gregory's presentation go smoothly.

"Thank you." Gregory stood and took the clicker. "As you all know, Ever Fund is interested in working with Lands. The presentation you gave us was intriguing—my mother in particular is excited about this proposition. We believe it's important for both parties to be on board, so part of our process is to give a reciprocal presentation to highlight what we do. Additionally, with some input from Emily, I have some suggestions to help along the return on our investment—assuming we all decide to move forward."

Emily jumped in. "Thank you, Gregory. You're here because the park needs cash. We have a lot of maintenance, some potential upgrades, and it's beyond time to open Under the Waves. The construction site keeps sitting stagnant, but it's all so close to the finish line. Ever Fund would be a huge help in making that happen. We're eager to hear what you have in mind, then we can hopefully move things forward soon."

"We hope for the same," Gregory said. "Allow me to get started."

She'd seen bursts of Gregory's personality on their tour around Lands, but he transformed while going through slides. Charisma, confidence, competence. God, Charlotte, who had nightmares about not being prepared, was a sucker for competence. While he may or may not be one hundred percent on board with working for his family, he came alive while delivering the notes about Ever Fund's history. Not for the first time, Gregory brought Chad to mind—that man could have a room on the edge of its seat for even the most boring topic. Gregory was so smooth.

His pride in his grandmother's business made Charlotte feel encouraged about how Ever Fund would work with Lands. Their portfolio wasn't what Charlotte would associate with a venture capitalist firm. More success stories for mom-and-pop–style businesses, like the burger trucks-turned-cute-diner Gregory had mentioned, than tech bros making apps—those sorts of clients were in there too, and Charlotte didn't miss when Gregory mentioned those were Ian's efforts to expand the firm's interest with more diverse clients, one of which was the deal Emily had spotted in her alumni newsletter.

Maybe this wasn't so bad, Charlotte thought. Wait, when did he roll up his shirtsleeves? She couldn't believe she'd been too absorbed in the presentation to miss that moment. And was that a hint of a tattoo peeking out below the pristine blue cuff? How dare he keep revealing these more laid-back parts of himself that also happened to be sexy. Charlotte wondered what the ink could be.

With the Ever Fund overview out of the way, Gregory clicked to the second part of the presentation: the part about Lands of Legend.

"After hearing from you about Lands of Legend and confirming details on the exact status of Under the Waves with Emily, Ever Fund is willing to invest up to two million dollars in the park."

Through wide blinks, Charlotte stole glances at her family. Emily had a small, content smile. Marianne looked cool, like she was offered millions of dollars on the daily. Frank, however, sat with his jaw hanging open. Yep, no poker face. Charlotte imagined her own face showed surprise, too. That would have been loose change in a couch at DreamUs, but here at Lands? Two million dollars could change everything.

Like a pro, Gregory let that number hang in the air and make an impression before he picked back up. "The majority of that would go toward opening Under the Waves with the two rides, the Manta Diver and Lost City. The remainder, if unused, will be allocated with approval from Ever Fund. I'll remain onsite at least through the opening of Under the Waves to ensure the work is carried out with maximum efficiency."

Charlotte interpreted that as Gregory being present to make sure no dollar would be wasted. And fine, they were investors. She wondered how they would recoup their costs, though; Charlotte could work her way around a budget, and while crunching numbers was never her most favorite task, she didn't have to pull out a calculator to know it would take a minute for Lands to turn a profit. She raised a hand.

"Charlotte, let's wait until Gregory is done before we ask questions." Emily looked at Charlotte with daggers in her eyes.

"No, it's fine. Yes, Charlotte?"

"When do you foresee Under the Waves and those rides opening?" She needed to know how long Gregory would be around, just because.

"I was getting to that." He clicked to the next slide with an opening date and summer revenue projections with and without Under the Waves. "Memorial Day Weekend."

Bold, Charlotte thought. Bold, but doable. It was January now. They'd have to plan around winter weather but with how far along Under the Waves was, a concentrated period of construction should do it. She looked around the table and saw her uncle's face flip through emotions while he took in that date and did the math. Surprise, reckoning—Charlotte could tell by how he was nodding his head—acceptance, happiness.

"You think that soon is possible?" Frank asked, voice wobblier than he probably preferred.

"Absolutely. Moreover, we would need Lands to commit to that date if we want to move ahead with a partnership. Having Under the Waves ready for summer business will be crucial to spiking attendance and start earning back the investment." He gestured toward the projections. "I think we can see a twenty percent increase in revenue in ticket sales after we open Under the Waves, which will be our first priority. I looked at several parks"—he paused to grin at Charlotte like a student who wanted a gold star sticker—"amusement parks *and* theme parks after our conversation this morning, Charlotte. Profits consistently see a big jump when parks open a new ride, let alone a whole new land."

Charlotte nodded emphatically. She didn't want to agree

with him, but he had done that homework correctly. Charlotte replied, "I know DreamUs is on a different scale, but that was always our experience. It brings in more crowds and you steadily earn back all the money you put into the new areas."

"That's our hope," Gregory said. "We want to make sustainable changes that continue to build the park's attendance and appeal over time. Ever Fund is in for the long haul; we know it will take a while for our investment to pay off. Of course, Under the Waves opening isn't the only contributing factor."

Click.

"I discussed some options for bumping up the bottom line with Emily."

That wasn't encouraging, Charlotte thought.

The screen jumped to the next slide and revealed a list, much like the one Charlotte had made to share with Frank and Marianne before running into Gregory derailed her. Except as Charlotte scanned this list, she noted how many ideas were counterproductive to one of her aunt and uncle's core tenets: keep Lands affordable for families. Ideas that were, for Lands, not great. Not right. Dynamic pricing that would drive the cost of park admission up on more popular days, increasing the prices for food and drinks by a substantial percentage, treating Under the Waves as an area that would require its own, separate ticket. Ideas that felt like nickel-and-diming their customers. And the last bullet point in the column of possible revenue levers to pull said, "Corporate events, weddings, including IP."

IP. Intellectual property. That screamed Emily. Charlotte would give up Sir Cinna-Swirls for life if Gregory could correctly define IP. With the latest Peak Fusion article fresh in her mind, she hoped that's not who Emily was considering partnering with.

The other column on the slide listed cost-cutting measures. Highlights included decreasing off-season offerings and cutting back on the associated staffing, outsourcing ride maintenance and landscaping, and converting most of the office staff into part-time employees instead of full-time employees with benefits. Charlotte didn't think any of it was concrete but it did perversely amuse her to see adding events and cutting staff mentioned in the same place. That made no sense.

"Some of this doesn't make sense." It's like her aunt read her mind. "We've discussed many of these ideas in the past." Here, Marianne stopped to serve Emily with a pointed look. "But we've dismissed them."

Gregory nodded. "I hear you, but we have to put everything back on the table in order to see the kind of change Ever Fund needs to gain back our investment. And respectfully, doing more of the same hasn't made a difference."

Charlotte's eyes couldn't get wider. Her aunt's face was wrought from steel, sharp and ready to cut if Gregory kept talking. Part of Charlotte wanted to egg Gregory on toward a verbal lashing, but the two million dollars on the table flashed through her mind.

"You know," Charlotte cut in, "I have a list of ideas, too. Ones that could increase revenue while supporting the park's values."

She kept her face angelic as she looked at Gregory and then Emily.

"As I said, I think everything should be on the table. From our discussion this morning, I look forward to hearing what you have in mind." Gregory gestured toward her.

"Oh, right now?"

"Ideally, yes. I know we're all eager to decide if we're going to be working together."

"Sure, Gregory." Charlotte stood up and thumbed open her phone. "Pardon the casual delivery, I was going to run these by you, Aunt Marianne and Uncle Frank, this morning, and I know you prefer to chat through ideas instead of making it all formal. But here we go."

It wasn't that Charlotte didn't have confidence in her ideas. They were solid and didn't work against what her aunt and uncle wanted. But with the pressure of the setting, Gregory's scrutiny, and Emily literally yawning, anxiety tightened across her throat. She cleared it and referenced her notes on her phone.

"First, we draw attention to our incredible restaurants and food stalls with a food-and-beverage pass that people buy in advance with tear-off tabs or something for them to use while they're here. It will offer a slight discount over buying each item individually, so they're still getting value, but will give guests a reason to commit to a potentially larger amount than they would otherwise spend on food. Second, we apply for an alcohol permit so we can serve beer and wine; it would be new to the park so we can set a nice markup from the beginning—marked-up alcohol is something people already accept because of sporting events and concerts, anyway. Also, we do add events but themed to go with the park and with plenty of staff to support it.

"And my favorite, we introduce an annual passholder program. This is—"

"An idea that will cause people to spend less money in the park," Emily interjected.

"No, it's an idea that will give us predictable, repeatable revenue and one that would be excellent to implement with the opening of Under the Waves. It's the type of added value that will tip people's decisions toward making the purchase."

Charlotte assessed the room. "That's only a start, but I believe all of those are doable and will be lucrative."

Gregory was sitting, writing notes in his paper notebook. "Thank you for sharing those, Charlotte. Sounds like there's potential there, particularly if we pair some of those with the cost-cutting measures I have."

The first part of Gregory's response had made Charlotte preen as she took her seat again, but then he'd kept talking.

"I'm going to do my best to go with the flow here," Frank said. "I know being a stubborn old goat hasn't been raking in the dough. But can we draw the line at cutting staff? We've built a strong community around the park. We don't want to set you and Ever Fund up to be the bad guys by making those kind of cuts, because we know everyone here will be so excited about moving ahead with Under the Waves. I bet if we asked the employees for ideas to increase profits, they'd be full of great ones like Charlotte's."

Her uncle gave her an indulgent smile. Charlotte beamed at the compliment but thought that Emily would probably add that compliment to her pile of grievances toward her cousin.

Frank then turned toward Gregory, eyes pleading in a way that Charlotte hadn't seen before.

Gregory, whose stick-up-his-ass nature Charlotte had experienced throughout the morning, softened his whole posture. He folded his hands in front of his face, wrinkle appearing between his eyebrows. "We *don't* want to be the bad guys. We almost never operate that way. I know it doesn't sound genuine to say we're here to help, but we wouldn't give you money otherwise. It is a business, however. But how about this? I will first consider every opportunity to make money without affecting the livelihood of the park's employees. Maybe we can shuffle some folks into Under the Waves to prep that land to open? I think we can figure it out, Frank."

Charlotte knew her family wouldn't leave employees hanging, but Gregory's comments were like a warm hug. Everyone at Lands, even the seasonal staff, knew each other. Most of the people in leadership positions had been with the company for years. She was glad they wouldn't be left in the cold.

"All right, then. Can we add into the contract that you

will talk with Marianne and me before making any significant staffing changes?"

"Absolutely, Frank."

Her uncle gave Gregory a firm nod.

"That's most of what I have, but while we're all here," Gregory said, "Charlotte, could you share a little more about the annual passholder idea? I didn't realize people would return to the same theme park multiple times a year."

His voice made it sound like that was the most bizarre choice a person could make. Charlotte again questioned Gregory's research methods. Then again, "annual passholder" wasn't a phrase he would have come across without specifically searching for it.

"Oh sure. Remember how I told you 'theme park adults' were a demographic?"

"I do."

"They make up a large percentage of annual passholders. In places like Orlando where theme parks are condensed, locals will go once a week. Maybe only to have dinner." If Charlotte didn't already spend so much time at theme parks because she worked in them, she would totally have an annual pass for Dreamland in Orlando.

But the concept was hard for Gregory to grasp. His perplexed expression was comedic. "Because that's fun?"

"Yes, Gregory. Fun. People have it all kinds of ways!" She noted Emily giving her a "cool it" look, and she schooled the exasperation in her voice. "Anyway, I'm happy to hear you're interested in this idea. I have a full proposal for the program. The community aspect is invaluable. Passholders may not spend buckets of money on every visit to the park, but we shouldn't count them out."

She'd watched DreamUs leadership push their annual passholders around. Company leadership would never say it outright, but DreamUs continued to try to discourage passholders from renewing with continually increasing prices and more limitations on the various passes' benefits. Social media, parks news sites, online forums—a passholder discussion blew up at least once a month.

"Okay, we'll make it a welcoming environment for them."

"And you'll work with me and the family to define what 'welcoming environment' means, right?" Charlotte prompted, hardness in the question. She would throw down for their potential annual passholder community, much like Frank with the park's staff, and Gregory needed to know she could hold her ground, despite their earlier hand-holding.

Gregory bit his bottom lip in frustration while tilting his head back ever so slightly. Charlotte felt that small movement in her goddamn toes, but she refused to let it knock her off course. She willed her eyes to bore through his skull until he answered.

"Sure," Gregory replied. "We can discuss the finer points."

Charlotte sat back in her chair and crossed her arms. "Excellent. I look forward to it."

"With that, I think we're done, unless there are any questions." Gregory looked around the table.

"Yes, I have one." Marianne pointed at the screen, bracelets rattling with the movement. "Please go back to the slide before this. Yes, that one. I know we talked about this stake in ownership for Ever Fund, and I'm not contesting that, especially since we plan to step away and retire after Under the Waves is up and running, but building on what Frank said about talking to us about staff, what kind of guidelines are there about Ever Fund—you—making decisions without consulting us?"

"On paper," Gregory answered, "Ever Fund does have the freedom to manage the business as we see fit, but we will consult the family whenever possible. In all my years with Ever Fund, we haven't bulldozed over anyone."

The phrase "whenever possible" was nebulous. Charlotte heard the words as a loophole that Ever Fund could exploit to do whatever they wanted, whether it aligned with the park's themes, or the family's values, or anything. She opened her mouth to further define that "whenever possible" but Emily gave her a look and jumped in.

"Yes, Gregory, we appreciate that," Emily said. "We know what we're signing up for if Ever Fund moves ahead with this deal and that you won't entirely shut the family out of decision-making. If this is going to work, we have to trust you and your company to make calls for the best interest of the park to keep it open. Does that work for you, Mom?" Emily turned pointedly toward Charlotte for the last sentence despite directing it to her mother. Charlotte nodded at her cousin. She got it, truly. Charlotte didn't want to see Lands of Legend close either. But she also didn't want it to become a shadow of what it had been for the last three-plus decades. Didn't want Ever Fund to cut corners when Gregory only learned about the difference between an amusement park and a theme park today.

"It does," Marianne said.

"Good. Anything else?"

Emily replied, "I don't think so. I'm confident about everything you showed us, and I'm looking forward to moving this along."

"Yes, thank you for the thorough review, Gregory," Frank said. "I think it's time we all take a break to process everything."

Gregory closed his laptop, relief on his face. "Thank you all for meeting today. I have no doubt Ever Fund can take Lands of Legend to its next successful phase and beyond. And you all have my email address if you have more questions. Charlotte, you can get my contact information from Emily if you need it."

"We'll be in touch soon," Emily said, walking out of the meeting room with her dad close behind.

"We will," Marianne echoed, lingering in the room. She

turned away from Gregory gathering his things and looked toward Charlotte. "By the way, I have something for you and I cannot wait any longer to give it to you."

Her aunt reached into her bag and grabbed a brown gift box stamped with white ferns; she thrust it toward Charlotte. "You're the worst at keeping surprises, Aunt Marianne," she said. Aunt Marianne was known for giving gifts year-round because she was too excited to save them for special occasions.

Fingertips under the edge of the lid, she paused to ask her aunt, "I can open this now, right?"

"Yes, that's why I gave it to you, honey."

Charlotte pulled the top from the box, unfolded tissue paper, and pulled out some fake leaves—you never knew what kind of wrapping material you'd find in a present from Aunt Marianne—and finally uncovered a picture frame. She brushed off the last of the faux leaves to reveal the picture and put her hand over her mouth. Her aunt had gotten hold of one of Charlotte's childhood drawings of Flossleaf the faery and framed it. The mat board surrounding Charlotte's rudimentary art had information about Flossleaf and the World of Faery in her uncle's tidy cursive.

"Aunt Marianne! This is perfect!" Charlotte said, sniffling.

"You like it?"

"Love it!"

"Your mom came across your drawings last week and we thought it would be nice to do something special with them," Aunt Marianne said. "And you've been back since . . . what, September? Consider it a very late housewarming present."

Charlotte was so moved she lost the ability to form words.

"Can I see?"

Charlotte had been so taken by the gift and all the memories it represented she hadn't noticed Gregory was still in the room. He was standing behind her so Charlotte lifted the picture up enough for him to see it, and it was like putting her tender heart on a platter for him to examine.

"This is a faery I met here at Lands when I was little. Probably the moment that I knew what I wanted to do when I grew up: make magic. And be best friends with a faery." Embarrassment caught Charlotte off guard so she added, "Obviously Flossleaf isn't real and a few different performers play her and—"

"I hope I get to meet Flossleaf. This is precious," Gregory said. "Thanks for showing me. I'll get out of your way."

Charlotte stepped over to her aunt to hug her as Gregory left, noticing he had that wistful aura about him again.

Chapter 12

Charlotte needed to unwind after her draining day. The tour, the meeting, the actual work she still had to finish. She couldn't bring herself to leave early but she decided she wouldn't work late. It was time for a night off. She drove herself to The Dragon's Breath, a bar and board game café that happened to make the best wood-fired pizza for miles. And they had a strict "no eating pizza while playing board games" rule that Charlotte respected.

Charlotte claimed a high-top table by the bar and ordered a hard cider and a margherita pizza. She checked to see if the owner, her friend Luke, was around, but he had the night off. Before she forgot, she sent off a quick text to Luke to say hello and ask about catching up, but then she made herself put her phone away.

She sipped her cider, dry and perfect, and stared at the blinking dragon above the bar. Just its head and front legs protruded from the wall so that it perpetually looked like it was trying to fly into the bar. It was as impressive as it was unnerving in the way that the best animatronics were. A buzz from her phone pulled her out of her dragon hypnosis and she didn't bother trying to talk herself out of fishing her phone from her bag to glance at the notification. She didn't have to answer whatever it was, but she should see what it was about.

An email preview notification glowed on her screen, an email from Gregory. She pushed it.

From: gbinns@everfund.com
To: charlotte@landsoflegend.com
Re: An Offer

Charlotte,

Thank you for showing me around Lands of Legend today. It's clear that you care deeply about the park and that you have extensive knowledge about and experience in the theme park industry. While Emily will retain her position as the park's manager, I'd like to offer you a permanent position in the park and put your experience to good use.

Would you be interested in taking on the role of Lands of Legend's Creative Executive?

Sincerely,
Gregory

Charlotte blinked several times, closed her eyes for a few seconds, and looked again. She wanted to make sure she'd read the email correctly. Her mind raced with a dozen thoughts: yes, she was interested; no, she had to leave the door open for DreamUs, but what a perfect opportunity this would be to use her knowledge; and oh boy, there was no way Gregory had discussed this with Emily. It was a lot and while Charlotte chased the thoughts around her head, she realized this must mean Ever Fund's investment was a done deal. She flipped to her text messages.

> **Charlotte: Hey! The meeting seemed to go well today. Did you agree to move ahead with Ever Fund?**
> **Aunt Marianne: Yes. I was going to tell you first thing tomorrow.**
> **Aunt Marianne: The presentation was really more of a courtesy. It's not like we have a line of investors lined up and Emily was already on board. Frank and I felt optimistic after hearing Gregory's thoughts.**
> **Charlotte: Yeah, I was surprised.**
> **Charlotte: Still waiting for the catch.**
> **Aunt Marianne: So cynical. But I get it. I think it's good though.**
> **Charlotte: We will see. But I'll keep an open mind!**

Charlotte wouldn't mention to her aunt that she didn't think Emily was going to be a positive influence on Ever Fund. All the more reason for Charlotte to consider Gregory's email.

> **Aunt Marianne: Good. That's all I ask.**
> **Charlotte: Lv you. See you tomorrow?**
> **Aunt Marianne: Yep! Lv you too. <3**

With a deep breath, Charlotte put her phone away. She focused on the pizza that the bartender dropped off at her table with the most flawless timing in the universe. Perfectly crispy crust, fresh basil, and tomato sauce with just a hint of sweetness. Charlotte forced Lands out of her mind while she ate.

But Gregory's email didn't leave her head for long once she finished dinner. She weighed every word while she drove home.

Then when she got to her basement apartment, she texted Melanie (she replied with a lot of emojis at first, including an eggplant). She asked Madmartigan's opinion; he gave an approving meow, but that probably had more to do with Charlotte holding treats. Her parents were out, so Charlotte couldn't ask them. She turned to a tried and true method: a list.

Pros:
- Help Under the Waves, a cool new land with leveled-up rides, open
- By extension, help Frank and Marianne's dreams come true before they retire
- Be around to stop Emily from being Emily
- It didn't have to be forever
- Yay full-time employment!

Cons:
- Working closely with Gregory
- Really closely with Gregory
- Seeing Emily more often

The Gregory part, the part of being around a suit who didn't understand theme parks, would be exhausting. Dream-Us had those types too, but as a Dream Mechanic, she was more often surrounded by creative idealists who didn't let numbers stifle their artistry. Staring into Gregory's green eyes and admiring his broad, square shoulders wouldn't make explaining the nuances of theme parks to him any more pleasurable. Well, maybe marginally more pleasurable. Okay, maybe working with Gregory was a pro. But she had to remember that the last time she'd worked with someone she was attracted to, things went off the rails.

But the Gregory of it all aside, she'd love to put Creative Executive on her résumé; it was always nice to future-proof her job experiences. Charlotte knew that with decision-making power and Ever Fund's cash infusion she could transform Lands of Legend in all the right ways. That would only help her successful return to DreamUs, and she could put an end date on her time at Lands. It was that simple. Charlotte pulled her laptop close and opened her email.

From: charlotte@landsoflegend.com
To: gbinns@everfund.com
Re: An Offer

Gregory,

I accept, though Creative Executive sounds like a demotion from Vice President of Fun. I want to remain flexible so let's set my contract to end on Memorial Day Weekend when Under the Waves opens.

Let's meet at Sir Cinna-Swirls at 10am tomorrow to discuss the rest of the details. We should talk to Marianne, Frank, and Emily afterward too so we can set an all-staff meeting and make sure we're being as transparent as possible with everyone about Ever Fund and what will and won't be happening.

Sincerely,
Charlotte

Her email chimed with a response immediately.

From: gbinns@everfund.com
To: charlotte@landsoflegend.com
Re: An Offer

Charlotte,

Do you eat cinnamon buns for breakfast every day?
That doesn't seem advisable.

Glad to hear you're accepting. That timeline works
for me. See you tomorrow.

Gregory

Chapter 13

Charlotte poured three cups of coffee in her parents' kitchen and pulled the last pieces of bacon from the frying pan to go with the eggs and toast she'd made. She'd decided an actual breakfast would make her stomach happier than only eating a cinnamon roll later.

"Good morning," she sang when Mom and Dad strolled into the kitchen. She gestured at the different platters with her tongs. "There's eggs, toast with butter and jam, and bacon. Oh and your coffee."

"Are more people joining us for breakfast?" Richard asked, grabbing a piece of bacon.

"Ha-ha," Charlotte said. "I'm making sure we all have plenty of protein and a solid meal. Some of us are starting a new job today."

Mom put down the plate she was making and hugged Charlotte. "You *are*?"

Charlotte detected the lack of surprise despite Alice's enthusiasm. Of course Gregory would have updated her relatives last night. "Wait, Uncle Frank and Aunt Marianne told you already, didn't they? You are all the worst."

Alice went back to assembling her breakfast. "I don't know what you're talking about, honey," she teased. "They're excited to have you as a full-time member of the team and we're excited for you and to know you'll be in town for longer."

Charlotte smiled, thinking about her aunt and uncle being so pleased that they had to tell her parents first thing. It further affirmed she'd made the right decision by accepting Gregory's offer.

"I'll be here until Under the Waves opens, so you're stuck with me until the end of May. I'm happy that they're happy. We'll see what Emily says."

Mom shrugged. "You know your cousin." Emily didn't have any kind of beef with Charlotte's parents, but they were aware of Emily's thoughts on all things Charlotte. "Anyway, I'm glad Marianne and Frank deemed Ever Fund a worthy partner."

"It all seems to have worked out like it was meant to," Dad added. "Congratulations, Charlotte. We know you're the right person to help see things through. It means so much to my brother—Lands always has, you know that— and it's . . ." Richard stared into his coffee cup. "It means a lot that you're doing this."

"It's my pleasure," Charlotte said. She got to assist her family, make some magic for all the guests who came to Lands, and add opening a new themed land to her experience. A real win-win situation for everyone. She sat down at the table with her family and started slathering apple butter on her toast when her phone buzzed on the table. Charlotte picked it up and saw Chad's name and dropped her butter knife. Then it buzzed again, this time with Gregory's name appearing. What did she do to deserve not one, but *two* annoying men bothering her during breakfast?

She put the phone on the table face down without looking at either message. They could both wait ten minutes.

Her dad must have noticed the change in her demeanor. "Everything okay?" he asked. "Hopefully you don't already have work drama."

"Um. Not drama," Charlotte said as she considered the best way to answer him. No need to mention Chad. Her parents were excellent at reading her, and she didn't want to hint at anything yet. "I'd say the venture capital firm's representative is interesting."

"Interesting?" Alice probed.

"Yeah," Charlotte answered. "Interesting. But hey, he holds the proverbial purse strings, so I can work with interesting." And the near-simultaneous message from her ex was a timely reminder to keep her work life and personal life separate.

Alice nodded. "You sure can. Besides, I know you handled a lot of egos along with bigger budgets and projects at Dream-Us. You'll do great and you'll be a huge help to Frank and Marianne in bridging the gap between Lands and this venture capital firm."

Charlotte was confident she could accomplish all those things, but she'd take all the words of encouragement to help battle the first-day jitters that had arrived with no warning. This was her family's labor of love, a place her uncle and aunt had dedicated most of their lives to. What if she *did* ruin it, like Emily asked her not to? What if she couldn't stop Ever Fund or Emily from making bad choices—or worse, what if *she* made bad choices by stopping *their* choices and then the park had to close without even opening Under the Waves?

She tried to continue a pleasant breakfast with her parents without sinking into panic. Panic that came on in full when she opened her messages while her parents cleaned up. Gregory was texting to confirm their meeting time; she replied with a thumbs-up. Then she opened Chad's text.

Chad: Hey. Good to see you at the Cosmic opening. I'm making some Paris plans and want to run something by you.

Her heartbeat accelerated. Was this it? The door to DreamUs swinging back open right after she'd made other plans?

Charlotte: Hey there. I'm all ears.

Charlotte couldn't bring herself to lie and say that it was good to see him, too.

Chad: Okay if I send you an email?

How very Chad to send a text asking to send an email.

Charlotte: Absolutely. I'll keep an eye out.

The anxiety over her new role and an incoming email from Chad about something to do with Dreamland Paris hadn't dissipated by the time she got to Lands of Legend, and Charlotte had to wipe her clammy hands on her pants before she got out of the car. She'd parked in this spot and made this walk past Owen's security station and into Lands countless times in the past—including yesterday. Sure, today she was beginning a position that would help determine the park's future—or if it had a future—but it was fine. She was fine.

She stepped into the park with time to spare before her meeting with Gregory. A lap around Emily's Carousel, she decided, would set her right. The ride was filled with dazzling mounts from the pages of fairy tales: a carved frog wearing a gold crown, a bench seat featuring the three bears who were, in the contemporary version, far too nice about finding Goldilocks invading their home, Puss in Boots, a unicorn that would look like it sparkled during golden hour.

She'd memorized each of the creatures and stories when she was a kid and rode the carousel on every one in order to choose her favorite, which ended up being the frog from "The Frog Prince." Seeing the figure soothed her nerves, so, Charlotte reasoned, climbing over the closed carousel's barrier and sitting on the jaunty frog would clearly erase her confidence issues and make everything okay. No one would see her since the park was opening on the later side today.

Charlotte set her bag on the ground inside the metal barrier and swung one leg over carefully—

"Charlotte? What are you doing?" a voice called from across the path. Specifically, Gregory's voice.

Of course he would be early, too.

She finished climbing over the barrier and turned to look at him. His tall, lanky body was silhouetted in front of Fairytale Land's buildings, the sun hitting him in a way that made him appear to be glowing. *Him and his full-ass suit*, Charlotte corrected in her head, today with the addition of a gray pea coat to ward off the chill. The sun would return later in the day, allegedly.

"I'm visiting a friend," Charlotte said.

Gregory turned his head left and right to look for said friend and crossed over to the carousel. "I don't see anyone else here, Charlotte. Are you allowed to be in there? It's closed." He nodded toward the locked entry gate.

Charlotte rolled her eyes. "First of all, yes, of course I can be in here. Nothing's running right now, it's perfectly safe."

He gave her a skeptical look.

"And there." Charlotte flung her arm in the direction of her frog. "My friend is right there. He was my favorite when I was little and I haven't said hello in a while."

Gregory leaned forward over the barrier. He peered past

Charlotte into the carousel and then shook his head. "I have no idea what you're talking about."

Charlotte hadn't even officially started the position and she had elicited quite the irritated tone from Gregory. It was kind of satisfying. "Come in here and I'll introduce you," she said. "Besides, you should get a closer look at one of our classic and most beloved rides."

Crinkles formed around his eyes while he considered. "Maybe, uh, we could wait until it's open?"

"Why would we do that when we could have it all to ourselves now?" she goaded.

"You're not going to let this go, are you?" he asked.

She shook her head.

"Fine," he muttered. "And then after this can we get to work?"

"I would argue that this *is* work, but yes, we can go plan all the things afterward," Charlotte said. She extended her hand across the barrier. "Now, come on."

He ignored her hand and unbuttoned his blazer before stepping over the barrier with ease—it was only a tall step given his height—and then setting his shiny briefcase next to Charlotte's well-loved backpack. His voice resigned, he said, "Lead the way."

"Look at you, breaking the rules on your second day here."

He froze, eyes open wide. "I thought you said it was fine for us to be back here."

This was too easy, Charlotte thought. She cackled. "I'm teasing."

"Oh. Funny."

"I have my moments," she said. "We'll board the carousel around this way."

As she led Gregory to the back, she went into a little of the ride's history. "So this opened with the park and then when

Uncle Frank and Aunt Marianne had Emily, they changed the name. Uncle Frank worked with a local builder to design and craft every animal you see here. They're all from fairy tales and Frank evaluates them every season and picks one to restore or repaint so they all get the chance to look their best. We have backups in storage past the office so the ride is never a mount down while he's doing repairs."

They'd reached the boarding spot by now, so Charlotte finished with, "It's also one of the most popular rides with guests too, partially because of its history but also who can resist a carousel? It's timeless."

"I'm surprised that, in these modern times, guests don't find the idea of a carousel boring," Gregory said.

"Simple is the answer sometimes. Classics are classics for a reason. And in our case, having the carousel go with the fairy-tale theming in the land elevates it beyond the usual carousel with colorful horses—which, to be clear, are also incredible works of art and *not* boring."

"Hmm," Gregory said.

"Come see for yourself." Charlotte wound through the quiet carousel, patting each mount on its head and naming its fairy-tale origins for Gregory before stopping in front of her frog. "This is my friend."

Gregory circled the frog. "From 'The Frog Prince,' right?"

"Yep."

"What made him your favorite as a kid?" he asked.

Charlotte thought. "Now I can look back and say I admire the frog's persistence in the face of such a rude princess— I have no idea why they ended up together, he deserved better—but back then, I liked his friendly face and of course his crown. My uncle always kept the gold paint fresh for me. I know it might be more interesting if I had some complex reasoning, but I was drawn to him. And when I was feeling anxious this morning, seeing him calmed me down. So, here we are."

Shit, she hadn't intended to let Gregory in on her experiencing anxiety. To stop him from inquiring about it, she walked to the side of the frog and hopped on board.

"Ahhhh!" Charlotte swung her body with too much vigor and the momentum started carrying her off the other side of the frog. Gregory stepped over to stop her from falling off and possibly breaking more than her pride by bracing his hands against her torso.

A warm blush spread over her face and neck. "Thank you," she said and she noticed Gregory hadn't let go, his strong hands propping her up. She cleared her throat as she straightened on the frog's back and held onto the pole. "I've got it now."

"You're welcome," he said. "But I thought you were a pro at this?"

She got defensive. "I haven't been on the carousel in a while and—"

"Charlotte. I'm teasing."

"Oh," she said. She was glad he wasn't *that* much of a jerk. "In that case, why don't you board that wolf right there?"

The big, bad wolf from "Little Red Riding Hood" was next to the frog. Gregory looked at it and then back at her. "Do I have to?"

"Yes, it's part of the experience. You have a lot to learn about theme parks in a short amount of time, so you should try one new thing a day."

"One," he grumbled. "I'll think about it."

He sighed with his whole body and then swung one gorgeous leg over the back of the wolf. Charlotte's blush got deeper as she, for reasons she couldn't fathom, imagined him in that position in a different situation. "There. Happy now?" he asked, looking down at her from his position on the wolf. His unruly hair fell across his face and between that and the wolf, he had a kind of annoyed, feral look that was decidedly attractive according to Charlotte's pounding traitor of a heart.

"I am, yes, I am happy now. Thank you for humoring me," she said. "How long is it since you've been on a carousel, anyway?"

Gregory looked down at the sculpted pommel on the wolf's back, made to look like fur since the animals on the carousel didn't have saddles like carousel horses. "I can't remember," he said. "Like I said, I think we went to an amusement park once, but if so, I was really little. I don't remember riding a carousel, even if I went on one. My family didn't do a lot of stuff like that. Too much work. So, I spent a lot of time with my grandpa as a kid and he preferred to get away from people and take me camping."

She noticed his shoulders had gone rigid, his voice quiet. That explained why he didn't take vacations to amusement parks or even a DreamUs park; it seemed like nearly everyone in his family was and had been super committed to Ever Fund. "Well, I'm glad you're getting the experience now," she said. "We'll have to come back when it's open and ride it. This all changes when the lights and music are on."

"I don't know, this is nice enough." Gregory shrugged. "I already feel silly."

"Why? Because you're an adult on a carousel? In a suit and tie?" Charlotte asked.

"Yeah, kinda exactly that."

"Haven't you heard that age is only a mindset, Gregory?"

"I've heard it, yes," he said, "but I don't believe it. Now, should we head over and start our meeting?"

"You know we don't stand on formality here. No suit necessary."

He wiped his hand across his face. "I know, Charlotte. But I'm representing Ever Fund and impressions matter."

"Get ready for a lot more of doing things like this while dressed like that."

Charlotte thought she had a ways to go before getting Gregory to understand activities like this were a vital part of the job, even more so when guests were in the park for them to observe. No amount of meetings in drab conference rooms were a substitute for being in the park and putting boots on the ground, going on the rides, trying the snacks, and playing. But today she would consider getting Gregory aboard the carousel a small triumph.

"We can go to our meeting now, but partially because I'm in dire need of a cinnamon roll," Charlotte said. "Give me one more minute with my frog prince."

Charlotte was hugging the frog's neck despite its hard unyielding surface when she heard the metal barrier around the ride rattle. She craned her neck and saw Jude, one of the carousel's operators, approaching.

"Hey, Jude," Charlotte called out, making sure he knew they were there but failing to not startle him.

Jude recovered from the scare and walked around the carousel where he could see them. "Charlotte, hi! I didn't expect to see anyone here, already on the carousel."

"See?" Gregory hissed. "I didn't think we were supposed to be here."

"It's fine," Charlotte whispered to him. Then turning to Jude, "I got here early and realized I hadn't seen my buddy for a while and wanted to say hi."

Jude beamed; Charlotte knew he took pride in operating the carousel and helping her uncle keep the ride gleaming. "I polished his crown just the other day," Jude said. "Would you two like a private ride?"

"Uh, absolutely yes! Please!" Charlotte exclaimed at the same time as Gregory said, "No, that's okay, we're good."

Jude looked between them. Charlotte spoke for both of them. "We would really appreciate that. Thank you."

"You got it, Charlotte." Jude grinned. "Give me two minutes and I'll fire 'er up."

Charlotte smiled at Gregory. "A roller coaster yesterday, a carousel today. What will tomorrow bring?"

His mouth stayed in a flat line. "Hopefully a peaceful day of sitting in my office."

"You've invested in the wrong kind of business for that. This is important on-the-ground research. In fact, you really need to go to a DreamUs park sometime and see how theming works on a larger scale. I'm going to figure out when we can go, okay?"

"We?" Gregory's eyebrows were almost in his hair.

Charlotte wasn't in love with the idea of accompanying Gregory to one of her favorite places, but she knew it would help open his eyes and give him needed perspective. Plus she knew every DreamUs park inside out. She would do that for Lands. "Yes, we. Who would be a better guide than me? Now hold on."

True to his word, Jude went back to the operator's stall and had the carousel's systems going in no time. He gave Charlotte a thumbs-up and then the overhead lights flipped on and bathed the carousel in a soft, flickering glow that made it look like hundreds of candles were set around the space. While it was more striking at night, the lights created an ethereal vibe even in the middle of the morning.

Next, the music. Rather than a typical carousel track, her aunt had worked with a teacher at Grove Tech back in the day who had composed a custom piece of music for the carousel. It wasn't tinny or typical; its soft bells and tinkles, a hint of sitar, and flutes made Charlotte think of '80s fantasy films in the best way. She closed her eyes and soaked it in, all the elements transporting her back through time.

She felt a gentle touch on her hand and opened her eyes. "You okay?" Gregory whispered. He'd stretched over to nudge her.

"More than okay," she replied, her lips curving.

"Just checking." He straightened back into his seat. "This music is beautiful and not what I would have expected."

"I think you'll see not a lot about Lands is what you expected."

"Yeah, I'm beginning to see that," he agreed.

The carousel started its gentle movement and after a few rotations Charlotte snuck a glance at Gregory. His posture had relaxed and while he wasn't smiling, he looked content. At peace.

Chapter 14

Charlotte chewed her turkey sandwich at record speed while she sat at her desk and got through emails, which still didn't include any messages from Chad. She kind of hated it, but it looked like she would have to follow up with him and do her best not to sound desperate. No, she couldn't risk looking desperate to Chad of all people. She'd make her follow-up breezy.

Not that her current schedule gave her a lot of time to overanalyze what Chad might want. Working with Gregory and her family the last few weeks to make a plan to take Under the Waves from a fragmented area with various construction in various states of progress to being open with a massive roller coaster with a water feature by Memorial Day was taking a lot out of her. Thank God they'd had the basic structure and detailed plans ready for the Manta, the land's star attraction, in place or it would be at least a year before it could open. That empty man-made lake had been an eyesore for a while, but now it was a godsend to have it done.

The accelerated timeline was both thanks to and because of Ever Fund. They were dropping a substantial infusion of cash into Lands of Legend's accounts, and if the near-constant wrinkle between Gregory's eyebrows was any indication, they wanted to see some kind of return on said cash sooner rather than later. Gregory had gone over the project milestones with Charlotte in excruciating detail; he had to, she knew it was part of his job, but numbers had never been *her* favorite part of the job—especially when she had a much larger coffer to pull from at DreamUs. They had budget limits, of course, but at DreamUs, the upper limits were often in the millions. As in, more than two million. Charlotte's team had also had room to be much more flexible. *Much* more. They were often running toward opening dates, true, but they had backup vendor after backup vendor in case anything went wrong with layers of contingency plans to set the ship to rights. Here, Gregory, Charlotte, and Emily ensured the trains ran on time, but it came down to them and them alone. Frank and Marianne were busy too, but they were more about polishing the bigger picture than managing the nitty-gritty.

She was exhausted beyond belief, more than at any point in her entire career, but Charlotte couldn't get over seeing the look in her uncle's eyes when he saw dozens of contractors on the Under the Waves site within a week of signing the paperwork with Ever Fund. And they were getting shit done. They'd engaged local construction companies too, and Frank enjoyed making the rounds to say hello to people he'd known for decades.

And that, Charlotte thought as she finished her sandwich, was worth eating lunch at her desk. She wouldn't be running at this breakneck pace forever.

She sent two more emails, one to the municipality board about permits and one to their social media manager to discuss a strategy for rolling out the Under the Waves news. Announcing the land and the Manta Diver would be huge for them and should lead into a spike in ticket sales, but (a) Charlotte wanted to give it more time to ensure they were for sure on track before they shared anything resembling an opening date—backtracking would be embarrassing, and (b) she wanted to make it part of a bigger message about Lands of Legend and how it was always growing and changing and maybe people should consider buying annual passes.

She was toying with the idea of a lifetime pass, too. Really any and all ideas that would bring in guests and money. And the next meeting on her calendar sparked another idea.

While walking toward the kitchen for that meeting with the head pastry chef, about treats they could sell in Under the Waves, Charlotte opened a note of revenue ideas on her phone and to a section labeled "Possible One-Time Events" she added:

- Themed dinner in Adventurer's Gate, maybe with some performers

Charlotte knew Holly, the pastry chef behind Lands's perfect cinnamon rolls, would relish the chance to stretch her culinary creativity. It was a bonus that she could have an event like this in her back pocket to offer Holly when Charlotte inevitably had to say no to some fancy and usually expensive ingredient the chef wanted to use in an everyday dessert in the park.

As if to prove her point, Charlotte opened the swinging kitchen door in time to hear Holly arguing with Quinn, the executive chef for the park. Holly had talked Quinn, her wife, into coming onboard after Quinn decided running a restaurant of her own was too aggravating. Quinn preferred running Lands's food and drink program, which she claimed had all of the benefits of having her own place with none of the hassle.

"We live in *Ohio*," Quinn was saying to Holly in an exasperated tone.

"And?" Holly asked.

Quinn crossed her arms. "Not exactly an abundance of seaweed around, is there?"

"We have to source plenty of ingredients that aren't grown in the area, Quinn."

Charlotte tried to step backward through the door instead of lurking while the pair bickered, but her sneakers squeaked and gave her away. Both Quinn's and Holly's heads swiveled toward her.

"Ah, Charlotte, right on time. Please explain to Holly that using a seaweed topping on handheld desserts in Under the Waves is not practical."

"It's actually a seaweed espuma," Holly said.

Charlotte held back a smile. She had become accustomed to ending up in the middle of these kinds of discussions and arbitrating, putting her foot down, or throwing her hands up as the situation required.

"What kind of dessert did you have in mind?" she asked Holly.

Holly opened a notebook and pointed to a colored pencil sketch (Quinn said Tom Hovey's illustrations for *The Great British Bake Off* had started a whole thing). "Chocolate bouchons with a swirl of the espuma on top. Think dark chocolate cakes—almost like brownies—with a silky, salty topping that tastes of the ocean. The contrasting colors would be *gorgeous*."

Charlotte looked at the delicate illustration and the fervent glow in Holly's eyes. It was never easy to pull back on an idea when Holly was so excited.

"Those do look beautiful and I'm sure they would taste amazing—"

"They do!" Holly interrupted.

"You know, Holly," Charlotte continued, "you're so talented at creating memorable desserts for our guests and using your background to put elevated twists on everyday items to get people out of their plain corn dog and ice cream sandwich mindsets. With so many people coming to the park, I know it's impossible to make everyone happy, but I think you give everyone a lot of choices to go with classics or to try something new."

Holly was beaming.

"That said, I feel like seaweed in this form might be too adventurous for everyday guests, and Quinn is right in that we do need to be conscious of the costs for standard menu items."

The pastry chef deflated. "Do most people not know what espuma is?"

"*I* don't know what it is," Charlotte admitted. "But I do like the idea of incorporating seaweed into the menu in Under the Waves. I defer to both of you, but maybe it could be in the form of a sprinkle or something so it's more cost effective. Plus, what do you think about having the seaweed and chocolate bouchons be a special item for the grand opening? We'll definitely be having a party and I know those would impress the guests."

"I could work with that," Holly agreed.

"We absolutely can," Quinn said. "Now, I know you had a couple other things to review with Charlotte, dear. I'll get out of the way."

Charlotte left the kitchen an hour later, having reviewed a list of ideas with Holly. They'd called Melanie halfway through the meeting her for opinion on a Jell-O concoction (Melanie voted absolutely not). Charlotte leaned against a counter after discussing the menu and drafted a brief email to Chad to get it over with. She kept it simple, light. "Hope you're well. Just seeing what you wanted to run by me."

There. Done. Painless. She grabbed a banana from a bowl

on the counter, swung the kitchen door open, and walked into Gregory with enough force to make them both take a step back.

"Ah, I'm sorry—"

"No, I'm sorry," Gregory said as he straightened his jacket. Charlotte noticed how the tailoring accentuated his everything; she couldn't relate to his dedication to business attire but she could appreciate it.

"I was just heading back to the office," Charlotte said. "What about you?"

"I thought I'd check in with Quinn, see how things are going in general."

Charlotte didn't realize Gregory had been checking in with Lands's employees on his own, not that he wasn't allowed. "Why?" Charlotte asked, her voice defensive. She was worried the venture capitalist asking people questions about their work might make them nervous. They'd had the all-staff meeting soon after Lands signed the contract with Ever Fund to reassure everyone about Ever Fund's future and their jobs, but that didn't mean people weren't humans who worried.

Gregory responded to the edge in Charlotte's question with one of his own. His jaw tensed as he said, "I thought it would be nice to get to know the people who work here."

He had a point.

"But you're only going to be here what, not even a full year, right?" she asked. Charlotte's confusion was genuine; at no point had Gregory seemed like the type to attempt bonding with his temporary coworkers.

He bristled. "Would you prefer I not talk to anyone except you, Emily, Marianne, and Frank?"

"No, of course not. I'm surprised you're interested, is all."

"Obviously I'm interested in the work everyone here does and any suggestions and thoughts they might have," Gregory said. "Remember how I can be good at my job?"

Working together so closely meant Charlotte had become aware of Gregory's skills. He was a competent force of nature in the office and applied his general business knowledge to the world of theme parks with ease. Hearing him talk with the many contractors and suppliers they were working with was as riveting as a true crime podcast. Charlotte would sometimes catch pieces of his conversations and wonder how anyone could say no to that charm, that logic. But then other times, he came across as a business robot and Charlotte hoped that wasn't the side of Gregory Lands's employees were seeing. Like she'd done with Holly, like she'd done countless times at DreamUs, Charlotte thought of how to phrase her thoughts without sounding like an asshole.

"You're right, you should talk with anyone you want."

"Gee, thanks for the permission."

Charlotte gritted her teeth. "If I may continue, it's good for the staff to meet you so they don't think of Ever Fund as a faceless suit from that one all-hands staff meeting that wants to change the park. In fact, they probably appreciate you introducing yourself and showing interest in their work, as long as we continue to make sure they know their jobs are secure. It can probably be a little scary if the new investor is popping up and 'checking in' without context, you know?"

The creak of the kitchen door opening prompted them both to step out of the entryway and into an alcove that Holly used as storage. Gregory chewed his lip, a habit that always grabbed Charlotte's focus both because it wasn't in step with tidy, confident way Gregory presented himself *and* because it made her curious about the texture of his lips.

"Casual communication isn't always my strength," Gregory admitted, the wrinkle between his eyebrows a deep trench. "I don't think I've been freaking anyone out—it wasn't my intention—but I know I don't always come across the way I mean to. What about instead you introduce me to everyone when we make our rounds in the park? Then I have you as a buffer; they know you and that should make it less weird. You can set up that I'm eager to meet people and learn as much as I can about them and the park."

He met Charlotte's eyes and added, "That's truly been my goal with talking to folks these last few weeks."

She took in what he said, feeling the slightest warmth when he mentioned their rounds. After they visited the Under the Waves construction site in the mornings, they'd taken to walking through different areas of the park. Gregory had asked one morning his first week there and it had become a habit; sometimes he posed questions, other times they went through the biggest to-dos on the park's lists and exchanged ideas—Gregory's observations had become more insightful as the days passed—and occasionally they walked in companionable silence. And every day, Charlotte reminded him about his agreement to try one new thing. The other day that new thing had been one of the stuffed dragon-egg pretzels; Gregory's moan of joy was still crystal clear in Charlotte's memory.

If Charlotte was being honest with herself, morning rounds with Gregory were her favorite part of the day. She loved showing Lands of Legend to him beyond their brief tour—its history, its many loving touches, its rides drove home how much she loved the park, how special it continued to be. How generations of families had come through the gates her uncle had built with his hands and that her aunt had helped paint. None of the sprawling theme parks she'd been in or worked in compared. And she could see Gregory was starting to get it.

"I know you care about your work, and I can see you're starting to care about Lands. So yeah, I think that's a solid plan for getting to know people. We can start on our walk tomorrow."

"Excellent," Gregory said. "I do think you could give me more credit."

"Oh yeah?" she teased.

"Yes. Like this much more." He bent his hand and put his index finger about inch over his thumb.

Charlotte reached over and pushed his thumb and finger together so they were almost touching. "Let's start with that much and see where we get."

Chapter 15

"I'm sorry, you're going to have to explain that to me again," Gregory said over the din of clanking metal, buzzing saws, and myriad other construction noises.

Charlotte was having a hell of a time explaining the concept of a photo wall to Gregory. She stood by his side and spread her hands across the in-progress mural in front of them, a realistic seascape that took no small amount of inspiration from Lisa Frank with hints of colorful mermaids in the background and the outline of a kraken in the water's depths. It was a work of art—a unique, instantly recognizable work of art guests would pose in front of and share online.

"It's a wall people will pose in front of for photos." Charlotte distilled the idea down as much as she could. "Maybe someone will nickname it. Like, one of the walls in a DreamUs park is called the bubblegum wall and people post pictures with it using the hashtag bubblegumwall."

Doubt swept over Gregory's face. "Because it's made of bubblegum? Like the one in Seattle? That doesn't seem sanitary. Or Instagrammable."

"Ew, gross," Charlotte said. "No, it's named that because it's the color of bubblegum. Here, let me show you."

She stepped closer until their arms brushed, and she unlocked her phone. After a few seconds of typing in the hashtag she had a wall of photos showing all kinds of people posing in front of the brightly painted wall.

"Here, look." She handed her phone to Gregory—or tried to, anyway. Instead of taking it, he cupped his hands under hers and lifted her phone up. It seemed like he found excuses to touch her in the same way she did with him. Nothing obvious, small moments here and there that could be excused as unintentional or unthinking. She insisted to herself that she was imagining things, but that was hard to believe when the warmth of his hands was against hers.

Right as he moved his hand to scroll through the images, a notification of another email from Chad appeared at the top of the screen. He'd gotten back to Charlotte's breezy nudge with a heads-up about potential work at Dreamland Paris; this must finally be the job posting. Charlotte raised her thumb to dismiss it so quickly she might have sprained it, feeling gratitude to her past self for turning off preview text for her messages and emails ages ago.

"Chad, huh?" Gregory asked while using his finger to move through the feed of images. "I saw a recent update from him on LinkedIn about being settled in Paris for DreamUs."

Charlotte could hear the unasked question: Why was Chad emailing her *now*? She felt guilty thinking about another job opportunity in the middle of so much work at Lands— not because of how she noticed the softness of Gregory's hands under hers. "Yeah, we've been trying to connect about some opportunities. You know my contract's only through the opening of Under the Waves."

Gregory stopped scrolling, the muscles on his other hand tensing under Charlotte's. "Right. You have to keep your eyes on the horizon." He cleared his throat and erased the flatness. "Now, here, I should have said I understand that people take photos in front of the wall, but why are there hashtags and why do we need one? I don't use social media much."

"I know."

"You do?"

"I assumed since I didn't see any of your—" Damn it. She'd basically just confessed to looking him up across social media.

Gregory lifted the corner of his mouth. "My what, Charlotte?"

Yep. Busted. "Your accounts, okay? I looked you up. For business reasons."

"That was almost convincing." He was fully smiling now, still holding Charlotte's phone with her. "But I can't give you too much of a hard time, because I looked you up, too. From my private Instagram account without my name on it. Pull up the search."

Charlotte, confused by this turn of events, followed his instructions. He reached his thumb over hers to type in "gbinz92" and the account that came up *was* private, but Gregory standing on the top of a mountain in what appeared to be in head-to-toe Patagonia, *with a beard*, smiled out from the profile photo. "If you promise not to make fun of my username, you can follow me. I mostly use this account to keep up with others and news."

"I won't make fun of the username, promise." Gregory had continued to open up as the weeks had passed but Charlotte knew this was a big step for him; she wouldn't trivialize it. But she had to ask. "What about that beard? Am I allowed to comment on that?"

"No, absolutely not."

"Okay. But just so you know, it suits you." The profile picture was so small but she could see how much the beard, the pullover, all of it suited him. She now longed for him to let his evening stubble keep growing. Overall hotness aside, he looked content. A huge smile split his face in the photo.

"Uh. Thanks. I really liked it." Gregory lifted his hand to his cheek, marked with a light blush, as if remembering having a beard. "Now help me out. Why do we want a hashtag for this wall?"

Charlotte took the hint. No more beard talk. She pressed FOLLOW on his account and got back to business, noting his use of "we." Gregory was becoming more invested in Lands with more than only money. "Photo walls are aesthetically pleasing, and people like to take fun photos. We're playing into a trend created by fans and when companies are overt about doing that, it can be a turnoff, but this is the first official photo wall in Lands. We won't push it. We'll let this gorgeous mural speak for itself and let it be a moment of discovery for everyone."

Gregory walked closer to the mural. "But we're hoping they'll make, I don't know, the ocean wall . . . a thing?"

"Exactly," Charlotte said. "Except, it's not gonna be hashtag the ocean wall."

He looked back over his shoulder. "What are your picks?"

"I leave it up to the people. We're making art and putting it in their hands. Like this." She held up her phone and snapped a quick photo before Gregory could protest. The midafternoon light was soft on the cloudy day and he was a sight in his suit, tight-fitting pea coat, and the safety gear the construction site required.

"Even with the mural only halfway done, it's looking perfect." She didn't mention how Gregory's presence in the photo enhanced it; she couldn't wait to see what the fully painted wall would do to his green eyes.

Enough of that, she thought. *Focus on work. Do not mix work and relationships together.* "So, you're clear on photo walls now, right?" she asked and started walking toward the Manta construction.

"As clear as I'm going to be." His legs were so long it only took him two steps to catch up with Charlotte.

They walked past a towering arch covered in unpainted swirling shells and graceful kelp carved from wood. It led into an empty structure with a dome roof right now, but day by day it was looking more like the mermaid palace her aunt drew. Mermaids would be inside, waiting to meet and interact with guests from their thrones—mermaid royalty who had been granted the ability to breathe air, obviously. Eventually they would add a tank so they could have swimming mermaids, maybe some synchronized swimmers, but that was for down the road. Charlotte put it on her ongoing list of experiences she'd like to add to Under the Waves. That particular list sat alongside another list of potential experiences for the whole park in the years to come. She reasoned that it made sense to keep the list going even if she didn't oversee the execution of everything herself.

The mermaid palace was so far along and the Lost City's entry was taking shape. Beyond the swooping art nouveau–style lines of the entrance, guests would wait in a queue that was part "moody under the water" vibes and part science lab that talked about the discovery of the Lost City of Atlantis and how this ride through the ruins was so remarkable, they'd decided to make it a tourist offering, inviting all the guests to come see the remnants of the great city and help protect a sacred artifact. Charlotte's lips curved as she recalled explaining the concept of a dark ride to Gregory. He'd thought the words indicated a horror-themed ride, which wasn't an unreasonable thought, plus some dark rides were scary. They were essentially an indoor ride in a guided vehicle through a themed environment, and that themed environment could be scary.

But now Gregory was using the ride terminology like a pro, and Charlotte was a proud teacher—a proud teacher who'd fallen behind. She jogged a few feet to catch up with him.

"It's wild to see how fast the coaster is coming along,"

Gregory said. They'd made it to the ride's footprint where framing and track had indeed multiplied at shocking speed, feeding right into the tunnel in the man-made lake. Besides local construction crews, they had engineers and contractors with experience from some amusement parks in Ohio who Gregory had persuaded to come work at Lands and between them all, the coaster was cooking.

"I'm impressed," Charlotte said.

Gregory pointed to the left at what would be the loading area. "Was that even there two days ago?! I realize this is probably pretty typical for construction at DreamUs parks and I've seen some real estate developments grow out of nowhere to complete in no time, but this is still blowing my mind."

"I've seen a lot of rides come together, but this is kind of blowing my mind, too. I know we, thanks to Ever Fund, threw a pile of money at all of this"—she gestured generally at Under the Waves—"but it's more than that. You pulled a solid crew together."

Gregory lifted a hand to protest. "I couldn't have done it without input from Marianne, Frank, Emily, and you."

"Don't be so modest. This site has come together in fragments before you. You brought chaos into smooth-running harmony."

"Harmony. Poetic."

"Don't be sarcastic, I'm paying you a compliment." Charlotte nudged him with her elbow and Gregory glanced down at the action, his expression unreadable, in its default grumpy look. Her comment was genuine; he'd made things happen from the first day he started work at Lands and this was the result. She added, "The crew seems super into their work here, like they're busting extra ass. Some of them have known my uncle for their whole lives and came here as kids and now bring *their* kids here, so I bet that's part of it, too."

"I also might have said yes to a rate that reflected the rush." Gregory was protective of Ever Fund's investment—essentially his mom's investment—but he wasn't a miser. Charlotte noticed he had the sense for when to spend money and when to pinch pinnies in the right ways.

"Speaking of saying yes to things"—Gregory turned to Charlotte—"I have an idea to run past you."

He had made some helpful suggestions lately—a plan for overflow parking, developing seasonal versions of the popular cinnamon buns, figuring out a crossover with the local, popular renaissance faire—so Charlotte was optimistic to hear what he had to say. "I'm all ears."

"Great. We know Under the Waves is going to be a success. The projections you put together based on the performance of thrill rides at other parks in the state are encouraging. I did have to adjust them slightly to account for those parks having more than one thrill ride—many more than one," Gregory said.

"Yeah, well, they're fantastic but they're amusement parks," Charlotte commented. "It's a different crowd."

" 'Crowd' being the key word. They draw in many more thousands of guests each year."

"I know Lands could eventually use more thrill rides. We've been over all of this, Gregory," she said. Charlotte didn't like where this was headed. She and her family had had a few conversations with Gregory, even a formal meeting, discussing what set Lands apart from those parks and why those differences mattered. They'd always known they weren't going to pull the thrill-seeking crowd away from the fastest, highest, or whatever superlative their newest roller coasters could offer. Any ride they added needed to be part of the story in whatever land they built it in.

"I'm not saying we should try adding random roller coasters—we don't have the budget or time for that—but what about some smaller, more accessible options for the sake of moving bodies through the gates? Maybe just until Under the Waves is ready."

"Okaaay," she said, crossing her arms. "What did you have in mind?"

"Quick wins, that's what I have in mind," he said, his body tensing. "We have more than enough space in the meadow for a few rides. Bumper cars, a scrambler, maybe a tilt-a-whirl. We could design special tickets and Quinn and Holly could come up with fun-fair food items."

Charlotte ground her teeth. "You want to set up bumper cars in Bluewhistle Meadow?!"

"Or something like it."

"Lands of Legend is not a fucking weekend carnival, Gregory!" she shouted, and at that moment, the sounds of construction paused. Her voice rung out across the site and everyone tried to pretend they hadn't heard what she said and weren't looking at her. Frustration was making her heart race and her arms vibrate. Charlotte had thought Gregory was getting on the same page and she was angry with herself for misreading the situation.

She lowered her voice. "I'm too pissed to have this conversation like a calm human right now, so if you'll excuse me, I'm going home for the day to hang out with Madmartigan and chill out." She started to walk in the opposite direction.

"Charlotte, wait. Before you go, you've mentioned Madmartigan a handful of times, and I have to know: Who or what is a Madmartigan?"

"Madmartigan is my cat, named after Val Kilmer's character in *Willow*."

Gregory's face was blank.

Charlotte gasped. "Wait, you've never seen *Willow*?!" Gregory shook his head.

She wouldn't normally take offense to someone not seeing a movie; instead she would be excited about them getting to watch and experience it for the first time. Not at this moment. She was livid on director Ron Howard's behalf that Gregory had never seen one of the best fantasy movies of all time. "Of course you haven't. It's a fun movie and you don't understand fun."

Charlotte inwardly cringed at the juvenile comment but it was too late. The baffling thing was, she'd noticed Gregory react to it, as stupid as the comment was. He appeared hurt.

"Hey, I'm sorry," she said. "I didn't mean that."

He averted his eyes to anywhere but her. "No, it's okay. It's not the first time I've heard it."

"It doesn't mean anyone who's said it, including me, was right." She thought Gregory could be stuffy, but after spending time with him, she didn't truly believe he wasn't fun. She saw glimpses, knew it was inside him to play.

Gregory shook his head as if to shake the thought off. "It's okay. I know I have my moments. I *am* wearing a suit with a high-visibility vest right now." He gestured down at himself.

"That you are," she agreed. "Now, I really am going to leave for the day and cool down. I didn't mean what I said about you not being fun, but I want to calm down before we keep talking about other additions. I understand where you're coming from. I don't want to, but I do get that things need to make money. But this isn't the way. We can't make changes that cheapen what Lands is, what Frank and Marianne dreamed of and built."

Gregory seemed like he wanted to say more but was holding it back. "I know. I'm only trying to find the best path forward that is also profitable. Let's talk more tomorrow."

Later that night after some pouting, chatting with Melanie, a comforting pizza from The Dragon's Breath, and even more comforting cuddles with Mads, Charlotte had calmed down. She picked up her phone one more time before she settled under the covers. She usually only texted Gregory about things like purchase orders, but she wanted to smooth over the edges.

Charlotte: For the record, I do like carnivals.

A reply came back within thirty seconds.

Gregory: I didn't think you disliked them.
Gregory: For the record, I think I would like 80s fantasy movies.
Charlotte: Hmm. You might? I don't know.
Charlotte: Glad we cleared both of those things up.
Gregory: Me too.

Three dots appeared and then disappeared. Charlotte wondered what else was on his mind that he was obviously hesitating to say when another message came through.

Gregory: Maybe you could show me Willow sometime?

Charlotte sat up in bed so fast that she startled Madmartigan, who was getting snuggly by her feet. She recognized Gregory's olive branch and she would grab it.

Charlotte: I WOULD LOVE TO SHOW YOU WILLOW.
Charlotte: Ahem.
Gregory: We'll find time soon.
Charlotte: Perfect.
Gregory: See you tomorrow. I expect to see photos of Madmartigan too.

If Gregory fawned over photos of Mads, Charlotte was done for.

Charlotte: See you then.
Gregory: 🏎🏁
Charlotte: Is that supposed to be a bumper car?
Gregory: See, I can be fun. Funny.
Charlotte: 😊

Gregory using emojis. The wonders never ceased.

She put her phone in "do not disturb" mode and tried not to overanalyze a possible movie night with Gregory. Not a movie night. A date. And while she did that, she opened his Instagram. He didn't have many posts. Most of them were of a relaxed Gregory from years ago, usually outside, glorious facial hair covering his cheeks. She glanced at their mutuals and it was only two accounts: the official Lands of Legend account and LegendDucklings, the account tracking ducklings at Lands in the springs, the one Charlotte had shown him on the day they met.

Charlotte thought she might be catching feelings. Feelings that didn't understand she'd be moving away after Under the Waves opened.

Chapter 16

Emily poked her head into Charlotte's office the next morning right as Charlotte was carefully reviewing Chad's email for the fifth time. It was indeed a link to a job opening for a creative executive at Dreamland Paris, and a note that said yes, she would have to fill out the application to go through the rehiring process and the position would report to him and he'd like to have her on his team opening the park. He encouraged her to get her application in as soon as possible and that they'd make a decision in early March. Charlotte was more than qualified and, with Chad's support, it seemed like the position was a sure thing. She'd have to make sure DreamUs could wait for her until after Memorial Day when Under the Waves opened—she wanted to honor her commitment to Lands—but that hadn't stopped her from daydreaming about moving to Paris and opening the park. Warring feelings came with that daydream as she thought about how much she liked Gregory's company, but also how much his carnival suggestion had annoyed her. If she left Lands, would Gregory and Emily make terrible choices without her oversight?

Would she miss Gregory? She was considering all the possibilities when Emily interrupted.

"Good morning. Can we talk?"

Charlotte hadn't slept well—not even Mads's purr was enough to comfort her anxieties about Lands, and her attraction to Gregory and the beard he didn't even have anymore, and pondering over the link Chad sent, so she'd snoozed her alarm three times and ended up rushing out of the house without coffee. She wasn't ready for other humans yet. Especially not Emily.

She told herself she should give Emily the courtesy of the benefit of the doubt since her cousin had been putting in as many hours as Charlotte and Gregory to help Lands succeed and make the most of the investment. She had been more supportive of Charlotte lately. Only last week she sided with Charlotte when Gregory asked about the possibility of changing the admission structure to be a flat fee with extra charges for ride tickets instead of all-inclusive.

"Morning," Charlotte said. "And of course. Coffee first?"

"Ah, I see that you're not at the talking-in-complete-sentences part of the morning yet," Emily said. "I could use some coffee, too. See you in the kitchen."

"I'll just be a few."

Charlotte pulled out her laptop and slung her bag strap over her chair, wanting to get set up for the day before she heard Emily out. While her laptop booted she texted Melanie. Her brain needed a break, and she needed to share updates.

Charlotte: I keep forgetting to ask you something important.
Charlotte: What the hell is espuma?
Melanie: Lol
Melanie: It's . . . Vegetable foam is the best way I can describe it.

Charlotte wrinkled her nose. She'd try any kind of food but the phrase "vegetable foam" wasn't doing it for her.

Charlotte: Hmm.
Melanie: Exactly. It's on a lot of fancy pants menus these days.
Melanie: One of Riley's favorite's if that tells you anything.
Charlotte: Thank you for saving me from googling it. I was scared.
Melanie: 😳
Melanie: Jk anytime.
Charlotte: Speaking of, have you talked to Riley lately?

Melanie's on-and-off relationship with Riley was what the phrase "it's complicated" had been invented for. When they were together, they made one hell of a team. Melanie a grounded, cheery tornado to Riley's kind but serious demeanor. Melanie had met him years ago while they were both attending Le Cordon Bleu; she'd burned out on the world of fine culinary experiences for reasons she refused to discuss with anyone, including Charlotte, while Riley couldn't let go and poured his all into his focus into food and not relationships.

Melanie's history was one reason why she didn't hesitate to call out Charlotte for focusing too much on work.

Melanie: No . . .
Charlotte: I sense a but.
Melanie: Not a but. Just a ¯_(ツ)_/¯
Charlotte: Let me know if you want to talk about it.
Melanie: I will, I promise.
Charlotte: Also I have two updates for you. 1. Chad

emailed me a link to an application for a DreamUs job in
Paris. 2. I might have a date with Gregory.
Melanie: !!!!!!!!! CHARLOTTE!
Melanie: Why is the date second! Have I taught you noth-
ing?
Melanie: Seriously though, those things are both messy.
MESSY. Let's talk later.
Charlotte: Messy is right. But maybe exciting too.
Melanie: But also, 🥒
Charlotte: 😊 Talk soon.

Thoughts about her best friend, vegetable foam, and egg-
plants in the front of her mind, Charlotte headed toward the
office kitchen with a grin. Emily had Charlotte's favorite mug
waiting, a vintage Lands of Legend mug with the park's logo
and information toadstool faded on the crackled glaze. It
was one of the park's earliest souvenirs. They had a few unused ones in the archives but Charlotte loved that this little
mug had survived the office kitchen and the constant re-
minders to never put it in the dishwasher over the decades.

"Thank you. You know, we should work on a retro line of
merchandise with this design." Charlotte lifted the full mug
from the counter with grateful hands and took a sip. "Ahh,
you made the coffee this morning." Marianne had learned to
make a killer latte, but both her aunt and uncle were hopeless
at making coffee that wasn't bitter, so Emily tried to beat
them to it.

"You know it." She leaned on the counter, soft cashmere
sweater at odds against the worn laminate countertop. Charlotte noted dark circles under eyes.

"How are you hanging in, Emily? I see you in meetings
with Gregory and around the construction site, but it's been
so chaotic I haven't had an actual conversation with you in a
while."

"Chaotic sure is the word," Emily said. She took a drink of coffee from her own mug and then pulled it against her chest and wrapped both hands around it like it was the only source of warmth in the room. "I am exhausted, like we all are, but it's worth it to see Under the Waves make so much progress—Dad's been chipping away at it for so long and I didn't think it was ever going to happen."

Charlotte nodded. "All that work he and your mom put in made it easy for the crew to jump in and execute all of it."

"I know Dad knows that, but I can tell part of him, well, he's upset with himself for not being able to finish it on his own after all this time. He's happier that it means Under the Waves will finally open and that Lands has a better chance of being around a decade from now, but taking Ever Fund's money is making him feel a little like a failure, like he hasn't made the right decisions over the years to keep Lands of Legend *viable*—that's Dad's word of choice lately, by the way. I think he learned it from Gregory; Mom's this close to banning it from conversations."

"I haven't heard Uncle Frank say it yet but it is quite the image," Charlotte said. "It's good of you to look out for your parents—"

"It's what family does," Emily said with a half shrug. The icy undertone in her voice meant the comment was likely a reference to Charlotte leaving Lands for DreamUs despite knowing Emily didn't have the same obsession Charlotte did for theme parks. Chad's text pounded in the back of her head, reminding her that she was at Lands to open the new area and would hopefully be back at DreamUs soon.

"Well, it's still a lot to carry. Remember to take care of yourself too, maybe take a day to chill," Charlotte said.

"We should all take that advice," Emily said.

She was right. Charlotte had brought up the idea of the

Dreamland research trip to Gregory again and she needed to find time for it on each of their calendars.

"So, what is it you wanted to talk about?" Charlotte asked, bracing for a repeat of Gregory's pitch from last night since he and Emily were the most likely of anyone to align on ideas to make the park money.

"I was talking to Gregory about—" Emily started.

Yep. "Let me guess, you think it would be a great idea to set up carnival rides in the meadow," Charlotte finished.

Emily furrowed her eyebrows and shook her head. "No, but I'd like to hear more about that when I'm done, if you'll let me continue."

"Yes, sorry," Charlotte said. She'd misread the situation; she told herself for the hundredth time to stop jumping to the worst possible conclusion.

"It's about Peak Fusion and *Heroic Patrol*."

Nope, Charlotte thought, this validated her tendency to jump to the worst conclusion. She put her coffee mug down and leaned into the counter. Clenching her stomach muscles as if bracing her body would make the conversation easier, she nodded at Emily to continue.

"Truth is, I've also felt like a failure, just like Dad. Like I haven't pushed hard enough for changes around here. I haven't pushed back enough. I know we've never wanted to include rides or anything from a movie or TV franchise in the park, but I also know it can mean a huge jump in attendance and money and help make Lands of Legend more of a destination than it currently is."

Charlotte blinked at Emily. "Yes, this is all true." Her tone was intentionally harsh.

Emily arched an eyebrow. In a voice just as hard as Charlotte's, she said, "Well, Peak Fusion read about Ever Fund's investment and sent an intriguing pitch over for putting *Heroic*

Patrol into the park. Ian, who you know went to business school like me—"

"Yes, I know that, Emily. We all know that. Anyone who talks to you for longer than five minutes knows that."

Emily stood taller. "Well, Ian in particular was very interested in hearing more from Peak Fusion. We are going to take a meeting with them and see what happens, and I wanted to let you know ahead of time."

Heroic Patrol was one of many franchises, intellectual properties, Peak Fusion owned; it started as a cartoon about a group of various superpowered creatures and beings who worked together to protect humans from all manner of threats. Charlotte didn't know it super well, but she knew the heroic group had a vampire, a mermaid, a Sasquatch, and others she couldn't remember. The cartoon had blown up, and the toys had their own aisle at department stores and a live-action movie was in the works.

But from what she understood, nothing about *Heroic Patrol* made sense for the theming in Lands. And that was on top of what she'd read about Peak Fusion trying and failing to make deals with other amusement parks.

"I see," she answered. "When is this meeting happening?"

"Tomorrow," Emily said.

"And your dad and mom are on board?"

Emily stared into her coffee mug as though she'd discovered something interesting. "They are skeptical. But they're willing to take the meeting."

"Because you and Gregory convinced them?" Charlotte asked.

Her cousin lifted her chin and met Charlotte's narrowed eyes. "Because I did. Gregory knows how they—and you—feel about adding IP to Lands. But I am obligated to point out the advantages for the business in the long term."

"What about the disadvantages, Emily?"

"How it could break the precious 'theme'? First of all, kids excited to meet *Heroic Patrol* characters wouldn't care about a theme." Emily was exasperated. "And Charlotte, you know I respect what Mom and Dad have built here, but if they want it to last, Under the Waves might not be enough. Even with that opening, Ever Fund's projections are a slow upward line. If *anything* doesn't go as planned or goes wrong, we're toast—as in, Lands might not make it for five more years toast. If that."

Charlotte knew Emily had a reasonable point, especially about kids not caring about characters not fitting the park's theme, but her cousin's casual dismissal of what made Lands extraordinary made a muscle under Charlotte's left eye twitch. "It isn't *only* about theming, Emily. Some gnarly news has come up over recent months about Peak Fusion's business practices, particularly regarding *Heroic Patrol* toy manufacturing and the latest *Heroic Patrol* movie. Beyond me not seeing how their stories could even make sense in Lands, I don't think we should be associated with them, despite the financial possibilities. Other parks, amusement parks, have turned them down."

"I have read about some of that, but I don't know how picky we can afford to be," Emily responded.

Charlotte took a calming breath. If things were desperate enough, apparently desperate beyond what Charlotte was aware of. "Look, take the meeting. Ask them a lot of questions. I'll think on some other ideas for repeat revenue to compete with whatever they say they will bring to the table. Hell, I'd rather do something with Gregory's idea for putting carnival rides in Fairytale—OH! A faery carnival!"

"What now?" Emily asked.

"You've given me an idea. Shit. I need to talk to Gregory," Charlotte said.

"Care to fill me in?"

"Not until I've fleshed it out more." Charlotte refilled her coffee mug, the Peak Fusion bullshit from Emily making her hand shake. She grabbed a towel to mop up the splash she'd made. She might not plan on being at Lands long term, but she wanted to protect her aunt and uncle's park for the future. A future Charlotte couldn't envision Peak Fusion being part of, even as a last resort. "Let me know how the meeting with Peak Fusion goes."

She walked away from Emily and the sour expression on her cousin's face.

Chapter 17

Hours later, after Charlotte had rushed through emails and the must-dos on her list, she opened a fresh presentation and dove in so she could show Gregory the scope of her faery carnival *and* what it would mean for his beloved numbers. Something like the faery carnival could be a foil to Peak Fusion, but it was only the beginning of an idea. When she knocked on his door toward the end of the day, the adrenaline of creation was still fueling her steps. Despite the lack of proper sleep, she was on her fourth or fifth wind of the day.

"Hey," she said. "Do you have thirty minutes?"

Gregory set down one of his notebooks and made a show of glancing at his watch and looking around his empty office, devoid of personal touches; Charlotte thought he could use a plant and made a note to bring him one—her dad always had cuttings propagating, surely something was suitable for the windowsill.

"Not like anyone else is here, or like I have anywhere else to be," he said.

"Great! I have an idea I want to present to you, sparked by what you said last night."

Gregory steepled his fingers in front of him, a perplexed expression on his face. "Interesting."

"You look like a super-villain right now with your hands like that," Charlotte pointed out.

He split his hands apart and rubbed his fingertips into his temples. "Isn't that what I am? A super-villain who wants to add evil, generic carnival rides to your park?"

"Please," Charlotte said. "Don't be ridiculous." Never mind that she had indeed thought of Gregory that way when he arrived. "Are you sure this is a good time? You look like you could use a break."

Gregory lowered his head and kept massaging his temples, making his hair fall into a curtain around his face. "Nah, I'm used to long hours on projects; my mom has a knack for giving me the projects that tend toward all-consuming. She doesn't do that with my brother."

"Why's that?"

"Because I can outwork Ian every day of the week and produce actual results. He's more about networking than executing. Ian would also argue that I'm not fun, but he doesn't step up to lessen my workload." Charlotte picked up on a hint of resentment. If she were the sibling in a family business doing the brunt of the work and getting "rewarded" with more work, she'd feel the same. His situation with his family business wasn't unlike Emily's with Lands. She didn't necessarily want to be part of it, but she still strove for its success.

"I see." Yeah, he definitely needed a break, and to see some of the town where he'd been staying and would be staying for at least a couple more months. "I think we need a change of scenery. You hungry?"

He lifted his head and Charlotte couldn't take the spark of excitement in his eyes. The gray flecks positively glimmered in the office lights. "Starving."

She grinned. "Me too. Come on, grab your stuff. Hope you like pizza." She glanced at his pale green button-down shirt. "And that you aren't a messy eater."

"I'm not," he said, "but pizza sauce is a test for even the

neatest of us. Okay if I run home and change and meet you wherever we're going? I can give you time if you need it?"

Charlotte looked down at her usual hoodie-and-jeans combo.

"Nah, I'm good. I'll go and snag us a table. It's a place called The Dragon's Breath, right on Main Street. Can't miss it."

"I've driven by and would not have guessed it was a restaurant."

"Bar, café, board game place—all of the above. Let me know when you're on the way from your place. See you in a few."

Charlotte returned to her office and took a few extra minutes to pack up and then run to the bathroom to check her hair and makeup—not because she cared what she looked like to Gregory because this wasn't a date or anything, but because she wanted to give him a head start.

Wait. Had she asked him on a date just now? And this on top of their pending movie night. No. He was Gregory, a work colleague, an uptight venture capitalist who had terrible ideas and was as likely to go behind Charlotte's back to put a scrambler in the park as he was to support her. Wasn't he? It's not like being a VC was his life's goal. And she'd been watching him try. Charlotte had seen him head into Fairytale Land's dark ride, A Selkie's Tale, on his own recently, not even as part of his trying one new thing a day. She was seeing him discover a sense of wonder and play in real time.

Would a date be the worst thing?

No, Charlotte argued with herself. It could not be a date. Getting mixed up with work colleagues had proved to be a terrible idea in the past. She was hopefully leaving for Paris by summer anyway. Besides, she was only making sure he saw a part of the world that wasn't his office at work or his temporary home. She was being a friend. And, she thought, she needed to get out too, so it wasn't entirely selfless.

Sure, she thought as she applied red-tinted lip balm to her naked lips and then smoothed her ponytail, *keep telling yourself that.*

Charlotte chose a high top near the front of the bar because a booth seemed to blur the line between professionals—work friends, even—meeting for dinner and a date. The lighting was brighter over the high-top tables, too. She made sure to pick a table with a prime view of the bar's titular breathing dragon.

When Gregory walked in, she almost fell off her stool and knocked her purse off its hook under the table in the process.

He wasn't wearing a suit. Or any part of a suit. Gregory was in denim and a short-sleeved, gray, slim-fit T-shirt with a slight V-neck. A V-neck! The sleeves showed a sliver of his mystery tattoo, but Charlotte was too focused on how the dark jeans rode his hips and how the notch in the top of the shirt showed a triangle of smooth skin in the middle of his collarbone.

He spotted her, waved, and walked toward the table. She picked up her purse to stop herself from staring. Gregory was handsome in a suit—hot, even. But Gregory in casual attire was downright dangerous. She'd never come this undone over a pair of jeans.

"That was fast," she said.

"I was extremely motivated by the idea of food that wasn't fresh from my microwave." He reached her and seemed unsure of how to greet her here, out in the world and away from Lands. He glanced at her, the other stool at the table, then her again before committing to the fastest hug in the history of ever. Fast but not so fast that Charlotte didn't register the pressure of his arms on her back, loose and awkward. His eucalyptus and foresty scent lingered between them as he stepped away and they both got situated on their stools.

She handed him two menus. "Here are the food and drink menus. You can't go wrong with anything."

She'd thought about choosing for them, but she didn't know enough about Gregory's food preferences and didn't want to cause an argument over olives or something.

"Any particular recommendations?" he asked.

She suggested a few pizzas and beers and ciders that paired well with them. "How do you feel about pickles?"

"In general, I like them," Gregory said. "On pizza, I'm not sold."

Charlotte tilted her head, considering. "They could be interesting on pizza, but I was planning to get an order of fried pickles for us to share if you're cool with that?"

"Absolutely."

Learning that Gregory liked fried food *and* owned a pair of jeans. What an illuminating evening this was turning out to be.

They placed their orders, Gregory choosing a pizza with a sesame seed crust and pesto base, Charlotte picking her usual margherita pizza. When their beers arrived, they raised their glasses.

"Here's to not being at work. I even put my phone on 'do not disturb,' " Charlotte said. "I'm proud of us."

"Good idea, I'm going to do the same," Gregory agreed, sliding his phone from his pocket and silencing notifications. He clinked the rim of his pint glass against hers.

Sometime around swallowing the first sip, Charlotte realized she had no idea what to talk with Gregory about if not work. It wasn't an uncommon problem for her regardless of the company. He was quiet too, intent on pulling condensation down his glass with a finger.

"So," they both started at the same time and laughed.

"You go ahead," Charlotte said, happy to turn over the conversation-starting pressure.

"That dragon above the bar is badass—almost looks like it could be part of Lands. I can't stop staring. Is it breathing?" Gregory said with an appropriate amount of awe.

"It is! The owner, Luke, did everything from sculpting it to building the animatronic elements," Charlotte gushed. She didn't love The Dragon's Breath only for its superior pizza; she was proud of her friend. "He's super creative. He's done a lot of animatronics work for my uncle at the park; he touched basically every creature on the Wintertide Trail. In fact, we should reach out to him about the mermaid palace. I bet he'd have some brilliant ideas for sea creatures for the interior."

Gregory sipped his beer and sat back in his stool, his face unreadable. "Sounds like you have a great relationship with him, so *you* should probably reach out."

Whoa, Charlotte thought. That comment seemed loaded. Was Gregory jealous of Luke?

Charlotte waved her hand. "Nah, I mean, we went to high school together; we're just old friends." Gregory visibly relaxed at the explanation. He *had* been jealous. Charlotte filed that thought for examination later.

"Anyway," she continued, "I like to see him get creative work. He loves running this place and all the community that comes with it, but sometimes I think he misses working in his shop and making things like the dragon."

"We should reach out next week, then," Gregory said. "Once we get past all our permit troubles."

Their fried pickles with a side of spicy ranch arrived. Charlotte pointed at the container. "You okay if we share that as long as we promise to not double dip?"

"As if I would do such a thing," Gregory said. He retrieved a pickle for himself and took a bite, a drop of pickle juice escaping down his chin. He flicked out his tongue to try to catch it. Charlotte followed every movement of his tongue with her eyes and Gregory noticed. Pink spread across the top of his cheekbones. "Good thing I changed," he joked as he wiped his chin with a napkin.

"Yeah, good thing," Charlotte agreed while she tried not to have further thoughts about his tongue. If Gregory in a short-sleeved shirt and jeans got her this worked up, she hoped to hell he never wore shorts in her presence. "I'm happy to know you own clothing that's not formal."

"It's not like I wear slacks to bed, Charlotte." Gregory's neck changed colors in front of Charlotte's eyes. "I mean, I wear clothes to bed but—"

"I'm glad to hear your PJs aren't a tie and nothing else." She couldn't not pick on him as even that *V* of skin turned pink. It was only fair since she was now thinking about Gregory and his bed; her own skin was probably changing colors.

"Seriously, though. You've been at Lands what, just about a couple of months now?"

"Something like that."

"You've seen how chill it is."

"Except for Emily."

Charlotte remembered Emily's cashmere sweater from earlier. "Yes, except for Emily."

Gregory grabbed another fried pickle, napkin in his other hand this time. "You're obsessed with my attire, aren't you? Is it because it makes me look like more of . . . how did you put it? A person who doesn't understand fun." His mocking smile showed Charlotte he was joking, so she did the most mature thing possible and lightly kicked him in the shin.

"Hey!" he protested.

"You deserved that!"

"Maybe." One half of his lips retained a smile and made him appear roguish, a face Charlotte hadn't seen on him before. She was a fan. "Anyway," he continued, "I am a bit boring. I'll give you that. And the suit thing started when I switched career paths to work with my family. It's like putting on a uniform. When I wear the suit, I'm Gregory, hard worker contributing to Ever Fund and pleasing my family."

"And when you don't wear the suit?"

"I'm me." He bit his lip. "Not like I'm leading a double life or anything, but it's a different life than I envisioned. When I switched gears and joined Ever Fund, my mom had me shadow Ian, and he didn't think I could swing it, that I could make such a hard left in plans and learn the job, much less do it well. I didn't feel equal to him if I showed up in 'chill' clothes. Changing my look was a way to convince him, my mom, *and* myself I could do it."

"Fake it until you make it?"

"Yeah. More or less."

A server brought their pizzas and in order to fit their feast on the small table, Gregory and Charlotte moved their glasses at the same time and the backs of their fingers brushed against each other. A spiky current pulsed through Charlotte's body from the touch, made all the more striking by Gregory sharing more about himself with her. They were still talking about work, basically, but this felt personal.

Unbidden, her hand drifted to his shoulder, and she lightly tugged one of his long locks, silky and light. "You kept this, though. Doesn't scream VC to me."

He took a bite of his pizza and made a small happy sound. "You have to try this; it's delicious. Let's swap a slice?"

"Definitely." Charlotte wouldn't tell him she'd sampled every pizza on the menu.

"And the hair. Ian said the same thing." Gregory smirked. "So I kinda kept it long to spite him, but also, I like my hair this way and I don't want to make that part of me fit a box, too." He pushed that constant wayward lock behind his ear.

"So you changed career paths for Ever Fund," Charlotte said. "What did you want to do before?"

Gregory took a long drink and looked down at the table. "Don't laugh."

"I won't laugh." Charlotte wouldn't. Gregory's tone was serious so no matter what he said, she wouldn't judge.

He glanced up, the lighting making his emerald eyes dark. "I was going to be a park ranger."

Charlotte didn't know what she expected Gregory to say, but it wasn't that. It did, however, explain the mountain-man persona she saw on Gregory's Instagram. She turned the thought over in her mind, making sure her answer reflected what she thought—that it was cool as hell and that she liked how they were both park people, just different kinds of parks—but she started imagining Gregory in a uniform and how the patches would sit over his shoulders and the pants would—

"Charlotte?"

"Sorry. Uh," she stammered. Gregory didn't need to hear about her new favorite daydream. "I was just picturing you outdoors, like, on a hike or whatever. Why did you change course?"

He busied himself with carrying out the pizza slice swap, eyes downcast, a storm rolling in around him.

"Hey, it's okay, Gregory. We don't have to talk about it."

He gave her a grateful smile. "No, it's okay. My grandpa spent a lot of time with me when I was a kid. Ian too. While Mom and Dad were busy with Grandma at Ever Fund, Grandpa took Ian and me fishing, hiking, and camping all over the mountains and deserts in SoCal."

The love for his grandpa wove behind Gregory's words, loud and bright.

"I spent as much time with him as I could. Once Ian got to middle school and high school and got hung up on popularity contests and then Ever Fund—I still don't know how he was such a nerd *and* had the personality of a prom king—it was just me and Grandpa. He was the only one to really support me when I took a break after high school to hike the Pacific Crest Trail. My mom and Ian both lectured me. Ian's only four years older than me, it's not like he knew everything. Anyway, my grandpa gave me this huge gift in nurturing this appreciation for the outdoors, so when I finally committed to college, it was to put myself in a position to be a park ranger.

"But then, he got sick. Cancer. Things progressed fast. So fast." Gregory paused and Charlotte reached across the table and put her hand on top of his. When he didn't withdraw, she left it there. He continued, "After he was gone, I couldn't go on a hike without being devastated, even if it wasn't a trail we'd ever done together. I'm not saying it was right, but I was in pain, and I boxed up that part of myself. Got rid of my plants, quit school, and turned to the family business. That was years ago. And here I am. I've been away from that part of myself for so long and I do like helping businesses like Lands and working with my mom, so I've stayed." He shrugged and let his posture sag, as if telling Charlotte about his grandpa had taken it out of him. He gazed at the table, looking despondent.

Charlotte lifted her hand from Gregory's, wishing it was appropriate to give him a real hug. "What was your grandpa's name?"

"Patrick."

"It sounds like Patrick was incredible. Thank you for sharing that with me." Charlotte was touched to experience the softer side of Grumpy Gregory. "No pressure, but we have some gorgeous trails around here to hike."

"Can you call it hiking when the land is flat for miles?" Gregory picked up the slice of margherita he'd taken from Charlotte, seemingly forcing himself to bounce back from the sadness of his memories.

Charlotte butted her knee into his. "Don't hate on our lack

of elevation." She took a bite of the pesto pizza he'd shared with her. "This *is* good. And hey, you know I can relate to turning to the family business when my life was in fragments—not at all the same, obviously."

"Right," Gregory said. "But you love Lands and what you do here."

"I do."

"Whereas I'm doing this job because of my family and not knowing what else to do, and being too cowardly to figure it out. Not that it's a competition over why we're both workaholics."

"Sounds like we could both work on doing less work."

"That's going to be a process," he said, "especially with everything we have going on right now."

"It is indeed a process. Melanie's been a big help this last year in helping me see that work is not life, but I'm still figuring it out. All we can do is try."

"We can."

"I'll get us another round so we can cheers to it," Charlotte said. "Ooh, and you know what else, we can pick a date for that Dreamland research trip too, which I know is work-related but it's also fun."

"I approve," Gregory said. "Actually, wait."

Charlotte froze halfway off the stool and lifted his empty glass toward him. "You want something different this time?"

Gregory sat up straighter and ran his hand through his hair. It made his bicep flex and Charlotte tried to keep her attention on his face. He was looking at the table instead of her. "I was wondering if you'd like to leave and do that movie night instead."

She sat back on her stool. Unable to keep extreme excitement out of her voice she answered, "Gregory. Are you telling me you'd like to go watch *Willow* right now?"

He met her eyes. "As long as you'd be into it."

"Yes. Always. Mind going to your place? Having friends

over to my basement apartment in my parents' home is too weird."

A satisfied smile spread across his face.

"What?" Charlotte asked. She didn't need to defend her current living situation but she couldn't stop herself. "It's only temporary, don't judge me."

Gregory stepped off his stool and Charlotte followed suit as they walked toward the bar to close out. "It's not that," he said.

She crossed her arms. "Then what?"

He turned toward her, that smile still in place, forming those striking crinkles around his mouth. "You called us friends."

Oh, Charlotte thought, she had said that. She was surprised by the casual way she'd mentioned it. "Well, yeah, we are friends, right? Maybe we've only been work friends, but now we're hang out and eat pizza and watch eighties fantasy movies kind of friends."

Gregory's smile turned into a full grin, so bright it made Charlotte step backward and right into a bar stool. She wasn't sure anything was as beautiful as Gregory being unabashedly happy. He reached an arm behind her to steady the stool's wobbles and then splayed his hand on the small of her back to guide her.

"I think I'm going to like being 'hang out outside of work' friends, Charlotte."

They paid their separate checks and while Charlotte was confirming his streaming situation to make sure she wouldn't have to run home for her *Willow* Blu-ray, she realized she'd forgotten to bring up the faery carnival presentation. *How about that?* she thought. She'd had such a pleasant time getting to know Gregory better that she hadn't thought about the very reason she went to his office.

Chapter 18

"And that's the general idea. We could run the carnival for a limited weekend to make it more exclusive or stretch it across a few weekends. That would depend on performer and vendor availability." Charlotte clicked back to the presentation title screen and looked around the room at Marianne, Frank, Emily, and Gregory.

It had been three weeks since she'd crafted the presentation and then been so distracted by Gregory wearing a V-neck T-shirt, sitting near to Gregory on his couch while he was wearing that V-neck T-shirt, *and* watching *Willow* enthrall him, that she hadn't given it. And that wasn't the only thing. Life had been a lot. She'd polished her DreamUs application, sent it in before the deadline, and had nudged Chad about it a few times with only a reminder from him that they'd be making a decision at the beginning of March. That was almost here, and she was starting to refresh her emails more than was strictly necessary. It didn't matter that she'd set the Under the Waves opening deadline for herself; guilt over the application had made a home in one small corner of her brain. Charlotte's gut swung like a pendulum between being eager about the promise of going back to DreamUs and sadness about leaving Lands, her family, and even Gregory.

On top of that, there was the looming Peak Fusion meeting. It had been moved a few times because of everyone at Lands being so slammed with Under the Waves business. It was a never-ending swirl of permits, codes, and construction materials problem-solving. At least seeing tangible results was so rewarding it helped keep them all going and gave them energy for the task list that had no end in sight.

Charlotte gained a whole other level of respect for her family because they did it all. They had to. No giant corporation with a dozen specialized departments was by their side to sort out, for example, environmental safety. Frank and Marianne were walking vaults of institutional knowledge, and they had a mile-long list of contractors and friends who wanted to help. The couple conjured a miracle almost daily, and Gregory deftly handled the logistics to make sure it all got done.

A highlight in the whirlwind was Gregory. Since their dinner date (whatever they'd called it) he'd appeared an ounce more carefree. Charlotte barely noticed him wearing a blazer anymore. And they had held firm on two aspects of their schedule: their daily construction site and park walks—they met by the carousel every morning at nine—where they talked about work; and a weekly trip to Dragon's Breath for dinner where they agreed to not discuss Lands or look at their phone notifications. They'd even spent one Saturday afternoon there playing a board game (Charlotte had been delighted to discover Gregory's fierce competitive streak as one game turned into the best two of three), and another weekend afternoon walking through the woods (Gregory refused to call it hiking). Their plan was to work up to an entire day off.

And while she noticed moments when Gregory's gaze lingered or he needed to lean close to her for no discernible reason, she still wasn't sure if the attraction was mutual. She was, however, certain that they had solidified the "friends" label for their relationship.

"What do you think?" Charlotte asked.

"I had no clue what you meant when you mentioned 'faery carnival' a few weeks ago," Emily said, "but this is beyond what I could have imagined. My only suggestion is maybe we call it a festival since carnival can seem sinister to some people."

"And some people are you because of that haunted carnival we went to as kids?" Charlotte asked. She remembered her cousin hiding the stuffed animal Charlotte won in the closet because Emily insisted it was blinking at her.

Gregory looked up from his notepad. "A haunted carnival?"

"Oh, don't be silly, it wasn't haunted," Marianne said. "It was only a bit run-down."

"I noticed we never went back," Emily remarked.

"Only because the city didn't approve their permit again," Frank said.

"My point stands," Emily noted. "But it's the only one I have. Otherwise, I can see this bringing people in, and we can figure out how to leverage the festival to start Under the Waves promotions."

Charlotte hoped it would be enough to stave off any moves from Peak Fusion for *Heroic Patrol*, while not truly believing it would be.

"I agree," Frank said, standing and stretching his arms. "As long as we don't think it's too much to add on in addition to Under the Waves. We're all on our last leg and we still have a lot more course to run."

"That's what I was going to say, Frank," Gregory added. "It's a masterful idea and an excellent use of that field before we turn it into overflow parking." He beamed at Charlotte and she sat up straighter. "However, I'm hesitant to put more on anyone's plate or take away any of the attention the new land needs."

Charlotte rolled her chair away from the table and rubbed

her chin. She knew getting the festival (not carnival) into place would be a comparatively light lift against opening a whole new themed land, but no one had time to spare except maybe some of the hourly seasonal employees they could bring back early. Maybe they'd like the chance to add something to the park's story while getting paid, and she was sure she could work out a fair bonus. She shared her idea with the others.

"I love that," Marianne said. "I always hate that we can't keep everyone on year-round."

"That's settled then, yes?" Everyone nodded at Charlotte. "Okay, I'll pull some more details together. And then we still need to come up with a reason for why the faeries are celebrating and why they would do it for more than one weekend."

"Isn't because we want to have a special event enough of a reason?" Gregory asked.

Marianne looked at Gregory with pity in her eyes. "Oh, sweetheart." In this instance, the kind endearment could be interpreted as, "You've stepped in it now, buddy."

Uncle Frank saved Charlotte from answering, sparing Gregory from what would have been a much longer answer. "We're not the faeries, son. It's their story and that story is part of Fairytale Land. Coming up with a faery holiday that they are beginning to celebrate again will make it more memorable and interesting than hanging up a banner that says, 'Faery Festival This Way' and calling it a day. We want it to fit in with the theming."

Gregory wrote something down in his notepad. "That makes sense. Thank you for explaining."

"Any time, Gregory. I have a whole book of faery lore I've built over the years and you're welcome to borrow it," Frank said. He'd made a lap around the table and patted Gregory on the back.

"I'd love to borrow it, Frank." Charlotte hid her smile at the back-and-forth by closing her laptop and disconnecting it from the meeting room's screen. If only she could hide that smile from her heart.

"We're all good here, then, right?" Emily asked. "I have a call."

"We're great," Charlotte said. "Thank you all. I'll email you an update on the project by the end of the week."

The room emptied, but Gregory lingered and walked out with Charlotte. He nudged her with his shoulder. "Genius upgrade for my terrible idea," Gregory said. "You didn't have to give me any credit given the whole terrible part of it."

During the presentation, Charlotte had mentioned Gregory sparking the idea. "You're right, it was a terrible idea at first, but look what it's led to. I never would have come up with the festival otherwise, and I think it has potential to make a splash and to potentially expand in the future. It will be like attending a faeries-only version of a renaissance faire, and who wouldn't love that? Perhaps it could tie in with your idea for the local renfaire partnership?"

"Ooh, good call. Maybe we could talk more about it on our walk? We need to head over to the construction site again this afternoon. I'd like to share some thoughts."

"Yeah," Charlotte said. "I'd love that. As long as those thoughts aren't terrible." She nudged *him* with *her* shoulder. They were high schoolers, actually. Every brush with Gregory was like a gentle tug testing Charlotte's resolve to not repeat the Chad situation.

He smirked. "I'll see what I can do. Catch up with you in a few hours."

Chapter 19

They didn't make it far outside the Under the Waves construction site after they finished their walk-through. Gregory was helping Charlotte untangle the site-required hard hat's strap from her hair and she was picturing him grabbing her hair in a another, very inappropriate circumstance when her family approached, each of them wearing a different expression: Emily's was determined, Frank's was resigned, and Marianne appeared irritated. It was enough to kick out the delicious thoughts of Gregory's fingers in her hair.

"Charlotte, did you forget to put on sunscreen?" her uncle scolded. "You know better."

She'd slathered on fifty SPF, the same as every day, but she wasn't about to tell that to Uncle Frank and have him inquire further about why her face was so red. Imagining telling her uncle about the inappropriate thoughts she was having about Gregory increased the flames on her cheeks. Once she pulled the hat off her head, she fibbed, "I must have been too excited about the presentation this morning to remember to put it on. What are you all doing out here?"

"We need to talk," Emily said, crossing her arms, mouth in a flat line.

Charlotte shot a questioning glance at Gregory, but he

shook his head. He didn't know what was up either. "Did you all change your mind about the faery festival? You could have sent an email or a text."

Charlotte knew that was unlikely with the air of intensity hanging around all of them, but she could hope.

"It's not that, Charlotte. We just wrapped another call with Peak Fusion about *Heroic Patrol* and wanted to loop you both in," her uncle said, voice apologetic.

Charlotte's brain did one of its best things and went to the worst interpretation of what her uncle said: that they were in full-blown negotiations with Peak Fusion when she thought the meeting had been on hold. Emily *had* seemed more agreeable than usual lately—was this why? Because she was going behind Charlotte's back?! They'd butted heads, but Charlotte hadn't thought Emily would ever outright lie to her about something like this.

"*Another* call? I don't understand. Emily mentioned a meeting weeks ago but anytime I followed up about it, I was told it was moved given our busy schedules getting Waves open."

Marianne's eyes were soft but blazing. "I'm sorry. Emily led us to believe you knew we'd chatted with them. We only now realized that was not the case."

Competing questions hammered in Charlotte's head; she went for the lowest-hanging fruit first. She faced Emily, who stood tall, no trace of shame in her posture. "Emily, what's going on? Why tell me you were going to have the meeting and then lie to me about having it? And to your parents? Wait. Gregory, did you know about this, too?"

"He didn't," Emily answered for him. "He's been busy, so I've been going through Ian after the first conversation with Peak Fusion proved interesting."

"Excuse me?" Gregory straightened and adjusted his tie. His tone was measured, but Charlotte picked up on a dissonant trace that told her she was hearing Gregory being angry for the first time since she'd known him. "Busy. Yes, busy working here every day alongside all of you as the representative for Ever Fund. And you bypassed me."

"Yes, I bypassed you. I knew Ian would give me an answer more quickly and I knew he would get it. As the park's manager, it was within my rights. Especially with Mom and Dad on board. I won't apologize for it when these meetings could change so much for Lands."

"Honey, we wouldn't have been on board if we knew you'd been keeping information from your cousin and Gregory," Frank said with a strain in his voice. "I'm sorry, you two."

Charlotte saw the line of Gregory's sharp jaw tighten, his Adam's apple bobbing. Emily cut them both out and she wondered if it was also because Emily didn't think Gregory would keep a secret from her. Her veins boiled. "This is wrong, Emily, and you know it. You are the park manager, yes, but Gregory and I aren't your subordinates. This is key to park operations and no, talking to Ian isn't a substitute." Emily looked like she wanted to speak, but Charlotte cut her cousin off with a lifted hand. "I know you didn't come track us down to tell us about covering this up. What's going on?"

Emily squared her shoulders. "I don't know why you care so much, Charlotte. We all know you have one foot out the door. And no, it's not all. They've made an interesting proposal. It would be an addition to Under the Waves, another phase after opening, with a ride and small area themed after *Heroic Patrol*. They'd have their branding there and at the park entrance and offer character meet and greets. One of the Patrol members, Scylla, is a mermaid with superpowers so they think it could all focus on that—her, her history, and her aquatic home."

Frank added, "When we first talked, I didn't agree with it. I still don't. However, if it means building an even more secure future for the park, I could see extending the overall look and design motifs for Under the Waves into Scylla's Lair, or whatever we'd call it, but it would have a separate arched entry and signage."

"If that's the case, why not build a whole park of their own?" Charlotte was confused. "What's the point of coming to Lands with their offer if they don't want to be like the rest of the park?"

"Because we already have infrastructure with the existing park and we have construction crews with theme park experience on hand who we can roll right onto another project. It saves them from buying land and starting from scratch," Emily explained, tapping her boot.

"What exactly are they offering us for this and what are they hoping to get from it?" Gregory asked.

Frank sighed and pulled on the sleeves of his flannel. "It sounds too good to be true, and the money is the only reason I'm considering it. Based on what Ian said, the revenue projections associated with *Heroic Patrol* brand studies are appealing to Ever Fund. But that doesn't mean I like any of it." He paused to grab Charlotte's hand. "And I know you hate it, but I'm trying to think past Under the Waves and to what this park will be years from now. To keep this place going for years from now."

Charlotte squeezed her uncle's hand. "I get that you have to make hard choices, Uncle Frank. Being here in the trenches with you all these last couple of months has shown me exactly how much you've all put in to make Lands of Legend so incredible for so long. You've had to decide when and where to make compromises—even the compromise of agreeing to take money from Ever Fund."

"More compromises than you can know, kid," her uncle said.

"And Lands is still here because of that. Because of both of you." She grabbed her aunt's hand, too. "But please think about this one. Peak Fusion has an awful reputation—one I don't want to tarnish everything you've built here. Their cutesy stories seem like a facade for some real shit, and *that* is not worth it."

She spared a glare for Emily, who shouldn't have let things get so far.

Likely sensing the tension, Gregory spoke up, "Going forward, I have to be part of these kinds of conversations from the beginning. Ian can be present if you want, but again, he's not here. I—we, Charlotte and I—will take a look at Peak Fusion's proposal and then we can *all* discuss it and next steps."

Oh, how Charlotte couldn't resist take-charge Gregory. She could feel another kind of emotion roiling in her underneath the irritation with her cousin.

"Fine," Emily spat. "But we shouldn't take too long; they might pull the offer."

"Since they can't seem to get any amusement or theme park to take their IP, I don't think we have to worry about that," Charlotte scoffed.

"Let's set something up as soon as we can," Gregory interjected. "I'll check all of your calendars and reach out. Now, if you'll excuse us, Charlotte and I have to check out something in Adventurer's Gate. After you, Charlotte." He put a hand on the small of her back as they walked away.

When they were out of hearing distance of her family and Charlotte had brought her frustration down to a simmer from a raging boil, she made a request. "Let's not talk about work on the rest of our walk today, okay? Except to say that Emily was wrong to go to Ian. You would make time to hear any idea that could help Lands."

"I would. Thanks for saying that. Emily was also wrong to keep such a big potential change from all of us," Gregory answered. "I feel like she knew Ian would be an easy yes because of the dollar signs involved."

"Yeah, that sounds right. Glad we, at least, have each other's backs."

"Me too."

Charlotte jerked her head toward the office. "You know, let's grab our things and go get an early dinner."

"I support this plan."

Having Gregory's support, Charlotte thought, was becoming more and more important to her.

Chapter 20

Frustrations stacked up as the days passed. The meeting about Peak Fusion was tense, with Emily's decision to include Ian via video making it worse. Gregory could be surly and hard to read, but Ian acted like the heartless Scrooge Charlotte had first imagined Gregory would be. Even through a computer screen Charlotte could see how much Ian's and Gregory's features looked alike, but Ian's eyes were a lighter green, his hair pale brown, short, and carefully spiked. He wore a suit so fancy Charlotte couldn't tell the brand, and she could see how Gregory's appearance was a shadow of Ian's. Except for Gregory's long hair. Ian was brusque and haughty and, like Gregory had mentioned, motivated by dollar signs. Charlotte could see why Emily went to him about Peak Fusion and why they got along so well. But Emily and Ian didn't walk away from the meeting with a yes or a no from everyone else.

Peak Fusion waived licensing fees for five years following the opening of the land and agreed to pay for ninety percent of the construction fees associated with their area of Lands of Legend. However, their proposal stretched beyond a small corner off Under the Waves as Emily had mentioned. They wanted a few acres to build a whole Heroic Patrol Land and make it a hub for the franchise, stretching the lone, nebulous connection of the mermaid character to the Lands of Legend theming. The projections were robust, and to Charlotte's eyes, only somewhat inflated. This would be the first presence for *Heroic Patrol* in a park, and people would come to see it. Charlotte had no doubt about that. Peak Fusion's argument was that the bigger the land, the more irresistible it would be to fans.

Moving ahead with Peak Fusion would, Charlotte was loath to admit, mean a more secure future for Lands of Legend, a level above the boost from Ever Fund to get Under the Waves open. She could see that fact was tearing Frank and Marianne in two, even after Charlotte put together a small report that collected information about settled lawsuits for factory mishaps, articles about harassment on the *Heroic Patrol* sets, and reports about sexism in the story and art departments on recent tie-in video games. It painted an ugly, questionable picture, but Ian emphasized that it was all *alleged*.

Peak Fusion wanted an answer soon, and since they couldn't come to an agreement this time, they decided to reconvene. And in the meantime, there was the usual list: Negotiating with every vendor about errors and shortages. Figuring out the merchandise delays. It was too much. And this latest email, one more goddamn permit quibble from the city, this one over a water quality report. The most mundane necessities went into making a theme park function, and those mundane items could impact their set opening date. And Under the Waves had to open on time; Ever Fund required it as part of their deal. Under the Waves opening as planned wouldn't stop Peak Fusion, that would all be an added bonus according to Emily, but getting the new land finished would mean satisfying Ever Fund *and* making money.

Plus Charlotte needed Under the Waves to open so she could

move on. The beginning of March was here, and she expected to hear back about her application for Dreamland Paris any day now.

Charlotte stood up, slammed her laptop shut, then closed her eyes and inhaled a breath the size of the ocean and forced it out with a prolonged whoosh. She knew every business in the history of always faced setbacks and that the businesses that lasted overcame them, but it was hard to see the other side when the setbacks piled into an avalanche.

Gregory walked around the conference room table where they'd been working together and put his hand on Charlotte's arm. That small reassurance comforted her more than she imagined it would, which led to her imagining sinking against his tall frame for a hug. But that would cross a professional line and Charlotte wasn't sure if their affectionate friendship was on an "offering long hugs in times of crisis" level yet.

"I know this is a lot, Charlotte, but it's going to work out. Everything will come together; we'll make sure of it," Gregory said in a voice that walked the line between gentle and firm. "I'll call in some help from Ever Fund and between that and Emily, we'll cross every 't' the city and the contractors give us. It only takes time."

He was right. Separate, they were competent businesspeople who got things done; it's how Lands of Legend had come so far with Under the Waves and other plans to boost attendance in such a short amount of time. Together? They were damn near an unstoppable force, her theme park knowledge and his finance and business expertise overwhelming each of the many obstacles in their path. Even when they argued or Charlotte overexplained some nuance of theme park operations, they presented a united front to others.

But Charlotte was tired. And cranky. And one hundred percent overworked. They both were.

An idea struck her. "We need a break, Gregory. It's time for that full day off—kind of—and I have just the place."

"Do *not* say Sir Cinna-Swirls," he deadpanned.

"No, I have somewhere else in mind. It's time for that research trip I've been threatening. You up for an adventure?"

"Why do I feel like this will *not* be a relaxing break?"

Charlotte imagined a mischievous glint to her eyes as she grinned and rubbed her hands together. This would either be incredible or backfire in spectacular fashion. "Sure it will. A relaxing break during which you will take over twenty thousand steps in a day. Let me see what I can arrange."

Charlotte sent an email to Aparna, her former boss Jeni's executive assistant. Aparna had always been kind to Charlotte—they'd vented to each other about Jeni a *lot* over the years—and Charlotte knew Aparna would help her pull off a last-minute Dreamland trip. An escape.

Chapter 21

Gregory yawned as Charlotte pressed a coffee into his hand after they arrived at the Orlando airport. The shadows under his eyes had dulled somewhat on the flight. Even with tired eyes and rumpled hair, he was impossibly handsome in jeans, sneakers, and another V-neck tee, this time in a plum color. Charlotte had cautioned him to dress comfortably.

"I can't believe we got up at that ungodly hour and are going right from the airport to a theme park for a day," he groaned.

"Technically we're going right to the hotel to drop off our luggage."

Gregory responded with an eye roll.

Charlotte nudged him with her elbow. "I thought you were a morning person."

"There's a huge difference between seven in the morning and four in the morning."

"Yeah, fair. But you were the one who pointed out how we have limited time and how we shouldn't be away from Lands too long. We have to maximize our trip!"

He leveled a stare at her. Charlotte decided it was best to forgo further conversation. They'd landed in Orlando and stopped for necessary caffeine before summoning a rideshare to the Dreamland Resort area; Charlotte didn't think Gregory was ready for the chaos of the DreamUs-operated transportation system that ferried passengers between the airport and hotels.

The driver was quiet, thankfully, so the drive passed in peace with minimal traffic and Charlotte texted Melanie to let her know they'd arrived in town. Charlotte and Gregory were staying at Charlotte's favorite DreamUs hotel, Retro-Dream, with an airy mid-century modern design connected to the resort's monorail system. Aparna had done Charlotte the hugest of favors by somehow getting them into Retro-Dream. It didn't matter that it was early March and well before spring break; Dreamland was always busy. In addition to the hotel having a stunning design, they could go up to the second level right to the monorail platform and ride for two stops to Dreamland's main entrance.

When they arrived, Charlotte ushered Gregory in and situated him on a low couch in one of the lobby's sunken areas, the terrazzo flooring sparkling in the morning light shining through the massive windows. He didn't say anything, but Charlotte could tell from his appraising glance that he was impressed.

"Not what you expected?" she asked.

"Not at all," he said. "I thought there would be . . . I don't know, cartoon characters everywhere?"

"One of their resorts *does* have cartoon characters everywhere, but give me a little credit—"

"About this much?" Gregory held up his thumb and index finger, almost touching.

"You know what?" Charlotte said. "I appreciate a solid callback. *Anyway*, I know cartoon characters aren't your thing. And besides, this is my preferred DreamUs hotel. It's gorgeous. Remind me to show you the indoor waterfall and river in the lounge downstairs.

"For now, though," she continued, "have a seat. I'll get

things sorted and then we can drop our bags off with the bellman."

She approached the front desk, a dreamy wood-and-quartz design formed with elegant, curved lines, and gave her last name. The front desk clerk's face lit up when she saw Charlotte's reservation.

"Ah yes, Ms. Gates. I have your special booking right here, but your suite isn't ready yet."

"No, I didn't think it would be since it's so—wait, did you say suite?" Charlotte asked. Aparna hadn't said anything about scoring her a suite. As in a single room.

She smiled. "Is it just the suite under my name? Only one room?"

"Yes! It's one of our nicest rooms," the clerk—Erika, according to her name tag—enthused.

Charlotte knew it was. She remembered drooling over pictures of RetroDream's suites years ago—suites with a single king-sized bed.

"It *is* a beautiful room," Charlotte agreed, "but I think there's been a mistake. I believe I was supposed to have two rooms. Is it possible to downgrade and get a second room?"

Erika looked perplexed by Charlotte's request but said she'd take a look, just in case. After a few minutes of Erika tapping the keyboard and then stepping away to talk to another clerk, Charlotte didn't feel hopeful.

"I'm sorry, Ms. Gates, we don't have another room available. We're booked solid. The reservation had a note to 'give Charlotte,' that's you, 'the most special room possible.' The note also has a winking face emoji. I could look at another hotel."

The gears in Charlotte's head turned and she realized she hadn't communicated clearly enough to Aparna. In the rush to get the trip together on short notice, she hadn't specified two reservations. No, she'd mentioned wanting to show a special friend a good time so he could see the magic of theme parks. So, yeah, it was easy to see how Aparna had connected dots and thought it was a romantic situation.

Welp.

"I appreciate you checking, Erika. And I'm grateful for the gorgeous room. I'm just, uh, wondering, is the couch in the suite a pullout?"

Erika looked relieved. "It is! All the bedding is in the living room closet and it's supposed to be very comfortable."

"Then we'll stick with the suite," Charlotte said.

"You won't regret it," Erika assured her.

Charlotte wasn't so sure, but the suite had a separate bedroom with a door and they were adults. They could figure it out. Plus they were doing a full day at Dreamland; they'd be wiped by the time they dragged their bodies back to the hotel.

She finished pre–checking in—RetroDream would send her a text when the room was ready—and returned to Gregory, figuring she'd wait to break the news about one room but not one bed until after he ate breakfast.

Chapter 22

They got to the gates of Dreamland around ten thirty a.m., which Charlotte considered a triumph considering how they'd already led entire lives since they left for the airport before four that morning. She was a pro at exiting the airport and stepping directly into a theme park, but it was Gregory's first time.

"This is it, we did it!" she exclaimed as they approached the entrance. "Do you have your ticket pulled up in the app?"

Gregory nodded, his gaze focused dead ahead with intensity.

"Hey," Charlotte said, slowing down her purposeful walk, "do you need a minute? We can go sit down over there and rest before we head in."

"Thank you, but no, I'm okay, it's a little overwhelming is all. I figured I could ground myself by focusing on one spot in the distance."

"Like people do so they won't get motion sickness?"

"Yes, exactly that."

"So Dreamland is making your body feel ill or?"

Gregory groaned. "No, that's not—"

"I'm kidding, Gregory."

"Oh."

"I know it can be a lot. Even I feel that way sometimes."

"You do?"

"Definitely. You should see the park in the week between Christmas and New Year's. It's too much even for theme park pros. Wall-to-wall people, super-long wait times for rides and food, basically a zoo."

"Why do people come at that time, then?" Gregory asked.

They'd made it near the beginning of the line to get in at this point. "Because it's magical and decorated and they make memories," Charlotte answered. "Now, scan your ticket here and put your index finger here—don't forget which finger you used, otherwise it's a pain later."

Both of them successfully entered and then Gregory pulled out his notebook and wrote something down.

"A note already?" she asked.

"I wrote down which finger I used," Gregory said, in a voice so serious that Charlotte cracked up and couldn't get a hold of herself.

"What?" Gregory asked. "You said it was important!"

Charlotte wiped a tear from her eye. "Nothing," she said between giggles. "We've been awake since an ungodly hour so everything's hilarious, including you not trusting yourself to remember which finger you used. Now, I have an idea of what to do first, if you can trust me?"

Gregory turned his body to face her fully and receiving the force of his full attention was like being hit by a wave—a wave with piercing green eyes. He said, "I trust you."

Charlotte gulped her heart back into place and tried not to look as flustered as she felt. And given that Gregory was trusting her, she moved Twisting Teacups with its spinning cups down the list until they had time to fully digest their breakfast. Besides, she was eager to take Gregory through Exploration Isle, the area of Dreamland themed to look like a wild jungle, complete with crumbling ruins.

Her list of must-dos rattled in her head:

- Make sure they went on at least one ride in each themed area
- For sure take Gregory on Sullivan Slade's Adventure and show him every detail in the queue
- Stop by the zoetrope
- Get the largest popcorn possible
- Snag seats for the evening parade

"This way, then. We'll walk up Main Street and head to the left," she said, starting in that direction. "This park is obviously much bigger than Lands but the layout isn't dissimilar. This type of design is called hub-and-spoke, with a central hub and pathways reaching out like—"

"Charlotte?" Gregory interrupted.

"Hmm?"

"As always—well, most of the time—I appreciate your passion, but we've discussed the hub-and-spoke design before," he said in a patient voice.

"We have?" She looked sideways at Gregory and caught his grin.

"Yeah, you put it in a presentation so I would remember it," he said. Then his eyes softened. "But you can tell me again if you want."

"Well, if I put it in a presentation, then I know it's locked into your brain, but I appreciate your offering to hear it again. It's such an obvious and clever design for moving people!" Charlotte said.

They'd emerged past the shops and restaurant on Main Street, the buildings leveraging forced perception to appear taller than they were, to the hub. Before they stepped toward Exploration Isle, Gregory took Charlotte by the elbow and pulled her off to the side of the path. She glanced down at his fingers wrapped around her arm, soft skin against hers, sending warmth through her entire body. He let his hand linger despite already catching her attention.

Charlotte raised her eyebrows at him. "Yes?"

"Before we get too far into your meticulously planned itin-erary—and don't try to pretend you don't have a list running through your head right now," he said with affection, "I want to hear everything you have in mind, but I did some re-search and reading on my own, and we need to make sure to visit Hidden Jungle today."

His words pierced through Charlotte's skin and struck an ooey-gooey core she wasn't aware she had. Hidden Jungle, a pocket-sized extension of Exploration Isle, wasn't an overly remarkable section of the park. It was a quiet place to get away from the crowds, get a bite, and soak in the ambiance of the nearby Jungle River Cruise ride. Hidden Jungle had no reason to be on Gregory's radar, except for the not-so-minor detail that it was one of her final projects before DreamUs ended her employment. She and her team poured an outsized effort into the area, pulling in obscure elements of DreamUs parks lore to make it compelling for die-hard fans and stretching every cent of the budget.

Gregory making it a must-do touched her.

"Hidden Jungle, huh?" she asked.

Gregory gave her a mischievous sideways glance. "Yeah, I read on Melanie's blog that the bao is not to be missed."

Charlotte arched an eyebrow.

"And," Gregory continued, "I know a certain Dream Me-chanic who worked on it and seemed, from interviews, to be pretty proud of that area."

"I see," Charlotte preened. "She sounds pretty cool."

Gregory stopped walking and faced her, his face solemn. "She is."

There went that ooey-gooey core again. He'd watched in-terviews of her gushing about Hidden Jungle. She lifted her hand to touch Gregory's, still on her elbow. "Thank you. Also, I'm proud of you."

"For what?"

"You avoided committing the most egregious theme park foul of them all: stopping in the middle of a walking area. I didn't even have to remind you." Charlotte pretended to wipe a tear from her eye.

Gregory chuckled. "I do pay attention, you know! I wrote that rule down ages ago."

His smile was so earnest, the light crinkles Charlotte so adored forming around his eyes and his mouth. She couldn't help it; she leaned in and hugged him. Only a quick one, an impulsive burst of affection. She pulled away before he could say anything, but he'd reacted to the hug instantaneously, wrapping his arms around Charlotte where they belonged.

Where they belonged, Charlotte mused. Maybe that thought was on the theatrical side, but maybe, just maybe, it was exactly right.

She looked up as she turned and held out her hand. "Shall we?"

Gregory put his hand in hers and let her guide him.

They didn't hold hands beyond Charlotte pulling Gregory in the right direction, but even that few seconds made warmth wash over her. *You are not a teenager,* Charlotte thought. *Control yourself!*

She brought them to the entry of one of her favorite rides, and pointed at the sign. "Let's start here. The line will only get longer."

"Sullivan Slade's Adventure, huh? Isn't that based on one of the biggest IPs in the world?" Gregory asked, a confused expression on his face.

"Yes, and I love those movies." Charlotte noticed him taking out his notebook again. "Gregory, you look like a reporter about to grill me."

He shrugged. "I *do* have questions."

"I don't know if I've had enough coffee for this."

"Buy you a cup after the ride?"

Charlotte considered the offer. "Okay. Fire away."

"So, I thought IPs were a big bad and you didn't like seeing them in theme parks. Loathed it, even. The heated discussions we've all had about *Heroic Patrol* would support this."

"Ugh. I cannot with *Heroic Patrol* today, Gregory. We are escaping! But, what you said is both true and not true," Charlotte answered as they reached the end of other people waiting in line. "Rides or even whole lands themed around a movie, book, game, whatever aren't inherently terrible. In the right place with thought and care, and if Peak Fusion weren't gross, a *Heroic Patrol* land could be cute. When the level of immersion is right and the designers and engineers are fans who nail every detail, it can be incredible. This ride is a fantastic example of an IP done right—it's in Exploration Isle and it makes me feel like I'm on an adventure with Sullivan Slade and that I'm with him in scenes of a new story—"

"Hey, no ride spoilers," Gregory interrupted.

"I would never," Charlotte said, hand to her chest. "May I continue?"

Gregory extended his hand in a "please go ahead" gesture.

"Thank you," Charlotte nodded her head at him, smirking. "Rides or lands that build upon the placemaking and themes of an IP can be glorious. On the other hand, sometimes it's shoehorned in or it feels like an easy way out. Say, for example, creatives have an idea for an exciting original ride unlike anything else in a theme park. They get excited, put together presentations, and throw in all kinds of innovation. But then executives who control the budget either say an outright no or ask them to make so many compromises the idea isn't special anymore. Maybe those executives will then say, 'Why don't you design a ride around 'insert popular character or movie here'?' Or they'll see what IP-based rides in other parks are doing well and clone them. That's when it feels like throwing a logo on a ride for no reason, disingenuous and like an obvious cash grab."

"Isn't it always a cash grab? These places are businesses," Gregory said.

"True, but there's a way to do it that makes it about the guest and what they'll feel and experience, and not just the IP for the sake of the IP. Know what I mean?"

"I think I do," he answered.

Charlotte continued, "And then with a place like Lands of Legend, it would feel exceptionally fake because it's a home-grown, handmade park. Even if we look at a family-friendly IP featuring the themes of the park—which totally exists—adding it would feel like we've done it for the sake of making money. *Heroic Patrol*, for example, seems more of the shoe-horned, cash-grab variety of IP. Does a superpowered mermaid really have the right vibe for Under the Waves and Lands?"

She didn't pause to check Gregory's reaction. "And yes, I know Lands needs to make money to stay stable and open for years to come, but bringing in more people with our own ideas, ones like Under the Waves and the Faery Festival, feels authentic. It upholds the world we want to create for our guests."

"As usual, that was enlightening," Gregory said, pen scratching on notebook paper. He glanced up at Charlotte, something she couldn't quite place in his eyes. Before she could ask him about it, he pulled his phone from his pocket, scowling as he cleared a notification.

"Everything okay?" Charlotte asked.

He put his notebook away and then leaned back against the queue's railing, themed to look like lashed leaves of tropical plants, and sighed. "Yeah, it's fine. It's Ian demanding an update on our response to Peak Fusion."

"You know I understand family obligations related to business, but I vote for muting his texts until we get back."

"That might make him reach out to Emily instead."

Charlotte made a face. "Then answer if you must."

Gregory tapped at his phone. "I let him know I'm in the

middle of important research that will help me provide an informed response."

"Proud of you. And I have another suggestion. Pass me your notebook?" Gregory narrowed his eyes but obliged, and Charlotte unzipped her backpack and tucked it inside. "It will be here safe and sound for you tomorrow, but for today, no more notes."

"How will I remember everything?"

"Because you're living it." And, Charlotte thought, she'd remember everything because she was there with Gregory for the first time.

"I think it's kind of become my emotional support notebook, though?"

"As someone who makes emotional support lists, I understand and I promise to give it back if the situation seems desperate."

They shuffled ahead and when the line paused again, they each leaned on the queue railing. They faced each other, Charlotte's feet staggered with his, toes almost touching. He nudged her shoe with his. "Thanks for putting this together. I would never have pictured myself here and now I'm excited."

Charlotte glowed at the comment and at the earnestness on Gregory's face. The ends of his hair curled in different directions in the light humidity and his eyes were shining. "Gregory Binns, ready to play in a theme park—who would have thought?"

"Well, I've had an excellent teacher who helped me understand how cool theme parks are. Plus we're outside and do you see the foliage in this queue?" Gregory pointed at a leafy green plant and called out its scientific name like it was a friend. Charlotte adored it when he let go enough to be a big nerd.

She crossed over to lean on the rail beside Gregory. "Can I ask you something?"

He nodded. "You can. And it doesn't seem like the line is moving, so we have time."

"Do you think you'd ever go back to school and try to be a park ranger?"

"Oh. Just some casual existential theme park chatter, then."

She poked his foot with hers. "You said I could ask."

"I did. And I don't know. I can't say that going back to college as a thirty-two-year-old sounds appealing. But seeing you and your uncle embracing your passion does make me realize I need to stop going with the flow so much, because the flow is going to sweep me away and I'm going to look up and another eight years will have passed with Ever Fund. I don't want that."

Charlotte leaned closer until their arms touched. "Luckily it's never too late to find your way or discover new possibilities; I think the most important thing is being open to anything, and as far as I can tell, you *are* open."

One corner of Gregory's mouth lifted in a shy smile. "I try to be. I've learned so much these last few months. Without Ever Fund and Mom sending me to Lands, just think, I never would have known the difference between theme parks and amusement parks and how much more I like the former."

"Oh really?"

"Yeah, I'm surprised by how much I've enjoyed my time at Lands."

"I could take that the wrong way," Charlotte joked, "but I hear you. I didn't expect much from you when you showed up. You in your suit. You've settled in and I can see that you care."

"I do. I know I'm an outsider and basically the face of money, but I do want Lands of Legend to succeed for your family. And for you." He all but whispered the last part.

Charlotte put her hand on the side of her face in mock surprise. "Gregory! Do you think theme parks could be becoming your new thing?"

She was mostly kidding, but Gregory leaned down and whispered in her ear, his soft breath sending a vibrating chill down her back. "Actually, they might be."

"Oh hey," he said, "Looks like the line is moving again." He nodded toward the widening gap between them and the people in front of them.

Charlotte shuffled forward, noting the way her pulse raced at her thinking about a possible future with Gregory, one where they ran Lands of Legend. One that wasn't possible given her current hopes for the DreamUs job in Paris.

Chapter 23

The adrenaline from the ride made Charlotte bouncy as they exited Sullivan Slade's Adventure. She'd been on it dozens of times and it never got less joyful, not even when she knew every twist and turn. And she'd stopped herself from looking at Gregory every thirty seconds to see if he was having a good time, but now she gave him her full attention as they followed the exit tunnel back into the park. His hair was askew in all possible directions and his cheeks looked a little pink.

"What did you think?" she asked.

"That. Was. *Awesome!*" Gregory said in a spirited tone she wasn't sure she'd ever heard him use before.

"Isn't it?!"

"I can see why it's one of your favorites. I need to start a *Sullivan Slade* rewatch when we get back home."

Gregory calling Lake Sterling home didn't escape Charlotte's notice, but she didn't want to call it out. They had a million more things to see anyway.

As if Gregory heard her mind jumping to the next item on her list, he asked, "What's next?"

"Well," she answered, "we covered a lot of ground in that line. Should we find something else with an even longer wait so we can get into more deep conversations?"

"Ha," Gregory chortled. He chortled! Being at this theme park had a tendency to make adults lighter and freer and she was seeing it unfold in front of her eyes.

"We'll see about that, but first," he said, "I believe I owe you a cup of coffee. Hidden Jungle has coffee, right?"

"It does, though it's nothing fancy."

"Nothing fancy is fine. You can amend the deal to be for any kind of beverage."

"Perfect." Charlotte grinned. "And it's conveniently by the Jungle River Cruise so that can be our next ride."

Over the last two-plus months of working together, Charlotte had witnessed Gregory relax. Whether she was guiding him through the Wintertide Trail at Lands and helping him spot the hidden creatures, or they were sharing the conference table in the office bickering about popcorn flavors, his edges had softened. And here at Dreamland, she could see the final walls coming down.

Gregory's increasingly carefree vibe was making him hotter than ever.

She'd been sneaking stares at him finishing an ice cream float from behind her sunglasses, thankfully of the mirrored variety. He caught a drip of the pineapple soft serve from the corner of his mouth with his tongue and Charlotte entertained a brief fantasy of licking ice cream from Gregory's skin and had to press her legs together. In fact, she thought, it was the perfect time to stand and refill her water bottle. She held the empty bottle up to Gregory and said, "I'll be right back."

Charlotte wound through the seating area at Hidden Jungle to the refill station with Gregory at the forefront of her thoughts. He'd been up for anything she suggested as they explored the park, deferring to her expertise and advice, letting her divert from their plans and get to Hidden Jungle hours later than they'd planned. Charlotte didn't need or want her partner to be subservient or anything, but having someone who listened and went with the flow was such a stark difference from her past relationships, especially with Chad.

Not that she and Gregory had a relationship of any kind. Nope. They were work colleagues. She was probably going to leave for Paris after Memorial Day. So many reasons not to have feelings. She was only appreciating his flexibility and that she was having the best day possible with him. *That's it,* she thought, *it's about seeing him open up so much and be less rigid, more himself.*

She couldn't stop the smile stretching across her face as she returned to the table and saw Gregory leaned back in his chair, taking it all in without a tense line in his body.

"What are you smiling about?" he asked, his own lips curling.

"I'm at Dreamland," Charlotte said. "Why wouldn't I be smiling? Glad you liked your float. I told you pineapple soft serve is where it's at."

"I was skeptical, but yeah, that was amazing. Much better than plain ol' coffee. I've already made a mental note about bringing something like it to Lands."

Charlotte shook her head. "Of course you have. We're going to have a ton of mental notes to go through when we get back, aren't we?"

"Well, this is a research trip, isn't it? You took away my notebook, but you can't stop this." He tapped his forehead with his finger.

"It is research, you absolute dork." Charlotte nodded. "And speaking of, shall we continue?"

"One second." Gregory pointed behind her shoulder. "Is that a photograph of the esteemed members of the Institution of Travelers?"

Charlotte kept looking at him, rested her head on her hand, and gave him a look. She knew what picture he was talking about. If she turned around, she'd see herself in a photo with other Dream Mechanics who worked on Hidden Jungle. They'd put on explorer costumes and pretended to be members of a fictional group invented for DreamUs parks, the Institution of Travelers. That Gregory knew the name told her he really had watched interviews about Hidden Jungle. "I'm aware of that photo, Gregory. I didn't expect you to be, though."

He bit his lip. "I did my research."

"Looks like your research techniques have improved since your first visit to Lands."

"Rude," he joked. "Now, about that hat you're wearing in the photo, is it a—"

"Time to go." She held out her hand to take his empty cup but instead Gregory grabbed her hand with his.

"Please help me out of this chair, I beg you. I'm having an excellent time but my body is not used to the kind of abuse a day at a theme park preceded by a very early flight inflicts."

He said true words. The combination of walking, standing in line, jostling from rides, and then blending all of that with popcorn and ice cream had unusual effects on the body. She put all her weight into pulling him into a standing position and he stumbled forward; he steadied himself by wrapping his other arm around Charlotte.

"Oof. You're stronger than I thought," he said as he lingered in the half-hugging position. Charlotte was conflicted; she wanted to lean into it and make it a full embrace but she also wanted to maintain boundaries. He must have read the confusion because he pulled away first and acted like nothing had happened.

"Let's go see this zoetrope you mentioned," he said. "Then I'll know what a zoetrope is."

She nodded. "And you'll wonder how you ever lived without knowing. This way."

Chapter 24

Charlotte couldn't believe her luck! They'd seen the zoetrope, worked through her list, and now it was time for the finale of the day. She eyed an opening on the sidewalk big enough for both of them to sit and wait for the parade and fireworks. She realized parades were not for everyone, usually including her, but this one came with dazzling lights and an earworm of a soundtrack, and then fireworks came right after. She grabbed Gregory's hand and tugged him toward the open spot.

"How do you feel about sitting down for a while?" she asked him.

"I would pay money to do that," Gregory said.

"Welcome to the world of tired theme park feet. I'll warn you now, they will hurt even more after we sit for a while."

Gregory winced. "I think that's a risk I'm willing to take."

Once in front of the designated spots on the curb, she gestured grandly. "May I present your throne for the next hour or so."

She wished she had her phone ready to capture the withering look Gregory gave her.

"Charlotte, if I sit all the way down there I might not be able to get up. Or move again."

"I'll help you, it will be okay."

He groaned as they settled in. Charlotte got it; his muscles were new to the stamina required for a day in a sprawling theme park. At least he wasn't complaining about the sitting-on-the-ground part.

Charlotte folded herself and sat beside him and then stretched out her legs, gray sneakers peeking out from the bottom of her blue jumpsuit's legs. They'd had an amazing time. Charlotte hadn't had a full day of playing without work in a DreamUs park in forever. Sure, they were calling this a research trip, but it's not like she was opening a ride or doing a conference call from a ride vehicle. "See, this concrete's not so bad, right?"

Gregory smiled. He looked more relaxed than Charlotte would have expected. "Not at all. Now, tell me what to expect from this parade. There's no, like, audience participation, is there?"

"Not usually. But you never know," Charlotte teased. "If there is, I promise to shield you. I think you've experienced enough theme park essentials for one day."

Gregory nodded so hard Charlotte thought he might hurt his neck. "There is so much to do. Too much? How do people fit everything in all in one day? Especially if they have kids!"

"Well, DreamUs isn't exactly mad about people wanting to split their trip across multiple days."

"Ah, so it's intentionally designed to be overwhelming? I feel like I need a degree to fully understand the LinePass system."

Charlotte held up a hand. "LinePass and how it's evolved from a helpful free tool to being more about another way to increase profits is a whole conversation neither of us has the energy for—except to say it's the exact opposite of what we want to do at Lands. We don't want to upcharge for every convenience, and it's something I'm sad to see happening in Dreamland and other DreamUs parks. Especially when the tickets are not cheap and families save for ages to come here. Plus, systems like LinePass as it is now make Dreamland more overwhelming. It can be a challenge to help guests not feel the pressure of doing every little thing—people want to get their money's worth. For many, this is a once-in-a-lifetime trip and they don't want to miss out. It was always a constant conversation at DreamUs to balance what a guest wants and can reasonably do in a day and what we—I mean they—offer. But ultimately, the company had to kind of 'train' guests to let go of the idea of cramming it all into a single day."

She looked at Gregory up and down and said, "As you've experienced, going at full throttle all day is exhausting. I hope it's still been fun for you, but there is a thin line between delirious joy and delirious collapse."

He stared intently at the asphalt by his shoes and chewed on his lip, that loose lock of hair swooping across his forehead. Charlotte wanted to be closer and it was impossible to pretend otherwise. She scooted in and gently wrapped her fingers around his arm.

"You *have* had fun, right? You can be honest."

Gregory breathed in and turned his stare toward Charlotte. The impact of his full attention lit her skin on fire, especially where her fingers made contact with his skin.

"Charlotte"—he paused to cover her hand with his—"I've had the most fun. I didn't have high expectations because I'm me, but I should have known better. I can see why you loved being part of the company that makes all of this."

She did, she reminded herself. That's why she hoped for a positive response to her DreamUs application. But when Gregory removed his hand to gesture at the park, Charlotte found it difficult not to grab it and pull it back to her side.

"Thank you for showing me around. It wouldn't have been as special without you," Gregory said, serious and sweet in perfect concert, as only he could manage.

"I loved doing it. I'll show you around any theme park any time." Charlotte winked. She was sure the wink didn't look as cute as it felt, and also why was she winking and making showing him around theme parks sound like a euphemism?!

"I like the sound of that," Gregory replied and Charlotte was dying to know if he was attempting to flirt. She could ask, she thought, but no, that would be too awkward even for her.

"But," Gregory added, "no more spinning cups. In fact, no more rides with spinning objects, no matter what they are. Not worth losing my lunch or ice cream snack or whatever delicious thing I've eaten."

Charlotte nodded. "Yeah, that's fair. You have yourself a deal."

She held out her hand in the world's most obvious ploy to touch Gregory again. He clasped her hand firmly and pumped it three times and every nerve in Charlotte's fingers tingled.

"I love when neither of us drives a hard bargain," Gregory said. "Now, we have a little while until the parade starts, so how about I go get us snacks?"

"Snacks! As long as you don't mind torturing your feet, yes, please. It's a parade worth waiting for, I promise. And then fireworks!"

"I've learned to trust you." He smiled. "And speaking of people I've learned to trust, can you see if Melanie has any snack recommendations for this time of day and part of the park?"

Charlotte clasped her hands together. "You're learning. I'm so proud."

* * *

Peanut butter cookie pie and chocolate-dipped marsh-mallows devoured—Melanie said she couldn't be forced to choose between them—Charlotte and Gregory watched the last float of the parade roll down the street. Charlotte had stolen a number of glances at Gregory out the corner of her eye during the parade—enough that he'd finally assured her that yes, he was still having fun.

"Your first theme park parade is over now. What did you think?" she asked.

He started to respond but shook his head and lifted a napkin to the corner of her mouth and dabbed. "You had a little chocolate, just there."

"Oh, thanks." Charlotte knew her cheeks turned pink but hoped the nighttime lighting obscured it. She was weirdly happy that Gregory felt comfortable enough with her to wipe food off her face.

"Anyway, I liked the parade, though I can't wrap my head around how it's cost effective to do that every day. But mostly what I want to know is how long that music will be in head?"

"Ah, that. I'm sorry to report it is with you for life now. You'll hear it all the time."

"I figured as much," he said. "How long until fireworks?"

"What, you're not going to look at the Dreamland app?" Charlotte asked.

"Hey, it's a really well-designed app," he said, nudging her shoulder with his, "but no, I figured you could tell me."

Charlotte stood up slowly, her professional theme park feet screaming as she put weight on them again, and reached her hand out to help Gregory do the same. "They'll happen soon but don't rush standing. You'll regret it."

He grasped her hand and unfolded his long limbs, his sleeve falling back enough to tease more of his bicep tattoo.

Charlotte pulled and Gregory groaned, joining the chorus of people around them standing and stretching.

"You were not joking about my feet. I never want to sit again."

"The hotel has a mint foot rub in the rooms that is heaven."

Gregory grunted at her.

She offered her elbow and he wrapped his arm around hers. It was for stability, she told herself. "Keep your eyes up there." Charlotte used her free arm to point at a patch of sky above the castle and slightly to the left. "Next time we come to Dreamland, we'll watch the fireworks from that direction. Less of a crowd and a view that's as spectacular as this."

"Next time?" Gregory asked.

Oops, Charlotte hadn't been aware she had hopes for returning to Dreamland with Gregory one day and she certainly hadn't meant to voice them. She cleared her throat and dropped her arm, breaking contact with him. "Uh, yeah. You know, in case we need further research for Lands."

"Research, yes, of course. Always more research to do," Gregory answered, his lips twisting to the side.

Charlotte wanted to own up to her attraction to Gregory. She thought he'd reciprocate the feeling, but she didn't know—not even with what might have been an almost-kiss on the Jungle River Cruise earlier. She hated being wrong. Look where being confident in a relationship had gotten her with Chad. His cheating had broken her sense of trust in her own judgment maybe more than it had broken her trust in others. But as she looked at Gregory's profile, illuminated by the softest orange light, she thought he might be worth putting herself out there again. If nothing else to sate the warmth in her stomach that only grew more intense the more time she spent around him.

Gregory turned his head toward her, maybe sensing Charlotte staring at him, and his lips curled up at the ends. She tracked every micro movement. He lifted a hand to her cheek and brushed a wayward strand of hair behind her ear. The first firework cracked in the sky, startling both of them. They giggled at how easily they jumped, and swiveled their heads away from each other and toward the sky.

Booming music underscored each splash of color, some of the fireworks exploding in elaborate flowers of sparkles and others falling like rain. Charlotte leaned into Gregory's side as the illuminations popped in the air, painting the park in ever-changing hues. The backs of Gregory's fingers brushed against hers and neither of them pulled away.

Gregory laced his fingers through hers and Charlotte inhaled sharply. The presence of his hand in hers caused waves of joy and lust to radiate through her. Sharing this moment, in one of her favorite places in the world with Gregory, during fireworks, was too much. Not enough. Her knees might give out. She held Gregory's hand harder.

The tempo and volume of the music increased as the show's grand finale began. Charlotte had seen this show enough times she could see it with her eyes closed, but she never tired of the ending, the way little bursts of white light gave way to color gradation, the fireworks getting bigger and brighter.

Gregory turned to face her and lifted his free arm to gently turn her toward him. He stared into her eyes and then at her mouth and Charlotte thought swooning was a real possibility. She closed the space between them, still holding hands. He wound his other arm around her waist, and she reached up to brush his jaw with his fingertips.

His eyes were full of wanting, no doubt a reflection of her own. Charlotte tilted her head up and met his lips with hers. She closed her eyes, afterimages of fireworks glowing against her eyelids, matching the explosions ricocheting through her as she and Gregory softly, tentatively kissed, a kiss that became more sure by the second as she realized he wanted this, too. Gregory unlaced his fingers from hers and used both hands to pull Charlotte against him; she sunk her fingers into the hair at the nape of his neck, deepening the kiss. Charlotte whimpered, not quite believing a kiss could be like this.

When they finally pulled apart, the fireworks over the park's sky were over but they were still sizzling inside her.

Chapter 25

Everything that had been building between them, the kiss set on fire. Charlotte wanted to drag Gregory to a tucked-away alley she knew by the entrance and kiss him senseless, but her more practical self, which realized they were kissing in a sea of families, prevailed.

She broke the kiss and brought her eyes up to Gregory's. "So were there any other rides you wanted to go on?"

Gregory made a strangled sound. "Uh, I can think of a ride, if you also want to go on it."

"Gregory Binns! Are you saying what I think you're saying?"

"Hey, you said it first."

"I did no—Oh, I did but I didn't mean it that way. I was legitimately making sure you didn't want to do more things in the park."

Gregory reached for her hand and brought it the back of it to his lips. "Charlotte. No. I do not want to see more of the park. Do you?"

"Nope, I've been here. A lot. Let's get out of here."

He wound his fingers through hers. "You're the expert. Lead the way?"

"I've got this. Hold on tight; this crowd is large and full of over-sugared and overtired children."

She cut through the crowd with determination and the presence of a linebacker, aware of Gregory's closeness behind her. Thank goodness the hotel had messed up their reservation and stuck them in a single room with a king-sized bed. She thought both of them wanted the same thing tonight. Right? *No, Charlotte*, she told herself, *you were there for that kiss.* Everything about his body said he was very into it. They got to the loading area for the monorail that would take them to their hotel and Gregory leaned into her back and Charlotte realized, yes, he was still very into it.

She pulled their clasped hands to her waist and pressed against him, enough to make him gasp sharply. Charlotte smiled with anticipation. She couldn't wait to hear more of Gregory loosening up.

They boarded the monorail, squeezing in with everyone else exiting the park and going the same destination. Normally, Charlotte found these moments oppressive; she did her best to avoid leaving the park right after the fireworks. But this time she had Gregory as a distraction, their upper bodies jostling against each other every time the monorail glided around a corner.

After one particularly jarring turn, Gregory wrapped a steady arm around her waist. She leaned in more than she strictly needed to and enjoyed having this solid rock—this sexy, not-as-uptight-as-he-once-seemed solid rock—next to her for support. It made it easy to ignore the crowds. Two stops later, which took far too long, they stepped out of the warm monorail car, into the cool night air. So did a large portion of the crowds, also staying at RetroDream.

"Okay with taking a shortcut that is not actually shorter?" Charlotte asked.

Gregory glanced around them. "Would it get us away from so many people?"

"Absolutely."

She led him to a sidewalk no one was taking.

"No one else is going this way," Gregory said. He nudged Charlotte with his elbow. "Should I be worried?"

She stuck her tongue out at him. "Should you be worried that you're with a pro who knows what she's doing?"

"Right. My bad."

"In the summer, this walk means getting approximately one dozen bug bites," Charlotte said, "but this time of year, it's not so bad."

"Seems much quieter, too," Gregory commented.

It was almost too quiet after their day in the park, the loud fireworks, and the hum of all the people on the monorail. Charlotte shook her head, as if to clear out the noise, and tuned into what was around them: the gentle lap of water, a light layer of bug sounds, and their feet on the paved sidewalk.

Her fingers brushed the back of Gregory's and he took her hand and they walked for a few minutes without saying anything.

"Charlotte. About what happened."

"That mind-melting kiss?" She hoped he also thought it was mind-melting or she'd shown her hand for nothing.

"Uh, yes. That. It was pretty mind-melting, wasn't it?"

Whew, Charlotte thought.

"It was. Now what about it? I hope you're not about to say it was a mistake or that we shouldn't do it again," Charlotte said.

"No, it's not that. I really would like to do it again as soon as possible."

"So?"

"I want to make sure you also feel that way and that there's not any weirdness because of Lands or our roles there or anything. I just. I want to make sure you want this in the same way as me."

Charlotte stopped and jerked her heard toward the side of the path. "There's a bench over here, let's sit for a minute."

"I thought we established sitting and giving our feet a break was a bad idea."

"You'll survive."

Seated and facing Gregory, Charlotte took both of his hands in hers. "First of all, I don't kiss anyone because they are my boss or whatever."

"I didn't mean that—"

Charlotte held up a finger. "Let me finish. I've been attracted to you since the day I showed you around Lands and you grabbed my hand on Hydra's Fury. It wasn't just because you're gorgeous."

Here, Gregory blushed so brightly Charlotte could see it in the dark.

"It was because you were a fish out of water, but you tried new things anyway. You did something scary with a stranger. You opened yourself to possibilities. And look, I know we've butted heads, but that is sexy as hell."

Charlotte looked into her lap and let go of his hands. "So yes, Gregory. I want this. I think I've wanted this for a while."

He leaned in, put a hand on either side of her face, and pulled her in for a kiss, longer and harder than the first time, a kiss with force behind it. Charlotte hadn't seen Gregory passionate in quite this way—usually his energy was reserved for the perfect PowerPoint graph—and it took her desire to deeper levels. She groaned into his mouth and he answered with what sounded like a low growl.

She pulled back breathless. "Well, I'm glad we took a few minutes to discuss that. Now shall we walk very quickly to our room?"

"I guess this means you don't want to stop by the lounge for drinks like we talked about?" Gregory asked.

Charlotte raised an eyebrow.

"Kidding. But a rain check, okay? I want to see that indoor river."

It sounded like Gregory was saying he wanted to come back to Dreamland with her, and the thought wrapped itself around Charlotte's heart and squeezed.

Chapter 26

They fell back against the door to their hotel room, kissing and giggling while Charlotte fished her phone out of her bag to pull up the app that would open the room's smart lock. Thankfully, her phone had just enough charge to open the door, saving them a hike back to the front desk

Once in the room, they took off bags and shoes. "Every part of my body wants to commit a murder against me," Charlotte said as she flopped onto a chair.

"If that's how you, a professional at this, are feeling, imagine how much every bone in my body is screaming right now."

"I do not recommend looking at the step count on your watch tonight. You can look tomorrow when you'll feel triumphant about it, but tonight, it will confuse and possibly upset you to learn how you walked so much around one place."

"Sounds like expert advice," Gregory agreed. "I could use some more advice."

Charlotte perked up, expecting him to ask about something to do with kissing.

"How much will I regret making a cup of coffee?"

Oh.

"I mean, maybe if you do like half caf or something you won't be awake all night."

"I'd be fine with being awake all night." He took the chair next to hers and waggled his eyebrows, and the sight of Gregory being so chill was going to undo her.

"But I was talking about whether it would be like, sanitary, to use that coffee maker. I've read too many 'don't do these things in hotel rooms' articles that mention how gross the in-room coffee machines are."

"Huh, I wouldn't have pegged you as the listicle reading type," Charlotte said.

He shrugged. "We all have our weaknesses."

"I guess so," she replied. "To my knowledge, no one has ever died from drinking terrible hotel room coffee."

She stood up, cringing as her feet lit on fire. Charlotte bent over to kiss Gregory's cheek. "Why don't you risk it and make some coffee for both of us, and I'll take a quick shower before you?"

"Yes, again, full of expert advice. No one should go to bed with a day of theme park grime on them." His voice turned mischievous. "Whether they're going to sleep or not."

Charlotte took the quickest shower of her life, scrubbing away the layers of sunscreen, sweat, and God knew what else. Much as she loved theme parks, she couldn't deny that germs abounded. Feeling too shy to walk out in only a towel or a robe, Charlotte slipped on her pajama short set and picked up the sacred mint foot-rub tube.

Swinging the bathroom door open she said, "All yours."

She'd been so fast the coffee maker was still percolating, gasping away as it dripped into the pot below.

"Gregory?"

No answer. She tiptoed around the corner and saw Gregory stretched out in one of the chairs, arms folded, head leaned back, and eyes closed. And was that a trace of a snore? Of course, she thought, laughing softly. He was *out*. Without taking a shower. This was another reason it was a gamble to sit down in a comfy spot for too long after a long day of going on rides, waiting in line for said rides, and eating as many snacks as possible.

Charlotte turned off the coffee maker—no one would have to bet their life on hotel room coffee tonight—and flipped off the bathroom light. She opened the closet door, the loud creak not making Gregory stir at all, and pulled a blanket from the top shelf. Taking his probably sweaty shoes off seemed like a level of intimacy he might not be into yet so she left them on his feet and covered him in the blanket.

She got the last of the lights in the room and crawled under the covers. Charlotte rolled over once or twice, trying to see Gregory's outline in the chair through the bedroom door in the dark. Exhaustion swept over her, not allowing her body the luxury of reliving her and Gregory's kisses and not giving her mind the space for anxiety to swirl about what might happen next. Charlotte fell asleep almost instantly.

The aroma of waffles and bacon swirled into Charlotte's dreams, strong enough to make her eyes open. She propped herself on one elbow and took in the room through sleep-addled eyes, spying a full breakfast spread on the coffee table. Slowly, her brain cleared and she remembered where she was—and who she was with. Except she didn't see Gregory anywhere in the room and the bathroom door wasn't closed.

"Gregory?" she said tentatively.

No answer.

She stretched and scooted toward the edge of the bed—just as well Gregory had fallen asleep on the chair since she'd sprawled across the king-size mattress—and swung her feet out, glancing at the clock. It wasn't even eight yet. She padded across the floor toward the food and saw there were indeed two plates. Then she walked toward the bathroom and peeked in slowly, saying his name again in case he was, for some reason, lurking in the shower in the dark.

Empty bathroom confirmed, Charlotte prioritized hygiene, appreciating the chance to brush her teeth before Gregory appeared from wherever he went. She shrugged into a light robe and was deciding how rude it would be to eat without him when the hotel room door beeped. Charlotte froze, then bent her knees slightly to prepare to do something—attack a possible room invader, she guessed—but an arm holding a coffee cup came through the door.

"Here, I got it," she said and stepped forward to swing the door open for Gregory, who was juggling a whole container of drinks.

"You're awake." He smiled.

"Yeah, the smell of bacon could pull me out of a coma."

"You kinda do sleep like the dead," he said, walking the drinks to the coffee table. He took cups of coffee and a couple of different juices out of the holder. "I kept thinking I was going to wake you up while I was getting ready this morning, but I realized there was no way. You were out."

"Well, it was a busy day and we were both exhausted."

"Yeah, about that." He gestured at the chairs. "Come sit and let's dig in before it gets cold. I had it brought to the room, but I forgot about drinks and I didn't know what you might like besides coffee, so . . ."

"So you brought a breakfast beverage sample platter?" Charlotte teased but the thoughtful gesture made her feel fuzzy, like a soft sweatshirt on the first day of fall. It made her think that, when they got around to talking about last night, it wasn't going to be bad, that they'd both been on the same page and both wanted to return to it.

"Basically, yeah."

"I normally just do coffee, but that's only because I never remember to get juice. If I'm getting breakfast somewhere, I love orange juice."

Gregory looked pleased with himself and held up two cups. "Pulp or no pulp?"

"Pulp, please, I like to chew my orange juice."

He wrinkled his nose. "That makes one of us."

"The coffee is their daily flavor too—honeycrisp apple, I think. After smelling the coffee I started before I passed out last night, I figured it was best if we let the hotel coffee maker exist in peace."

Charlotte snickered. "That bad, huh?"

Gregory made a pained face. "Like sweaty feet mixed with bean water."

"I'm so glad you shared that as we're about to eat." It didn't stop her from picking up a fork and digging into the waffle she'd smothered with maple syrup.

They chewed in comfortable silence. Most hotel room service wasn't anything impressive but DreamUs resorts made delectable waffles so popular they even sold their proprietary mix so people could make the treats at home.

Gregory wiped his mouth with a napkin and cleared his throat. *Here we go*, thought Charlotte. "So, uh, last night," he said.

Charlotte speared a link of chicken-and-apple sausage. "Yes, about that." She bit off half the sausage, refusing to show her hand first.

Gregory looked alarmed at how much food she'd shoved into her face but recovered quickly. He put a hand on Charlotte's bare knee. "I hate that I fell asleep."

Charlotte hurried through the last couple of chews and swallowed hard. "Yeah, me too. But I was out as soon as I closed my eyes, so maybe it was for the best."

"Oh," Gregory said and withdrew his hand. "I was worried about that—that I missed my chance."

Charlotte was sipping her coffee, which gave her time to process that he was disappointed they hadn't been able to follow their kisses up with more. She wouldn't leave any room for misunderstanding. She put her cup down, stood up, and took one step to loom over Gregory before sitting in his lap and putting each of her hands on either side of his sharp jaw. He wrapped his arms around her.

"You haven't missed your chance, Gregory. *We* haven't missed our chance."

She pulled his face closer and leaned into his lips, showing him with a kiss how happy she was that he wasn't going to try to brush off the heated embraces of last night as a mistake, or a business liability, or some other excuse. He answered her lips with equal fire and when he slipped his tongue into her mouth, Charlotte thought she might melt into a puddle.

They took their time, lingering with each kiss, each movement of exploration. Gregory brushed her robe down her arm, baring her shoulder, and left a trail of kisses along her collarbone. Charlotte moaned in pleasure.

"I want to hear that sound again," he said, voice raspy, and pulled her closer into him, helping her arrange one knee on other side of his legs, straddling him. She could feel that he was enjoying this as much as her, and she lightly ran her nails over the exposed slice of skin above his pants, earning a groan.

"Charlotte," he breathed.

"Yes?" she asked.

"This is all— You're okay with this, right?"

"More than okay." She pressed her hips down and leaned in to kiss his neck right below his hairline.

"Thank fuck."

Charlotte pulled back. "Gregory! I have never heard you say 'fuck'!"

Gregory cupped his hands below her bottom and stood, lifting her. Charlotte wound her legs around his thighs. "There's a time and place for everything, Charlotte. Now, can we move to the bed?"

"Yes, immediately, please."

Chapter 27

Charlotte lay on her side, arm draped over Gregory's chest—Gregory's rather chiseled chest, it turned out. She'd made note of the muscles on his biceps before, but it didn't occur to her that whatever he did to build those muscles would apply to other parts of his body. She rubbed her hand over his pecs and stomach, marveling at the dips and lines, mentally cataloging every hair.

Gregory twitched and said warmly, "That tickles."

She rolled back so she could look up at him and his lips stretched into a lazy smile. His hair was brushed loosely to the side but it was clearly tangled and he had the look of a boneless being.

"I thought you were sleeping," she said.

"How could I sleep when you're naked and this close?"

He had a point. Relaxed as she might be, every nerve ending on her body was on full alert, ready for a sign that he was up for another round. She couldn't not be aware of the many places their skin touched right now and had touched in the past, however long it had been since they'd left the breakfast and their coffees to go cold.

She stretched her head over Gregory's torso to look at the clock. It was past eleven, so they'd been in bed for a few hours.

Wait, it was past eleven. She'd never slept in that late at Dreamland, or any other DreamUs theme park, and she could get used it.

Charlotte rolled away from Gregory and onto her back. He sighed and turned to curl in next to her. She kissed his forehead. "We're meeting Melanie for lunch at one thirty," she whispered into his hair.

"So we should start thinking about getting out of bed, then? Nope, not a fan," Gregory said. "But I have been looking forward to meeting Melanie."

"She feels the same."

Gregory propped his head on his arm, showing off the tattoo of stippled mountains and trees wrapping around his bicep, honoring his grandfather and the San Gabriel Mountains they adored so much. Charlotte pressed her teeth into her bottom lip. She wasn't sure if it was the tattoo itself— she'd never been so mesmerized by a tattoo before—but she'd never imagined that the rigid and structured Gregory would be a tattoo guy. And it wasn't his only one.

A delicately shaded devil's-claw bloom adorned his shoulder blade, its leaves falling gracefully over his shoulder toward his collarbone. One time, Gregory explained as Charlotte had traced the art with her fingernail, his grandfather had taken him to the Mojave Desert to see a wildflower superbloom after a rainy winter. He'd walked a young Gregory along the edges of superbloom, showing him every different wildflower, all of them exploding with color. Gregory said he knew a tattoo couldn't capture the vibrancy of the wildflowers that day, so he had the tattoo artist do the art in shades of black and gray. That way he could imagine the color instead. The story had made Charlotte hold him close and cover the tattoo in kisses.

Kisses she was thinking about now. She cleared her throat. They had to get out of bed and get moving, and that meant she had to stop.

Gregory was looking at her like he was waiting for an answer.

"Sorry, could you repeat that?" Charlotte said.

"Someone's a little distracted, huh? I can relate." He looked Charlotte's mostly sheet-covered form up and down. "But I was saying, I was surprised Melanie wanted to meet me. I know I haven't been the easiest person to work with these last few months."

Charlotte focused on a spot on the ceiling. "You've had your moments. I have too, to be fair. But even when you've been stubborn, you've generally had a reason and you've been open to me sharing data to change your mind. I think Melanie respects that. Plus she always loves inviting people to restaurants in the park, especially people who might not think theme park food is anything more than hamburgers and fries—I know you don't think that anymore."

When she glanced back over at Gregory, he looked thoughtful. "How should we handle this with Melanie?"

"Handle what?" Charlotte asked.

Gregory moved in and brushed his lips against her bruised ones. "This," he whispered.

"Oh! This! Right!" Charlotte exclaimed. "Well, Melanie's been saying I should bone you almost since we met."

Charlotte had not meant to say that much aloud.

Gregory raised both eyebrows. "Oh, she has, has she?"

She may as well own up. "I may have mentioned the color of your eyes once or twice. And your jawline. Also your biceps."

He looked smug. "So I wasn't alone in my attraction?"

"Tell me more," Charlotte said.

"When you wear your blue-light glasses in the office and push them up your nose, I have to step out of the room. The way your flip your hair to the side makes the air smell like your rosemary-and-lavender shampoo and I always try to take the deepest breath possible. And when you wear skirts your legs, even your ankles, are indecent. Those are very uncomfortable days for me—uh, in a good way."

"Gregory," she said. "One, that is very sweet. I was not aware you noticed me in that way. Two, we are naked in bed. Why are you blushing?"

"I don't know. I guess I never thought I'd be able to tell you any of those things. I thought you disliked me. A lot."

She picked up his hand and kissed the back of it. "It's a good thing we cleared that up, then, isn't it?"

He exhaled sharply. "Yes. Very good thing."

Need and want pooled in Charlotte's belly again but she pushed them away. She said, "It's time for us to get ready. I'll shower first."

"And I'll get us more coffee."

If Gregory kept doing things like that, she might just fall in love with him. The L-word had popped into her thoughts, uninvited and unwelcome. She shook it out of her head. She should make sure he even wanted to date first before she let her mind wander in that direction.

The scent of pizza and wood-fired dough drifted outside the restaurant's entrance and Charlotte thought it might lift her onto her toes, like in a cartoon. They were a little early, so she led Gregory to stand under the restaurant's awning and pulled out her phone.

Charlotte: We're here. Under the awning.
Charlotte: Can't wait to see you. <3
Melanie: SAME! Just walked through the gates and will be there soon!!!

"Melanie will be here in a few," she told Gregory. They'd held hands all through the park on their walk here and Charlotte couldn't believe how right and easy it had felt. Chad had never been much for public displays of affection, no matter how mild, and never anywhere near DreamUs or its parks, so it made the simple pleasure of feeling Gregory solid at her side all the more novel and wonderful. She leaned into him under the awning.

Charlotte saw platinum hair with strands of purple and green weaving through the light crowds and grinned as Melanie approached. She dropped Gregory's hand and stepped out from under the awning to crash into Melanie's open arms.

"I am so happy to see you!" Charlotte squealed.

"I know, so am I! We have to do better about visiting each other more often!" Melanie replied.

"Agreed. Glad we're hanging tomorrow, though."

"Me too." Melanie popped her head to the side to look at Gregory. She lowered her voice. "Pictures didn't do him justice. And yes, I saw you two holding hands. I will need all the details. You look really happy and kinda glowy. And you haven't mentioned work yet."

"We've been talking for less than a minute!" Charlotte protested.

Melanie smiled innocently. "I stand by what I said."

Her best friend stepped out of their embrace and over to Gregory. Melanie thrust out a hand. "Gregory. It's nice to meet you. I've heard so much about you."

He shook her hand. "Likewise. Also thank you for the snack recs last night. That peanut butter cookie pie was one of the best desserts I've ever put in my mouth."

Melanie preened. "It's true. I *am* excellent at what I do. Speaking of, I'll check in for our table. Get ready for amazing pizza."

"You know, I like how much we eat pizza together," Gregory said.

"Hard same," Charlotte answered.

The host, who Melanie seemed to know, led them through the sunlit space and into a small alcove with a stucco finish on the walls. The restaurant's whole vibe was Italian villa in the summer with faux finishes and plants everywhere.

"You scored one of the best tables in the place," Charlotte said as they sat down and scooted in.

Melanie shrugged. "It's what I do. Let's look over the menu and then I want to hear what you've thought of Dreamland so far, Gregory."

"Only if you tell me what's best to order here," he teased. Granted, they'd only sat down two minutes ago, but she already felt good about her best friend and her whatever-Gregory-was were getting along. She nudged her leg against his under the table, feeling him press back.

Melanie asked Gregory a few questions about his preferences and gave a short list of picks. Charlotte thought it was one of the many elements that helped Melanie rise above other food writers: she didn't give blanket recommendations. When she had the chance for a conversation, she tailored her choices toward the person's likes and dislikes. If someone hated beets, as Charlotte did, it didn't matter how much Melanie gushed about the beet ice cream from the fuchsia stand around the corner from the restaurant.

Orders placed, Melanie looked at Gregory and then Charlotte. Her mischievous smile said Charlotte would get an earful later, but Melanie was too kind to ask questions about their relationship over lunch. "So, tell me about your impressions of the parks, Gregory. Have you gathered a lot of research for Lands?" Melanie said, giving Charlotte a pointed look when she said the word "research."

Gregory took a swig of his prosecco, and Charlotte realized she was admiring his throat. It was like the morning's events had unlocked every bit of attraction to Gregory she'd felt from the day they met and now she had no reason to suppress them. She uncrossed and recrossed her legs and put her chin in her hand, waiting for his answer.

"It's been a lot to take in, but I don't mean that in a bad way or anything," he said. Charlotte could tell he'd flipped into über-analytical mode. "I'm impressed with the attention to detail, especially when it comes to accommodating all the crowds. The layout effectively funnels the crowds, even when people move in the same direction en masse. Leaving after the fireworks last night did get a tiny bit claustrophobic, but everyone was at least moving. It's clear a lot of thought was put into absorbing bodies and then dispersing them so no one feels crushed," Gregory observed. "Even when it came to ordering food, whether through the mobile app or waiting in line, it all moved quickly. I think there are definitely some points we can take back to Lands."

"You should see those lines when there's a new souvenir popcorn bucket. They've yet to perfect that process," Melanie smoothly commented. "I know I'm the one who asked about research, but what I really want to know is what you thought of the rides, the theme park of it all."

"Ah." Gregory smiled. "I've been known to get too hung up on the details." Charlotte nodded emphatically.

"I had way more fun than I thought I would," he continued. "My feet may never be the same, but it was worth it. The attention to detail I like so much in operations applies to all the rides, even the queues. With Charlotte's help I saw how the stories and themes connected."

Gregory stopped to grin at Charlotte and she thought she was going to dissolve into goo, and none of the workers deserved to clean goo off the floor. She caressed Gregory's arm. "Hey, give yourself a little credit," she said. "You asked questions you wouldn't have even thought of a couple of months ago."

"I did notice more of the fun parts, I guess, than I would have before." He turned his attention back to Melanie. "But mostly, I feel like I finally 'get' it."

"Get what?" Melanie asked.

"The magic of theme parks," Gregory answered. "I've seen it at Lands, but we've been so focused on the budget and Under the Waves and all the business of running it that I haven't appreciated it properly. Not since Charlotte showed me the ropes, really. But here, I don't have to worry about any of those parts and I can take in how much people are enjoying themselves and escaping. Even from only a day in the parks, I can see why working for DreamUs and being a part of giving this much joy to so many people is appealing."

Gregory put his hand on Charlotte's knee under the table as he said the part about DreamUs. He hadn't shared any of that with Charlotte yet and she found it moving and sweet. She'd have to make sure to show him how much she appreciated it later.

They continued discussing the highlights of Gregory and Charlotte's trip and before long, their food arrived and they swapped slices of pizza and divided salads and pasta in order to try more things. Melanie had trained Charlotte in the art of maximizing ordering.

"We've been talking a lot," Gregory said as they dug in. "Melanie, Charlotte tells me you used to be a pastry chef in Europe."

Charlotte focused on the slice of prosciutto-and-basil pizza in front of her to hide her wince. Gregory had dived right in with the most sensitive possible subject, though he had no way of knowing that. She looked up and mouthed a "Sorry" at Melanie.

Melanie shook her head almost imperceptibly, letting Charlotte know it was okay. "I was," she said, putting down her fork. "It feels like another life. I went to culinary school right after high school and trained under some talented chefs— talented chefs with giant egos. I moved around restaurants and got stuck in this cycle of competition for no good reason and eventually the stress got to me. It got to the point where I didn't like anything about baking anymore. Once upon a time, coming up with new desserts and perfecting recipes was my refuge.

"I was excellent at my job," she continued, "but it wasn't worth my mental health, which started to affect my physical health, too. Truly there are not enough kind or chill people in fine dining kitchens. So I came back home to Orlando—my mom was not and is still not thrilled with that choice—and cheered myself up with coming to Dreamland and the other parks. Once I realized how amazing the food is, I started my own site focused on reviews and recommendations."

"She's not selling herself well," Charlotte said. "Melanie's crushing it. She has her site, an incredible social media presence, and theme parks around the world reaching out to hire her as a consultant."

"Like Lands," Gregory said. "I'm surprised Charlotte hasn't tried to wrangle you to come work for Lands full-time."

"Oh, she has." Melanie grinned. "She got Emily ready to offer me a job and everything. But I wasn't ready, am not ready, to run a kitchen again. I did recommend Holly, however."

"You did," Charlotte confirmed, "and she's been terrific. But I'll just say, the door is always open. You have so much to offer Lands and there's always a place for you."

Charlotte meant those words; Melanie would bring a whole new energy to the park staff. Besides, Uncle Frank *adored* Mel and they'd bonded when she consulted for the park. Charlotte also thought how nice it would be to know

Mel was there overseeing things after Under the Waves opened and after Charlotte was gone.

"I'll keep that in mind," Melanie said. "Oh my gosh, kind of related, Charlotte, I have to tell you about who's back in town."

Charlotte leaned in. "Who? Tell me!"

"Riley," Melanie said.

"Like, *Riley* Riley?"

"Do we know another Riley?"

Charlotte couldn't believe Melanie's ex and onetime professional rival was back. It had sounded like he was entrenched in his life in Italy.

"I can't believe you didn't text me!" Charlotte scolded.

"I only found out a couple of days ago because I read about him opening a new restaurant nearby in the paper."

This was not good. "Okay, Mel, we have to discuss this in depth tomorrow."

Gregory was leaving a day ahead of Charlotte so she could have some one-on-one time with her best friend.

"Yes, please," Melanie said. "But now let's talk about dessert. We can share a couple things."

Gregory looked at Charlotte. "We're not going on any motion-intensive rides today, are we?"

"We don't have to," she replied.

"Then I'm in for dessert," Gregory said.

The rest of the meal passed in easy conversation, Gregory and Melanie getting along wonderfully. Charlotte hadn't known that was important to her until she experienced a sense of relief. Lord knew she'd sent Melanie no shortage of texts complaining about Gregory, but Melanie saw through it all along.

They lingered outside the restaurant after they'd paid and Melanie told Gregory about some treats from the caramel-focused store down the path that would travel well. Then she turned to Charlotte.

"I'll see you tomorrow. We have a lot to talk about," Melanie said and then hugged Charlotte tightly. Melanie dropped her voice and said, "You look maybe more relaxed than I've ever seen you and I need details."

"Deal," Charlotte whispered back.

Melanie waggled her eyebrows at Charlotte. She leaned over to shake Gregory's hand. "I'm glad I finally got to meet you."

"Likewise," he said.

Then Melanie pulled Gregory in for a hug, clearly surprising him. She must have whispered something to him because Gregory's face went serious, and he nodded.

They waved goodbye and Charlotte led Gregory toward a chill boat ride. "What was that about?" she asked, cocking her head toward Melanie's departing form.

"Hmm?" Gregory blinked a couple of times. "Oh, that. She said she was happy for us and that I'd better treat you in a manner you deserve and that if I don't, she'll destroy all my spreadsheets."

Charlotte guffawed. "If anyone could figure out a way to do that, it would be Melanie. Just so you know."

Gregory reached for her hand and tugged Charlotte toward an alcove off the path. He faced her, hands on her arms and smiled. "I have no intention of losing my spreadsheets, Charlotte. I want to give this, us, a chance and see what happens."

Charlotte's mind spun thinking of all the ways it could go wrong between them and possibly affect Lands of Legend's continuing existence. She couldn't put her family's business on the line. Besides, she'd had firsthand experience mixing business and pleasure and it hadn't gone well. But if she left for Paris, they wouldn't be colleagues anymore. She looked down, very interested in the scuffed toes of her theme park–

tested sneakers, figuring out how to say what she wanted to say.

"I really like you, Gregory. It turns out I have for a while, but I've been trying to ignore those feelings."

"Me too, I think. I didn't want to—"

"No, let me finish. You know about what happened at DreamUs. With Chad. I am not saying I think you're like him. I trust you," Charlotte said, finding the last words to be truer than she'd believed. "But there's a lot at stake for my family with Lands and I can't put all of them at risk. Though I am planning to leave after Under the Waves."

Gregory let his arms drop. "I see. I shouldn't have assumed."

"No, you shouldn't have. I mean, yes, you should have. Just come here, would you?" Charlotte grabbed him around the waist and hugged tight. She could feel his muscles tense.

"If you would have let me finish," she said, lightly poking his side, "I was going to say I also want to give us a chance. But I want to set some boundaries, I guess, about the park and make sure our work there will be okay, whatever's going on with us."

Gregory relaxed. "Note to self: Let Charlotte finish talking before jumping to conclusions."

"Mmm-hmm, good idea."

"That sounds reasonable to me. There's a lot riding on Lands for your family and mine. We can't let this fully distract us."

"I think *some* distraction is good," Charlotte countered. "Probably healthy. We both work too much, you know?"

She wrapped her arms around his neck and brushed his lips with hers, intending it to be a sweet and gentle kiss. But the sensation spurred a reaction in both of them and while Charlotte let herself get carried away during the fireworks last night, she didn't want to do the same in the bright afternoon with many people passing by.

Gregory broke the kiss first anyway. "Distractions. Yes, some are good. Like now—maybe we can find some distractions back at the hotel instead of doing more rides today?"

Charlotte put her hand to her chest. "Gregory. Are you saying we should skip research and 'work' and go to our room? Because I agree."

His lips spread wide, his lone crooked tooth the first to appear in his smile. "Who are we, even?"

"I don't know," Charlotte said, "but I'm a fan."

Chapter 28

Charlotte leaned against Gregory, savoring how nice it was to be able to do something so simple and how much she liked having him to lean on. She hadn't known how much she was craving that. They sat on a bench by the hotel's porte cochere, waiting for the shuttle that would take Gregory to the airport. Charlotte sighed, not ready for him to leave. She was more bummed than anyone should be when they were this close to Dreamland, but she wasn't ready to say goodbye to Gregory—no, more accurately she wasn't ready to let go of this trip with Gregory, this moment when they'd discovered their feelings for each other. And also spent hours exploring each other's bodies. She'd see him tomorrow, sure, but it would be back in Ohio and back to work and all that came with it—including her family and how they would tell them about their new relationship, and if they would care. Also Charlotte lived in her parents' basement and as private as the space was, she felt weird about inviting Gregory over.

It was all going to be different, Charlotte thought, but maybe in a good way. They were both committed to seeing where things went. Changes were afoot, and historically speaking, she had a hard time with change.

As if sensing her distress, Gregory squeezed her hand. "I realized I didn't ask what you and Melanie have planned for today."

Thinking about her time with Melanie was the perfect topic to reanimate Charlotte.

"So much! Let me open the list on my phone." She swiped and tapped, pulling up her beloved list-making app. "First, we're going on a roller-coaster crawl to hit all our favorites in the parks. Mel doesn't care for Wonder World's coasters but over here at Dreamland, most of the coasters aren't too bananas."

"Still," Gregory said, "now I see why you didn't eat much breakfast."

"That and . . . well, we were kinda otherwise occupied," Charlotte admitted.

Gregory kissed her cheek. "True. Sorry for interrupting, please continue."

Charlotte glanced at the app. "Then we're taking a break from the parks to drive out of town a bit to get some perfect, giant cookies. I'll bring some back with me, don't worry. And to wrap up the day, we'll come back here and use the monorail to stop at hotels with the best bars on property."

"That's a lot to do in one day," Gregory said. "Even for someone as efficient as you. I'm impressed."

"Melanie and I are pros at this point. Our visits always end up being shorter than we'd like so we've learned to optimize our schedules and also do activities that give us plenty of time to catch up and talk," Charlotte explained. As much as she texted and chatted with Melanie, nothing compared to spending time in person with her best friend. Excitement for spending the whole day with her best friend quickly overrode any glum thoughts she had about Gregory leaving.

The shuttle arrived and they stood up.

"Any big plans after you get home today?" she asked.

"I'm going to go to the park after I drop off my things and unpack. I have some ideas I want to put into my models and have them ready to share with you when you're back."

"You could take the rest of the day off, you know. Do some exploring around Columbus, maybe?" Charlotte suggested.

"I have a better idea. How about I come pick you up at the airport tomorrow so you don't have to deal with that and then we can go to Stauf's and The Book Loft?"

Gregory *had* been paying attention to Charlotte all along. She'd only mentioned those places to him a couple of times. Thoughtfulness like that was definitely one of Charlotte's love languages.

"That sounds perfect," she said. "I'll see you then." They kissed and she waved goodbye, then returned to the empty hotel room, maybe lingering over the pillow Gregory had used and breathing in the woodsy smell. It had been beyond satisfying to wrap herself in that scent—and in his arms. Charlotte shook her whole body, as if to expel the heady emotions inside her. It was time to finish getting ready for her day with Mel.

Charlotte carried two iced coffees in the largest possible size to a bench next to the entrance for Canyon Frontier Railroad, its large pastel rocks reminiscent of the hoodoos in Bryce Canyon National Park reaching into the sky behind her. This early in the day the line wasn't too long, so they'd need to finish their coffees before they entered the queue since the drinks could not ride the coaster with them.

Melanie strolled into view, a paper bag with her half of their first snack: a Flaky Delight. Leave it to DreamUs chefs to concoct the best version of the croissant-doughnut treat that Charlotte had ever eaten.

Charlotte stood and when Melanie got close enough, she pulled her friend into a hug.

"You know you could have put the coffee down first," Melanie chuckled. Charlotte still had one cup in each hand.

"Put the coffee *down*? Never," Charlotte said.

Settling on the bench and swapping an iced coffee for a cronut, Melanie took a loud sip of her drink. "Ah, that's better. Okay. Now, Charlotte. Tell me everything."

Charlotte grinned as she filled in her friend on everything that had happened since she and Gregory kissed during the fireworks.

"I knew it would happen," Melanie insisted. "I didn't bring it up *too* much since you've been kind of busy and also kind of frequently annoyed with him, but it was only a matter of time."

Charlotte raised her eyebrows. "Ha! You brought it up enough!"

"I just want you to be happy; it's what you deserve after stupid Chad. You need some more nonwork joy in your life—though I guess Gregory is extremely connected to your work. How's that going? Or how's it gonna go? Especially with your DreamUs application out there."

As usual, Melanie had homed in on Charlotte's biggest anxieties about all of it. Charlotte took the lid off her cup and took a fortifying gulp of chilled coffee.

"That's a good question." Charlotte talked it out, working through it with herself as much as with Melanie. "Everything about our relationship or whatever you want to call it has been entwined with Lands and will be for a little while. He's been receptive to a lot of my suggestions and he takes his work seriously. The pressure he puts on himself for his family, mostly his brother Ian, is really something. Family baggage. Always a thing."

"That sounds familiar. Your family is the best except for Emily, but Lands and all the expectations that come with it and all your memories of it, that all counts as baggage, too.

'Baggage' isn't always negative. It's the accumulation of memories and obligations and things you carry around with you."

"When you put it that way," Charlotte acknowledged, "I can't argue with that. Gregory's brother has a lot of similar traits to Emily's—for example, I already told you they both went to the same business school. Gregory's trying to do his best for Ever Fund, even if he doesn't want to stay there and I can see he cares for Lands. I think working at Lands has given him back a part of himself he locked away. He wants Lands to succeed for his company and for my aunt and uncle—"

"And for you," Melanie added.

"Okay, and for me. I do worry he'll see appeal in this Peak Fusion offer, and maybe I'm wrong to question it if Frank and Marianne are still considering it."

"It's not like IPs are automatically bad. Think about all the cool rides we love that exist because of IPs."

"I know, but I can't tell if anyone wants it for Lands beyond money reasons. Which are potentially valid. But if an addition like a whole *Heroic Patrol* area is what it takes to make Lands long-lasting, would it even be Lands anymore? I wish they'd wait for Under the Waves to open and *then* evaluate things before making a decision like this," Charlotte said.

"So if Gregory were to get on board with Peak Fusion, what happens with you two continuing to do whatever you're doing?"

"I don't know," Charlotte admitted. "It's so new, like brand-new, we haven't put any labels on anything, but we've said we both want to see where it goes."

That implied a relationship, didn't it? Charlotte thought so. Certainly more than only being friends and coworkers with benefits. But Melanie had a point. If her working relationship with Gregory faced any roadblocks, it could all implode. She said as much to her friend.

"Yeah, it might," Melanie said. "But it might not. Mostly what I wanted to get at is to tell you to try not to let your fear get in the way, and to remember that relationships need dedication and attention."

Charlotte looked away, remembering how she'd let her obsession with her work get in the way of so many relationships with friends and family in the past. Thought about her lack of friends in Los Angeles despite her years there. How she'd worked hard since she met Melanie to give Mel the attention and love she deserved but still failed sometimes. How Melanie had experience in a relationship with a partner who thought working with her in a kitchen counted as spending time with her.

"I appreciate the advice and the reminder," she told Melanie. "I know you've lived that with Riley. Speaking of! He's opening a restaurant here and he didn't bother to tell you?"

"Eh, he might have tried. I've had his number blocked." Melanie shrugged.

"Blocked? I didn't realize the most recent break-up was that bad."

Her friend studied her cup's paper straw like it was the only thing in the world. "It wasn't, not really, but I didn't trust myself not to reach back out, and we both needed a break from that cycle. We always ended up in the same place: me heartbroken, him still focused on his career in Italy."

Charlotte touched Melanie's knee. "Do you think that cycle could change with him opening a place here?"

Melanie leaned her head back to rest it on the top of the bench. "I don't know, Charlotte. I can't seem to keep my head straight when it comes to anything involving Riley. I guess I could start with unblocking his number and sending him a message. Maybe."

"Only if you feel like it, Mel."

"I know, I know." Melanie drained the rest of her coffee.

"I think I'd rather that than somehow run into him somewhere. I'm going to think about it."

"I'm here for whatever you decide, and if you need back-up, okay?"

Melanie nodded. "Thank you."

"Now, how about we get in the line for Canyon Frontier Railroad and start our day while you catch me up on all things Mel. I want to hear about your consulting gig for that theme park in Tennessee."

"Oh, that. This line isn't long enough to cover it." Melanie laughed and grimaced at the same time. "But let's see how far I can get."

Working around lines and occasionally using the park's paid LinePass system meant Charlotte and Melanie made it through their roller-coaster crawl in record time, even with posing for increasingly ridiculous photos with the signs in front of every coaster. High-fiving after their last ride and plopping onto a bench in the shade, Charlotte and Melanie sprawled their limbs dramatically.

"We did it!" Melanie exclaimed.

"We sure did. I hate admitting it, but I feel like maybe my body doesn't process riding that many roller coasters in a row as well anymore," Charlotte said. Even with breaks between the coasters to walk, wait in line, and travel between parks to get to the next one, her bones had had enough high-speed twists and turns and hills for the day.

"Honestly, same," Melanie replied. "None of these coasters were as intense as Cosmic Catastrophe Coaster—that's the only reason I could do a whole roller-coaster crawl with you—but all of them together add up. Maybe next time we do a chill-ride crawl and only go on . . . I'm thinking gentle boat rides. "

"Yes, one thousand percent, yes," Charlotte said. "Still, if

I'm gonna be this exhausted and very mildly nauseated, I'm glad it's with you."

"Likewise, friend," Melanie said.

Charlotte glanced at her watch to check her step count, so she could be unreasonably proud of herself for it, and saw she'd missed a text from Gregory letting her know he'd landed safely. He'd sent her dozens of texts and emails as a work friend, usually nitpicking over some small detail or maybe sharing a font he thought would be perfect for a sign in Under the Waves, but this was the first text during this next stage—whatever it was—for them and it made Charlotte unexpectedly swoony. She sighed happily.

"You okay over there?" Melanie asked.

Charlotte pulled out her phone in response and showed her the text. Melanie looked at her questioningly. "And you're happy he made it back?"

Charlotte explained why the message touched her and Melanie widened her eyes and patted Charlotte's hand. "Oh babes, you're in for it, aren't you?"

Charlotte shook her head no. She was in denial, reluctant to give what she was feeling power by acknowledging it, but she knew Melanie was right. As usual. Charlotte told her as much. The feelings she'd had for Chad could be called fondness with some intense attraction. Their relationship had never kindled anything like this.

Melanie nodded and said without a trace of arrogance, "I know I'm right. You deserve happiness and only the best. Just do your best to keep your love for Lands of Legend separate from your whatever for Gregory. Business, family, dating all wrapped together should come with a warning sign, so that's what I'm being: a talking warning sign, telling you to guard your heart above all, okay?"

Charlotte turned Melanie's advice over in her mind and thought she could manage everything, or at least try to. She leaned in to hug her friend, grateful to have someone at her side who would always tell her what's what—even if it wasn't something she wanted to hear.

"Why are you the best, Mel?"

"I *am* pretty terrific, aren't I? And I'll continue being terrific by driving us to get obscenely massive cookies. Sound good?"

"Absolutely yes," Charlotte answered and interlocked her arm with Melanie's as they walked out of the park. Today, she would enjoy hanging out with her friend. Tomorrow, she would return to a reality balancing the new, dazzling thing developing between her and Gregory, the nonstop to-dos for Under the Waves, and her possible return to DreamUs—a return she was starting to feel less sure about the more she considered this new thing with Gregory.

Chapter 29

"You were not joking about the cookies," Gregory said, his eyes wide as he approached the island in the Lands of Legend office kitchen, where Charlotte had made a decorative spread of the six almost half-pound cookies she'd brought back in one of her carry-on bags.

"Gregory, I never joke about food. Especially dessert. You should know that by now." She winked at him and then swiveled her head around the space to make sure no one had seen. They still had to figure out how to act at work.

Gregory raised an eyebrow and came up next to Charlotte, brushing his fingers along the back of her hand. "No one's here yet. Kind of nice that the office is empty."

"Oh, hmm, that's interesting."

"It is, isn't it?" He leaned down and gently pressed his lips to hers, and Charlotte grabbed his tie and pulled him closer. They'd been existing in a content bubble since he'd picked her up at the airport yesterday; he even parked and came into wait at arrivals instead of retrieving her from the curb like a piece of luggage. He gave her what, as far as she could tell, was one of his dearest gifts to share with another person: time.

Their trip to Dreamland had knocked something loose be-tween them, like the last rock that needed to fall in order for the avalanche to sweep down the mountain. It was the sex, yes—dear God, was it the sex—but also another layer of intimacy. Hours of working together, arguing, and talking about their families in the last couple of months had brought them closer than Charlotte realized. It was all so comfortable, so quickly. Gregory smiling at her in the airport. Going with her to The Book Loft and winding through its many small rooms stuffed with books. Then sitting down with her at her second-favorite Stauf's location, the one in what used to be a church, the colored light filtering through the stained-glass window making his eyes look like green suncatcher crystals.

After a perfect morning of hanging out and holding hands, they'd decided to take the rest of the day off—aside from checking emails a couple of times since the Under the Waves opening was ten weeks away and every little thing needed to be addressed in a timely manner. Gregory dropped Charlotte at home, where she didn't invite him in because Dad was around and she wasn't ready for anyone else to know about their change in relationship status. Her parents had met Gregory when they swung by the park one afternoon last month when they'd wrapped up work early. They'd wanted to see how Under the Waves construction was coming along *and*, Charlotte suspected, they wanted to meet Gregory and see what he was about. Since then, they'd made comments about how he seemed to be a "nice enough young man" more than once—usually the morning after Charlotte and Gregory's standing weekly visit to The Dragon's Breath.

So, to avoid too many questions, she'd left Gregory's car, tossed her bags in her space, given Madmartigan many pets and treats, showered and changed, grabbed her laptop, and headed to Gregory's place.

The perfect morning turned into a perfect day as they nestled side by side on his plush couch to check emails and discuss business and then moved to his even more plush bed to discuss a different kind of business. Charlotte had eventually left to go home for dinner and Madmartigan snuggles, reluctance dogging her steps.

They hadn't discussed what to say or do while at work, so when Charlotte now heard the office door open downstairs, she pulled away from the kiss, instead standing on her tiptoes to whisper into Gregory's ear. "I know all the best, secret places to make out in the park, just saying."

Gregory chuckled and whispered back. "Yes, but *how* do you know them?"

Charlotte relaxed her feet and stood flat. She smirked. "I did grow up here as a teenager. Now, pick a cookie before everyone else comes up. I recommend the Eternal Flame, it's seasonal and the blend of spices is . . ." She blew a chef's kiss to indicate how exquisite that blend was.

"Sold. I'll take a quarter of it."

Charlotte fake-gasped as she walked to the other side of the island for cutlery and plates. "When people bring doughnuts into the office, you cut them in half, don't you?"

"Charlotte, these are half-pound cookies! My blood vessels will explode if I eat that much sugar at once." He hesitated. "And yes, I do cut doughnuts in half."

"I knew it!" Charlotte said.

"Knew what?" Emily asked as she walked into the open space.

"Gregory cuts communal office doughnuts in half," Charlotte said in an accusatory tone.

Emily rolled her eyes. "Of course he does! He probably uses a fork too, so he doesn't make a mess. Uh, no offense, Gregory."

"Why would I take offense at being tidy and not getting flakes of doughnut glaze on my tie?"

"You're right, we should all aspire to this," Emily replied. Gregory's head was down as he cut a triangle of cookie and Emily made a "can you believe this guy?" face at Charlotte, who couldn't contain a snort. She and her cousin didn't often joke together as adults, and for a second, it reminded Charlotte of how close they were when they were little, and how much she had looked up to her cousin.

Gregory caught her staring. "What?"

Charlotte pressed her lips together. "Nothing! Hey, Emily, I brought back Divine D's, please help yourself to more than a quarter of a cookie."

Cookies made perfect peace offerings, and Emily loved sweets almost as much as Charlotte. "That won't be a problem. I see a peanut butter crunch and it's all mine. I love a cookie so giant I can eat it all day long."

Hey, they still had that one thing in common.

"So, I saw some emails about electric-line shenanigans while we were gone. How's that going?" Charlotte asked.

Emily put her chosen cookie on a plate and started pushing buttons on the espresso machine. "It's going. The Manta is going to require a lot of juice so we're going back and forth about adjustments to the power grid."

At that, Gregory straightened. Emily saw and held up her hand. "I know you have a million questions popping into your head, Gregory, but I need to have a few calls this morning, and then I can let you know if it's going to require more time or money."

He nodded.

"Now," Emily said, "I want to hear about Dreamland. I'm sure Charlotte was the best possible tour guide. Did you have any epiphanies about theme parks?"

Charlotte wasn't able to stop the warmth spreading up her neck, probably turning it an incriminating pink hue. Emily couldn't have known about her and Gregory's mutual epiphany about each other, but the question felt loaded, so Charlotte leaned into it. "Yeah, Gregory, any particularly memorable moments jump to mind?"

The delight of making Gregory squirm mitigated the blush burning her skin.

"Uh, several." He busied himself with looking for a mug in the cupboard. "I, uh, was really moved by the fireworks."

"You know," Emily commented, "you don't strike me as a person who would be into fireworks."

"I'm, uh, not normally. But something about these fireworks were special."

Charlotte bent her head down and smiled. "We did have the perfect viewing spot," she added. "That makes a big difference."

"Okayyy, so you were both really into the fireworks. What else?" Emily asked. If only she knew *how* into fireworks they were, Charlotte thought.

"Well, I haven't walked so much in a single day in a while, if ever, and the rides were all impressive—except for the Twisting Teacups."

"Yeah, I'm still sorry about that," Charlotte said.

"I recovered eventually. But besides that one, I enjoyed the rides and seeing all the thought put into the story and details. And while that was all enlightening, what I found most educational and wonderful was the guests."

"How so?" Charlotte asked.

"Everyone at the park was making memories. I could tell they were experiencing the world around them, soaking it in. I was struck by the moments of joy, big and little, happening all around us: The kid crying happy tears hugging that costumed bear character; the group of friends passing a box of popcorn back and forth while laughing; and Charlotte, remember that cute couple we talked to, celebrating their twentieth wedding anniversary at the parks because they always had so much fun when they visited? Then there was that mom we met on the bus bringing her baby for the first time and talking about how it transformed the parks for her. Sure, some kids threw temper tantrums and some people were impolite, but the guests are what made it magic."

Charlotte felt moisture in her eyes. She and Gregory had reviewed his mental notes at his place yesterday and blue-skied about some aspects of Dreamland he thought they could maybe incorporate into Lands of Legend, but he hadn't told her all of that. She'd lost touch with the most important part of creating a theme park and Gregory had just reminded her that it was always about the guests.

"Wow, you've been listening to Charlotte, haven't you?" And with that comment, Emily pulled Charlotte out of her reverie.

"I can't take credit for that," Charlotte said, blinking the tears back into her eyes where they belonged. "Gregory got there all on his own."

Emily changed the subject, starting in on construction updates, and when Charlotte looked away to top off her coffee, Gregory mouthed to her, "Are you okay?"

Charlotte nodded. She was better than okay.

Chapter 30

The next week melted into a productive haze peppered with meetings, wrangling utilities, and wandering around Lands with Gregory. Their walks continued to start with them checking on the progress of construction in Under the Waves and giving notes, but now they tended to end with Charlotte leading him into an out-of-the-way corner where she could bury her fingers in his soft hair and drag him close. She could no longer pretend she was going to maintain any kind of work-and-dating line. This rush of sentiment and happiness with Gregory defied logic and lists. It was worth chasing.

They'd make their new status public soon since Charlotte didn't like keeping secrets from her family, but for now, it was only theirs and she liked it that way. It didn't keep her from testing Gregory's poker face during meetings when she'd sneak in an occasional knee squeeze. If she didn't stop, her aunt and uncle were going to ask why Gregory had developed a twitch in his face. At least they could blame it on stress. Even in the brief time since they'd been back, Charlotte and Gregory had addressed one problem after another—everything from conversations with the municipality about the additional load on the power grid that Emily had mentioned, to a delayed delivery of concrete stamps Charlotte wanted to use to add a permanent scavenger hunt element to the land, to putting off giving an answer about Peak Fusion to Emily and Ian for one more day. The phone calls, pages over the walkie-talkies, and emails never ended. They closed each day exhausted, and Charlotte wished they could go back to the Dreamland bubble and never leave.

But not really. The work might be draining, but she took pride in it. Still, as she ran through her day's list while lounging in her own bed one morning after they got back from Dreamland, Charlotte had to remind herself that adoring the work didn't mean it should be her whole life.

To that end, she closed her list app and opened her messages.

Charlotte: Hey, want to wrap up work at a reasonable hour later today and have a picnic?

Three dots appeared immediately.

Gregory: Picnics. Eating food on the ground on purpose?

She scoffed.

Charlotte: That's typically how it works.
Gregory: I know.
Gregory: I'm teasing. I love a picnic.
Gregory: Where did you have in mind?
Charlotte: A small clearing in the state park we hiked at.
Gregory: That we walked at.
Charlotte: Fine. WALKED at.

Charlotte: The spring ephemerals are in bloom now too.
Gregory: Charlotte.
Charlotte: Hmm?

Gregory: You cannot casually drop the words "spring ephemerals" in texts and expect me to contain myself around you later.

When they were at The Book Loft, Charlotte had gotten him a book on Ohio's native wildflowers, and he'd been sharing fun facts with her ever since. His sincere glee over the flowers blooming right now was so sweet.

Charlotte: I learned from the best.

Gregory: 😊

Charlotte: See you at work soon. We have the latest attendance projection numbers to review.
Gregory: I can think of a lot of things we have to review.

Madmartigan stepped onto her chest, somehow channeling every bit of his mass into two paws pressing on her sternum. He rubbed his face against her phone and pushed it out of the way. She let him settle and welcomed the excuse to stay in bed a little longer.

She headed to the office around midmorning in a leisurely mood, dropping off a cup of coffee to Owen and detouring to wind through Forgotten Beasts while she sipped a coffee of her own. The early spring air was crisp this early in the day with a light breeze rustling through the branches, so completely perfect she wished she could bottle it.

When she got to her desk, she opened her laptop, logged in, and then cracked open the nearby window. Her eyes scanned over the subjects of her still-loading emails: Under the Waves graphics, a storage bill, Dreamland Paris.

No, she thought, one of these things is *not* like the others. She stopped skimming and focused, opening her eyes wide enough to displace a contact lens. The beginning-of-March deadline had passed, and she hadn't bugged Chad for fear of coming across as needy. But now? Now Chad was finally getting back to her? The timing.

She needed more coffee before she faced whatever her ex had to say about her job application.

As she dumped out the dregs of the pot someone had started earlier it the morning—her uncle, if she had to guess by the potent and bitter smell—she heard her new favorite voice.

"Thank God someone else is making the coffee," Gregory said from behind her. "Frank is a hell of a nice guy, but his coffee-grounds-to-water ratio leaves much to be desired."

"You're telling me," Charlotte said as she stood on her tip-toes to reach the filters.

Gregory reached above her and handed a filter down. "Allow me. I'll also move them to a place that doesn't require a step stool to access."

"Thank you," she said as she took it. "You know, there's always the option of *not* drinking the coffee when Uncle Frank makes it."

"Nah, I don't want to offend him," Gregory said. "Plus even terrible coffee is still coffee. It's nothing a little—no, a lot—of half-and-half can't fix. But enough coffee talk."

"Mmmhmm." Gregory stood in front of her and leaned toward her, placing one hand on either side of her on the counter. Charlotte looked down to each side.

"Wow, you really *were* turned on by me mentioning wild-flowers." she said.

He answered by dipping his head down and pressing his lips against her neck right behind her ear. The feel of his breath had Charlotte arching into the kiss and he had his hands on her bottom in a second, lifting her onto the counter. She wound her arms around his torso and pressed against him while he trailed kisses around the base of her neck and collarbone. But the line of heat igniting along her skin brought Chad's email to the front of her mind. That could mean the end of moments like this.

She couldn't make out with him with this on her mind. Breathless, she said, "Gregory, I support this uncharacteristically impulsive behavior, but let's save it for later."

He paused and nodded. "You're right. Not here." His voice was a growl. "Later." He kissed her forehead.

Charlotte hoped for many laters but knew it might depend on Chad's email. She'd once been so excited to get a reply about the possible job, but now she was afraid to open it. Afraid of the decision she'd have to make.

Chapter 31

Charlotte thought about Chad's email all day, through meetings and a dozen other competing priorities for Lands. While it loomed large in her mind, Charlotte was and wasn't ready to open it, so she told herself she was waiting for a distraction-free moment. That finally came toward the end of the day when she was waiting for Gregory to finish a call in his office.

To: charlotte@landsoflegend.com
From: csandusky@dreamus.com
Re: Dreamland Paris

Charlotte,
I'm sorry it's taken me so long to follow up with you. It's been crazy busy with the move and elopement and getting things going here. Early construction is underway already! Your application finally got through all the right channels and back to me for next steps—you know how long things can take here.

I think you'd make a great addition to the team. I'd love to offer you the Creative Executive position

here for Dreamland Paris. That is, if you're not too
busy with Lands of Legend.

Let me know when you want to talk more about
the job.

-C

There it was. Exactly the opportunity she'd been waiting for.

When she'd run into Chad at the opening of Cosmic Catastrophe at Wonder World, she'd been beyond irritated when
he said he would be heading up the Dreamland Paris portfolio. She could admit some of that had been jealousy. And
now he'd offered her exactly what she'd been wanting. If it
was still what she wanted.

All the emotions she had when she chased her job at
DreamUs the first time years ago crashed to the front of her
mind. It felt like she was at the same crossroads. Once again
choosing between her family park with its beautiful but small
footprint or DreamUs, where she could collaborate with the
most respected and talented minds in the world of immersive
entertainment and reach millions with her work, every bell
and whistle at her disposal.

Not every part of the equation was the same. DreamUs
had laid her off once. She did, on some level, understand it
was an unfortunate business decision, but it had still felt like
a betrayal. Plus how would her family react this time around?
What would happen here after Under the Waves if her aunt
and uncle retired and Emily was in charge?

"I'm shutting down my laptop now, I promise," Gregory's
voice called out.

And then there was Gregory.

Gregory, who'd come into her life not knowing what a
theme park was, never having been on a roller coaster but

who, despite being far out of his element, kept his mind open, who took notes whenever Charlotte or her family answered his many questions, who was slowly rediscovering and reclaiming himself.

Gregory, who she was pretty sure she was falling for. Had fallen for?

"I'm ready! Sorry about the wait." Gregory closed his office door and leaned down to kiss her on the forehead. "What is that smile about?"

She took his hand in hers. "Come closer and I'll tell you."

Gregory's eyes sparkled as brought his ear closer to her lips, and Charlotte changed her mind about saying anything and turned to kiss him. She didn't want to ruin their picnic when she hadn't made a decision about anything yet.

"Let's go. I'm going to grab a bag from the fridge, and I'll follow you home—but in a less creepy way than that sounded."

"You can follow me home anytime, Charlotte."

Charlotte parked beside Gregory outside his place and then transferred picnic supplies to his car while he went to change. With snacks and wine nestled into their proper places in the picnic basket she'd borrowed from her parents, she went to place it in the backseat. A green file folder that must have escaped Gregory's briefcase—the honest-to-God briefcase he carried every day, the adorable nerd—was in the way. She picked it up, intending to take it inside to him, but a gust of wind caught the papers.

"Shit!" she exclaimed, and chased them around the driveway to collect them.

Charlotte wasn't trying to read anything but then the words "Heroic Patrol" jumped at her from a label on the folder. It was an unresolved topic despite pressure from Peak Fusion to let them know what was going on, but Charlotte didn't know why Gregory would have a whole folder on it.

Unless things had progressed. And the label was in Emily's handwriting. Her chest grew tight; her gut dropped to her toenails. She glanced at the door to Gregory's place, then back at the folder, and decided to ask him about it before she flipped through its contents.

"Gregory," she called as she poked her head in the door.

"Sorry, two more minutes and I'm ready."

She followed the sound of his voice to his kitchen, where he was digging through his pantry. "I have the perfect bottle of wine in here somewhere."

"Gregory," she repeated in a quiet voice. "I need to ask you something."

"Here it is!" He held out the bottle. "Do you need to ask me if I have a wine opener because obviously—"

He stopped in his tracks when he saw the green folder she was holding.

"You left this in the car," she said. "I moved it to put the picnic basket down and was going to bring it in, then wind happened, and it has Emily's handwriting on it. Can you just tell me you haven't been having separate conversations about Peak Fusion?"

Gregory set the bottle of wine on the kitchen counter and closed his eyes.

"Gregory?" Charlotte didn't like how her voice had gotten small.

"I can't. I mean, we have," Gregory said as he looked down at his feet.

Charlotte paced to the other side of the island, needing to put distance between them and flexed her fists. His reaction spurred her to open the folder. The top piece of paper was concept art putting *Heroic Patrol*'s superpowered mermaid, Scylla, right into the Atlantis dark ride in Under the Waves, sticking out like a sore thumb. This was different from shoving *Heroic Patrol* off into its own corner, and she hadn't been the biggest fan of *that* option. Were they selling Lands to

Peak Fusion? What was this about? Outrage rose in her like the temperature increasing in a thermometer; she tracked its progress and grounded herself by pressing her fingertips on the kitchen island's surface, the granite a cool balm. But this was a sticky anger, the kind she knew from after Chad cheated on her. It settled under your skin in a way you could feel and added an edge to your voice, ready to jump out at any moment and attack whoever set off the slightest trigger. Right now that was Gregory, who, like Chad, had also betrayed her.

She held up the art to Gregory, only to uncover another piece that had the superhero team's talking dog sitting in Forgotten Beasts. "What. The. Fuck, Gregory? I thought you were on my side."

Gregory folded his arms and sighed. "I *am* on your side, Charlotte, but you're not the only stakeholder here. I have to think about the park's owners and the person who will be staying around to run things. You're not even planning to stay! And I'm the one responsible for the return on my family's investment. Me, as Ian recently reminded me."

His grumpy and firm tone took Charlotte back to their early disagreements. "So that's it? Ian pushes you around and you give in? When did you even have time to talk about this?!"

"That's not fair, Charlotte. He and Emily were moving forward without everyone again because they thought we were taking too long. I inserted myself so there was a voice of reason. I would never let them put whatever this talking dog is named in Forgotten Beasts."

"But you'd let them throw *Heroic Patrol* into Under the Waves?"

"If it's what Frank and Marianne agree to, then yes."

Charlotte pushed away from the counter and rolled a scrunchie off her wrist into her hair; she was overheating from fury and felt like she was on the edge of a panic attack.

"You didn't answer my question, Gregory. When did you have time to discuss this?"

He looked at the ceiling and closed his eyes. "The other day."

"After Dreamland? After this?" She gestured her hand back and forth between them.

"Yes, after Dreamland." His voice became a whisper. "After us."

Gregory shook his head. "I'm sorry for keeping you in the dark, but give me some credit, Charlotte. After all this time together, do you think I don't care about Lands of Legend's success—your family's success? Especially when I know how much you care about this place? We all want this park to stay open for years to come."

"Business decisions aside, this is a discussion I've been excluded from despite how upset you were about Emily leaving us out of Peak Fusion conversations before."

"I-I know," Gregory sputtered, "but we all thought you might have this sort of reaction, and I wanted to jump in and mitigate what I could before telling you what Emily and Ian had been up to."

The words hit Charlotte like a slap and while a tiny rational part of her understood their hesitation given how she had reacted, this was not a moment to be rational. Her voice got louder. " 'We' all thought? As in, all of you just assumed I'd melt down instead of acting like an adult. I care, too. Yes, the idea of a *Heroic Patrol* logo near Lands of Legend breaks my heart, but this is worse. You all wrote me off."

Charlotte thought back to the end of last July and Chad telling her that she was too emotional about DreamUs laying her off. Back to over a decade ago and Emily telling her she was too obsessed with theme parks and too good for Lands, too ambitious when it came to pursuing a career at DreamUs. Now once again, people close to her thought she was too much.

"Charlotte, you're leaving, remember? And I thought I was being helpful, protecting you."

No, his betrayal wasn't exactly like Chad cheating on her, but it pierced her heart all the same considering the steps she and Gregory had taken toward a new path together.

A tear slid down her cheek. "I see."

Gregory crossed to her side of the island in a heartbeat and wiped away her tears with his thumb, catching one after another. "We wanted to see what the next steps looked like, what Marianne and Frank wanted to proceed with, before we brought it up again to you—and that was wrong. I'm so sorry we haven't been honest about this with you, Charlotte."

"Me too," she answered. She covered his hand on her cheek with her own for a moment, dropped it, and stepped back. Tears done and voice hard she said, "It sounds like maybe I'm holding you all back from some lucrative opportunities."

"It's not like that."

"No? It sure seems that way from where I stand, but I'll get out of the way." Charlotte took a breath. "I think my work at Lands is done." She turned away and walked toward the front door, ignoring the sounds of Gregory following her.

"Charlotte," he said as she was opening the door to leave. She looked over her shoulder. "Can we talk about this?"

"I need some time," she said and closed the door. She got in her car, glanced at the picnic basket she'd put in Gregory's car, and thought about fetching it. Nah, she thought, it would make its way back to her parents and if, in the meantime, it resulted in Gregory's car smelling like moldering cheese, she wasn't mad about it.

She sat back in the driver's seat and closed her eyes. It wasn't how she expected the evening to go, but instead, she could pick up a pizza from The Dragon's Breath and go home to snuggle Mads. She plucked out her phone to order dinner and her email inbox greeted her; before she could exit, Chad's message from earlier jumped out. It turned out that his offer couldn't have come at a more perfect time. She didn't have to vacillate over what she would do anymore. She opened a draft to reply.

To: csandusky@dreamus.com
From: charlotte@landsoflegend.com
Re: Dreamland Paris

Chad,

I'm glad to hear the plans are moving along even if it's chaotic. I appreciate you all reviewing my application and offering me such an exciting position. I have been very busy with Lands, but as it turns out, I'm open to other opportunities. Let me know when you can talk tomorrow.

Charlotte

Chapter 32

Charlotte stayed home the next day to stew and to have a video call with Chad. Not long after nine, a text lit up her phone.

Gregory: Hey, I'm waiting by the carousel. I have a coffee for you.

Charlotte debated ignoring it. She compromised by waiting fifteen minutes to reply.

Charlotte: I won't be in today.
Gregory: I see. Can we talk later?
Charlotte: Like I said, I need time.
Gregory: Okay. I'm here. Just let me know.

She prepped for the video call, but based on Chad's email, the job was hers so this wouldn't be a formal interview or anything. She was glad her previous experience had made them forgo interviewing her. Her fantasy of making a huge splash by being part of the Dream Mechanic opening team for Dreamland Paris was coming to fruition. Guilt over submitting the application had gnawed around the edges of her mind while she'd waited to hear back from Chad. But being cut out of the Peak Fusion conversation only made her more open. It looked like Emily was getting her way, and she didn't want to be part of that version of Lands.

Chad was too self-centered to consider Charlotte having any other reason to return to DreamUs besides working for the best company and team out of Paris, the most incredible city in the world in his opinion, so Charlotte didn't have to explain a thing about her change of heart toward working at Lands. She only had to choose a start date, and she chose soon. Like, within the week. They could do without her for the last two months of working toward the Under the Waves opening, and she didn't want to be there. Not with the knowledge that they'd been sneaking around her.

Making plans to go work in Paris for an unspecified amount of time yanked Charlotte's emotions in different directions. Mostly promise and excitement. She'd wanted this and planned for this. Going back to DreamUs had a luminous edge; with Dreamland Paris in early stages, Charlotte could put her thumbprints all over the park and use the DreamUs influence to craft memorable experiences for the millions of guests who would eventually visit.

But underneath that brilliant shine crept thorny vines of regret over leaving Lands of Legend and her family for a bigger company *again*. She'd repaired her relationship with her aunt and uncle after she left for DreamUs the first time, and she hated to think about being distant from them again. However, she thought they would understand this time with everything going on; plus she'd mentioned her exit date to them. They weren't taking her opinions into account anyway, so what would they care if she left two months earlier than planned?

She still thought Peak Fusion sucked, but if her family was on board and if it helped them out, maybe they should pursue it. But Charlotte didn't have to like it. Let them make their terrible choices. She'd make it easy on them and take herself out of the equation. Then they could open Under the Waves and Emily and Ever Fund could plot the park's future without her opinions or overreactions complicating things.

Job officially accepted, plane ticket and temporary place to stay sorted (she'd be rooming with one of her peers on the team), Charlotte drafted separate emails to her aunt and uncle, her cousin, and Gregory, and scheduled them to send later in the day. She'd have a conversation with her mom and dad tonight and then leave in a few days. No reason to drag out the inevitable.

Her conversation with her parents went well, with Alice and Richard expressing support while still exchanging looks that said they were worried about Charlotte. And then later that night, after her scheduled emails were sent, her phone buzzed with texts. Emily's said only good luck and that she wished Charlotte well. Sure she did. She was probably thrilled to have her troublesome cousin out of the way. Aunt Marianne, who hadn't seen the email but had heard from Emily, apologized and told Charlotte they hated to see her go but that she understood. And Gregory. He called. Charlotte ignored it. He texted. She ignored him. But even though she was pissed, it would be cruel to leave the country without saying goodbye in person.

Charlotte: Carousel in the morning? Nine?
Gregory: I'll be there.

Charlotte got to Lands early so she could grab a few things from her office and toss them in the car before Gregory arrived. When she walked to the carousel, arms wrapped tightly around herself, he was waiting in a wrinkled V-neck and rumply hiking pants, hands in his pockets, damp hair glistening in the early light. He looked haggard, like he hadn't slept.

"Hey," she said, stopping a few feet away from him.

"Hey," he replied, voice raspy. His head was bent but he looked up at her through his lashes, green eyes clear and pained. "Thanks for texting me back. I know you said you needed time, Charlotte, but Paris?"

"Paris. You know I wanted to go back to DreamUs."

He took a step forward and reached out for one of her hands, which she gave him, knowing she'd kick herself for this later, for such a fresh memory of his skin against hers. "I thought we'd have longer. Until Under the Waves, at least. Time to figure out this and what it might be."

She swallowed a tacky lump of sadness and lingering anger. "We would have, but things have changed."

He laced his fingers with hers and pulled her hand to his chest, thumb caressing the back of her hand. "I won't try to talk you into staying. I know this was your goal all along. I'm going to miss you. And I'm sorry for my part in all this."

"I'm sorry, too." She allowed herself the indulgence of stretching to kiss his cheek and started to question if she was making the right choice. Yes, he'd been wrong, but this still hurt. "Goodbye, Gregory. Good luck with Under the Waves."

As she broke from him and turned away, she heard him whisper, "It won't be the same without you."

Chapter 33

Charlotte didn't have much of a settling in period. She'd arrived in Paris and after taking a day to recover from jet lag, she'd started work. The DreamUs headquarters was on the outskirts of the city, with the park site a short train ride away. Charlotte had become a pro at working on the go, hopping back and forth between a desk and the mounds of dirt slowly taking shape between fiberglass and steel.

Paris, sparkling as the city was with no shortage of sights for her to see, faded into the background as Charlotte worked and slept on repeat, not even noticing how quickly she'd returned to giving herself to the job. Pointedly not questioning why she was so eager to exhaust her mind every day.

She hadn't left any loose ends in the work department at Lands; Charlotte had worked with her family to make sure she'd handed off all her responsibilities. Other than those communications, she hadn't known how to interact with them. Aunt Marianne seemed to take her choice in stride and, after a heart-to-heart, she texted Charlotte often about progress on the construction and with updates on the Faery Festival. Uncle Frank didn't text, but he'd joined the heart-to-heart with Aunt Marianne and they were okay. Emily hadn't reached out, hadn't apologized, and honestly, that was fine. She probably didn't think she had anything to apologize for.

And Gregory. She didn't even know what to do with Gregory. Or without him. When she looked out the office window at the city around her, all she could think about was how much she missed their weekly pizza nights and how much she wished he were there. He emailed occasionally when he needed a small something for Lands that Charlotte had forgotten to pass on, but she didn't reply. But after he'd sent her a photo of a brood of baby ducks waddling through Bluewhistle Meadow, Charlotte finally replied, suggesting the transition would be easier if they weren't in touch for a while. She did it to spare her foolish heart, which kept pining for his gray-flecked eyes, the crinkles around his mouth, and his friendship.

Melanie was on the market for freelance work and had offered to help Lands scoot toward the Under the Waves opening, but she made her thoughts on Charlotte's choice clear. Charlotte had called her from the airport while on the way to Paris, waiting so long to tell her best friend on purpose, and Melanie had threatened to somehow stop her from boarding the plane. Melanie, as ever, hadn't hesitated to call Charlotte on her shit. While she understood Charlotte's frustration and sense of being betrayed by Gregory and her family, Melanie couldn't believe her response was running away to Paris. Running away to the company that had once laid her off and sent her into an existential spiral. Running away to work with Chad, who had contributed in a very big, very negative way to said existential spiral.

Melanie's words were weeks old by now, but they still played loud and clear in Charlotte's head in quiet moments, like today when she was alone in the office for a round of virtual meetings with other Dream Mechanics at the DreamUs office in Glendale.

Charlotte: Saw this in the patisserie window and thought of you.

Charlotte sent a photo of a decadent-looking éclair with the text to Melanie. Her friend didn't always answer her texts, but Charlotte kept trying.

Melanie: !!
Melanie: Please have one for me and report back.

Charlotte smiled.

Charlotte: You got it.
Charlotte: But if you come to visit, you could try for yourself.
Melanie: And hang out in Paris by myself while you work the whole time? Nah.
Melanie: (I promise I'm saying that with love).

Charlotte couldn't argue with Mel as she looked out the office window at the lights glowing against the darkening sky over the city. The time difference with the home office meant some late-night meetings—meetings Chad usually took from his apartment with Jeni, who had moved to Paris but left DreamUs to work at a marketing firm. Charlotte opted to stay in the office alone because she couldn't bring herself to set up a desk in her already small bedroom. She didn't want to add up the number of hours she spent at the office or on-site, though. It would be staggering.

Maybe tonight, when she was done with work, would be the night she would meander through the neighborhood on the way home. She could pretend she wasn't lonely and stop for an indulgent late-night dinner—one probably with large quantities of wine.

Melanie's jab about not visiting because Charlotte would be too preoccupied with work haunted Charlotte the next few days. She was in Paris, and Paris had much more to offer than her small apartment, the DreamUs office, and the park's construction zone. It was criminal that she hadn't given the city any special attention.

She committed to disconnecting from work and putting her desire to continue wallowing aside for a full weekend by exploring her neighborhood and maybe visiting a museum. Two days. Charlotte could do it. She put it on her calendar to make sure her team knew she wouldn't be available.

When her weekend off arrived, she flipped her phone into "do not disturb" mode, and walked out of her apartment and down the building's rickety spiral staircase with purpose. Charlotte strolled to the lone place in her neighborhood she had become acquainted with so far: the boulangerie around the corner. Normally, she got her coffee and croissant to go, juggling the butter-stained bag as she navigated to the office on the train and getting crumbs everywhere.

Today, she would eat here, sitting in the nook by the window that she eyed every time she came in. She placed her order and sat down at the bistro table overlooking the street outside, not so bustling this early on a Saturday. When her café au lait arrived in a cup a reasonable person could call a bowl, Charlotte picked it up with both hands and took a careful sip. She closed her eyes and leaned back into the chair.

Slowing down was good. Why was it so hard for her to remember to do it?

Charlotte put down her drink and picked up the flaky croissant that arrived with it. As she peeled a layer of the pastry away, a sense memory swept her back to Sir Cinna-Swirls on Gregory's first day in the park. Recalling his formal posture back then and thinking of the ways he'd softened since punched her in the core. She put the pastry back on its plate as if setting it down could wash the wave of sadness and regret away.

They'd gone from bickering coworkers to friends, to

lovers, to people who lived across an ocean from each other and didn't talk.

No, Charlotte told herself. *Pastries make you feel happy. They do* not *leave room for sadness.* With that resolve, she devoted every fiber of her attention to dissecting and savoring the croissant.

It still tasted like nothing.

A long walk to the Musée d'Orsay would set things right. She'd wanted to visit the museum for ages, and its appearance in the *Doctor Who* episode about Van Gogh that made her cry buckets only moved it higher up her list. She ordered another drink to go and stepped out into a spring morning with air so light it buoyed her steps.

After confirming the route on her phone, Charlotte opted to turn off the navigation and instead meander in the museum's general direction. She followed narrow sidewalks to cobblestone alleys and stepped into the brightening sun to see if it would wipe the heaviness from her shoulders. And it did. For a while.

She was in one of the most beautiful cities on the planet. Old buildings crowding the streets, loud church bells punctuating the hustle and bustle, smells of rich food wafting through the air, history oozing out of every crack—and she was here alone. Charlotte didn't have anything against solitude; it was an old friend. But here in this place, in this moment, she felt empty. No family. No Melanie.

No Gregory.

She wandered into a green space, sat on a bench, and asked herself what the hell she was doing there.

Chapter 34

Two weeks later, it was the end of April and Charlotte stood at the edge of what would become Dreamland Paris's own version of Exploration Isle before the construction team started their day. She held a steaming cup of coffee close while she walked the perimeter of the land, with structures taking shape and the bones of the land's main attraction becoming more noticeable.

Aside from the difference in scale, Charlotte could have been back on the Under the Waves site at Lands of Legend. How many times had she started the day with a cup of coffee and Gregory, walking around and noting the progress happening?

Some of Charlotte's colleagues were around, but they were evaluating the areas they were responsible for, each land developing simultaneously. The scope that had appealed to Charlotte at first had now become overwhelming. She was so focused on this new version of Exploration Isle she'd lost sight of how the whole park was coming together.

Still, under her supervision, Exploration Isle and its big-ticket attraction had remained ahead of schedule and under budget, with almost no creative compromises. The night before, she'd had a meeting with an executive who called out her progress as the most notable in the park. In the past, triumph from that kind of accomplishment would fuel Charlotte for days and make her think she could take on anything in the world. And now, well, it made her think of how satisfying it had been to problem-solve with Gregory.

Instead, as her email dinged and she made a makeshift desk from a slab of unpainted faux rock to review a recent report and updated concept art to go with it, it hit her how hollow it all felt. It didn't mean anything. She thought of how she'd start her day at Lands of Legend, in the office kitchen, exchanging hellos with coworkers and catching up on their lives. It was cozy. Warm. Not a construction site where she sat alone.

None of this was right.

None of it.

She closed her laptop and peeled her personalized hard hat from her head to set it aside, the safety wear suddenly stifling her. Charlotte pulled her phone from her back pocket and called the only person she knew who would understand and who would answer at such a late hour. Melanie answered on the first ring.

"Hey, there. Isn't it some ungodly morning hour there?" Melanie asked.

"Hey. And kinda. Construction crews start early and I wanted to beat them to it today."

Melanie chuckled. "Of course you did. But I'm guessing you didn't call to tell me about construction crews and what they're doing, especially since I know you signed a novel-sized NDA saying you would not talk about those things."

"Yeah," Charlotte said. "I think I maybe had an epiphany and you were the first person I wanted to tell."

"Let me sit down for this; one second."

She heard Melanie rustling around on the other line and could picture her friend getting cozy in her favorite daisy yellow chair.

"I'm all set," Melanie confirmed. "Please epiphany away."

"Okay, so you know how I came back to DreamUs."

"Yes, I'm aware," Melanie said, voice kind and supportive.

"I was wrong. I thought Lands didn't want or need me and my opinions. And I thought coming back to DreamUs was the only way for me to make a difference." Charlotte had believed it was how she could fulfill her goals of delivering the maximum amount of magic and escape to people who needed it. DreamUs had near endless resources in terms of money, workforce, and sway with local governments around the world. Her fellow Dream Mechanics were doing huge things, remarkable things. Magnificent attractions and experiences poured out of them, and their innovations would bring joy to the world, Charlotte had no doubt. She would always cheer them on.

She covered the highlights for Melanie and finished, "I've had the perfect place to have an impact, to make memorable moments and be on hand to see how that work affects people. Lands of Legend was right there. It's been there all along."

Charlotte paused to sniffle. "Do you think . . . I can fix this, right?"

"You absolutely can," Melanie reassured her. "You'll have some work to do to convince your family you're for-real all in and will not, once again, run away to DreamUs if they dangle a fancy title and cool opportunity at you."

"Yeah, I know," Charlotte agreed.

"And to be fair, they did mess up. Gregory and Emily weren't the only ones not being fully transparent with you; your aunt and uncle could have been upfront, too. You did overreact, kinda spectacularly, by leaving town for another continent on short notice, but I'm saying lots of factors were at play. You made the choice you made and you can't undo it or cancel it out, but you can make another choice to make it right and see what happens."

Charlotte stood from her seat on the ground and paced.

"You still there, Charlotte?"

"Yeah, Mel. I'm thinking about how to fix this."

"Look, you have good intentions and you're a smart human. You'll figure out the next right thing and how to make it up to the people you need to make it up to."

"Thank you, Melanie."

"I've got your back, even if that means telling you when you've made a mistake, but I could maybe work on being a little gentler about that."

"No, I need your bluntness," Charlotte said. "Now, if you'll excuse me, I've got some things to take care of."

She gathered her things and secured her hard hat on her head. As she tightened it, she muttered to herself, "Charlotte, you've been an idiot."

Not quietly enough, based on the raised eyebrows she got from the foreman who had arrived and was giving her a concerned look. Charlotte shook her head. "All good, sorry about that."

Except that was a lie; nothing was good. She'd looked past what she had to her flawed ambition not once, but twice. Charlotte had a lot to get in order so she could return to the life she now knew she'd always been meant for. She picked up her phone and made a list:

- Buy a one-way ticket home
- Call Mom & Dad, then Marianne & Frank
- Pack
- Leave enough room to bring home a crap ton of Ladurée macarons to go with apologies
- Text Gregory? Email him? Something
- Make a thorough document detailing the status of projects for coworkers
- Give notice to Chad, in person

Wait, she thought, she was starting with the wrong part of the list; she should give notice to Chad immediately, both to set things in motion and to get a sense of closure. She glanced at the shared office calendar and sent a meeting request for the soonest available time on his schedule.

As soon as she got to the office an hour later, fifteen minutes before her meeting with Chad, a shadow appeared over her temporary desk. Chad. "What's with the last-minute meeting request?"

She looked up and willed the sass washing over her to stay on the inside.

"You'll find out in approximately fourteen minutes," she said sweetly. Keeping the sass contained around Chad was a futile effort.

"I'm free now." Chad shrugged, the gesture sending a ruffle through his rigid posture. "What's up?"

Fine. "Let's go to your office."

"Oh, that serious, huh?" Chad appeared taken aback. "Let's go, then."

Charlotte closed her laptop, stood, and followed—not so much followed as trailed behind. He was most of the way to his office already.

While they'd been civil and managed to work rather well together during Charlotte's time in Paris, their relationship didn't approach anything that resembled friendship. They stretched the textbook definition of "professional colleagues"; nothing said professional colleagues had to be more than polite to each other.

She stretched the brief walk to compose herself before entering Chad's office, where he leaned against the window behind his desk and gestured at the chair. "So," he prompted. "What's on your mind?"

"It's time for me to go home," Charlotte said, voice direct and firm. She'd flipped into business mode, like she was giving a presentation to executives. And she sort of was. A presentation for quitting.

Chad crossed his arms and looked down. "I see. Is everything okay?"

That, Charlotte realized, was concern in his voice, and he wasn't faking it.

"Thank you for asking," she replied. "Everyone's okay. Everything is okay. As far as I know, anyway. But as challenging and interesting as my time here has been—and I appreciate that I had the opportunity to come back and help make cool things—my place is at Lands of Legend with my family and the park. I can make as much magic there as I can here *and* get to see the results of that work every day."

Chad moved to his chair and sat down. "I'd argue that you can't make as much magic there based on attendance numbers alone, but I know what you mean. It's not a numbers game. Charlotte, I know I've been a jerk in the past—"

"You think?" The words flew out before Charlotte could stop them.

"I know," Chad said. "About many things, including Lands. But I get it. Your family built that place from the ground up and sure, it's quaint in scale, but that doesn't make it less special. I can see how it would be rewarding to help the park grow and to be present to watch it happen, react to feedback and observations immediately. I'm a little jealous of it."

Charlotte furrowed her eyebrows. This didn't sound like the Chad she knew. "You are?"

He laughed. "Sure. I mean, not enough to leave all of this and the Dream Mechanics and try to find work at a smaller park or anything."

That was more like it, Charlotte thought. "No, I didn't think so."

Chad leaned back in his chair and folded his arms behind his head. Eyes toward the ceiling as if imagining a palace in the sky, he said, "I have a lot of work to accomplish here to make Dreamland Paris the best and brightest of all the parks, then I can keep moving up until I'm running the Dream Mechanic division."

"So only some small plans, then." Charlotte didn't blame him. She'd once had grand ambitions of her own about rising through the Dream Mechanic ranks. And despite Chad's many, *many* flaws, he was talented and generally knew when to tap others in when he wasn't an expert.

Chad half-shrugged, a nonchalant look on his face—the kind that indicated he was so confident he didn't second-guess himself. "I have it all laid out. I don't suppose I can do anything to convince you to stay? Development has thrived under your management; you bridge the gap between creative and engineering unlike anyone else on the team."

That kind of flattery, while it sounded honest, was part of what had led Charlotte to Paris and back to DreamUs in the first place. "No, Chad. This is it for me."

"Okay then, let's set another meeting for tomorrow about the best way to wrap up everything you have pending." He pushed his chair away from his desk, stood up, and extended his hand. "It really has been good to work with you again. Just like old times, except without all the 'in a relationship' stuff."

She shook her head at his verbal use of air quotes and then his hand. "You know, it hasn't been the worst." Charlotte found the statement to be true as she said it.

He rolled his eyes. "Talk to you tomorrow."

Charlotte stopped by her desk to throw her laptop in a bag; nothing was stopping her from going home to start packing.

Chapter 35

A desperate desire to get back to Lake Sterling pushed Charlotte to be extra efficient in wrapping up her work in a week. She'd still promised to be available remotely for another week so it was a full two weeks' notice, but she was ready to go home. In her last week, she tried to take in Paris and enjoy it. The city's streets still had a hollowness for her, but since she had a plan to get her life back on track, Charlotte felt more like a tourist who could explore temporarily instead of a woman who had left parts of herself in another country and was uncertain if she could get them back.

One afternoon after a stroll by the Seine, she called Marianne at a time they'd both agreed on. It was the day after she'd given notice to DreamUs, and she wanted to see if Marianne and Frank were open to her returning to Lands. Charlotte heard a tinniness on the line that indicated they were on speaker. "Aunt Marianne, hi! How are you? Are you on speaker?"

"Hey, honey. I'm here with your uncle Frank in our office. We're busy but okay."

"Well, as long as you're not pushing yourselves too hard."

"Charlotte," Uncle Frank said sternly, "that's the pot calling the kettle black and you know it."

She laughed. "You're not wrong. And that's kind of why I

wanted to talk. I was wrong to come here. I thought this was what I wanted. Needed after everything that happened. It's beautiful here and the park is going to be amazing, but it's not home. I'm not at home. I was wondering if . . . you would have me back at Lands? For good this time. Like, in it for the long haul."

She got silence in response. Then the sound of a door opening and closing.

"Hello? Are you guys still there?"

"Yes, Charlotte, we're here," her aunt answered. "Your uncle just brought Emily in to say something to you."

"Oookay."

"Charlotte. Hi. I owe you an apology."

"Emily, let me stop you there. I don't want an apology only because your parents are making you. That's—"

"They're not making me, Charlotte. I've been putting it off. Look, I was wrong." Her cousin sighed, the speaker-phone exaggerating the sound. "The more we talked with Peak Fusion, the pushier they got. They wanted us to ink the deal and announce it before Under the Waves opened, and Gregory pushed back on the timing. It turns out it was all a PR move. You can say, 'I told you so.' "

"I already did when I brought all of that to your attention, but I'm not going to rub it in."

"Hmph. They would have gone through with everything they said, but the date they wanted to announce in a couple of weeks suspiciously coincided with the drop of an article in *Ride Report*, exposing all of their dirty laundry. They tried to hide that tidbit of information, but Gregory did some digging and told them off in a spectacular fashion. And then told off Ian when Ian still tried to go behind our backs."

"That's . . . Wow." Charlotte didn't know what to say.

"Beyond that," Emily continued, "it wasn't the right fit. I was focused on the profits and not the heart of the park and I pushed Mom and Dad."

"Now Emily," Marianne jumped in, "we're adults capable of making our own decisions. We got so hung up on the idea of building a long future for Lands of Legend that we didn't take enough time to think about whether it was the right decision. And we definitely should not have kept secrets from you. I know we've talked about that, but I want to reiterate that we are sorry. Gregory, too."

Charlotte closed her eyes and tried to formulate a satisfactory response.

"Charlotte, you still there?" Uncle Frank asked.

"Still here. I'm happy it didn't work out, but I know you saw that as a *viable* path forward."

"Ha ha," Frank deadpanned. "It's fine. We have other, better ideas for Lands. The Faery Festival was a success, so there's a plan to expand that. And Gregory's contracting some students from Grove Tech to put together a daily puppet show. All sorts of things brewing. And Charlotte?"

"Yes?"

Marianne picked up the thread. "We'd love to have you back to help us with all of it."

Emotion gripped Charlotte's throat. "I would like that. Working for DreamUs again was amazing, at first. I had resources again, a team of people, a seven-figure budget, every supplier you can imagine."

"Point taken, Charlotte," Emily interrupted.

"No, I wasn't trying to make a point, only stating facts. And what I was getting to: I had all of that but no magic. No Flossleaf. No information toadstool. No kids wide-eyed, looking for the source of the dragon's heartbeat on the Wintertide Trail. It hasn't been right. Dreamland Paris will be special, I know it will, and people will travel from around the world to visit and make memories. But people travel to Lands to make memories and Lands is where I'm meant to be, where I want to be."

"Then hurry up and come home, Charlotte," her aunt said. "Lands isn't going anywhere."

"And," Emily added, "maybe we can talk about your role more. I think I'm going to go back to New York for grad school."

"Oh! I see," Charlotte said. "I'm overwhelmed with feelings right now, you guys. I can't wait to see you soon."

"We love you, Charlotte," Marianne said. "See you soon."

Chapter 36

Charlotte sat cross-legged on a rug, surrounded by some furniture and boxes in her new apartment, Madmartigan nestled into her lap. Since she was trapped and absolutely could not move the precious angel baby, she leaned back and looked around the cozy space. Moving into her own place after her return from Paris and establishing herself as a permanent resident of Lake Sterling felt like the right way to show her aunt and uncle she was committed to Lands. Plus, her mom had needed to assemble her stained-glass triptych for Under the Waves and took over the basement studio as a bigger space for her art. It had only taken Charlotte a day to find her new place too, so it felt as if it was meant to be.

"I'm just glad you got to move with me, Mads," she whispered to him and stroked his silky head. Her dad had insisted that Charlotte take the cat, who apparently did a lot of yowling at the basement door while Charlotte was away. Charlotte promised Richard he could come and visit Madmartigan anytime.

Charlotte and her cat had officially moved in earlier in the day; her parents had helped her lug the boxes and furniture across town. They'd filled up the one-bedroom apartment quickly and Charlotte didn't need too much more to make the place her home. In her head, she ran through the miscellaneous items she still wanted to get:

- A giant bookshelf
- Cat tree
- Cozy chair
- A slow cooker
- Probably another throw blanket
- Gregory

Wait, what? Brains always veered off in directions you didn't want or need them to. Ugh. She leaned back and lay down on the rug; she'd left her legs crossed so she wouldn't disturb Mads, but he stirred and walked across her torso to loaf on her chest. "What are we going to do about Gregory, bud?"

Madmartigan chirped. Cute, but not at all helpful.

Charlotte had only texted Gregory after the phone call with her family but not since being back. She opened her messages to reread that conversation. She'd gone back to their messages dozens of times in Paris, watching how their texts shifted over time from colleagues to friends, to lovers, then back. A written history of their relationship in letters and emojis.

Charlotte: I heard what happened with Peak Fusion and that you told them off.
Gregory: You tried to warn us.
Charlotte: I'm not messaging to gloat.
Gregory: Didn't think you were.
Gregory: It felt good to tell them off. Ian, too.
Charlotte: ???
Gregory: Tell you more when you come back.
Gregory: I mean, not that I know you're coming back.

Charlotte: Surprise!
Gregory: See you soon?
Charlotte: Yes. I'll let you know when I'm back.

She missed him, but instead of texting him about being back, which felt too pushy for some reason, she'd emailed him. But he was legitimately busy with the Under the Waves grand opening coming up in two weeks, so Charlotte tried not to make up her own story about his lack of response. She didn't want to corner him, but she did need to see him in person and to talk through everything. Including getting back to work at Lands and what that would look like. So she reached out, but for business reasons this time.

To: gregory@landsoflegend.com
From: charlotte@charlottegates.com
Re: An Offer

Gregory,

Hi, I'm back. I know I emailed that already and I know you're busy but I think I can still be of assistance with the grand opening party for Waves. Would you be available to meet me at Sir Cinna-Swirls tomorrow afternoon? I have an idea to present to you.

Best,
Charlotte

She closed her laptop and made a promise to herself to not check her email again for an hour, even setting a timer to hold herself accountable. To occupy herself, she called Melanie for an overdue catch-up on everything that had happened since Charlotte returned to Lake Sterling. Melanie hadn't let her off the hook for her decision to return to DreamUs, but she also understood it. She related, even. She sometimes considered going back to the world of fine dining despite it causing her so much stress that it affected her physical well-being. Still, Melanie had a way of being straightforward while also offering reassurance and support. Charlotte was lucky to have Mel in her life.

After they said goodbye and Melanie confirmed she'd be in town for the grand opening of Under the Waves, Charlotte plugged in her phone in the other room and then walked a full lap around her apartment while eyeing her closed laptop on the couch. It had been well over an hour; the timer went off while she was talking to Melanie and Charlotte had dismissed it.

She opened the laptop and then closed her eyes while she waited for her email to refresh. Charlotte finally opened one eye to see what new messages had made her computer ding: a shop drop email from Lost Petal Pottery (which was excellent timing because Charlotte needed some coffee mugs for her new place); a note from Luke asking her to stop by and sample some new pizza flavors; a reminder to go paperless for her new rental insurance.

Still nothing from Gregory. Gregory, who typically fired back email responses so fast that it was almost annoying.

Charlotte left her email open and ordered takeout for dinner. As she was walking out the door to grab her food, her laptop dinged. She raced across her apartment, telling herself it wasn't an email from Gregory and she needed to pick up her food while it was still warm. But she had to check. Just in case.

She clicked on her email and saw Gregory's name in her inbox. It made her gut plummet to somewhere around her heels. She opened it.

From: gregory@landsoflegend.com
To: charlotte@charlottegates.com
Re: An Offer

Charlotte,
It's nice to hear from you. Welcome back. You're right, I've been busy and not as on top of things as usual. The plans for the grand opening are coming along, but I want to make it as successful as possible. To that end, I'd like to hear your idea.
See you at Cinna-Swirls at 2.

Sincerely,
Gregory

She sent back an immediate confirmation and skipped out of her apartment. Nerves still gripped every single one of her organs, but he answered. She could make things between them right.

Chapter 37

Charlotte paced in front of Sir Cinna-Swirls the next afternoon, practicing what she wanted to say, yes, but also kicking herself for not giving equal attention to what she'd say to Gregory outside of business talk. Should she keep it strictly to Lands and the grand opening? Should she spill her guts about how she'd agonized over her poor choices and say how much she missed his insightful questions, careful input, as well as his biceps, eyes, and tattoos? How much she'd missed him?

She'd have to read his overall vibe before deciding, and that annoyed her because she'd prefer to have all of her possible words rehearsed and ready.

The inner monologue was becoming dizzying when Gregory approached, looking buttoned up and stiff in his dress and his movements. The formality alone was enough to make Charlotte want to crawl into a hole and send out a message offering to have this meeting in a virtual setting. *Pull yourself together*, she told herself. *You are capable and professional and you want to see Lands succeed.* She could put aside personal feelings.

"Thanks for meeting me," Charlotte said.

"Of course," Gregory replied as he opened the door.

Charlotte caught a whiff of his woodsy cologne as she walked in, and wished she could preserve that scent somewhere inside her heart. She walked toward what had become their usual table—the table they'd sat at the day they met and had returned to numerous times to plot and bicker—but Gregory headed toward another in the corner.

So, she thought, maybe not the time to lay her heart bare. She'd read their last text exchange completely wrong. Best to stick to the business at hand.

"Do you want to get anything before we start?" she asked.

"Why don't you get settled and I'll place an order?" he said. "I know what you like."

Charlotte would take that as encouraging if not for his flat voice—a voice that said he wanted to go back to being colleagues. Okay, then. She told her cracking heart to harden. "Thank you, that sounds good."

She shook it off as she pulled her laptop out of her bag, opened it, and placed it at an angle where they both could see the screen. Navigating to the presentation and pushing her emotions to the side, she thought, *For Lands!*, and then chuckled at a mental image of Gregory as Aragon.

Gregory came back with cinnamon rolls and coffee just then. "What did I miss?"

"You know in *Return of the King* when Aragorn is facing Sauron's forces and he beautifully says, 'For Frodo'?" Charlotte answered.

"Of course I do, it's classic," Gregory said. "Those are fantasy movies I *have* seen."

"Well, that's what I was thinking of, except it's us fighting for the theme park and saying, 'For Lands!' "

"And who is Sauron in this scenario?"

"You know, I hadn't gotten that far."

Gregory gave her a half smile. "I've missed the weird and wonderful journeys your brain takes when you're stressed."

Ha, Charlotte thought. He *had* missed her. The words drew an underscore under her heart while her brain had mild whiplash from the back-and-forth.

"Yeah, well, it's constant entertainment up there." She took a cinnamon roll and iced coffee. "Thanks for these."

"I know how much sugar and caffeine help your process, so really it was in my best interest. Now, what's your helpful idea?"

Back to business they went.

"Right, that." Charlotte chewed a bit of her pastry and washed it down with a long pull of coffee. Gregory hadn't been incorrect about her process. She popped the presentation's first slide onto the screen.

"Emily caught me up on the details of the grand opening, including the guest list. You've all put so much hard work into this and done a fantastic job already, so my suggestions are only finishing touches. The icing on the cinnamon roll, if you will."

Gregory rolled his eyes.

"I saw that," Charlotte called out.

"You were meant to."

"Now, I think the guest list is a little lacking for the kind of reach and impact we want to achieve. It's all solid—especially the members of the regional press and locals who have been Lands supporters for the longest. But here's where we can boost things."

She navigated to a slide showing influencer data she'd gathered with Melanie's help.

"Influencers?" Gregory asked.

"Influencers," Charlotte answered.

"Emily and I did consider the influencer route while you

were gone, but we decided their tastes were too flashy for Lands."

Charlotte had noticed the emphasis Gregory had put on the words "while you were gone." She persisted. "I can see why you would think that. A lot of theme park influencers focus on places like Dreamland and Wonder World, and you're right that those companies go all out with complimentary stays, dining, and gift cards, and throw every little thing at the influencers."

"Which we can't do."

"No. But we can give them something the other parks can't." She paused, both for dramatic effect and for another bite of cinnamon roll. "An underdog story."

Gregory leaned back and crossed his arms. "Do you think it's wise to position Lands as a place in need of pity or saving?"

"I don't think that would be wise, but we wouldn't be doing that. We'd be giving them an opportunity to help a small family business continue to grow and make them feel like part of that family. Sure, we can't pay for their travel or anything, and this is kinda last minute, but we can add a new tier of annual pass just for them with a 'welcome to the Lands family' kind of message—in a sincere way, not a gross quid pro quo way."

Gregory looked thoughtful. "Wouldn't giving them an annual pass be a lot of value to give away?"

"No," Charlotte insisted, "because they put their lives online, at least the theme park portions of them. If they like Lands enough to come back and use their pass, chances are high that they'll post about and share videos on whatever platform happens to be popular at the time. It's a win for us. Here, look."

She knew Gregory responded to data, which she'd pulled

together and double-checked last night. Charlotte showed him the numbers and sample posts from influencers about theme parks not owned by mega corporations.

"The only risk involved," she told him, "is that we obviously don't have any say in what they post. If they, for some reason, hate the Manta or anything else about Lands, that could have the opposite effect of what we want. But that could happen with any guest."

"Not every guest has tens of thousands of theme park fans hanging on their every word," Gregory pointed out. He chewed his lip. "This could completely backfire."

"It could," Charlotte conceded. "But I believe in Lands and Under the Waves and the work you've done."

"The work *we've* done, Charlotte."

She glanced down and smiled. "Sorry, that *we've* done. It will charm people. I believe in all of it, don't you?"

"You know I do."

"Then the risk is minimal. Words like *quaint*, *intimate*, and *cozy* might come up, but we embrace those qualities about Lands. We don't want to be like a giant theme park."

"No, we don't," Gregory agreed.

Charlotte hadn't meant her words to be a test, but she knew that past Gregory believed Lands should emulate bigger parks instead of leaning into what made it unique. His answer demonstrated how much he'd come to appreciate Lands of Legend.

While Gregory mulled the idea over, she finished her cinnamon roll. Then he asked, "How much value would we be giving away with the comped annual passes?"

She clicked to the slide with a range based on how many influencers took them up on the offer.

Gregory blinked repeatedly and pressed his lips together. "That is not a small number, Charlotte."

"I'm aware. But think of the possible results and it will support the return on Ever Fund's investment."

He leaned forward into his hands and rubbed his hairline with his fingertips, taking a minute before replying. "You're right, it's worth it. Do you need any help with the outreach or invites?"

Charlotte glowed with triumph. "Nope, I have a plan for that. I got some help ready in case you said yes."

"Of course you did. And I'm guessing you already have ideas for the new annual-pass tier for these folks?"

"Yes, right here. Do you want to go over them now or should I email them to you?"

Gregory glanced at his watch, a beaded bracelet snug against its leather band. "Why don't you email me everything? I need to—"

Charlotte's hand shot out, not of her own volition, to grab his wrist and look at the gemstones circling it. Aunt Marianne. It had to be. "Gregory. This is a gemstone bracelet. When did you start wearing a bracelet?"

He glanced down at the bracelet and a fond smile played across his lips, bringing out those lines around his mouth that Charlotte adored. "Recently. Marianne slid this onto my wrist after a stressful update call with Ian a couple weeks ago. Red jasper. She said it's helpful for boosting confidence and she thought I, quote, 'could stand to be reminded that I've got this.'"

Hearing about both Marianne's gesture and Gregory's reaction to it lit up Charlotte's everything with a heartfelt glow. "Aunt Marianne has a knack for knowing what people need."

"Yeah, she's great." Gregory's face appeared conflicted as he pulled his arm away. "Sorry, but I do need to go check on a few things in the office."

She hid her disappointment because she wasn't ready to leave his presence yet. He'd relaxed more as they'd talked and she could see the stress underneath the surface, but couldn't tell if it was all Lands-related or if any of it was about them. "Anything I can help with?"

"I think you have plenty to keep yourself busy with," he said. "Your office is kind of covered in supplies for the grand opening, anyway. I mean, assuming you want your office back?"

Charlotte's family had supported her returning. She had her job. But hearing that Gregory was okay with her coming back? It meant something different. Maybe that they could be friends again. Or more than friends. Charlotte would prefer more than friends, but this meeting had felt like Gregory drawing a line between them and labeling it "business only."

"I do. But that's okay, I'll work elsewhere. I should get to it," she said through a fake smile. She gathered her things and they walked out of Sir Cinna-Swirls.

"Let me know if I can help, and text me if it's timely," Gregory said.

"Of course. Likewise, let me know what I can do as we get closer, okay?"

"I definitely will."

Unsure of how to end the conversation, Charlotte treated it like a meeting and stuck out her hand for a shake. Gregory surprised her by taking it and pulling her into a tight hug. She gave into her wants, burying her face in his chest and inhaling deeply. He whispered, "It's really good to have you back, Charlotte."

He let go and walked away, leaving Charlotte staring after him. Okay, maybe not business only, but he was still holding back. She tried to see things from his perspective: She'd left abruptly, though he acknowledged he and Emily made a mistake by keeping secrets from her, but she hadn't communicated much while she was on another continent. And she hadn't expressed *to him* how much she missed him. Plus he had the most going on with the opening in two weeks—an opening crucial for both Lands and Ever Fund. She could be patient. See what happened. If nothing else, it seemed like they could still be friends. And while that wasn't enough, she would take it.

Chapter 38

Gloomy morning light filtered through the gauzy curtains Charlotte had hung in her apartment, Mads blocking some of the light from his perch in front of the window that provided prime cat-television programming. She woke before her alarm, already buzzing with the excitement of the grand opening of Under the Waves. Memorial Day Weekend started tomorrow, and Uncle Frank and Aunt Marianne's longtime dream was coming true after years of hard work, ready to greet guests for the first time. And Gregory and Ever Fund had got them over the last hump. The thought of Gregory sent a million sensations through her mind and heart: gratitude, sadness, hopefulness. He'd warmed up ever so slightly in that meeting and that hug at the end had meant something, right?

But in the last couple of weeks, they'd only interacted in regards to the big event. There hadn't been another hug or even a brushing of arms. An invisible barrier stood between them. Charlotte missed sharing their days together: work headaches, laughter, coffee—all of it.

She pushed the covers back, stood, and kissed Madmartigan on the head. "It's going to be the best day, buddy. And that doesn't look like rain to you, does it?"

"Meow."

"I didn't think so either. I can feel your excitement from here, Mads. Shall we get you some food?"

He dutifully led Charlotte to his bowl and after he was crunching his kibble, Charlotte thumbed open her phone. It was early but it hadn't stopped Melanie, her parents, her cousin, *and* her aunt from sending her messages. She needed to remind her family about the efficiency of group texting. Charlotte brewed coffee and made toast before she answered their questions, soothed worries, and put in a pastry order with Melanie. God love her, she was stopping at Three Bites Bakery, Charlotte's favorite, on her way from the airport. She'd decided on an assortment of sugary goodness and was pressing SEND when the phone rang, startling her into a comedic and unintentional game of cell phone hot potato. Once she'd saved it from a free fall, she clocked Gregory's name flashing across the screen.

Eyes wide, she answered. "Hey! Hi. Good morning?"

Gregory laughed and she felt the sound of it in her toes. "It is indeed morning. I didn't wake you up, did I?"

"No, I'm already on the coffee portion part of the day. I was too excited to sleep in."

"Same," Gregory said. "I've been up for hours."

"From excitement?"

"A little of that. More like anxiety, worry—pick a synonym. It's a big day for Lands and . . . it's a lot."

"Yeah," Charlotte agreed. "It *is* a lot. But take comfort in knowing that you're making a big dream come true today."

"I know. Though that's part of the pressure."

"It's all going to go great," Charlotte reassured him. "We're prepared for any scenario." And they were. Charlotte knew the importance of the backup plans having backup plans, and she'd helped make sure they were ready for anything weather, crowds, or malfunctions could throw at them.

"I know."

"Can I give you a tip?"

"Please," Gregory said.

"When the time comes to let guests in, find a place to stand off to the side and watch their faces as they enter. It's always magical."

"What if they make bad faces?" Gregory asked.

"Never happens," Charlotte said.

"Would you, uh, stand with me, Charlotte?"

She sat down hard on the nearest chair.

"Stand with you? For, like, moral support?"

"Uh, moral support, yes, but more than that. I think this evening would be infinitely better if we were together for it. What I'm trying to say is, will you be my date for the grand opening?"

Charlotte swallowed a ball of emotion. "I will."

"Meet you at the park in an hour, at the Under the Waves entrance? Then we can talk?"

Having a "talk" with Gregory wasn't how Charlotte had imagined this wildly busy and important day of all days starting, but she would take it.

"Can't wait. See you soon."

They hung up and Charlotte held her phone in front of her, mouth agape. That was definitely not a business-only conversation. She jumped out of her chair with a huge grin on her face, walking toward the shower with a literal skip in her step. The day had gotten a hundred times better.

Charlotte got ready, packed her outfit for the grand opening—since she probably wouldn't have time to run back home to change—and sent a handful of texts and emails to make sure everything she was responsible for was on track for the day. She put out extra food for Mads and gave him goodbye scritches before heading out.

As Charlotte walked through Adventurer's Gate and toward the iridescent tunnel that marked the entryway to Under the

Waves, she spoke quietly to herself to calm her nerves. "Charlotte, you can do this. It's going to be fine. Great, even."

Gregory asking to talk on this busy day had to be a positive thing. Had to be. She took a deep breath and walked into the tunnel. The lighting and sound weren't on just yet, but even so, the cooler air and dimmer light supported the feeling of walking into a new space. On any other day she'd be scrutinizing the shifting gradation of the paint and the texture of the tunnel walls, making sure they looked as they should, but today Gregory stood at the end of the tunnel. He was in worn black jeans and a black V-neck T-shirt, running his hand through his still-wet-from-the-shower hair, and holding something Charlotte couldn't make out in his other hand. The morning sunlight made him shine. He spotted Charlotte and his face transformed, glowing, kind, and open. He looked like everything she'd been missing. Everything she'd been waiting for.

"You're here," he called.

"I'm here." Her answer echoed in the tunnel. She walked closer, her eyes locked on his and as she reached hugging range, he held out the object in his hand. Charlotte laughed. "Is that what I think it is?"

He chuckled. "If you think it is a bouquet of cinnamon rolls, then yes. I may have plotted with Holly."

"A mini cinnamon roll bouquet. Gregory, you goddamn genius." She took the pastry bouquet and brought it to her nose as if it were roses. "This is so much better than flowers."

"I hoped you would approve."

"I do, and I guess I'll have to eat them immediately since I don't think I have a cinnamon roll vase."

"I'll keep that in mind for next time."

"Next time?"

Gregory took her free hand, the one not clutching her magnificent edible arrangement. "Next time I'm short-sighted and don't trust you enough to communicate clearly with you and then ignore you when you're trying to tell me what you want and need. I don't intend for there to be a next time, though."

Charlotte nodded and intertwined her fingers with his. "And next time I don't talk to you to find out what's going on and go chasing after what I *think* I want and need, I'll try to take a few before acting rashly and I'll bring you . . . I don't know, what kind of apology gift works for you?"

"You, Charlotte. Just you."

He stepped toward her and opened his arms, and Charlotte propped the bouquet between the slats of a nearby bench to walk right into Gregory's arms and sink into him. She buried her head in his chest and inhaled the scent of his eucalyptus woodsy cologne as he rested his cheek on her head. "I'm so sorry, Charlotte."

"No, I'm sorry, Gregory. I messed up and abandoned you and Lands and everything we worked on together for so long. I thought the grass was greener, but no, it's just the right amount of green here."

"You did run, but you had a reason to. We shouldn't have shut you out. I could have handled things better, too. A lot better."

"You could have. We both have to communicate in the future and agree to not keep things from each other based on assumptions about how the other person will react or anything else."

"I could not agree more, especially since I just did it again. I was assuming from your switching to emails instead of texts and not bringing up anything about us at Sir Cinna-Swirls that you weren't interested in figuring this out," Gregory said, tightening his arms around her.

"No, I didn't want to push you. I couldn't get a read on your feelings and email felt like it gave you more of an option to keep work boundaries. I don't know. Then it seemed like you were in business mode only at Cinna-Swirls. We're idiots, in other words. Appreciate you being the one to pull their head out of their ass and call me."

"Glad we settled everything," he said. "Now what?"

Charlotte pulled back and looked up at him, losing herself in those forest-green eyes. "Now I need you to know something." She took a deep breath.

"I'm all ears."

"I love you." There, Charlotte put it out there. Her time feeling untethered in Paris proved she wasn't falling in love with Gregory when she left; she had fallen for him.

Gregory wrapped his arms around her waist, lifted her off the ground, and gave her a spin. He set her down and locked eyes with her. Happiness infused his voice as he said, "Thank goodness, Charlotte, because I love you, too. You being gone made it crystal clear how important you've become to me, and how much I like having you by my side. We make a strong team—but more than that, you make me want to loosen my tie and take on the world. You remind me that I have the power to do anything I want. And right now, what I want is to work with you to make Lands be the best it can be, and to help give others the kind of magic I've experienced here."

"Is that all you want?"

"No, I want as much of this as humanly possible." Gregory pulled her close and gave her a soul-cleansing kiss, their lips connecting with urgency and longing and a promise of a bright tomorrow—many bright tomorrows.

Charlotte broke the kiss and collected herself. "So, big day for us. We made up, first I love yous, and now we're going to open a kick-ass theme park land and rides."

"Solid plan."

"I know. Planning is a talent of mine." Charlotte paused, considered her recent missteps and added, "Most of the time."

Gregory leaned down, took Charlotte's cheek in his hand,

and kissed her. She stretched up into the kiss and wound her arms around his neck. When they finally broke apart, both of them were a little out of breath.

"That's better," Gregory murmured.

"Definitely better. Remind me, how's our schedule this morning?" she asked.

"You know as well as I do that it's packed," Gregory said. "Unfortunately. It's an entire holiday weekend, after all. And the way I want to make up with you, we're going to need more than five minutes." He ran his fingertips lightly around the inside of her waistband and Charlotte's toes curled inside her shoes.

"You're coming home with me tonight, okay?" she said.

They kissed again and Charlotte felt his lips curl into a smile. "You couldn't keep me away. Then we take the day off on Tuesday. Maybe get to the next movie on the eighties fantasy list—*Labyrinth*, wasn't it?"

"If we have time, sure."

"Why wouldn't we have time on our day off?"

"We have a lot of catching up to do." She tugged on the bottom of his shirt and lifted an eyebrow. "But right now, we have so much to get done."

Charlotte pulled on his hand and retrieved her bouquet. "Good thing someone provided us with plenty of sugar. Let's get to the office. Everyone else should be here soon."

Chapter 39

They hit the ground running after they made up, starting with Gregory showing Charlotte that her office was cleaned and ready for her return. She'd been working from home and the conference room since she got back.

The day slipped by in a blur. Charlotte, running on sugar from the cinnamon bouquet she'd had to sample immediately and the pastries Melanie brought with her, coordinated with her family, Gregory, the park's staff, and Mel. She knew what needed to be done and by whom and answered questions with confidence, no checklists needed. They made it through every aspect of preparation, from ironing tablecloths at Aunt Marianne's insistence to ensuring careful placement of Charlotte's mom's incredibly detailed stained-glass triptych, with minimal stress and hiccups.

An hour before guests arrived and after everyone was changed and ready for the event to start, Charlotte found her uncle and aunt sitting on a bench outside the Manta's exit. Its carved wood looked like cresting waves with pale foam roiling at the top of them; fronds of carved seaweed wrapped the bench's legs. It was one of a kind, carved by Uncle Frank years ago when they first had the idea for Under the Waves and then stained by Aunt Marianne. It was one of the last items they'd placed. Seeing the couple sitting on the bench in the land they'd worked to bring to fruition for so long was enough to make Charlotte's eyes well with moisture.

She smiled as she approached them. "I knew you still had that bench, but where have you been hiding it? I haven't seen it in forever."

"Of all places, it's been in our bedroom," Uncle Frank said, giving his wife the kind of warm and intimate look that came from decades of partnership. "Marianne here insisted it should be somewhere she could look at it every day."

"I did. But when I said that, I didn't know you'd choose the bedroom, because it doesn't go with our decor even a little."

Frank elbowed Marianne and teased, "Hey now, I'm sophisticated. I have taste."

"If you think so, dear, I'll let you hold on to that." She patted Frank's knee.

"Well, regardless of whether it matched your bedroom's design," Charlotte said, "I'm glad it's finally here where it belongs. Where it's always belonged. Do you know how many people are going to take pictures of this bench? It's practically a throne."

"You think?" Frank asked.

"I *know*," Charlotte answered. "And I want anyone who poses for a selfie here to know about you two, so I had a little something made."

She reached into a tote bag and pulled out a brass plaque, aged with faux verdigris to look like it had been in the ocean for ages. The plaque was engraved: THIS BENCH WAS MADE BY FRANK AND MARIANNE GATES, TWO DREAMERS WHO ANSWERED THE CALL OF ADVENTURE IN THEIR HEARTS AND BROUGHT MAGIC TO ALL.

Charlotte handed it to her aunt and uncle. "Under the Waves needed this finishing touch to show all you've done for not just our family, but every family who visits Lands."

Frank scrubbed his face with his hand, and Marianne stood to embrace Charlotte. "Thank you. We love you so much and we're so happy you're here to stay—for good, this time. And you know, we aren't the only dreamers around here."

Marianne nodded her head over Charlotte's shoulder, to where Gregory was standing. "Aunt Marianne, I think you're right."

Charlotte broke from her aunt and leaned over to kiss her uncle on his forehead. "I'm glad you're happy with how everything's come together."

"It couldn't be more perfect, Charlotte."

She left them sitting on the bench fussing over where the plaque should go and walked over to Gregory, gorgeous in a gray pinstripe suit with a seafoam-green tie.

"What do they think of everything?" he asked, his voice anxious.

"They're over the moon to see this last piece of their come to reality. I think what we've done has given them permission to close the chapter on this part of their life," Charlotte said.

"Like, in a good way, not a *we've taken over everything and they feel useless* kind of way, right?" His voice was frantic.

"Gregory."

"Hmm?"

"How much caffeine have you had today?"

"I lost track."

Charlotte pulled back and squeezed his biceps with her hands. "Well, it's time to cut you off. Everything's all set. My aunt and uncle are thrilled, Emily is pleased, it's all done. You don't have to worry."

"That's easy for you to say! You've been at a theme park grand opening before. What if the mock sushi makes someone ill? What if the rides don't run for half the night? What if—"

Charlotte placed a finger on his lips. "Then we'll have many amusing stories to tell later. It's going to be okay; I promise."

Gregory nodded. "When did you become the practical one?"

Charlotte shrugged. "Don't worry, I'm sure you'll be the one calming me down about something in the near future. Speaking of one of us calming the other one down, how are you feeling about riding the Manta? I know you've been skipping the test and soft-opening rides."

"Marianne was supposed to tell you I've gone on it a million times and loved it," Gregory whined. "Would you believe me if I said I wanted to save my first ride and authentic reaction for the grand opening?"

"Hmm," Charlotte teased. "That's very thoughtful of you, as long as you enjoy it, of course."

Panic filled his eyes. "*Why* would you say that, Charlotte? Do you think I'm not going to like it? Am I going to throw up and/or cry in front of everyone? That would be a terrible headline!"

"That would also be an amusing story, but no, you're going to love it. The designers brought Uncle Frank's vision to life beautifully. We'll ride together and you can crush the life out of my hand if you need to. But maybe don't eat until after we ride it. Deal?"

"Deal." Gregory stopped and turned to Charlotte. "Have I mentioned how stunning you look this evening?"

Charlotte had chosen a sleeveless ocean-blue maxi dress for the night with silver-sequined sneakers. She'd left her hair down in waves and clipped in barrettes that looked like abalone shells.

"My ocean goddess." He lifted the back of her hand to his lips.

Charlotte grinned. It was going to be an excellent evening.

Before the festivities started, Charlotte led Gregory and Melanie to a spot around a sculpted coral reef so they could see the guests approaching.

"The guests will be coming in there," Charlotte said as she

pointed. "We've designed the land so they enter through the tunnel that simulates going under the water and then they'll step into this open space and be able to take the whole area in. It helps add to the sense of wonder when you compress and then release the space like that. Of course you both walked through there multiple times today, so you already know that. I've probably already said that. I'm rambling. Okay, I guess I *am* a bit nervous."

"Babes, it would be weird if you *weren't* nervous." Melanie slid an arm around Charlotte's shoulder and surprised her by putting an arm around Gregory's shoulders, too. "Feel the nerves, but remember to be proud, too. Look what you both did. Together." She moved her arms and spun around to face them. "Together you two can do anything you want. Remember that, okay? And remember that I knew it before anyone."

"Hey, I knew for a while," Charlotte said.

"Yeah, but you didn't want to admit it."

Gregory tucked Charlotte into his side. "Melanie's right. You didn't. We didn't. We got there, though." He kissed her cheek.

Frank, Marianne, and Emily joined them. "I see you brought Gregory and Melanie to the best spot in the house," Uncle Frank said.

"You know it," Charlotte answered. "Where are Mom and Dad?"

"Right over there. They wanted to watch *you* watch the guests arrive," Aunt Marianne said. Charlotte waved at them.

"Remind me," Emily said, "who all did we invite again? I know I helped make the list but all the prep has scrambled my brain."

"Local press, theme park influencers, teens from local schools, people who love the thrill rides at Rushing Vortex up north, and friends and family, of course," Gregory rattled off.

"That's a lot of people," Emily answered. "Definitely the

biggest party we've ever had here at Lands. And that's in no small part due to you for pushing us, Charlotte—in a good way, to be clear."

Since Charlotte got home, she and Emily had started repairing their relationship. It would take a while to get back to where they were as kids, and Charlotte wasn't sure if they'd ever be that close again. They'd see. "Thank you," Charlotte said. "I want this party to be a success, and I can't wait to see how many guests come to Lands this year just to ride the Manta Diver and see all of Under the Waves."

Marianne tapped Charlotte on the shoulder. "Here they come."

Charlotte moved next to Gregory and squeezed his hand. "You ready?"

"As I'll ever be."

The first wave of guests walked into Under the Waves— Charlotte had planned it carefully so the influencers and press who wanted to take a million photos and videos would have time in the morning to explore before the park opened so they could film all they wanted. That meant they ideally wouldn't be holding up phones and cameras all evening long. She didn't want selfie sticks obscuring the faces of all the people coming in.

First up were their younger guests and harshest critics: teenagers.

Charlotte watched them take in Under the Waves. Some of them were clearly not impressed, but she could see others' expressions transform from curiosity to surprise and delight. Nothing beat this feeling and she didn't have to be at a theme park with a multimillion-dollar budget to get it. Her uncle had designed Under the Waves with such thoughtfulness and care and with everyone's input, Charlotte's experience, and Gregory's finance management finesse, they'd made the attraction look amazing.

The walkways appeared to be made from grains of sand with shells, fossils, and bits of seaweed embedded into the flat surface. Caustic lighting that cast reflections of moving water across the walkway—bioluminescent spots would glow at nighttime—adding to the feeling of wandering the sea floor and seeing what was out there. Gentle wind chimes secured in the trees gave the space a background sound of crashing waves, and the splash-play area, though not open to guests for the grand opening, was on to add to the sound design.

It was all perfect.

They stayed in place as the bulk of the guests entered, magic hour starting as the last group came in. They hadn't wanted to risk having an event in the middle of the day in case it was too hot; they had plenty of shady spots in the land but this was better. At this hour, everyone would see the sunset and twilight glow illuminate the faux sea cliffs.

Some influencers Charlotte knew from her DreamUs days stopped in their tracks, taken with something about the space. Other guests barreled in, eager to see it all. Proud-looking staff directed them toward the ribbon-cutting stage and seats in front of the Manta. They also offered drinks and small bites—Melanie had helped Quinn and Holly develop a tasting menu representative of what would be available in Under the Waves all the time, but with a celebratory flare for the event. Melanie refused to let them go for the easy trick of serving blue drinks to represent the ocean and calling it a day; she used the word "elevated" frequently. And as ever, Melanie was right. Charlotte noticed a lot of people positioning phones to photograph their snacks—especially Holly's chocolate bouchons with the seaweed espuma swirl on top.

Guests also gathered in a crowd around Owen and their corgis. The photos they'd shown Charlotte of Mabel and Olive dressed as mermaids didn't do the pups justice. With mermaid tails crocheted from sparkly yarn and crowns of seaweed and shells, the dogs looked ridiculously adorable. People came over to fawn over them with pets and ask for photos, and Mabel and Olive were eating it up. Owen art directed everyone for the best possible shots, a huge grin on their face.

This could only happen at Lands of Legend. Relief that she'd come to her senses in time to be part of this coursed through her body, followed by a comforting sense of rightness and belonging.

When the final bunch of people trickled in, Charlotte led everyone toward the ribbon-cutting stage. "It's time to officially get this shindig going and get these folks on rides. Remember, Uncle Frank and Aunt Marianne, you're kicking things off after I introduce you."

Marianne patted Frank's hand and inhaled deeply. "We're ready."

Charlotte made sure her parents, Gregory, and Mel were seated in the reserved front row before taking the stage.

"Hi, everyone! Thank you for joining us for the grand opening of Under the Waves!" Charlotte beamed into the microphone. When the applause died down, she continued, "This addition to Lands of Legend has been a long time in the making, but I'll let the minds behind all of Lands tell you about it. Please welcome Frank and Marianne Gates, the founders of Lands of Legend."

Charlotte made way for her aunt and uncle and then took a place offstage.

"We're so happy and grateful to have you all here," her aunt started. "Lands of Legend has always been a project of love for Frank and me." Here, she took her husband's hand. "Frank had a vision for this park back in the early eighties and built it piece by piece, sharing his imagination with all of us. Lands kept growing and our family grew alongside it; our daughter Emily and our niece, Charlotte, practically grew up here. We've all contributed over the years and made it through some tough times."

Marianne's eyes watered and she paused for a moment. "Honestly, I was beginning to wonder if we'd ever see Under the Waves become real. As some of you know, it's been a real stop-and-go addition to the park. Frank's idea for the Manta was ambitious—even I questioned him about the practicality of all of this a few times. But thanks to support from everyone we know and love, and from Ever Fund, specifically Gregory Binns, here we are. We couldn't be more thrilled. Frank, do you have anything to add?"

Charlotte waited since she knew her uncle wasn't big on speaking in public. Frank took a moment, looking down and swiping a hand under his eye. "I'll just echo you: Thank you to everyone who made this happen. I've had my doubts about whether we'd open this last part of Lands of Legend before we retired, but I shouldn't have strayed. Now, what do you say we wrap this up and go on rides?"

The crowd cheered. Charlotte walked with her aunt and uncle to the deep blue shimmering ribbon tied across the entry to the Manta Diver and handed them oversized ceremonial scissors. Together, they cut the ribbon and entered the queue. Charlotte ushered her cousin and parents in after them. Melanie wasn't ready for the Manta yet, so she hung back. Gregory approached with slow steps.

"Do you see how happy everyone looks?" Charlotte asked, sliding an arm around his waist. "Under the Waves is perfect, Gregory. Perfect."

He put his arm around her shoulders and looked out on the crowd for a moment before facing her. "It is nice to see, but I'm more concerned with how you're feeling. It's been a long day. A long, what, five months?"

"Almost. But we did it. Together." She stepped closer and

ran her thumb over one of his laugh lines. "We make a good team."

He leaned in and kissed her, sweet and brief. "I can't wait to do more of this with you."

"This?"

"Everything, Charlotte. Everything."

She extended her hand to Gregory. "Me too. Including this." She nodded toward the Manta. "May I have this roller-coaster ride?"

He clasped her fingers. "Always."

Epilogue

Late afternoon sun spread dappled light across Bluewhistle Meadow. Charlotte stood and leaned against a tree, pressing her lips together in amusement as she watched Gregory taking way too much time to straighten a blanket on the ground. He stepped back to assess his wrinkle-free blanket placement and a grin spread across his face when he saw her. Charlotte's knees fully felt it.

"Hey there, handsome." She walked toward him. "I didn't know this is what you had in mind for date night, but I'm here for it."

He opened his arms to hug her close. "I've owed you a picnic in this meadow for a while. And I know it can be hard to leave the house once we get back from work, so this seemed like the smartest idea. Just this once. I need to grab one more thing. I'll be back in five minutes, okay?"

"Anything I can do to help set up?" she asked.

"Absolutely not. Sit down, grab a pillow. As someone once told me, close your eyes and listen to the park," Gregory instructed.

Charlotte settled onto a plush pillow and smiled at the memory of showing him around the park last year. He'd come a long way since then—she'd noticed him wearing a short-sleeved Henley in the office last week. Short sleeves! At work!

He did have a button-down, collared shirt at the ready by his office door, but he didn't go formal all day every day.

She'd come a long way too, she reflected. Her life was more balanced, especially since she and Gregory, with Mad-martigan, had moved in together in a cozy old farmhouse not far from the park, on the edge of a forest. They camped on their own property sometimes.

Yes, Charlotte still loved her work. Especially since she'd proved to her family she wanted to stay for the long haul and run the park with Gregory, who'd formally left Ever Fund not long after the Under the Waves opening and realized that yes, co-running a theme park had become his thing. He'd incorporated his passion for the outdoors and the environment too; the vibrant pollinator garden on the edge of Bluewhistle Meadow, humming with bustling insects, was only one small way he'd put himself into Lands. Gregory and her dad were constantly planning landscape additions emphasizing natural elements; they even wanted to turn the now-annual Faery Festival into a Faery Flower and Garden Festival. Finally retired, Aunt Marianne and Uncle Frank kept going on road trips around the States. And Emily, free from her self-imposed familial obligation, was happier, lighter, and about to return to New York for grad school

So yeah, Charlotte still gave a not-small part of her heart to Lands of Legend—and it showed in the park's increased attendance—but her work was no longer the whole focus of her life. She created boundaries, learned how to delegate, took days off. Not like at DreamUs when she'd amass so much PTO that her boss would have to force her to take time away, and then she'd be online working anyway. But no longer. She and Gregory had even gone on a vacation to Los Angeles, partly to close up his sad and empty apartment but mostly to play tourists in the town they'd both lived in for years, but only lived to work in. A concert at the Hollywood Bowl, ice cream on the Santa Monica Pier, rambling the wild

paths at Descanso Gardens—L.A. had more to offer than office walls, as it turned out.

The healthier stance toward work post–Under the Waves
opening had helped her relationships. She connected on a
deeper level with Gregory, Melanie, Emily, and her whole family by being more present. Madmartigan benefited from her
more chill state of mind too, coming to expect and demand
snuggle time with her every evening as she relaxed on the
couch.

Charlotte closed her eyes and breathed. Life felt just right.

"Charlotte, did you fall asleep?" Gregory stage whispered.

She opened her eyes and saw him leaning over her, eyes
shining with warmth, picnic basket in hand.

"I wouldn't dare. Who am I, you?" she teased, thinking
back to the night they'd realized they wanted to be together.
"But I bet I could. It's quite peaceful out here with the park
closing for the day."

She sat straight up, her mind racing and already forming a
list. "In fact, this reminds me. I had a thought about Bluewhistle Meadow picnic packages ages ago and forgot. It could
be a great offering for passholders or even a special event on
its own. We could set up picnics across the meadow—I know
Melanie would have amazing suggestions for the menu—and
do shows for them, like Shakespeare in the Park, but our version, and we could—"

Gregory, who had sat next to her, folding his long legs behind him, pressed a finger to her lips and gave her a look. He
raised an eyebrow, as if asking if he could remove his finger,
and she nodded.

"It's an excellent idea," Gregory said, "And I see potential
there."

"Right?" Charlotte gushed as she reached toward her bag
to grab the notebook she kept in it for this reason. "I'm going
to write it down so I don't forget and then maybe we can discuss it more tomorrow?"

"I'd love to." Gregory smiled.

Charlotte quickly scribbled enough words to jog her memory tomorrow, and gasped when she looked up. Gregory had spread out an elaborate cheese plate in front of them in record time and now he was placing lanterns with small battery-operated flickering candles at the blanket's corners.

She gazed at him and once he was settled on the blanket again, she leaned over, put her hand on his neck, and pulled him in for a gentle kiss, his soft lips yielding against hers.

Charlotte pulled away and looked into his eyes, the green soft in the lingering golden hour. "This is beautiful. Thank you for doing all of this. You even got Brie for me. I know how you feel about Brie."

He leaned forward and kissed her on the tip of her nose. "It was my pleasure. You deserve Brie and so much more."

They both giggled and Charlotte plucked a blueberry from the edge of the spread and threw it at him.

"Before we dig in," Gregory said, "I'd like to, uh, ask you something."

Hearing Gregory sound anything less than one thousand percent confident put Charlotte on edge; she was still working on not jumping to the worst possible conclusion first.

She straightened. "Anything."

Gregory twisted his arm behind him, picked something up, and opened his palm to reveal a small, carved wooden box.

Charlotte's jaw dropped.

Gregory cleared his throat. "I, um, was wondering— as long as I always include Brie in our cheese plates, have Sir Cinna-Swirls and also pizza with you once a week, and love you for always—if you would do me the honor of marrying me?"

Charlotte's eyes started watering when he started speaking and a tear slipped down her cheek. "Yes! Gregory! There is no other answer. Only yes."

He opened the box to reveal a vintage ring with hexagon-cut labradorite surrounded by small diamonds.

"AHHHH! It's *perfect*! Gregory!"

He plucked the ring out and slid it onto Charlotte's finger. A perfect fit.

She scooted closer and wrapped her arms around him, in disbelief that this thoughtful man who smelled of evergreen trees and comfort was hers.

"I love you, Gregory," Charlotte whispered into his ear.

"And I love you right back, Charlotte," he replied and then kissed her thoroughly.

They pulled apart and Charlotte laughed. "You know this means going on roller coasters for the rest of your life, right?"

Without hesitation, he replied, "I wouldn't have it any other way."

Acknowledgments

I can't believe this book is real! Thank you, dear reader, for picking it up, going on Charlotte and Gregory's journey, and visiting Lands of Legend. As a theme park nerd, it was a dream to make up a place like this. I definitely didn't procrastinate writing in favor of coming up with rides that didn't make it into the book—I would *never*.

I couldn't have made it through this process without the support of so many lovely humans. Thank you to my agent, Eric Smith, for being into this idea when it was but an incoherent pitch, cheerleading me the whole way, and answering my many questions about publishing. There is so much I do not know. Thank you to Norma Perez-Hernandez for seeing the potential in *Thrill Ride* and acquiring it for Kensington. Thank you to Alexandra Sunshine for taking my messy draft and helping me pinpoint how to improve it and make the story and characters better—like, so much better. I loved our conversations. I so appreciate the thoughtful ideas you bring to the table *and* your opinions on pastries for breakfast.

I must shout out production editor Carly Sommerstein at Kensington as well as copy editor, Steven Roman, and proofreader Amanda Kreklau, for helping *Thrill Ride* be the best it can be, and Jane Nutter for getting this book in front of people. Thank you so much to Michelle Grant for the stunning cover! Blessings to David and Curtis at P.S. Literary and all the other talented folks at Kensington for making my first romcom come to fruition. Oh, and massive ups to Jacob McAlister for designing the gorgeous map for Lands of Legend.

My sister read this book in its earliest form and gave me the encouragement and gushing I needed to continue. Thank you, Nicole, for reading and for sharing all your favorite baked good spots with me when I visit.

This book would not exist without the general enthusiasm of the theme park fan community, of which I am proudly a member. Thanks to Chris Hayner and Carlye Wisel for listening to the nugget of the idea for this book after a busy press day at the parks. Additional thanks to Carlye for sharing thoughts about both themes and parks with me. Scott Trowbridge, I'm grateful for your insight into storytelling and into some of the nitty gritty of theme park operations.

Thank you to a couple of special places in my community: the Flatiron Writers Room for giving me a quiet place to finish my proposal for this book and Izzy's Coffee for being an excellent place to write with coffee and bagels at hand.

Last but not least, thanks to my supportive husband, Aaron. I'm glad I have someone in my life to nerd out over Imagineers with and who fully supports year-round *Haunted Mansion* décor. You're my favorite person to go to a theme park with, and I'll always share my popcorn with you.

Visit our website at
KensingtonBooks.com
to sign up for our newsletters, read
more from your favorite authors, see
books by series, view reading group
guides, and more!

Become a Part of Our
Between the Chapters Book Club
Community and Join the Conversation